JULIA
UNBOUND

ALSO BY CATHERINE EGAN

Julia Vanishes

Julia Defiant

JULIA UNBOUND

THE WITCH'S CHILD, BOOK 3

CATHERINE EGAN

ALFRED A. KNOPF

NEW YORK

Text copyright © 2018 by Catherine Egan
Jacket art copyright © 2018 by Gustavo Marx (girl), Shutterstock (background)
Map copyright © 2018 by Robert Lazzaretti

All rights reserved. Published in the United States by Alfred A. Knopf,
an imprint of Random House Children's Books,
a division of Penguin Random House LLC, New York.

Knopf, Borzoi Books, and the colophon are registered trademarks of
Penguin Random House LLC.

Visit us on the Web! GetUnderlined.com

Educators and librarians, for a variety of teaching tools, visit us at
RHTeachersLibrarians.com

Library of Congress Cataloging-in-Publication Data is available upon request.
ISBN 978-0-553-52488-8 (trade) — ISBN 978-0-553-52490-1 (ebook)

The text of this book is set in 13-point Adobe Jenson.

Printed in the United States of America
August 2018
10 9 8 7 6 5 4 3 2 1

First Edition

For Gillian—

All the way through every story

I am waiting for you under the streetlamp

Let's go

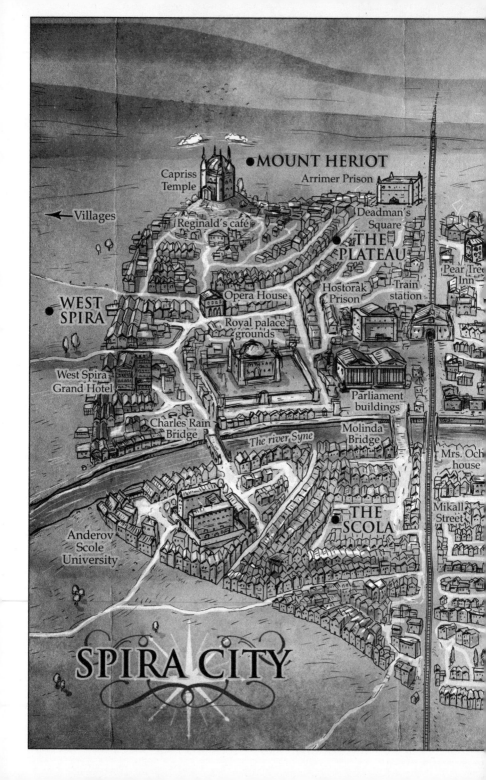

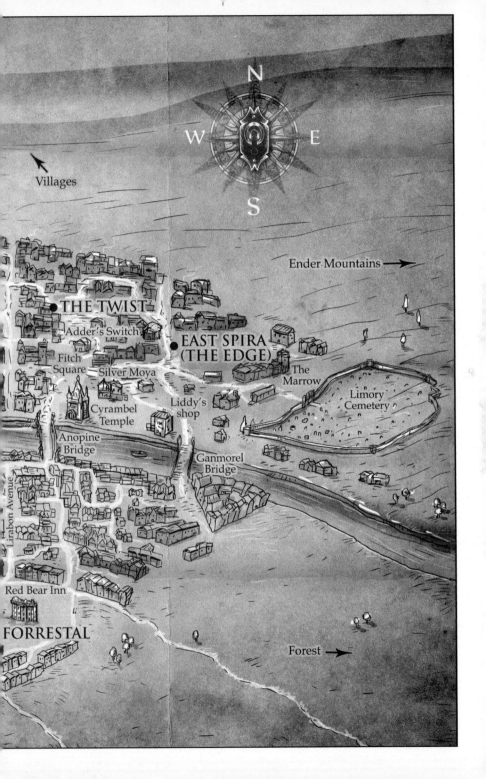

PEOPLE, PLACES, AND THINGS

Ammi: A witch; Julia and Benedek's mother

Professor Baranyi: A scholar and friend to Mrs. Och; once jailed for heretical writings

Benedek: Julia's brother

Dafne Besnik: A noble girl chosen by Casimir to marry Duke Everard and become queen of Frayne

Bianka: A witch; Theo's mother; drowned by Mrs. Och

Casimir (Lan Camshe): One of the Xianren, seeking to reassemble all three parts of *The Book of Disruption*

Csilla: Part of Esme's gang; a former actress turned con artist; Gregor's lover

Esme: Spira City crime boss, now one of the leaders of the burgeoning revolution

Idir Faruk: A witch; Zara's ex-tutor and Lady Laroche's friend

Frederick: A brilliant young student; Professor Baranyi's assistant

Gennady (Zor Gen): Youngest of the Xianren; Theo's father; imprisoned by Casimir

Gregor: An ex-aristocrat con man working for Esme; Csilla's lover

Agoston Horthy: The prime minister of Frayne

Lady Laroche: A witch; the head of the Sidhar Coven in Frayne

Lidari: A general of the Gethin; Marike's associate

Liddy: An elderly shoemaker with a large network of mysterious connections; Julia's friend

Emil Lorka: A famous artist and Wyn's hero; a member of the revolutionary set

Marike: A witch; the first Phar and founder of the Eshriki Empire

Mrs. Och (Och Farya): Eldest of the Xianren; fatally injured by Julia in Kahge

Pia: Casimir's enforcer

Ragg Rock: A name for both the hill between the world and Kahge and the mud woman guarding it

Silver Moya: A witch called to act as a gatekeeper between the world and Ragg Rock

Lord Skaal: Half-man, half–Parnese wolf; in Agoston Horthy's employ

Theo: Gennady and Bianka's toddler son, with a fragment of *The Book of Disruption* bound to his essence

Dorje Tsewang: A mysterious Xanuhan woman working for Zara

Sir Victor: A nobleman forced into a contract with Casimir; his daughter is a hostage in Agoston Horthy's court; a double agent

Wyn: An orphan and a crook; Esme's adopted son; Julia's ex-lover

Zara: Claimant to the Fraynish throne and leader of the revolution

King Zey: The dying king of Frayne

The Ankh-nu: A double-spouted clay pot made to transfer the essence of a living being from one body to another

The besilik mirror: A mirror with magical properties, used for searching inside someone's mind or unearthing memories

The Book of Disruption: The first written magic and origin of magic in the world, said to have been written by Feo, spirit of fire, and broken into three pieces by the other elemental spirits

The Eshriki Empire: A powerful witch empire three thousand years ago whose rulers called themselves the Phars

The Gethin: A now-extinct army of creatures brought into the world from Kahge and given physical form by Marike, the first Eshriki Phar

Kahge: A magic-infused reflection, shadow, or image imprint of the natural world, created when *The Book of Disruption* was split into three

The Lorian Uprising: An unsuccessful revolution in Frayne eighteen years ago, intending to supplant King Zey with his more moderate brother, Roparzh

The *nuyi*: A parasite that embeds itself in the brain and conquers the will of its host—used by Casimir to assert control over those in his employ; called his "contract"

The Sidhar Coven: A Fraynish coven of witches—of which Julia's mother, Ammi, was a part—involved in the Lorian Uprising

The Xianren: Immortal siblings, sometimes allies and sometimes enemies, each charged with protecting a portion of *The Book of Disruption*—Casimir (Lan Camshe), Gennady (Zor Gen), and Mrs. Och (Och Farya)

JULIA
UNBOUND

NAGO ISLAND

I wake up with his hands around my throat.

ONE

She is a burnt husk on the bed, a charred and twisted branch, like something left behind after the fire has raged through. But she is somehow alive, if you can call it that. Her breath comes in and out in slow, laborious rasps; her blackened chest rises and falls. At first I wonder why they don't cover her, but then I imagine it must be painful to have clothing or blankets touching that seared flesh.

When her breath rattles to a halt, the two men at her bedside lean forward. And then: another gasp, the burnt chest heaves. They relax—deflate. I call them men, but they are not really men. They are the Xianren, ancient, immortal siblings—or as close to immortal as any living thing can come. There is no true immortality. Their sister dying on the bed is proof of that.

A hunchbacked woman with fair, graying hair and sad eyes sits in the corner of the room. I know her. The last time we met I fired as many bullets as I had into her, for all the good it did. She has a cartridge pen in her hand, and she is writing in a book that lies open on her lap—writing magic. The room smells of damp earth. Her gaze flickers toward us and rests on me, appraising, curious. The brothers do not look up. It becomes obvious that they did not hear us come in at all—too bent on their sister's every breath. Pia says, in her broken-glass voice, "Here is Julia."

They look up: Casimir, his face livid, all sharp edges and dead stone eyes, and Gennady like a broken lion, huge and golden-hued. I've been here a week, but they have been sitting vigil, and I was not summoned to see them until now, no matter how I begged for news of my own brother. I've been locked in a tower room playing cards with Pia, waiting. We got in the habit of cards on the long sea journey from Yongguo: King's Heir, Four Realms, Evil Eights, Diamond Jack. It's true that I count Pia my enemy, when I pause to count my enemies, but she's all I've had for company for over a month now, and we had to pass the time somehow. One can't fill every hour counting enemies.

Casimir rises, a flash of panic on his face that surprises me. Surely he is not afraid of me? But maybe he is. After all, look what I did to his sister.

"I told you—" he snarls at Pia. Her knees buckle; she steadies herself against the doorframe. The mechanical goggles fixed over her eyes swivel in and out. The hunchbacked witch—I know her only as Shey—looks back and forth between Pia and Casimir. When Casimir speaks again, it is to me, and his voice is unnervingly calm: "You left a mess behind you in Yongguo."

4

"I'm here for Dek," I say.

I am waiting for the moment when I can pull this man out of the world and destroy him like I did his sister. I *will* end him—but her scorched body on the bed and the horrible sound of her breathing shake my resolve more than I'd expected.

He points a trembling finger at her. His voice might be steady, but *he* is not steady, not at all.

"Look at what you have done to her."

We all look at her. I used to think about forgiveness. I used to want it for myself. But I'm past all that, and I forgive nothing.

Her breathing comes to a choking stop again. The silence stretches out. Gennady moans. I make myself watch. If I did this, and if I was right, then I don't get to look away.

"Save her," Casimir says to Shey—somewhere between a plea and a command.

"I can only ease her pain."

"She is not dead yet. You *can* save her!"

Shey keeps writing in her book and says, "Not for long, and even if I could, it would cost me too much."

His face twists. His voice comes out a shriek: "Do as I say, witch!"

Shey puts her pen down and looks at him. The color drains from his face. I can see in that moment that he's afraid; he's overstepped. She picks up the pen again—a weapon, in her hand.

A gurgle, a cough, a gasp from the carcass on the bed.

"She killed Bianka," I say to Gennady.

He raises his head slowly, like it's too heavy for him. "Bianka is dead?"

I nod, and he sags forward. He will blame himself, I reckon, and rightly so. Between the three of them—for they each played a part—the Xianren destroyed Bianka. If not for Gennady, though, she would never have been involved at all.

"My sister has been asking for you," says Casimir.

I can't quite see how she would manage to ask for anything, but I walk to her bedside. I find her eyes open in what used to be her face. Her hand moves suddenly, like a snake, closing wetly around my wrist, her grip stronger than I would have expected. I stifle a scream. With the next tortured exhalation, she says: *Julia.*

I'm sorry. That's what leaps to my lips, but I shut my teeth over the words. I'm not sorry. Die, old thing. Just die.

"I tried to," she whispers. "Everything . . . depends on. You *must.* The *book,* Lidari. Don't let him."

And then she stops breathing again, eyes rolling around frantically, and her enemy brothers bend over her, stunned by their grief because death has never truly touched any of them before in all of their thousands of years as sometime allies and sometime foes. But she's not dead—she's still holding on to me. I yank my wrist free.

She heaves another breath.

"Is that it?" I say.

Casimir pivots and shoves me away from her so that I stumble backward, nearly falling over. I regain my footing

6

and whip my knife out of my boot. Just instinct, that. We stand staring at each other, and then Casimir says coldly to Pia: "Why is she armed?"

Pia shrugs. "What is she going to do with a knife? Cut your throat?"

"Get her out of my sight." He turns his back on me and my useless knife, bending his long body over his sister again.

Shaking, I slide the knife back into my boot lining. Pia's boot, actually; everything I'm wearing is hers. I could have asked for other clothes once we got here, but the truth is I prefer dressing like her. It feels like wearing a kind of armor. And what *am* I going to do with a knife? The witch, Shey, watches us go, pen poised. Pia takes me back to the room at the top of the castle where I've been passing the days since my arrival.

I slump in a chair and drop my face into my hands, trying to blot out the sight of Mrs. Och's ruined body, her eyes still the same in that face that is no longer a face. *The book, Lidari.* I feel sick at being called Lidari—the monster that may or may not be trapped inside me—and bewildered by her message. Was she asking me not to let Casimir assemble *The Book of Disruption?* As if I need to be told.

Pia slings herself into the chair across from me, takes out a pack of cards, cuts and shuffles the deck, deals out.

TWO

I wake up with his hands around my throat.

"She's gone."

The whites of his eyes shine in the dark room. He squeezes. My fingers find my knife under the pillow. I can't kill him with a knife any more than he can strangle me—we are just playing at murderous rage. Much as we may want to kill each other, we each have something the other wants. Someone.

He makes a sound that is almost a sob.

"We buried her at sea. My sister! Och Farya, the oldest living being in all the world! The first among the Xian-ren, child of the spirits! *You* snuffed her out, her light, her greatness—you stupid girl, you *nothing*." His breath is hot on my cheek. I get the knife between us, holding it to his throat, but he doesn't even notice. *What is she going to do with a knife?*

He hisses right in my ear: "I will make you pay and pay and *pay* until the world stops spinning on its axis." As if he can't help himself, his fist closes hard on my throat, his nails driving into my skin. Gagging, I vanish out of his throttling hold, out of my body, away from the world.

From early childhood I've been able to pull myself one step out of the world into what felt like an invisible pocket just for me, where people wouldn't notice me at all. Handy skill for a thief and spy, and I reveled in it. But it was here in this very castle—months ago, though it seems much longer—that my little vanishing trick revealed its full and terrible range. I prefer not to remember, but my nightmares sometimes take me back to Casimir's flat eyes, his fist knocking me to the ground, his boot smashing into my face, his elegant hands breaking my fingers one by one, snapping my wrist. Then it was like a wall fell away and the space I vanished into went on and on, all the way to Kahge, a hellish reflection of the world, a place where I am changed, monstrous—and powerful enough to kill an immortal. It is a place where none can follow me, unless I take them there.

I've saved myself a hundred times this way—and nearly gotten myself killed just as often—but I'm no closer to knowing what it means, why I can do it. I don't need to vanish to Kahge to escape Casimir's hold on my throat, though. With my perception hanging overhead somewhere—nowhere—I can make him out in the dark: sprawling on the empty bed, hands closing on nothing. He gives an awful laugh and goes staggering out. I return to myself—to my body, to the bed—and I lie there, my heart pounding out the seconds, the minutes, the hours of the rest of the night until dawn lightens the room and I can hear the gulls crying.

THREE

Pia takes me to see him in the morning. He is having his breakfast on a stone terrace overlooking the sea. He doesn't mention visiting me in the night, although the purpling finger marks on my neck and the gashes from his nails are visible reminders. He gestures at the chair across from him. Freshly baked fruit tarts, strings of sausages, and neat little omelets are laid out on the table. He pours me a cup of coffee, the steam rising up between us. I'm not one to let murder and mayhem come between me and a good breakfast. I sit down and dig into a gooseberry tart.

Casimir looks me over as if he's really seeing me for the first time, then runs a finger along his cheek to indicate the scar on mine. I have so many new scars since the last time we met.

"Who cut you?" he asks. "I should like to shake his hand."

"He doesn't have hands anymore," I answer.

He laughs appreciatively and takes a sip of his coffee.

"Let's talk about the little boy," he says.

We're getting right down to it, then—what we want from each other. Casimir wants Theo, and I have hidden him away. I want my brother, and Casimir has stolen him from me. No doubt he imagines a simple trade. Once I gave him Theo for a bag of silver, but I am so far from being that girl now.

Of course, it isn't *Theo* Casimir wants so much as what is inside him—a fragment of *The Book of Disruption*. The only fragment Casimir doesn't have. If he can get ahold of Theo and get the text out of him, he will be able to reassemble that book, the first written magic in all the world. The consequences are too huge to imagine—Kahge would be pulled back into the world, and who knows what Casimir could or would do with such power? Mrs. Och was so afraid of this that she was willing to kill Theo—an innocent child, barely two years old—to prevent it. I can't really wrap my head around the idea of a changed world—*Casimir's* world. Maybe I lack imagination. I'm here to get my brother back, but it won't be by trading Theo. I keep my face blank, force down my mouthful, and take another bite.

"Si Tan, the grand librarian of Yongguo, has searched high and low, but he has not found the boy. If Si Tan has not found him, he is not in Yongguo. Where is he?"

I keep shoveling food into my mouth.

"He won't be able to hide from me forever. There is no corner of the world I can't reach into."

That's why he's not in the world, fiend.

"Frederick took Theo, but I don't know where," I lie around a mouthful of gooseberries.

I have to play Casimir's game. He knows what I can do. If my brother is alive—and I would know, surely I would *know* if he was not—I have to tread carefully.

"I find it hard to believe you have *no* idea where the child is. Pia, how long do you think it would take you to get the truth out of this mangy pup?"

"Not so very long, my lord."

"And what would the damage be?"

"Extensive, my lord, and permanent," says Pia.

Some days I almost forget to be afraid of her—I am so used to her by now—but her dispassionate assessment of what it would take to torture Theo's whereabouts out of me makes me feel ill. I'm gambling on the hope that even if they force the truth out of me, as I know they *can*, they won't be able to reach him, but I wish I could be more certain of that. I finish the tart, scraping the crumbs up with my fork.

Casimir grins, showing too many teeth. "You have a good appetite."

"You have a good cook," I reply.

He leans back, folding his hands behind his head. I imagine driving my knife into his chest as I start on one of the omelets.

"What are you, Julia?" he asks.

Sometimes I think not knowing the answer to that question is the worst of it. But maybe I'm wrong. Maybe the truth is worse. I don't answer him because I can't, but I try to look as if it's because I don't want to.

"Ammi—always with an extra trick up her sleeve," he sneers.

Is that what I am? An extra trick up my dead mother's sleeve? Maybe the more relevant questions are, who was my mother and is she really dead?

"My sister came to believe that you are the latest incarnation of Lidari, Marike's paramour, or companion, or whatever he was to her for the hundreds of years he spent at her side."

He spits out the name *Marike*. The feud between the Xianren and that long-ago witch is the stuff of legend. She was the first witch ever to challenge the power and authority of the Xianren. As the first Phar of the Eshriki Empire, she once imprisoned the Xianren, stole the fragments of *The*

Book of Disruption, and tried to assemble it herself. Turned out only the Xianren can assemble and read the Book, so it was a wasted effort on Marike's part and sparked a few millennia of ill will. Never a good idea to get on the wrong side of someone who is going to live forever.

"If you are Lidari, I've already killed you once," he continues. "But I am skeptical. I remember him well, and you have nothing of his manner, his clarity of mind, or his wily, dispassionate nature."

I shrug and keep eating, but I file all that away—the bit about clarity of mind and wily, dispassionate nature. Doesn't sound like me.

"My sister was raving for days before she died. She claimed that your mother brought Lidari back into the world—a deal between the two of them, to destroy me." He says this calmly, but his eyes turn an even flatter gray than usual. "So Ammi brought him back, and she very nearly *did* destroy me—but there has been no sign of Lidari since. Only a daughter who can vanish and cross all the way from the world to Kahge and back again. Or so my sister said."

He seems to think I know more, and I wish I did. I try not to think of it—the possibility that Lidari is buried inside me somehow, waiting to reassert himself.

"Lidari would want revenge," he says, watching me carefully.

"I have my own reasons to want you dead," I say, and he laughs like I've made a good joke.

"Let us put the question of killing me out of your head

13

for now. I am not fading like my sister was. You can't harm me in any of the ways you might harm a mortal man, but perhaps you think that in Kahge you *could* harm me—if you could take me there."

"It does sound fun," I say. My heart is pounding like a war drum under my falsely light tone. I'm still and waiting at the center of the whirlwind.

"I lost myself last night. Later I found your skin under my fingernails." He spits on the stone terrace, like he's spitting out the taste of the memory. "Disgusted as I was, it occurred to me that I might make use of a bit of your skin. I called for Shey. She used the flesh and put this upon me." He unbuttons his shirt and reveals a symbol tattooed over his sternum. "She wondered that I should have any need to fear you, but she did as I asked all the same. The needle used to write the spell was cast into the sea. I tell you that only so you don't bother looking for it." He grins at my expression. "I can see I've alarmed you, but this is only a matter of self-protection. Try to touch me. You could throw that knife at me, if you like."

I pick up the knife next to my plate and look it over. He spreads his arms wide. I glance at Pia, but she is peering over our heads, expressionless.

I hurl the knife at him. It veers off to the side, clatters to the ground.

He reaches across the table. "Take my hand."

"I don't want to take your ugly hand," I say, shaken.

"This is a demonstration. Take my hand."

I reach for his hand, but my own hand is repelled by some force I can't see. I make another grab; again my hand flies back toward me. Casimir gives a satisfied nod.

"So I can't touch you," I say. "No great loss."

"Not with your hands, nor with anything else," he says. "I thought it wise to get that out of the way. Now we can focus on the important things. If I don't find the boy soon, Pia will have to get his whereabouts out of you. I hope it won't come to that, as it would likely destroy you, and I have other plans for you. I'd like to keep you in one piece if I can. Bodily, at least."

I finish the omelet, mop up what's left on my plate with a piece of bread, and wash it all down with black coffee. When I'm sure my voice will come out steady, I say again: "Where's my brother?"

The mask drops, and Casimir opens his mouth. His lips flatten back against his gums, but no sound comes out into the air. Instead, a deafening roar erupts inside my own head, jolting me out of my seat. He opens his mouth wider, and the sound grows, exploding against the inside of my skull, blotting out everything else. I am up and flailing—I cannot see; I clap my hands over my ears, but that doesn't help at all, as the sound is coming from within, not without. The roar rises to a terrible pitch, a piercing wail that shatters me. I hit the ground, my whole world a howling darkness, the volume unbearable; I know nothing, I remember nothing; it hurts it hurts it *hurts*.

And then silence.

I pull in a shaky breath. Blood is pooling inside my mouth—I must have bitten my tongue. I open my eyes. I am lying on the terrace, and Casimir is bending over me, the knife he was eating with pointed at my throat, his awful eyes fixed on mine. A sound comes out of me, like the whimper of a wounded animal. Something wet is trickling out of my nose.

"Unlike me, you are easy to kill," he says softly. "A knife in the right place. A blow to the head. A bit of poison. A high ledge. There are so many ways to kill you that it positively boggles the imagination. I did not know what you could do the last time we met. But I am ready for you now."

He walks away from me. I roll onto my side and wipe my sleeve against my nose; it comes away red and sticky with blood. I make another sobbing noise and hate myself for it. Everything hurts.

"Think yourself lucky that you still have a brother after taking my sister from me." He stands rigid at the parapet for a moment, and then without turning around he says to Pia: "Take her now. Take care of the whole thing. I don't want to look at her again."

"Come," says Pia, helping me up. When she sees my expression, her voice drops slightly, losing its shattering edge: "Your brother will be fine. You should worry about yourself."

FOUR

Two men are bent over a diagram spread across a table. They look up when we come in. Dek sees me, and his face falls.

"Oh, Julia," he says. "I'd hoped it wasn't true."

I shout something inarticulate, bounding across the room and throwing my arms around him. The temptation to pull him right out of the world and away from this place is tremendous, even though I know they would never let me near him if there weren't a catch of some kind. But oh, the relief and the *joy* of seeing him, well and whole and unharmed. It registers a moment late—something changed in his face, his arms around me, *both* his arms. I pull back, suddenly sick with fear.

"What's happened? What have they done?"

My brother was strong and fast once, a beautiful boy with a laughing face and bright eyes, and I followed him everywhere. Eleven summers ago, Scourge swept across Frayne, striking thousands in our city alone—including my brother. It was rare for a child to survive, but our mother was a witch, and she turned the illness back. Ma was never the same after that, and the Scourge ravaged the right side of Dek's body before she was able to stop it, the arm and leg left withered and useless, the eye eaten away, that side of his face marred by scars and blots.

Now the skin there is smooth and shiny, paler than the rest of his face. There is a glass eye in his empty eye socket—brown, but a lighter brown than his other eye, so that his face appears to show two Deks: the real one, and a false, fairer copy. He looks a little strange, but he does not look like a Scourge victim. He does not really look like *himself*.

"Your crutch . . . ," I say, and he laughs. He is standing on two legs. The arm that normally hangs thin and useless at his side is still wrapped around my shoulders.

The laugh is genuine, but his voice sounds so sad: "Julia, I'm sorry. . . . You're hurt."

Yes. No. How can I answer? The glass eye disturbs me; I can't look at it.

"Not badly," I say, though my head is throbbing—I hit it on the terrace, throwing myself to the ground. I pull his arm off me, take his right hand in mine, and look at it. Metal hinges at the knuckles. He flexes the fingers.

"What's going on? And who is *this*?" I ask.

"My name is Savio," says the other man, bowing. I can't place his accent. He is an innocuous-looking fellow, with light brown skin and large, liquid eyes—unusually wet-looking, as if he were on the edge of tears. "I am Casimir's mechanic."

He unbuttons his cuff and rolls his sleeve up to show me the silvery disk in the skin of his wrist: Casimir's contract.

I look at Pia.

"He is good at what he does," she says, spreading her arms as if to display herself. Pia was once sent to assassinate

Casimir. She told me that after he broke her—bodily and in spirit—his mechanic put her back together. Rebuilt her into something new. Put Casimir's contract inside her.

"So you can walk now?" I say slowly.

"Walk. Run. Jump. Dance," says Dek, but I can't figure out his expression. That glass eye is throwing me off, making him unreadable. "With some practice, anyway. He was just showing me the diagrams. It will take a bit of getting used to. The limbs feel heavy, and the nerve connections are still new. I'm tripping and dropping things a lot, but he says it will get better."

Dek is a gifted inventor himself, but neither of us ever dreamed that such a thing was possible—the building of new limbs.

"Why?" I ask.

The mechanic gives me a quizzical look, so I make myself elaborate: "Why did you do it?"

"As a gift," says the mechanic. "Casimir can be good to you or he can crush you. Let your brother be a lesson in both."

I'm cold with terror now but unable to find the right question. I look at Dek as he casts his eye down and begins to unbutton his shirt. The fingers of his right hand above the hinges are pale and waxy, working clumsily with the buttons, while his other hand, the one he's relied on for years, is deft. He can unbutton a shirt easily with one hand—he's using the other deliberately, for practice. He opens his shirt to show me the long, lurid scar down the middle of his chest.

"What is it?"

"I have fastened to your brother's heart a sac of poison," says the mechanic, and I feel my stomach plunge with every word. "The sac will degrade naturally inside the body. It has been one week already. It will take another twenty days. Once the sac degrades and the poison touches the heart, he will be killed instantly."

There it is. Dek buttons his shirt up, his face showing nothing.

"Can it be taken out?"

"You understand"—Savio shows me again the silvery disk in his wrist—"I cannot do anything without Casimir's consent. You could threaten my life, torture me, and still my contract would simply prevent me from removing the sac of poison. I cannot operate until Casimir says it is to be done. But when he bids me do it—then, yes—it is a complicated procedure, not without risk, but I could remove the poison and he would live."

I should have been expecting something like this. Except of course I had no idea something like this was even possible. I knew they would try to hold Dek hostage in some way to compel me, but I thought I would find a way around it, that I would rescue him, vanishing us away from whatever threats Casimir devised. I did not imagine the threat placed inside Dek's body.

"So Casimir will have you remove it when I let him put his contract in me," I say.

The mechanic inclines his head. "Has Pia explained the contract to you?"

"I've seen it."

"The contract takes ten to fourteen days to grow toward the brain," says the mechanic. "Once it embeds in your brain, it is fully functional. In the interim, the poison inside your brother is Casimir's insurance policy. The sac of poison will take longer to degrade than the contract takes to reach your brain, I promise you. As soon as the contract is complete, binding you to Casimir, I will remove the poison and your brother will be fine. Better than fine. I must recommend against seeking somebody else to perform the surgery. It would be all too easy for an ordinary surgeon to puncture the sac and kill your brother. Likewise, poison fixed inside the body is too delicate and dangerous for a tool as clumsy as witchcraft to safely extract."

"Are you so sure I can't compel you?" I ask, low.

He looks frightened—clever man—but he says: "I am not brave, but my contract will prevent me. If you harm me, I will be unable to perform the surgery when Casimir permits it."

"It's true," says Pia behind me. "His instructions were explicit. He cannot do it without Casimir's consent."

Casimir has found a way to protect himself from me and a way to compel me. For now I'm at his mercy.

"Don't do it, Julia," says Dek wearily. "There's no way for this to end well. It's all right. I mean—I'm all right."

I turn to Pia again. "So Casimir puts his contract in me and then what? Tells me to go fetch Theo for him?"

"Yes," says Pia. "If he doesn't find Theo himself. First he

wants you back in Spira City. Frayne is still an important piece in Casimir's game. The king is dying, power is shifting, and Casimir is too careful a man to let his influence there lapse. The coming weeks will be key in determining the future of Frayne."

Dek shakes his head at me, one sad doomed-man eye, one glass-nothing eye, but I'll find a way, I will.

"He won't keep his word," says Dek. "You know that."

"I killed his sister," I say to Pia. "He wants revenge."

"Casimir wants to control you more than he wants to punish you," says Pia. "He wants Frayne in his power and he wants you in his power. He wants *The Book of Disruption* above all, but that is an uncertain venture, and he will try to get it without risking any of the power he has already accumulated. Casimir *always* plays the long game. Make yourself useful—better yet, indispensable—and your brother will reap the reward."

"Julia, I'm done for." Dek is so calm when he says this, holding my hand in his good hand, his *Dek* hand. "I've made my peace with this. I won't let you throw your life away."

But I think Pia is right about Casimir, and whatever Dek says, I've just watched him practice buttoning a shirt with his new hand—what is that, if not hope for a future? I'll find a way, but I need time. Ten days is time.

"I have conditions," I say to Pia.

FIVE

Dek is so determined not to let me go with the mechanic that, in the end, Savio has to knock him out with sleeping serum while Pia holds him. I slam my heart shut like an empty box as they take him down. It's something I've gotten better at—like the vanishing.

The light overhead is an electric light, the mechanic tells me. It is blazing white, too bright to look at. My arm is strapped to the arm of the chair, my body bound. Ridiculous, of course—as if these bindings are what will keep me in the chair.

I say as much: "It's no use tying me up. Hasn't anyone told you that?"

"It's so that you don't jump or twitch," says the mechanic. "But it shouldn't hurt. I've numbed your arm."

Indeed, I feel nothing at all below the elbow. He unscrews the lid of a jar on the table, and with long tweezers, he pulls something out of the jelly: a little amber bead, the size of a pinhead, its waving tentacles thin as thread. My throat clenches as he places it on my wrist.

"What *is* it?" I make myself ask. "How does it bind me to him?"

I watch with fast-rising horror as the thing crawls across my wrist and then burrows into the skin, disappearing. I feel a faraway burning sensation. The amber bead is gone, a tiny bulge under my skin, and behind it a glint of silver appears in the little hole it has left behind it, edged with blood.

"They are called the *nuyi*," murmurs the mechanic, leaning over my arm. The drop of silver is spreading, and I can smell my skin burning around it. "A sort of parasite. It attaches to the brain and conquers the will. They secrete this substance to seal themselves inside. We used to put them directly into the brain via the ear, but we found that all too often the body rejected them and they died, or the patient went mad and died. They attach most effectively if inserted when smaller and given a chance to grow inside the body as they move through it. It will strengthen, feeding on your blood, and your body will not fight it by the time it reaches the brain."

That doesn't answer my question as to how it works, but I suppose I didn't expect a real answer.

"So I can pull it out before it reaches my brain?"

I know the answer to this, because I've seen it, but I'd still like his assurance.

"Before it attaches to the brain, it can be surgically removed," he says carefully. "But then your brother's death would be assured. I hope you will not be so rash. Your brother is a remarkable young man. I would like the opportunity to save his life. There are worse fates than serving Casimir."

The silvery disk is hardening. The mechanic cleans the area and wraps a bandage around it. I think of Ling in Tianshi, the girl my brother loved, the fraying bandage on her wrist. The girl who pulled the *nuyi* out.

24

"What about you?" I ask him. "When he put the contract in you, were you willing?"

He raises his wet eyes to mine and says tonelessly, "I regret nothing."

A shudder seizes me, and I close my eyes against the blaze of electric light. I'll cut my own throat before serving Casimir. But it won't come to that. I just need to get home, get Dek away from these people. I hang on to that thought: *home*. I have ten days to figure this out. This is Day One.

DAY 2 TO DAY 4

JOURNEY

⤿

"Tell me how she died," he says.

SIX

Though he'd expressed his desire not to see me again, Casimir walks down to the jetty with Gennady. Gennady's freedom was one of my conditions. There are things I need to ask him. I hadn't expected Casimir to so readily agree to let Dek and Gennady leave with me. He holds all the cards; he doesn't *have* to make concessions. Maybe he's glad to be rid of them. Maybe he believes I'd make good my threat to pull his contract right out of my wrist if he didn't let me take them. Maybe he doesn't think it makes a difference.

Dek, Pia, and I watch their approach from the deck of the boat. They don't look a bit like brothers. Casimir is spindly, spiderish in his gleaming boots and bulky fur cape. His doublet, wrists, fingers, and neck glint with jewels, and his skin looks as if it is stretched too tight over his sharp bones. Gennady is the youngest of the Xianren—the adventurer, the seducer. While Casimir is tall for a man, Gennady is a giant. Now he looks like an injured bear. Pia tells me that all his power has been cut out of him, his ability to transform or speak any magic stripped away by Shey, his veins full of her writing, shot through with silver and ink.

With what appears to be some effort, Casimir looks at me. I am still wearing Pia's things—her tall boots, her leather trousers and jacket adjusted for me on our long sea voyage. She is surprisingly good with a needle and thread. My hair has grown out a bit, but it is still too short to pin up, so it just hangs in my face, a ragged mop.

"You'll have to prettify her somehow," he calls to Pia. "She can't turn up at the Fraynish court looking like that."

"I'll see to it," says Pia.

"If she fails to convince, you might as well cut her throat," he adds carelessly, and Pia gives a brief nod of assent. It's a petty threat, as Casimir's threats go, and I ignore it.

Gennady lumbers up the gangplank onto the boat, shouldering his way past Pia. I wonder if he's remembering how she snapped his leg like a twig. Pia goes down to speak with Casimir. He bends close to her, murmuring into her ear, and then she returns to us on deck. The crew raises the gangplank; they let the sails unfurl and catch the wind. Casimir does not stay to watch us sail away but turns and walks back to his fortress, a gray rock squatting on a gray rock.

SEVEN

Dek and I huddle together by the starboard gunwale, faces pointed into the salty wind. The question of what we are going to do next has fizzled to the agreement that we will try to find Esme—Spira City's most renowned crook and our longtime employer. She'll help us, if she can. Now he is telling me about his journey from Yongguo.

"It was like a big metal cylinder. We climbed through a hatch in the top, and then the hatch closed and it traveled under the water. It took less than two weeks to reach Nago Island, so it traveled tremendously fast, whatever it was."

"And they had Mrs. Och's body too?" I ask.

"I suppose they must have, but I never saw her. I was locked up. I didn't try to escape, obviously. How could I, underwater, in the middle of the ocean?" He flexes the new hand, staring at it like it is a species of animal he's never seen before. "I wouldn't have let them take me—but Pia had Ling. She said she'd let her go if I came quietly. I couldn't just let them kill her."

My throat constricts as I remember slamming Ling against the wall, the way she pulled the *nuyi*, bloody and gleaming, out of her arm. He doesn't need to know that she was in Casimir's employ, and I don't tell him. We watch the gray water rocking on either side of the boat, the horizon tilting back and forth. The unsteady world.

"I found Ko Dan," I tell him at last. "But it wasn't him who put the *Book of Disruption* fragment in Theo at all. Somebody had stolen his body using the Ankh-nu—that little double-spouted pot I told you about. Si Tan said only Marike could use the Ankh-nu. He said she'd been using it to live forever, switching from body to body, and when he saw that memory of mine, the one where Ma had the Ankh-nu, he thought—"

"Julia, stop," he says.

"I'm just telling you what Si Tan said," I continue in a rush, pushing past his resistance. Because who can I say this to if not Dek? How do I face any of it if he doesn't know? "He thought our ma was Marike. And Mrs. Och thought Ma hid Lidari inside me, and that's why I can vanish, cross over to Kahge. I'm not saying I believe it, but if it *is* true, Dek, then . . ." I break off. *Then she's still alive.* But somehow I can't say it. Not with the way he's looking at me.

"What are you saying? That *Ma* was the first Eshriki Phar, leader of the greatest witch empire the world has ever known, a witch who found a way to live forever? Do you realize how completely mad that sounds?"

I shake my head.

"Don't you remember her?" he says more gently, and there's something like pity in his good eye now. "On the barge, at the Cleansing?"

"It might not have been . . . I mean, if she could change bodies."

"But then who was it on the barge? The *look* on her face, Julia. We saw her drown."

"But she was so calm. Didn't you find that strange? How she never seemed afraid?"

"She looked terrified," he says, and then we just stare at each other.

It was ten years ago and easily the worst moment of our lives. Does either of us really remember her expression from a distance, through our own terror and helplessness? Why the difference?

"I stand by what I said before," he says. "We don't know if the vision you had of Ma with the Ankh-nu was real. You're making a huge leap based on stories from people you've no reason to trust and a sort of dream."

I can't explain it—how real the vision was, how sure I am. If I say more I'll burst into tears like a child. So I just say, "You're right." And I tuck it away in a corner of my heart to think about later, because thinking on it too much is like handling broken glass or burning twigs—a few moments only and I need to put it aside.

"Here's what I know," he says. "Our mother is dead, and you are my sister, Julia. You have to believe that."

I shrink back from the look on his face. "All right," I whisper.

He turns back to the water. There is something awful in his expression that I don't know how to interpret. I feel like he's gone a million miles away. I tuck myself against him for comfort. The sea is so deep, the sky is so high, and whatever lies beyond it all goes on perhaps forever. All I want is some hope that we will survive this. I don't know how to think about Ma, or what I am. I just want to be Julia and Dek in the city again.

EIGHT

The four of us sit together in the cramped galley for supper. The cook has worked wonders in a kitchen the size of a cupboard. We are served honeyed duck cooked with apples, black spiced rice, miraculous little soufflés, and Sirillian wine from Casimir's own wine cellar.

"Good wine," says Dek. He raises his glass, with the slightest glimmer of Dek-like humor—a toast to the absurdity of our dinner party.

I raise my glass as well. Pia stares at us, mechanical goggles whirring, as if this is some foreign custom she doesn't understand. Her normally sleek helmet of black hair is rough and tangled with wind and salt, making her look even more lunatic than usual. Gennady empties his plate in approximately two bites and slugs back his wine. The glass looks like a thimble in his big hand.

"So how does this contract work?" I ask Pia. "Can Casimir see me or hear me?"

"It does not work at all yet," she says. "Not until it reaches the brain. And then it is simply a matter of will—his over your own. You'll see. It is an interesting experience."

Gennady gives a grunt of disgust, pours himself another glass of wine, empties it.

"Four of us," says Pia. She takes out a deck of cards, letting them fly from one hand to the other. "We could play Salto Mortale."

"What would the stakes be?" asks Dek.

"I have nothing," says Gennady.

"One of your pretty blue eyes, perhaps?" suggests Pia. "A finger? Not bad. The finger of an immortal. I'm sure witches would pay a fortune for it. An ear?"

This is the sort of conversation I've gotten used to. Pia can be quite disgusting.

"I could bet my glass eye," says Dek, laughing along. He is drinking too much, too fast.

Pia deals out. "If you'd rather not shed blood, we could bet our secrets. What else do we have of value, after all?"

"I don't have any of those left either," says Gennady.

"Then whoever loses the hand tells what they love most or what they fear most," says Pia.

I lose first. What I love most: Dek. What I fear most: losing Dek.

When Dek loses, he looks at his hinged hand and says, "I fear . . . that my sister, who is worth a thousand of me, will try to sacrifice herself for me, which would be a tremendous waste. I fear . . ." His face twists suddenly. "Oh, stars, I could go on and on. I have an awful lot of fears, now that I stop to think about it."

He says nothing of love. He pours himself another glass of wine. He's keeping up with Gennady, who is twice his size and immortal besides. Pia gathers the cards, letting them dance between her hands in a whirling shuffle. The little room sways, the gas lamp sputters.

I lose again, drawing all spades but none that are any good to me. My answers have not changed. Gennady loses next, the queen of hearts hobbled by twos and threes of the wrong color.

"What I feared most has come to pass already," he answers. "Irrelevance, and nothing left to love. Or not enough left of me to feel love. There is nothing to fear without love. Fear is love's shadow, the other side of its coin."

Pia does not lose. Not once.

"She's probably cheating," says Dek. "Let me deal."

It's hard work for him, with his clumsy new hand. He gives up and does it one-handed. Still Pia wins.

"Pity we're not playing for gold," she says.

Dek rises unsteadily.

"I'm going out for some air." He kisses me on top of my head. "I love you, Julia."

I look up at him in surprise. Pia's goggles whir. Dek disappears up the narrow steps, and the three of us sit in silence for a moment. Then Gennady says, "He's probably going to throw himself into the sea."

The truth of that lands like a blow—the way Dek was staring at the waves earlier, the way he's been drinking so resolutely all evening. I rocket out of my seat and up the steps after him. Pia is right behind me.

It is dark, the sky and the water barely distinguishable. I hear a shout from a deckhand and then I see Dek, a shadow by the gunwale. He raises a hand in a little half-wave and tips himself over the side. A blow to the side of my head sends me reeling face-first into the deck. I can't see, can't breathe, scrambling in what might be the wrong direction, trying to get to my feet. I can hear the water, and I lurch toward it, try to call him, but it comes out a pitiful, airless squeak: *"Dek."* I find the gunwale with my hands.

"Easy, girly. She's got him."

That's the deckhand, helping me up. I blink and blink until I can see the moving darkness of the water, Pia's white hand on the rope, the shape in her arms, my brother, my brother. Air pours into my lungs and then I can scream.

The deckhand hauls Dek over the gunwale, and Pia pulls herself after. I don't even help. My brother choking up water in front of me. I crawl over to him and lay my head on his chest.

"No," I weep. "No, no, no."

His arms close weakly around me.

꩜

Dry and wrapped in blankets in our little cabin below, he no longer seems the least bit drunk.

"I won't let you sacrifice yourself for me," he says, terribly calm.

"That's not my plan either!" I sob. I can't get control of myself. I can't wipe from my mind the sight of him disappearing over the side of the boat. I hold the cold cloth Pia brought me to the side of my head. I only figured out afterward that she'd hit me to stop me going in after him.

"Then take that thing out of your wrist."

"I'm not going to let it get to my brain. We agreed! We'll get to Spira City, find Esme and the others, come up with a plan. There might be a way to get this poison out of you or . . . I don't know, something else. I *swear* I'll take it out before it gets too far. We have ten days."

He fixes his good eye on me.

"How could you?" I choke at him. "How could you almost leave me like that?"

"Eight days now," he murmurs. "I don't want to die. But I don't want to sit around with a sac of poison next to my heart waiting to die either, and I'm frightened for you."

"I haven't given up yet. Don't do that again. Not when we still have a chance."

"This is what you call a chance?" He almost smiles.

NINE

My panic recedes slowly as he sleeps, but there's no hope of sleeping myself and the cabin is stuffy, so after a few hours of staring at him, I go up on deck. My breath catches in my throat at the immense, rippling darkness of the sea stretched out all around us, the sky a web of starlight. The silence is vast.

"Tell me how she died," he says, making me jump.

Gennady is hulking by the mainmast, a huge shadow against a huge shadow.

"You can't sleep either?" I ask, trying not to sound as if I'd nearly leaped overboard with fright.

"Tell me," he says again.

So I tell him. I try to stay detached from the words I'm speaking. It tears open such a gaping hole of rage and grief in me to think of Bianka disappearing in the canal, how I tried to save her and could not, my brave, beautiful, sharp-tongued friend—if I can call her that. I wanted so badly for her to be my friend, and I think maybe she was, by the end.

"And where is my son?"

"Safe."

Hounds, I hope it's true. I left Theo behind in Ragg Rock, the hill between the world and its shadow, with only a very injured Frederick and the made-of-mud woman-creature who guards that place to take care of him.

"I asked you *where*."

When I say nothing, he grabs the collar of my coat—Pia's coat—with his big hand and growls at me: "He is my *son*! Tell me where he is!"

I am shocked at the anger that comes exploding out of me then. I had not thought I was so angry. I shove him hard—which is basically as pointless as shoving a wall, but he lets go of my coat—and I shout: "He's in danger because of *you*. He was nearly killed because of *you*. You left Bianka behind, and she's dead because of *you*. You've done nothing for either of them but put them in harm's way, and it cost Bianka her life and may yet cost Theo his too. You let a stranger put something hugely powerful and dangerous inside your son and then you *left*. Did you know the pictures he draws come to life? He might draw a monster that will eat him up! So don't *my son* at me! I know a thing or two about rotten fathers. Maybe you were there for his conception, but you've forfeited any claim you ever had. Bianka asked *me* to protect him and I'm doing my bleeding best and you'd better just keep out of it."

He takes a step back. "I tried," he mutters.

"Oh, don't be pathetic," I snap.

We stand there in silence, the stars hanging overhead like a spectacular, uncaring map of the unknown, and I begin to feel a little bad about my outburst.

"Why did you ask my brother to let me go?" Gennady asks me.

"I promised you, before. I said I'd come back for you and get you out."

"Too late," he says. "I still had some power then. Shey has taken everything. Now I am nothing."

"Well, you're free, anyway. Isn't that worth something?"

"I will never be free."

"Oh well, don't bother thanking me, then." I have so little energy for pitying Gennady, pitiful though he may be. "It's not really an altruistic rescue, anyway. I have questions. How did you meet Ko Dan?"

"He sent me a letter," says Gennady. "I'd heard of him, of course—his fame was growing. Casimir was hunting me. He had already stolen our sister's fragment of *The Book of Disruption,* and he wanted mine as well. My part of the Book had become a shadow that clung to me always—I could not separate it from myself in order to hide it from my brother. Ko Dan told me he could help."

40

Mrs. Och once told me that *The Book of Disruption* was written by the spirit of fire and then split in three by the other elemental spirits, who were frightened of its power. I'm not altogether clear on this bit, but supposedly breaking the Book in three involved a huge magical explosion that created Kahge—a reflection or echo of the world, made of magic. Kahge is also a kind of giant drain, through which magic is slowly flowing out of the world. When Casimir called Mrs. Och *child of the spirits*, he meant it literally. The Xianren think they were birthed by the spirits to protect the three fragments of the Book and keep them separate—and for thousands of years, that is exactly what the Xianren did. As a long-term plan, it clearly wasn't very solid, though, because look where we are now.

"So Ko Dan told you that if you had a child, he could put the text in the child," I prompt Gennady. I could tell him what I know—or think I know—about Ko Dan. But I want to hear his story first.

"Yes," he says. "The shadow had attached itself to my essence, taken root in it, but a child would carry enough of my essence that the shadow—the text—could be transferred."

"Using the Ankh-nu."

He looks at me in surprise, but he keeps talking.

"Yes. I found Bianka—I chose her to be the mother of my child: a witch, a survivor, clever and loving and *strong*. I kept her secret. When she was pregnant, I sent word to Ko Dan. We met him in Sirillia after Theo was born. I told him Bianka was Sirillian so that he would not think to look for

41

her in Frayne. I gave Bianka a sleeping draught at night, and Ko Dan came to our cabin on the coast to do the magic. It was surprisingly simple and painless, though I felt different without the shadow. Theo seemed unharmed. I knew that Ko Dan intended to cut Theo's throat right away in order to destroy the Book fragment—bound to his essence, the fragment had also become mortal. I felt guilty harming a monk, but once the magic was complete, I knocked him out, tied him up, and left him down at the quay."

"Are you sure Ko Dan meant to kill Theo?" I interrupt. If Ko Dan was actually Marike, and if Marike is actually my mother . . . I refuse to believe she would take the life of an innocent child.

"We had spoken of it," says Gennady. "He believed it *had* to be done to protect the world—one life for many. I understood the argument, but I thought I could hide Theo for his natural life, which after all is not very long. I thought Bianka could protect him. I was wrong, and now I wonder if it would have been better to let Ko Dan take his life. Think how many have been killed already in Casimir's search for the text—and how many more will be killed, what hell will come to earth, if he assembles the Book."

"You immortals are all alike," I grind out between my teeth. "Tell me the rest."

"I worked a spell on Bianka and Theo to cloud their essences from anyone searching. As soon as Bianka woke in the morning, a little groggy but none the wiser, we went to the train station. Halfway to Frayne, I told her I was going to get something from the dining car. I jumped off the train. I thought . . . I hoped she would just think I had abandoned her, and she would raise the child and they would be all right. I didn't reckon on Shey, how she was able to dig things out of my mind."

"What a fool you were," I say, which is cruel, but it's hard to listen to him talk of how he lied to her and left her, when I know just what he left her with: no choices. She fought to keep Theo safe until the only choice left was to let go of him and sink. She left Theo to me, and here I am on a boat heading to Frayne with Casimir's contract creeping up my wrist.

"You are hardly an example of a brilliant strategic thinker yourself," he says. "What did you think you would achieve, coming back to Nago Island?"

"I came for Dek."

I'd hoped for more. On the sea journey from Yongguo, I stared at the water and sharpened my knife and tried to make plans. Killing Casimir was Plan A, but I knew it was a long shot. I thought that if I could steal and destroy one of the other text fragments, Theo would no longer be any use to Casimir. But where to begin? What would they look like? How would I know? Then I thought: *I will murder Shey.* Casimir might not be able to change the fragments into text without her. But maybe he would find another way. And how would I kill her? I shot her five times before, and she did not die.

"Remember that he has your brother," Pia would sometimes say to me, when she saw me looking too fierce and thoughtful. In the end, it made no difference; Casimir was ready for me, and I am leaving his island defeated. But I'm alive, and so is Dek, and Casimir doesn't have Theo yet. I've got a week to come up with *something*.

The stars are beginning to fade, the first hint of a paler gray lightening the sky in the east. A dark hump on the horizon solidifies into the Sirillian coastline, and I go down to check on my brother.

TEN

We reach Nim the following evening. The buildings are seashell pink, spilling down the hillside toward the bright water. People stare at us in the streets, moving out of our way fast, whispering behind their hands. A little boy throws a stone, too frightened to aim properly, so it bounces against Gennady's shoe. Pia pivots toward him, and everybody scatters, the boy's heels flying. The innkeeper charges us double and takes Pia's silver with eyes cast down. In our first-class berth on the train leaving at dawn, the ticket master's hands shake when he takes our tickets or brings our coffee. The dining car falls silent when we seat ourselves for lunch.

When he bore the marks of Scourge, Dek was an outcast wherever he went, like all Scourge survivors—feared and shunned. In Spira City, he could not leave the house except by shadow of night, covering his face with a hood. Now he is the most ordinary-looking in our group. Even I am

44

attracting stares—a girl in trousers and boots, my ragged hair practically standing straight up from the sea-salty wind, my face scarred, my nose crooked, broken by Casimir's boot months ago. I used to wonder how Pia could go anywhere at all, looking as strange as she does, but now I see for myself that it is simply by having lots of money and displaying with her papers a certificate bearing the royal seal and proclaiming her a guest of the Crown in Frayne. People may whisper or throw stones or even report her, but the law will not touch her. A mob could have a go, if they dared, but she'd make short work of them, I reckon.

The farms, forests, and towns of my country pass by outside the windows of the train. Sometimes I spot a ruined shrine in the woods, some remnant of what used to be before Agoston Horthy became prime minister of Frayne. We reach Spira City after nightfall, passing through the tidy buildings of Forrestal, then the brightly lit bustle of the Scola. Cyrambel Temple looms darkly by the river Syne, where our mother was drowned, and Dek takes my hand.

When I remember that Cleansing, the first I ever watched, I think Dek must be right—we watched her drown, she's gone. But when I think of the vision I had of her with the Ankh-nu, I have a million questions, and I wonder if it's possible that she is still alive. I don't know if there is more hope or fear in the question. Because what does it mean if she was not who we thought? If she'd lived thousands of years before us, done terrible things, left us behind? If she was only Ammi, then she loved us and she died brutally, unjustly. If she is Marike, she may not be dead, but she may not have loved us at all.

We get off the train in the Plateau and stand together on the platform.

"You're confident your brother will not attempt to take his own life again?" Pia asks me.

I look at Dek.

"Not this week," he says calmly.

Pia's goggles swivel at him, and then she turns back to me: "I will be in the same suite you remember at the West Spira Grand Hotel. I've taken the whole tenth floor, so you may choose your room. Clothes for you have already been delivered. We need to find a ladies' maid who can make you look . . . appropriate."

"I know someone who can help," I say, thinking of Csilla. "If she's back in Spira City, that is."

"You will *need* help," Pia says, looking me over.

"Why do I have to play dress-up? Can't I just go around vanished?"

"There will be plenty of that. But you will need to be able to talk to people as well. Tomorrow Sir Victor Penn Ostoway will take you to the opera and introduce you as his niece, visiting from the countryside."

"Sir *Victor*?" I cry.

"He has been in Casimir's employ for some months now. I thought you knew."

"I did. I suppose I hadn't expected to see him again."

He is a high-up official in the government, a sort of

antimagic official. I met him when I was posing as a house-maid in Mrs. Och's house. He'd been bitten by a Parnese wolf and turned to Mrs. Och for help. In the end, Casimir's witch Shey cured him, halting his transformation into a wolf—in exchange for his taking on Casimir's contract.

"Pretending to be a noble girl is hardly my area of expertise," I say. "I tried it in Yongguo, and Si Tan saw through me in about three seconds."

"Si Tan is very perceptive," says Pia. "Most people aren't. Find your friend and ask her to come in the morning to help you dress. Good night."

Then, to my amazement, Pia turns and walks away from us. Dek and I gape at each other. For a wild moment I feel like a dog let off the leash, free to bolt. But of course the truth is that Casimir's leash is working its way under my skin and sitting next to Dek's heart. There's no running away.

"Well," says Dek. "I wasn't expecting *that*." He looks at Gennady. "What about you?"

Gennady looks weary and confused, and I feel rather sorry for him after all.

"There might be a revolution," I tell him. "I thought you liked those."

He makes a sound that might be a chuckle.

"Come with us," I say, though I don't really know why I'm offering. "We'll find the others. If he's here, you could tell Professor Baranyi about Mrs. Och. I don't fancy delivering that news myself."

"He was her assistant?" he asks. "Or companion?"

"Something like that," I say. I've never been sure what he was to her, but I know he loved her.

We walk from the station into the winding streets of the Twist. Laughter, quarreling, music, and the smell of food drift out from the bars, and tears rise to my eyes unexpectedly. For all that there were terrible losses and hardships, I was happy here once.

Esme's building on the east side of Fitch Square is empty, no sign of anyone having been here in months. It says something about what high esteem she is held in that no squatters have set up here.

Esme took us in when I was seven and Dek was ten. She was always more a boss than a surrogate mother, but she saw us fed and clothed, taught us to read and write and do our sums. She raised us, more or less, from that point on. As the most feared and respected crook in the city, she also trained us and made use of our skills. I think of her stern face by firelight as I struggled to copy out a poem I hated, stolen jewels across the table with our lesson books, a hot supper in my belly. She'd lost her own son to Scourge, and I think that's why she took Dek in, but she saw something in him too—that flash of brilliance. Tough as we were, we still needed a place to call home, someone strong at our backs. She gave us that.

"This is where you lived?" Gennady asks, looking curiously into the little room where Dek and I used to sleep. Roaches scuttle out of the way underfoot. The parlor upstairs is cleaned out, Wyn's attic room abandoned. There is nothing but a bare bedframe and an empty desk left behind in Esme's room. Dust gathers in the corners, and cobwebs hang in sheets where the ceiling meets the walls.

"It's not that they didn't come back at all," says Dek. "All my papers are gone, and Esme's too. Somebody *was* here and took everything."

"But no note for us," I say.

"Where else would they go?"

"Let's check Mrs. Och's place."

None of the hackneys we try to flag down will stop for us—I don't know if that's Gennady's size, me wearing Pia's clothes, or how sea-battered we all look, but we end up walking all the way to the Scola. Gennady opens the gate to his dead sister's house. The windows are bright, so *somebody* is here. My heart speeds up a little—as if Mrs. Och might be there and answer the door, as if the past few months had not happened at all—but I muster my courage and we bang the brass knocker. Voices sound within, and footsteps. The door swings open, and there is Gregor, Esme's longtime associate, his face lighting up at the sight of us. I shout and throw myself into his arms. I'm immediately a little embarrassed, but it is so good to have friends in the world, people who are on our side.

"Hounds, it's good to see you," I say. He looks better than I've ever seen him—leaner, the pouches under his eyes less prominent, and his gaze clear, not fogged by booze. He's keeping away from the drink after all. Good old Gregor.

Then Esme and Gregor's lover, Csilla, join him in the entry-way, and I am yelling like an idiot, hugging them all. Esme cups my face in her big hands and kisses my forehead. She looks just the same—as tall as Gregor, dressed like a gentleman since ladies' clothes do not fit her, hair a helmet of white, her chiseled face peculiarly ageless.

"You're all right, then?" she asks me.

"I am," I say, which isn't true but feels it at the moment. "Is Wyn here too? He met up with you?"

"He did," says Esme. "He's staying at a pub in the Edge. We only got back to the city last week."

Gennady is hulking behind us, looking miserable. I try to draw him into the foyer with us. "This is Gennady. Theo's father." Like I'm in the habit of introducing strange, enormous immortals to my gang.

"Good," says Esme briskly. "Come meet the others."

I don't have time to ask who *the others* are. She takes us into the front parlor. Professor Baranyi is there, and Princess Zara, who we rescued from Yongguo, with little Strig in her lap—the owlet Bianka turned into a cat, now stuck somewhere between the two, a feathery, squashed-face, owl-eyed little kitty. But my eyes go straight to the two strangers in the room.

One of them is a young man with coal-black eyes and skin nearly as dark, dressed in a rather dandy dinner suit and ruffled cravat. He is sitting on the sofa, folding squares of colored paper into complicated little three-dimensional animals, but he offers a distant smile. Next to him is a fair-complexioned woman in a fashionable gown. She is older than the man, perhaps in her fifties, her black hair shot through with silver, but there is a youthful vigor in the way she holds herself. She is smoking a cigarette in a long pearl-handled holder, which she puts down in an ashtray when we come in, waving the smoke away and crossing the room with a quick, limping gait to greet us.

"*Julia!*" she cries, and her voice is rich and warm. "I cannot tell you how happy I am to meet you at last."

DAY 4, EVENING
WELCOME TO THE REVOLUTION

But here she is, her head still attached
to her neck after all.

ELEVEN

The woman clasps my hand and kisses my cheek, the corners of her dark eyes curling up with her smile. She has an upper-class accent. Her hands are warm and soft. She smells of cigarettes and brandy and expensive soap. I stare at her with my mouth open while she moves smoothly on to Dek.

"And you must be Benedek. You look very well—both of you. Better than we'd feared!"

In fact, we look very confused. Princess Zara gives me a wave.

"I'd get up to say hello," she says, "but I hate to disturb the cat!"

"It's not really a cat," I say.

"Oh, I know. I heard about that."

"Zor Gen!" says the elegant lady—*not* kissing Gennady. "I am glad to see you also. Please, sit, all of you. You must be tired! I'll have the cook bring something to eat and drink. Will you speak to her, Csilla?"

Csilla nods and goes out.

Dek and I are standing there gaping like fools, but Gennady is unimpressed. "Do I know you?" he rumbles—which is just what I am thinking.

"We haven't met," she says. "But I have heard a great deal about all three of you, and I'm sure you have heard some mention of me too. At least, I *hope* so. I am Ariane Laroche."

"Lady Laroche?" Dek gives me a startled look.

"I'd heard you were ... well, we were told you were ... *dead*," I say, not finding a polite way to come to this point.

Lady Laroche—leader of the Sidhar Coven. The coven my mother was once a part of. The coven that brutalized Pia and sent her to kill Casimir. In Tianshi, I heard Agoston Horthy's lackey claim she'd been caught and executed. He was promising to send the grand librarian of Yongguo her head. But here she is, her head still attached to her neck after all.

"*Not* dead," she says, holding her arms out and executing a startling twirl, as if to prove the point. She picks up her cigarette. Indeed, she is tremendously jaunty for someone supposedly executed over a month ago. "Not dead at all, though I *was* captured and taken to Hostorak. A low point in my career. What a dreadful place!"

There is a short pause, and then the man on the sofa drawls, "She's waiting for you to ask how she escaped."

She laughs, swooping the hand with the cigarette in the direction of the young stranger and his paper animals. "Excuse my rudeness. May I introduce Mr. Idir Faruk?"

He rises to shake my hand as if I were a man, then Dek's, then Gennady's before returning to the sofa. Idir Faruk: there is no explanation of him beyond that.

"How *did* you get out of Hostorak?" asks Dek obligingly. The dreaded prison for witches and folklore practitioners is reputed to be impenetrable.

"Idir is tired of the story, so I'll be brief. I keep a needle in my dress, always. I knew I would be searched, so I stuck it into my heel and it went unnoticed. I went to my cell with it. The cells in Hostorak are coated with silver, to impede magic being worked inside them, but not all of us are strongly affected by silver. I used the needle to write a spell on my own flesh. When my captors returned to take me to the river and drown me, I turned into a bat and escaped. Would you believe, though, that of all the possible dangers involved, my *heel* became infected! I nearly lost my foot!"

Dek and I exchange a look at *turned into a bat*. What kind of witch *is* this?

"And now you're all staying here?" I ask Esme. "The old place is empty."

"We weren't sure it was safe," she says. "But I am staying in the Edge. We're here for a strategy meeting tonight."

"Welcome to the revolution," says Lady Laroche, with a slightly lunatic grin, and I finally sit down next to Mr. Faruk. Dek sits with me.

In comes Mrs. Freeley, the cook when I was posing as a housemaid here, with Csilla behind her. Mrs. Freeley is unchanged—a mountain of a woman with shrewd little eyes.

She rather frightened me when I ostensibly worked for her, but her expression now is more amused than anything else.

"You look a mite different from the last time I saw you," she says, putting a platter of biscuits and coffee down on the table. "Julia, is it, now? I've been telling myself I should've known that no maid with any training could've been as incompetent as you were in the kitchen. It's quite a mixed bag of tales I've been hearing about you."

I attempt a smile.

"Where is Mrs. Och?" asks Professor Baranyi, hunched on the settee near the princess and watching me guardedly. "Where are Frederick and Bianka and Theo?"

My mouth goes dry. Might as well get it over with.

"Mrs. Och and Bianka are both dead."

A stunned silence follows. Lady Laroche alone doesn't look terribly shocked. She sucks on her cigarette and blows a plume of smoke out into the room. Mrs. Freeley sits down in the one empty chair—not like a servant at all, and I suppose I had gathered by the end of my performance as housemaid here that she was not really—or not merely—a servant. They are all staring at me, waiting, and so I tell them.

"Mrs. Och killed Bianka. Threw her into the Dongnan Canal in Tianshi. She meant to kill Theo too—she was going for him with a knife—so . . . I killed Mrs. Och. Or, I hurt her badly, and she died later."

At first my voice is shaking, but I pull myself together. I did what I had to do. I still believe that. I refuse to be some simpering girl wracked with guilt.

The princess has stopped stroking Strig, her lips parted in horror. Csilla bursts out, "Oh, Julia!" and then covers her mouth. I daren't look at Professor Baranyi.

"I rather think you're bringing us in at the end of the story," says Lady Laroche. "Your friends have told me about your journey to Yongguo—how you hoped to find the monk Ko Dan. But I thought Mrs. Och was *protecting* the witch and her son."

"She was," I say. "Until she wasn't."

I explain it stumblingly—how Mrs. Och lost all hope of helping Theo, and Si Tan persuaded her to destroy Theo and that dangerous text fragment. I tell again, my voice hollow, how she drained Frederick of his strength, took Bianka and Theo on the water. How she tossed them into the canal and swung her blade at Theo when I fished him out.

"And I stopped her," I say. "I killed her."

"Pray, *how?*" asks Lady Laroche. "My understanding is that immortals are rather difficult to kill."

Gennady answers for me: "She took my sister to Kahge and plunged her into the fire there until she was burnt to nearly nothing. It might not have killed her if she were not already dying. But it hastened her end."

I allow myself a glance at Esme. I should have told them before now what I can do. Well, now they know. She meets my eyes steadily, and I realize that she already knows a fair bit when Lady Laroche says, "*Kahge!* Incredible! Professor Baranyi told us about this *remarkable* ability you have. I confess, I wasn't sure whether I believed it, but if the Xian-ren say it is true . . ."

I wonder what else the professor told them. If they know about Lidari. I wonder what Esme thinks. But she kissed me at the door like I was just Julia.

"I've known Mrs. Och for more than twenty years," says Mrs. Freeley. There are tears in her eyes, but her voice doesn't waver. "She would never have done such a thing if she'd had a choice. This girl . . . last time she was here she kidnapped the little boy. Now she's back to say his mother's dead and claiming Mrs. Och's responsible for it. How do we know she's telling the truth?"

"Careful," says Esme, her voice dropping a pitch to that dangerous place that sometimes precedes violence.

"You weren't with us in Yongguo, Mrs. Freeley," says Gregor, more diplomatically. "We all respected Mrs. Och, but I don't doubt Julia's telling. Professor—it has the ring of truth, does it not? We all know Mrs. Och was entirely capable of—"

Professor Baranyi stands up and goes out without look-ing at me.

"We understand that you were left with few choices, Julia," says Lady Laroche. She glances at Mrs. Freeley, who presses her lips together and says nothing. "And where *is* the child now?"

"With Frederick," I say. "I don't know where."

Princess Zara is watching me closely, stroking the owl-cat. With a nasty jolt I remember that she can tell when somebody is lying. So she knows I know where Theo is. But she says nothing.

Dek takes over to tell his part—being captured in Tian-shi, the surgery and the sac of poison slowly deteriorating next to his heart. He tells them about the contract in my wrist, the thing that will crawl toward my brain over the coming days and conquer my mind entirely. The parlor is quiet as a tomb while he talks. We certainly know how to bring the fun to a party.

"I've heard rumors about Casimir's contracts," says Lady Laroche. "Show us, Julia."

I roll the sleeve of Pia's shirt up and pull off the bandage to reveal the red streak running from the metal disk in my wrist to the little itching lump that has nearly reached the inside of my elbow now. It's *moving*, and alarmingly fast too. Lady Laroche clenches her jaw around her cigarette holder.

"Why not just pluck it out now?" she asks.

"I'll pull it out as soon as we find a way of getting the poison out of Dek," I say. "Given how fast it's moving, I'd say I've got a week tops to figure something out."

Lady Laroche kneels before the sofa, skirts rustling, and takes my wrist in her hand to examine the little lump. "It's alive, isn't it?"

I shrug, feeling queasy.

"The Xianren can tell us about the *nuyi*," says Mr. Faruk, directing his words to Gennady. "Once upon a time they posed a terrible threat, and the Xianren joined together to destroy them, is that not so?"

"What *is* it?" asks Esme. "Let's get that straight first."

"A kind of parasite," says Gennady. "Each nest has a queen, and only the queen is truly intelligent. Her soldiers execute her will, however far they may roam from the nest. The queen herself is too large to enter the brain without killing the carrier, but her small soldiers burrow into living beings, take over their will, and serve the queen through the body they have come to dominate. At first we didn't know what was happening. Once-benevolent kings, generals, coven leaders would turn ruthless and power-hungry. It had been going on for centuries before we discovered the *nuyi*. We destroyed all the nests we could find, killing the queens and thus releasing the many tribes and kingdoms that had fallen under their power. If they are not quite extinct, they are not nearly the threat they used to be." He gives a snort that might be laughter. "Trust Casimir to keep a few as pets."

"Yes, he's really one for the hijinks, isn't he," says Dek dryly. "A regular barrel of monkeys, that brother of yours."

"So where is the *nuyi* queen?" I ask.

"*Casimir* is the queen," says Gennady. "I do not know how he maintains his control over the *nuyi*, but he functions as the queen of his own nest. They are linked to his will, and they obey it. He keeps the soldiers alive and puts them inside anyone he wants to control."

"So all our problems end if we kill Casimir," I say bitterly.

"Easier said than done, my dear," says Lady Laroche. "We've tried that. Still, it is a worthy goal, and I would like to help you."

"As will I, if I can," says Gennady. "I am ready for the end of the Xianren. Including myself."

Lady Laroche gives him an appraising glance. "I think we can be of use to each other, Zor Gen."

"Perhaps I can be of use to you," he replies. "You are no use to me."

"Don't be so sure. My goodness, what a lot to think about. Julia, you've really *no* idea where the little boy is? We could help keep him safe."

I shake my head, avoiding Zara's gaze. I don't know this woman, and I'm not going to trust her with Theo's life.

Lady Laroche grinds her cigarette out. "Pity. So, Casimir wants you spying on the Fraynish court."

"He doesn't trust Agoston Horthy," I say.

"Indeed no, and nor should he," says Lady Laroche. Her eyes are bright. She looks like she's about to suggest a picnic at the seaside. "How do you feel about being a sort of double agent, Julia? If you are able to pass along information to us as well, it could be very useful."

"As long as Casimir doesn't figure it out, I feel fine," I say.

"Good. In the meantime, we must see what we can do for Benedek. It may be that the right surgeon and the right witch together can help us. If we cannot take the poison out, perhaps we could prevent the sac from deteriorating, or counter the poison somehow. I will send a telegram first thing in the morning to a friend who might be able to help. We need expert opinions."

I start to warm to her a little. She sounds so assured that I wonder if she might really be able to help us after all. There are powerful people in the world other than Casimir, and she probably knows them.

The night grows deeper as we talk. Mrs. Freeley says nothing but glowers at me while the others fill us in on the nascent revolution. Gregor and Csilla have taken a house in West Spira, just north of the university, where they are throwing illicit parties with the purpose of wooing members of the upper classes unhappy with Agoston Horthy's regime. Esme is working with a group of revolutionaries stationed in the Edge and sounding out allies in other parts of the country. When the grandfather clock on the third-floor landing strikes one, we are all still gathered in the parlor, the owl-cat asleep on the princess's lap now. Professor Baranyi has not come back.

"It's late," says Lady Laroche with a theatrical yawn.

"Mr. Gennady, you're welcome to stay here," says Mrs. Freeley, pointedly excluding me and Dek from the invitation. "I know Mrs. Och would've wanted her brother to be comfortable. I'll make up the room in the cellar for you. We had a nobleman staying there before, and it'll afford you the most privacy."

She must mean the room Sir Victor stayed in, struggling with his nocturnal wolfism. I think after his long imprisonment, Gennady might prefer a room that didn't have chains on the walls, but at least he won't have to wear them. Lady Laroche looks vaguely surprised at Mrs. Freeley's offer but doesn't argue. I wouldn't want to be the one to tell Gennady he's not welcome either.

"Julia and Benedek have traveled a long way," she begins.

Mrs. Freeley locks eyes with her, and to head off the conflict I say quickly, "I'm to stay at the West Spira Grand Hotel with Pia. Speaking of which, Csilla, d'you suppose you could come there tomorrow morning, first thing? Tenth floor. I need somebody to help me dress up like a noble girl."

Csilla is leaning against Gregor on the settee—either that or propping him up. She assents immediately, smiling away the tension in the room: "Of course. I've always wanted to dress you up a bit. This latest outfit of yours is ghastly."

"I'd like to see Wyn," says Dek, rising. "He's a night owl—I reckon he's still up. Where's this pub he's staying at?"

"It's called the Marrow, in Rat's Row," says Esme. "I've another meeting tonight, down in Forrestal, but if you're going to the Marrow, perhaps you can take a message for me to a fellow named Torne."

"Hang on, *who?*" I cry.

"Torne," says Esme, frowning at me. "He's one of the few surviving leaders of the Lorian Uprising."

"At the Marrow?"

"Yes."

I feel an odd little quiver of . . . what? It starts out queasy, but there's something else in it too. Anticipation?

"I know the place," I say.

TWELVE

East Spira—more commonly known as the Edge—is like the grimy hem of the city, trailing in the dust. It is a desolate place, reeking of desperation. Beyond it, Limory Cemetery climbs the foothills toward the jagged Ender Mountains. The Marrow has a street-level door with no number, and no one answers our knock. Dek picks the lock, and we go down the narrow staircase toward the voices at the bottom.

The last time I was here, on an errand for Professor Baranyi, I barely got out with my stockings still on. I swore then that I'd come back and torch the place someday. I won't deny a little thrill at descending the familiar staircase. I could barely defend myself back then, but now—well, I'm positively looking forward to seeing the men who assaulted me.

At the bottom of the stairs is a wide room with a few dirty tables and chairs and, at the back, a long bar. Above the bar is a balcony with a few more doors in the hall behind it. The way up there is not apparent; I think I remember a door behind the bar, but the light is bad. I recognize the woman cleaning glasses at the bar, her wrinkled bosom barely fitting into her dress, a great scar down her face—I've one to match it now. Time, debauchery, and violence have done such a number on her that it's impossible to imagine what she must have looked like once. She doesn't recognize me, of course. I look different, and was surely not very memorable, anyway—just another girl in the wrong place, an afternoon's entertainment.

Half a dozen men are slouching at the tables. I spot Graybeard, the one who hit me and ripped my coat getting it off me, and I feel a hot thrill of anger.

"We're looking for Wyn," says Dek.

"Are you now?" says the woman, her wide grin revealing a nearly toothless maw.

"And who might you be?" asks a fellow at the bar with tattoos on his forearms—element symbols.

"His friends," says Dek.

"Wyn!" roars the fellow, so loud that I jump in spite of myself. He grins nastily at me, and I give him a sweet smile back. *Just wait, you bastard.* Somebody spills a drink and curses, somebody laughs, a squabble ensues. A door off the balcony above opens and out comes Wyn—beautiful Wyn—tucking his shirt into his trousers and leaning over the banister, his face lighting up when he sees us. Behind him, out of the same door, looking tousled and happy, her hair loose around her shoulders, comes a fair-haired girl I've never seen. Of course.

"Hounds, is it ever good to see the two of you!" Wyn shouts. "Hang on, I'm coming down!"

The two of them disappear back inside, and a moment later Wyn emerges alone behind the bar. He grabs Dek in a bear hug and then pulls me into the embrace as well, so that all three of us are hugging and laughing.

"I was afraid I'd never see you two again," says Wyn, and pulls back to look us over. "This new look suits you," he says to me. "We just need to get you an eye patch and a parrot. And *you*—you've . . . you're . . . flaming hounds, what *is* all this?" He grabs Dek's arm, touching the hinges at his knuckles, laughing in disbelief.

"Long story," says Dek, but he's laughing too.

A man with a ferret on his shoulder comes sauntering over, hand on the gun buckled to his belt, and says, "Introduce us to your friends, then."

I remember him too. He didn't take part in the attack on me, but he didn't stop it either.

Wyn introduces us. Of me, he says good-humoredly, "You don't want to mess with Julia here!" and they all laugh. I feel myself sneering.

Someone outside our little circle says, "I know you."

The men go silent. Torne has come in, and even if none of the others recognize me, *he* does.

"You've a good memory for faces," I say. "The same can't be said of your fellows here."

"Hang on," says Wyn, confused.

"You worked for Casimir," says Torne.

"I did," I say. "And now I do again."

I flash the contract at my wrist, and he flinches.

"What . . . ?" says Wyn.

Torne draws a gun.

"Wait!" says Wyn.

I vanish. Torne is spinning in circles looking for me, all

the men shouting and drawing weapons now, Wyn yelling, "Calm down, it's fine, it's just something she can do! *Julia!*"

"Julia, stop it!" cries Dek.

I reappear next to Torne, just for a second. I twist the gun out of his hand, and I'm gone, leaving them in a total uproar that I hear only faintly through the blur of my vanishing. I don't like to upset Dek, but otherwise I am enjoying this immensely.

I find Graybeard, a hazy silhouette yelling obscenities, and I reappear behind him, pressing Torne's gun under his chin. "Nobody move!"

Torne holds up his hands for silence, and they all go still, pointing their weapons and their angry, scared faces at me. I'll say this: if there is an upside to finding out you're a monster, it's terrorizing the people who once terrorized you.

"You remember me," I say to Torne. "But nobody else does. Even though they tried to rip my dress off less than a year ago. This one hit me in the face. Seems to me you ought to remember a girl you've punched. Or perhaps you do it so often that they all blur together."

Wyn and Dek's expressions change, turning murderous.

"What do you want?" asks Torne.

"I want to have some fun," I say. "I want to dangle this fellow from the roof beams by his ankles and throw lit matches at him for sport. I want to burn this place *down*."

"Julia," says Dek. "What happened?"

"These fellows had a go at me last winter," I say.

"Which ones?"

"This one," I say, giving Graybeard a little shove so he grunts. "Most of them."

I didn't know Wyn had a gun on him, but he takes it out now—he's nearly as quick a draw as Esme—so he's got the muzzle of it right under Torne's missing ear, and I think, *Good old Wyn*; I may not have been able to trust him as a lover, but I've always known he'd stand by me when it counted most. The others swivel to point their weapons at him. Dek sighs.

"I *persuaded* Esme to work with you lot," says Wyn scathingly. "Time to unpersuade her, I reckon."

"Calm down," says Torne. "Esme agreed to work with us for a reason. If you want a revolution, we are indispensable."

"You're not indispensable," says Wyn. "And we're not working with villains and brutes."

"We can discuss some form of punishment for the guilty," says Torne, his voice level.

I laugh and shove Graybeard away from me.

"Punishment *now*?" I say. "You mean they *weren't* punished? I'm shocked! Well, I like my idea with the roof beams and the matches."

I've lowered the gun, but I see movement—it's the tattooed brick wall of a fellow who held me when Graybeard hit me last time. I let him get close and then I vanish, pulling away so far that he stumbles into nothing. Then I bring myself back, grab Graybeard again, and pull him with me right out of the world.

Oh, this pulsing, triumphant fury. It's a little *too* much

fun. I pull him through and through and through, and we land hard in a Spira City that is burnt and shadowy, the air smoking.

Kahge.

Something like a crocodile but black and indistinct is crawling toward us down an alley. The doorways are all on fire. Graybeard screams and screams, eyes rolling wildly, and the joy goes out of me all at once, like a match going out. I'm too familiar with mortal terror to enjoy watching it. I drag him back and drop him, sweating and gibbering, on the floor of the bar.

"Demon!" he sobs, pointing at me. "Help me—she's a demon!"

"Nobody move," says Torne again, and nobody does. Wyn still has his gun pointed at Torne, but he and Dek are staring at me like they don't know who I am. And of course—how would they know?

"Julia," says Wyn, very softly. "What do you want to do?"

I look around at the men, sweaty and pale, frightened of me, and I'm *glad* I got to come back here and terrify them.

"We have some catching up to do with Wyn," I say to Torne. "We'll talk about your *men* and punishments later. For now, keep them away from me."

He says, with no trace of a smile, "I think they will stay away from you by themselves."

Wyn lowers his gun, and Dek says to Torne, "We've got a message from Esme, by the way. We still ought to give it to him, Julia, don't you think?"

I nod. He hands Torne the folded-up piece of paper. We looked at it on the way over, but it was in some kind of code, unsurprisingly. Torne takes it from him with a murmur of thanks.

"Where can we talk?" I ask Wyn.

He takes us upstairs to a bleak little room with a stove, where his girl has gone back to bed, her flaxen hair poured over the pillow. I don't know how to feel about it. It's not that I can't handle the idea of Wyn with somebody else by now. I had to make my peace with *that* while we were still together. Maybe I'm just getting used to not minding so much.

Wyn brings out a bottle of rum and three glasses, and we sit around a greasy table dotted with crumbs while he pours us each a drink.

"Are you going to be all right here?" I ask. "I mean, after pulling a gun on Torne . . . have I gotten you in trouble?"

He shakes his head. "Esme is top dog. Nobody's going to mess with me."

I'm wondering if I overdid it down there, if I've frightened my own brother and my oldest friend. But then Wyn raises his glass and flashes his old heartbreaker grin.

"Hounds, Julia. I always thought the vanishing was a neat trick, but you've become downright scary."

"I have," I agree.

"You could've *warned* me you were going to pull that," says Dek.

"Well, I wasn't sure," I say. "But I couldn't resist."

"Bleeding stars, their *faces* . . ." Dek gives a snort of laughter, and we are all laughing then, so hard I'm not sure I can stop, doubled over in my chair, tears streaming down my cheeks. Monster I may be, but I adore these two, and the three of us together feels something like home.

Telegram to Lord Casimir, Nago

Island: SAFE ARRIVAL STOP OPERA

TOMORROW STOP JULIA COOPERATIVE STOP

DAY 5

RATS

But then sometimes I feel as if
my body is only a disguise.

THIRTEEN

For a moment I can't remember where I am. Sunlight is pouring through the window, and Pia is silhouetted in front of it, having drawn back the curtains. I came to the hotel a few hours before dawn, not much wanting to sleep under the same roof as Torne's men. Funny that rooming with Pia would seem less of a threat. Or maybe *funny* isn't the right word for it.

"The maid is filling you a bath," she says. "You stink."

I'm still in my clothes—*her* clothes—sprawled on top of the covers of this absolutely enormous four-poster bed. I groan, which makes me feel slightly better, so I do it again, and Pia laughs.

"Get up," she says. "Wash. It's already midday. Your friend is here, and you've got an opera to go to."

"My friend?" I say, sitting up. And then I remember that I asked Csilla to come.

I peel Pia's clothes off in the bathroom and step into the

tub. The water is so hot I have to lower myself into it inch by inch. I sink up to my neck and then dunk my ratty mop of hair underneath as well. Settling back in the water, I examine the red-mud scars on my arm and my side—slices taken out of me by monsters I may have more in common with than I'd like to believe, stopped up by the mud of Ragg Rock. The *nuyi* has reached the inside of my elbow, a tender lump creeping under my skin. My body is changed—damaged, patched up, invaded by the otherworldly. But then sometimes I feel as if my body is only a disguise, barely real, if I can shed it so easily. I *want* it to be mine, though—to be real, to be *me*. What am I, if not the body I inhabit? If that body is something that can disappear and change, what part is *me*? I stretch my muscles, roll my neck, and feel, as I still sometimes do, that surely I *am* Julia, I *am* this body that feels so much. I stay in the tub, letting the warm water soothe me, until the bath starts to cool and I hear voices from the other room.

FOURTEEN

When we were in Yongguo, I sometimes asked myself, what would Little Julia, aged ten or thereabouts and believing herself so tough and so brave, have thought if she could glimpse a few years ahead and watch her future self scaling walls and rescuing a princess halfway around the world? It amused me to think of it. And still my life keeps producing scenes that just a few months ago would have been unimaginable.

Like this scene. I am wearing a silk dressing gown and drinking coffee on the tenth floor of a West Spira hotel room. The balcony doors are open to let in the early-summer breeze. There are trunks full of expensive dresses all over the place. Pia is stretched out on the sofa, her booted feet up on the arm of it, reading a telegram, while Csilla, corn-silk curls tumbling over her creamy shoulders, opens trunk after trunk, pulling out gowns, shoes, shawls, boxes of jewelry. "You can't wear this, not unless we stuff the bust," she'll say, or, "This one will suit you well, but you'll need a good, tight corset," or, "Stars, it's *much* too hot for velvet; let's find something suitable to the season."

"I saw your friend Torne last night," I say to Pia. "D'you remember? You told me you knew him."

"Yes," says Pia. "I did."

"He doesn't strike me as a nice man."

She looks up at me, goggles whirring. "He isn't."

"The first time I saw him, he got very nervous when I mentioned your name."

That makes her grin.

"Who is he?"

"He worked for the Sidhar Coven years ago as a sort of liaison," she says, putting the telegram down. "He's not a man-witch, but he ran messages, took care of various nasty jobs, and linked the witches up with revolutionaries in the city. He was in charge of me, back when they considered me their attack dog. He was my keeper, you might say."

"So he's afraid you might take revenge?"

"I already have. He and I passed a day in a cellar together, not long after the Lorian Uprising. I let him live, to match the mercy he occasionally showed me, but I cut off his ear as a souvenir."

"Ugh!" Csilla looks up from a ruffled, cream-colored gown that I hope to heaven she doesn't try to make me wear. "Enough about cutting off ears and horrible men. Hang on—here's something." She puts down the ruffled gown and holds another dress up to show us. The top and shoulders are pale lace, cut modestly. It has a satin sash right under the bust and a long, flowing skirt in navy blue.

"Simple, elegant, but not too eye-catching," she says. "That's what you want, isn't it?"

"That is what Casimir wants," says Pia, barely glancing at the dress. "I do not know anything about ladies' fashions."

"No, I suppose you don't," says Csilla, regarding her curiously. "It seems a shame not to dress her up a bit more, though. Everything here is so banal, nothing interesting or *new*."

"She is a spy," says Pia. "She's not supposed to attract attention."

"But why does Casimir want her to spy on Agoston Horthy? I thought they were allies," says Csilla.

"Agoston Horthy is proving unreliable," says Pia. "There is a revolution brewing, as you know. You might warn your friends it can't end well. Horthy will take care of this would-be coup as efficiently as he took care of the Lorian Uprising. But once things settle down, Casimir wants Horthy replaced with someone he can control more easily."

"*Really?*" says Csilla, fascinated.

"I've said too much," says Pia to me. "I'll have to kill her."

Csilla and I freeze.

"Joking," says Pia, without smiling.

"Well, I promise not to breathe a word of it to Agoston Horthy," says Csilla, recovering fast. "Come on, Julia, let's try this on and see how you look."

"I'm going to look ridiculous," I say. "Especially with my hair like this and the scar . . ."

"I worked in the theater for years," says Csilla. "Don't you think I know how to cover a scar? I've got hair extensions for you as well. I'm going to make you look lovely. Or simple, elegant, and not too eye-catching, in any case."

Indeed, over the next hour, Csilla transforms me. First she nearly kills me with the corset, and I have to beg her to loosen it, pointing out that I can't spy if I'm fainting from lack of oxygen. She squashes me into the dress and a pair of satin shoes, painstakingly fastens the hair extensions and arranges it all into a sweeping updo, and then spends another half hour painting my face. When she is done, I do not look like myself at all. The scar on my cheek is still a visible line if you look closely, but it doesn't jump out anymore, blending into the stiff, powdered mask of my face. I admit I'd half hoped I might look pretty at the end of all this pinching and prodding and pulling and powdering, but in fact I look stunningly ordinary—like a dull, plain girl who can afford nice dresses but has no taste.

Dek gave me five little darts of sleeping serum in a leather purse last night, and now I tuck the purse into the top of the dress, tugging the fabric around it so it doesn't look too lumpy.

"What do you think?" Triumphant, Csilla spins me to face Pia.

The goggles swivel in and out. "You look like a rich girl," she concedes.

"You think I'll pass as Sir Victor's niece?" I pull an exaggerated simper, curtsying, and Pia smiles. An odd smile, I think at first—and then I realize it is odd because it is genuine.

"It will do," she says.

FIFTEEN

An electric hackney is waiting outside the hotel in the late afternoon. Csilla has already left, accepting money from Pia with the smoothness of somebody accustomed to unusual, well-paid transactions. The window drapes are closed, and the hackney is dim and stuffy. I climb in and sit myself down across from Sir Victor Penn Ostoway III.

"I barely recognize you," he says. His hair is grayer than I remember it, though it has only been a few months since I last saw him.

"I barely recognize myself," I reply.

"I was sorry to hear that you were coming."

"He got me in a tight spot," I admit, pulling my lacy sleeve back to show him the glint of silver. "See what we've got in common now?"

A flash of anger crosses his face and is smoothed away, replaced by a look of exhausted resignation.

"Good luck," says Pia, slamming the door and banging on the side of the hackney. The driver pulls away.

"Disgusting creature," mutters Sir Victor, and it takes me a moment to realize he is talking about Pia.

Sir Victor is one of Agoston Horthy's top officials, routing out magic wherever he can find it. It is not by choice; his daughter, Elisha, is a witch, and he has served Horthy for years in exchange for her life. Now that he is bound to Casimir as well, Shey having cured him of a Parnese wolf bite, he is a sort of double agent, I suppose—still working for Horthy but also reporting on the prime minister to Casimir. The strain of it shows.

"So we're off to the opera?" I say. "Could be worse. Bit early for an opera, though, isn't it?"

"There is a party before the opera," says Sir Victor. "And a party afterward, which will take up most of the night."

"Hounds," I mutter. I haven't slept nearly enough.

"King Zey's condition is declining rapidly," continues Sir Victor. "I will introduce you to his heir—Duke Everard. He arrived in Spira City last week. He is the king's second cousin, and will be crowned as soon as Zey dies, which his doctors believe will be a matter of days."

"A second cousin? Is that the best they could find?"

"Zey had no children and only one brother—Roparzh—whom he hanged," says Sir Victor. "His cousin, the former Duke Everard, was killed in a riding accident some years ago, making young Luca, the current duke, heir to the crown. He is barely twenty, but Zey's father was crowned at about the same age and ruled for sixty years. Duke Everard's castle is on the Isle of Corf, a rather remote northern island that Ingle and Frayne used to dispute. This is the first time he has come to Spira City since his father's death. His mother is . . . a rather difficult personality, according to gossip."

"I thought I was supposed to be spying on Agoston Horthy. What has this duke got to do with anything?"

"Your job will be twofold. You will indeed be reporting on Horthy's movements, his correspondence and conversation, whom he sees, where he goes. But Casimir would also like to be sure of the new king. The Everards have always been loyal to the Crown, but the mother is problematic, and the duke himself has grown up far from court. He's said to be a flighty fellow. The right wife would likely wield a good deal of influence, and Casimir has chosen one. Her name is Dafne Besnik. I know her father, Lord Besnik, quite well. He has raised his children to share his views and his intolerance. Casimir wants to know the character of the new king-to-be, and he would also like you to help bring Duke Everard and Dafne together. You are to befriend them both. You may spy on the duke, learn of his tastes, and help guide Dafne in topics of conversation that will interest him. She is a great beauty, which ought to make things easy."

"Usually does," I say. "Am I really meant to play matchmaker? That's hardly where my talents lie."

"You will be Dafne's companion at a few events. Help

her to shine, and tell us what you can of your impressions of the duke. He will be more open with young people like himself."

"Is Agoston Horthy going to be at the opera too?"

"No," says Sir Victor. "You'll look in on him tomorrow. This evening, be one of the young people."

"I don't know how young aristocrats behave."

"You are meant to be from the countryside, so you needn't have city manners."

For the rest of the ride, he tells me about my new identity, my family and home. I try to pay attention and not get distracted thinking about the *nuyi* creeping up the inside of my arm, the sac of poison deteriorating next to Dek's heart, or how we will get out of this mess in less than a week.

The hackney glides to a halt. Sir Victor helps me out.

We are outside the opera hall. I've seen it before, and it has never failed to astound me, wide marble stairs leading to intricately carved doors, pillars soaring up to the roof. The roof is made up of several smaller domes around the vast main dome, all shining a brilliant turquoise in the sunlight. Ridiculous as it is, I feel a flutter of excitement that I will get to see inside this place, reserved for the top echelons of Fraynish society.

Sir Victor gives me his arm, and we start up the stairs. He bends his head toward me and says softly: "There are rumors flying that Zey's niece has returned to Frayne to claim the throne."

"Is that so?" I say.

"Horthy has asked me to investigate. He told me that Mrs. Och herself helped smuggle the girl out of Yongguo, but that the lady has passed on."

I look into his questioning eyes, and I think I *do* owe him an answer to that.

"Mrs. Och is dead," I say flatly.

"I am sorry to hear it," he murmurs. "She was a great lady."

I make no reply, and he takes me on his arm through the carved doorway into the opera hall itself.

SIXTEEN

The inside of the hall makes my jaw drop in spite of myself. Carpeted staircases swoop up in three different directions. Everything is gilded and seething with intricate decoration, the impossibly high ceilings depicting scenes from Scripture in brilliant color, and all of it glowing by the light of dozens of chandeliers. We are immediately caught up in a swirl of elegant, perfumed people—powdered wigs and gleaming watches, monocles and feathered hats, silk gowns, silk cravats, shining shoes and shining jewels, and wet, toothy smiles. I have never been in such a mass of well-fed, well-dressed people before.

"Yes, he's here, I *know! Very* handsome!" a woman is hissing to her friend as we pass by.

"Ah, here are Lord and Lady Besnik," says Sir Victor, in a voice I've never heard him use, rich and happy. "Good day, my friends! May I present my niece, Miss Ella Penn Witzel."

I step forward and curtsy. Sir Besnik is, I decide from a glance, the kind of man I'd hate to be stuck near at a party. His face is like a pale stone slab—large and blank and hard-edged. There is no hint of humor or kindness in his expression or in his small blue eyes. He stands leaning forward slightly, as if he intends to loom over whomever he comes into contact with. His wife hangs on his arm, her hair swept up in an elegant flaxen whorl on top of her head, diamonds dripping from her ears and throat and wrists. She looks alarmingly bloodless, like a wax model of a woman.

"Miss Ell-a, we have heard *waaanderful* things about you," says Lady Besnik tonelessly. I find myself searching for a pulse in her desiccated neck. "Dafne has been simply *da-hyyying* to meet you."

"Indeed I have," says Dafne warmly. I look her over—this girl Casimir has picked out to be queen. She is wearing white lace with hints of violet, her dress showing off a tiny waist and a full bust without being too daring. Her hair, like her mother's, is so blond that it is nearly white, her eyes a stormy gray with dark lashes, her lips a sweet little bow, and her expression just lively enough to give her face character without tripping over into mischief. I can't think she'll need any help from *me* winning over the heir to the throne. Spending time with this perfect specimen of young womanhood is hardly my idea of an exciting job.

"The *aaah*pera is not really Dafne's *i-dee-yal*," says Lady

Besnik in her nasal drone. "She is well trained in *myuuu-sic*, and yet she would prefer to be at temple in silent contemplation of the *Naaameless* One."

"Oh, but even in a place like this, I find I can turn my mind toward the Nameless One, and His great silence embraces me in the midst of all the noise and celebration," says Dafne, slipping her arm through mine. "Don't you find?"

"Ye-es," I say, feeling a bit panicky. "What instrument do you play?"

"The harp," she says, blinking her big gray eyes at me. I almost want to laugh. Of course she plays the bleeding harp.

"Have you been to the opera many times?" I ask, thinking I might play up the country bumpkin angle. Snobby girls love to brag about their worldliness and talk down to girls they think stupid or uncultured.

"My mother loves the opera" is all she says.

"We are *haaanored* to be sharing a box with Duke Everard," says Lady Besnik, staring at nothing. "Have you met the duke, Sir Victor?"

"I have," says Sir Victor. "There he is with his mother, the duchess. I will introduce you."

I follow their eyes to a tall fellow with a head of unruly copper curls. He is chatting enthusiastically with a silver-haired, hawkish-looking lady.

"I have heard she is a very *faaahn* horsewoman," says Lady Besnik with a sniff. "A bit ec*centr*ic, they say."

"Eccentric how?" I can't help asking.

"Haven't you heard the story?" asks Dafne. "Why, it was

a great scandal in her day. She ran away from home when she was just about our age, didn't she, Mother? She dressed as a boy to enter a falconry contest, and she won! But then her identity was discovered, and she was sent home in disgrace, her reputation ruined. Somehow or other, though, she met Duke Everard—the elder one—when she was *twenty-eight* and considered an old maid, unmarriageable due to her wild ways. He was five years younger than she was at the time, but they fell in love and married, and she has been Duchess Everard ever since! They say she still has falcons, and that she nearly lost her mind when her husband died. Imagine!"

I quite like the sound of this duchess, and watch her with interest, chatting animatedly with her son. She looks an ordinary enough lady here, in spite of the fierce expression— well dressed, well laced.

Lady Besnik clucks her tongue. "Such *taaahk*, Dafne! One should not listen to *gaaassip*."

"Oh, indeed not, Mother," agrees Dafne. "I am not gossiping. This is all *fact*. I cannot imagine how the elder Duke Everard *dared* to marry such a woman. Look how devoted her son is to her, though!"

"She is reformed, I daresay, and the Nameless One is forgiving," says Lord Besnik in a bored rumble.

"Yes indeed," says Sir Victor. "Come—let's say hello."

The young duke and his mother look up as we approach. Her expression narrows, but the duke takes us all in with a lively interest. He is as tall as Sir Victor but wider, with

broad shoulders, a block of a chest, and great thick legs—
the kind of figure that looks very fine now but will likely go
to fat as he gets older. His boyish good looks are a little in-
congruous with his bulk—a merry grin, cleft chin, tumbling
curls in need of cutting, and something puppyish about the
eyes, which are such a light brown they are almost amber.
He certainly cuts a dashing figure to present to Frayne as
the new king. Then again, we are all so used to thinking
of the *king* as an ancient, holy, white-haired man that this
merry-looking boy might not strike anybody as even remotely kingly.

"Duke Everard! Duchess! I am glad to see you again."
Sir Victor shakes the duke's hand, bends to kiss the duchess's gloved knuckles. "May I present Lord and Lady Besnik,
their daughter, Miss Dafne Besnik, and my own niece, Miss
Ella Penn Witzel."

"Charmed," says the duchess coolly, but the duke shakes
Lord Besnik's hand enthusiastically—so enthusiastically,
in fact, that Lord Besnik looks a little rattled—and then
swoops to kiss Lady Besnik's hand with a great smacking
sound. There is hand-kissing all around. Even through
my glove I can feel the warmth of the duke's mouth, which
makes the genteel hand-kissing feel slightly inappropriate.

"I've heard talk about you," he says to Dafne. "They say
you are a fine harpist and a great beauty. I should love to
hear your playing someday, as your beauty has clearly been
undersold."

She looks startled for a moment—this is rather bold—but

then ducks her head and thanks him. Duchess Everard gives her son a stern look.

"Why don't we leave the young people to talk," says Sir Victor. "Duchess, I've been wanting to show you the portrait in the anteroom of your ancestor Lord Castilly."

She looks irritated, but she says, "Thank you, Sir Victor," and off they all go, she in her dark dress like a crow next to Lady Besnik's white silk. We are left to ourselves—the duke, Dafne, and I—but I sense that everyone around us is watching us.

"How do you find the capital, my lord?" asks Dafne.

"I haven't seen much of it yet," he says. "I've seen the opera house and the palace and the parliament and some *very* fine houses. However, I believe there is, between each of these places I keep on being taken to, this thing called the *city*. I've only caught glimpses out of a carriage window thus far." Then he leans toward us conspiratorially and says, "Don't you get the feeling that you are being *watched*?"

"*You* are being watched," says Dafne, smiling at him. "Everybody is wildly curious about you!"

"I suppose so." He sighs. "I feel very silly dressed up like this. Do *you* feel like you're in costume? You carry it very well."

He directs this to Dafne, of course. I do not carry it particularly well. And neither does the duke, I have to admit. He looks as if he's been stuffed into his gleaming waistcoat and cravat. His trousers are too tight on his muscular thighs, which is becoming but not very *royal*.

"Oh, I'm used to events like this," she says. "It must feel odd to you, though. I hear Corf is very beautiful."

"It is," he says. "But we live simply. The castle is rather a shambles and the weather is fierce, so we dress for warmth. The town of Corf is charming, but there is no opera house. This will be my first opera, in fact. Do *you* like the opera?"

"Very much. I think you'll enjoy it," says Dafne, and makes some banal comments about the opera we are going to see. The duke looks immediately bored.

"What rhymes with *bereaved?*" he asks, à propos of nothing.

"*Deceived,*" I say, a bit too quickly.

He laughs—a lovely bright burst of laughter that makes the eavesdroppers around us jump, and warms me to him somewhat. It is difficult to dislike a person with a truly happy-sounding laugh.

"Well done. But I'm composing a sonnet about a nation bereaved, so that's not the word I'm looking for."

I think it's a very apt word in that case, but don't say so.

"What about *achieved?* Or *conceived?*"

"*Conceived* might be good," he says, pulling a little note-pad and cartridge pen from his pocket and scribbling something.

"You're a poet!" exclaims Dafne. "How marvelous!"

"A very bad one," he says. "Do you read poetry?"

"I admire Simon Gavell very much," she says. He looks disappointed by this answer. I've no idea who Simon Gavell is.

He turns those gold-hued eyes on me. His gaze flicks to

my scar and then back to my eyes. "What about you, Miss Penn Witzel?"

"I don't read much poetry," I say.

"And yet such a knack for rhyme!"

"Isn't there more to poetry than rhyming? You just told me my first rhyme was no good."

"It was unfair. You didn't know the subject. What rhymes with *wealth?*"

"*Filth,*" I say, and then laugh. "Not a good rhyme. Perhaps *stealth.* Oh, stars—*health,* I should have thought of that first."

He beams at me. "You see? You're a natural!"

"I can't make a poem out of that, though."

Dafne is staring hard at me, and I think I ought to shut up and go back to being quiet and unpretty.

"Perhaps the world needs more poetry about filth and stealth and deceit," he says.

"I can't think *that's* what the world needs," I say.

"Are you interested in philosophy?" he asks us.

"I am *interested* in everything," says Dafne. "Only very ignorant."

I am both ignorant of and uninterested in it, but I just say, "Likewise."

"I've been reading a book of philosophy that suggests that the wealthy are less worthy than ... well, the filthy, you might say ... because they squander their wealth on selfish pleasures, while others suffer. Edwin Corr. He was trying to take Rainist principles to their logical conclusion, but he went to prison for writing it! The book is banned!"

"Oh!" Dafne raises a gloved hand to her lips, and I wonder why the heir to the throne is flaunting his reading of banned books to us at a first meeting.

"I've shocked you," he says, a bit hopefully, I think.

You'll have to work harder than that, friend. But I let Dafne answer.

"You are a freethinker," she says, rallying. "I admire that."

"Do you?" he asks, as if he's genuinely curious.

"I do." She sticks her chin out a little, and he smiles, tucking his notebook back into his waistcoat pocket.

"My mother thinks people in the city are narrow-minded," he says. "I am conducting an investigation."

"Your mother is unfair to us!" cries Dafne.

There is a shriek from across the hall.

"Is it normal to scream at the opera?" asks the duke, but then there is a chorus of screaming and shouting, and the people at the other end of the hall start running in all their finery, clinging to their hats and wigs. As they approach, the ground seems to be moving under them. A horrified yell leaps from my own lips.

Surging among the well-shod feet of the aristocracy are hundreds and hundreds of rats, long and black and swift, pouring across the carpeted floor. I look around and see an alcove with a glowering bust a foot or so above us. I grab Dafne by the hand and pull her over to it, then clamber up.

"Come on," I say, grabbing her wrists. The duke gives her an indelicate boost from behind and I pull her up, so that we are squeezed on either side of the great bronze head of some dead nobleman.

"Stay there!" he shouts at us. "I've got to find my mother."

His broad back disappears into the surge of bodies.

"What on earth . . . ?" gasps Dafne. "What is *happening*?"

The hall clears, a sea of rats streaming behind the fleeing aristocrats.

"Witchery!" I hear somebody shout from outside, and another voice takes up the cry: "*Witchery!*"

SEVENTEEN

Mrs. Och's house is dark except for a glow from the front parlor window. The roof is spiked with roosting crows. One of them swoops low over our heads with an angry squawk as Dek and I approach.

Mr. Faruk opens the door almost the instant I knock. He is dressed in traditional Eshriki garb—a white robe embroidered with gold thread and open at the chest. I remember seeing the rich dressed this way in Eshrik, and it seemed quite natural there, but it is rather startling in Mrs. Och's foyer. He greets us cordially and leads us into the parlor, where a lamp is blazing.

Lady Laroche is at the tea table in front of a game of Conquest, puffing on a cigar.

"What a pleasant surprise!" she says. "Julia, you *do* look fine! Csilla knows her business!"

My ribs and feet are aching from the press of the corset and the pinch of my shoes. I went straight from the opera house to the Marrow to find Dek. We ate supper with Wyn and then came here. I haven't even been back to report to Pia yet.

"What's with all the crows outside?" I ask.

"Prudence," says Lady Laroche. "It's better that visitors don't know what a full house we have."

"What do they do? Peck people's eyes out?" asks Dek.

"They give warning. Mrs. Och certainly *was* prepared for unwelcome visitors. Did you know there are tunnels in the cellar with enchanted doors? We've been searched once already, but as far as the Fraynish Crown knows, Professor Baranyi has returned to Spira City to claim the house Mrs. Och left him in her will, along with her fortune, and he still employs Mrs. Freeley, and they live here alone. Do sit down, please."

"Mrs. Och left Professor Baranyi the house?" I say, surprised.

"She left him everything," says Lady Laroche. "He paid your friends what Mrs. Och promised them, by the way, and they have generously put those funds toward the revolution."

"He hates me, doesn't he?"

"Yes. But he is grieving, and sometimes it helps to hate somebody."

"Is he here now?"

"No. He is dining at the university, and I hope winning some of the literati to our cause. The princess and Gennady have both gone to bed. I was about to go to bed myself, since the game is at a stalemate." She gives a theatrical yawn and grinds her cigar out in the ashtray. "You've only just caught us."

"You know what's funny?" says Dek, settling down on the sofa as if she hasn't just said she's going to bed. "We've come from the Edge, and we didn't see a single rat on the way over here. That part of the city is usually crawling with them."

Lady Laroche raises a thin eyebrow.

"And *yet*," I say, "the opera house is still full of them. And the parliament buildings, and half of West Spira."

The opera never took place. Everybody fled, but the scene outdoors was chaos too, more rats than I have ever seen in my life, traveling in swift packs, dark-furred and malevolent-looking, biting ankles and climbing up suits and dresses and into hackneys. Having grown up in the Twist, I'm hardly squeamish about rats, but I confess I didn't think twice about getting out of there.

"Did you witness it, Julia?" Lady Laroche asks eagerly.

I describe the scene at the opera, and she laughs, clapping her hands, girlish in her delight. "I wish I could have seen it!"

Mr. Faruk manages to give the impression of rolling his eyes without actually doing so, then holds up a porcelain pot and says, "Coffee?"

"Don't you have anything stronger?" asks Dek.

"I'd like coffee," I say, elbowing him in the ribs. He elbows me back.

Mr. Faruk glides out of the room to fetch extra cups.

"I am glad you're here, Benedek," says Lady Laroche. "We've found a doctor at the university who will take a photograph of the inside of your chest tomorrow. Difficult to imagine, I know, but I've been assured it works. Then we will be able to see where the poison is attached. This doctor will analyze the photographs and see if there's anything to be done."

"Hounds. How do they photograph my insides?" asks Dek. "Is it magic?"

"Not at all! It is a new technology," says Lady Laroche.

"Casimir's mechanic was quite sure nobody but him would be able to take the poison out without killing Dek," I say anxiously.

"We won't do a thing unless we can be sure it's safe, but we ought to have a look," says Lady Laroche. "They may be bluffing. Suppose there is no poison at all?"

"They opened up his chest," I say.

"I'd like to see a photograph of my insides, anyway," says Dek. "See if my heart is as black as I think it is."

"Getting at Casimir will be the more difficult part," says Lady Laroche. "I tried to have him assassinated and failed—and that was before he employed a witch of such legendary power."

I think of Pia, and my insides quake. I don't want anybody to die for me, or suffer a fate like hers.

"I think an assassination plot is probably pointless," I concede.

Mr. Faruk comes back in with cups and pours us coffee.

"Thank you," says Dek, and then he adds to Lady Laroche, "And thank you for helping me."

"You are Ammi's son," she says simply. It is as if a mask drops away for a moment, and her ironic flair is gone. "I wasn't able to protect Ammi, and I will live with that sorrow for the rest of my life. If I can help her children in any way, it will make me very happy indeed. I loved her dearly."

"But you sent her to kill Casimir," I say. I don't mean to accuse her. Or at least, I don't think I do. But I can't help saying it.

"No," she says, startled. "I did not know what Ammi intended. I would *never* have sent her on such a mission. She was too dear to me."

That surprises me. I'd assumed my mother was acting for the coven. Lady Laroche only sent Pia, then. Pia, dear to nobody.

"Casimir thinks you were behind it," I say.

"I'm sure he does, but he is wrong. Oh, I certainly wanted him dead. But I never asked Ammi to do it."

Mr. Faruk studies the board and makes a move.

"Blast," says Lady Laroche, glancing at it. The mask comes back up, sardonic and amused. "*Blast*," she repeats, more emphatically. "You've cornered me."

"Three moves," says Mr. Faruk, smiling.

"Yes, I see. All right, I surrender."

She turns over the king with an index finger and sighs. "I've yet to beat Idir at this game. One day!"

"So are you part of the Sidhar Coven?" I ask Mr. Faruk, since I haven't figured out how he fits in. I've been assuming he's a man-witch, now that I know such creatures exist.

"No," he says. "I was the princess's tutor in Eshrik for a few years. We kept in touch after she moved to the monastery in Tianshi. I came as soon as I received word that she was on her way to Frayne."

"Word from who?"

"From Princess Zara. She sent me a letter from Xanuha saying that she was with a group of Fraynish revolutionaries on her way to claim the throne. I wrote to Lady Laroche and came immediately to see if I could be of service."

This is the most I've heard him speak yet.

"So . . . you're *not* a man-witch, then?" I ask.

"I am a witch," he says. "We are rare, but nonetheless we favor *witch* over *man-witch*."

"Oh."

"Idir is part of a sect that believes the first Eshriki Phar Marike is still alive," says Lady Laroche laconically, and I choke on my coffee. "He is waiting patiently for her return to power, but is granting us his company while he waits."

Dek gives me a hard look, but I ask anyway: "Why do you think Marike is still alive?"

"The evidence," he says simply. "The witch executed as Marike by the Sirillian Empire claimed to be a farmer's wife from Vassali, and indeed it was discovered not long after that a farmer's wife from Vassali had gone missing. There have been many credible reports from those who harbored Marike afterward."

"A thousand years ago," scoffs Lady Laroche. "Pretending to be Marike is quite a popular pastime among a certain kind of witch. I can't tell you how many Marikes I've met in my time."

"Have you heard of the Ankh-nu?" I ask them.

Mr. Faruk says, "Of course. The vessel Marike made to bring the Gethin into the world."

"My mother had it," I say in a great rush. "She used it. Not long before I was born, she used it to bring Lidari back into the world from Kahge."

Lady Laroche is looking at me like she's suddenly realized I'm completely mad and must choose her words carefully. Dek is quietly seething next to me.

"Lidari," she says. "That's a familiar name."

Mr. Faruk laughs. "Modern Fraynish witches tend to neglect their Eshriki history. A mistake, if they aspire to power themselves!" To Lady Laroche, he says: "Lidari was the first among the Gethin, but he too lived in many bodies and stayed by Marike through the centuries."

"Until Casimir killed him and sent him back to Kahge," I say.

"So Casimir claimed, yes," says Mr. Faruk.

I'm thinking of the vision I had of my mother in Ragg Rock with the Ankh-nu—less a vision than a memory, but it was Lidari's memory, I'm sure of it. *I've got it*, she said. So had she lost it? Or am I on the wrong track?

"My *mother* brought Lidari back to the world," I repeat. "Mrs. Och thought she put his essence in *me*. I saw one of his memories."

"A vision that could have been planted by a witch," interjects Dek.

"No." I shake my head. It's easier to pose this theory to two strangers than to Dek, so I look at them rather than him. "This witch was looking through my memories, and one of them wasn't mine. It was Lidari's. But inside *my mind*. The creatures in Kahge thought I was him too."

For the first time since I've met him, Mr. Faruk looks intensely interested. He has gone stiller than usual, like a cat poised to pounce.

"I found Ko Dan in Tianshi too," I say. "But he claimed *he* didn't put the *Book of Disruption* fragment in Theo. He was held prisoner, and someone took his body. Who do you know that can borrow bodies and take them over?"

"You think it was Marike," says Mr. Faruk softly.

"Yes." My hands are shaking, and I clench them together. "Si Tan thought that our ma . . . that *Ammi* was Marike. She had the Ankh-nu because it was *hers*. *She* got her old friend Lidari out of Kaghe and went to take revenge on Casimir. Then years later, she borrowed Ko Dan's body, like a disguise, and used the Ankh-nu to put Gennady's part of *The Book of Disruption* into Theo."

Lady Laroche bursts into amazed laughter. "Ammi? No. It is impossible."

"That's what I said," says Dek.

"But how can you know that?" I'm nearly shouting.

"If Marike were alive, why borrow the body of a monk in Yongguo? Why not just do what she wanted directly?" says

Lady Laroche, leaning closer to me. She is glamorous from a few feet away, but up close I see the frayed skin around her fingernails, the chewed edges of her lips.

"Gennady would never have agreed to let *Marike* work magic on him or get near *The Book of Disruption*," I say. "All three of the Xianren considered her an enemy. Ko Dan was an excellent disguise."

"You don't believe it, though," says Mr. Faruk to Dek.

"No," says Dek stiffly. "I know that my sister is my sister. I know that my mother was my mother. All this about Marike and Lidari . . . no, I don't believe it."

"It is rather far-fetched," says Lady Laroche. "But perhaps . . . if I could get a besilik mirror, I might manage a memory retrieval. That would answer the question."

"A besilik mirror!" exclaims Mr. Faruk. "You are full of surprises."

"I have a friend who could get me one, I think." Lady Laroche gives me a feral sort of grin. "Would you like to do a bit of digging through your memories, Julia, and see if we can find traces of this Lidari?"

"If there's something inside me, I want to know," I say unsteadily.

"Come back tomorrow," says Lady Laroche, suddenly brisk. "I will go into the city first thing in the morning for the mirror. You don't approve, Benedek?"

"I don't like the idea of more magical prying inside Julia's brain," he says. "But it's up to her."

"I see the best of Ammi in both of you," she says.

That seems to make Dek uncomfortable.

"Can we get back to the rats for a minute?" he says abruptly. "I'm not clear on the *point* of having them swarming all over West Spira."

Lady Laroche grins. "Just giving the denizens of West Spira a little scare."

"And people say I have odd hobbies," he says.

Her eyes glitter, and she says, "Every witch must reckon with what she is, alone and terrified, before she finds her people. I *know* the aristocracy, I grew up among them. I had servants and governesses, I was dressed in silks and lace, I was taught how to sit, how to stand, how to speak, how to tinkle a pretty tune on the piano, how to laugh and, also important, how *not* to laugh, and every moment felt like drowning." She pauses, a faraway expression on her face. "My mother had a cabinet full of very fine old ceramics on display—a gift to our family from the Brezhian queen. When I was five years old, I went downstairs in the middle of the night, broke into the cabinet, and smashed them all to bits."

"I'll bet you were whipped," says Dek.

"Oh, I was," she says, almost fondly. "My father beat me within an inch of my life. But I had tasted something akin to freedom. That same evening, I set fire to the house. I was locked up for months after that. I learned, over the years that followed, that they would go to any lengths to subdue me, to tame me, and I knew that they would break me if they could. I got older, wilier. I learned the art of pretense. I learned how to seem to be what they wanted. By the time I knew I was a witch, I was already adept at keeping secrets. I married a rich idiot and lived the life of a fine lady for a time, intending to burn the aristocracy down from within. Still, I cannot describe to you the relief when my identity as leader of the Sidhar Coven was revealed. I never had to pretend again—and I have *never* forgotten how it felt, the tremendous joy that could not be whipped out of me when I smashed those prized ceramics—my first act of true rebellion. What I mean to say is that I am not squeamish about destruction. If you want to change something, the easiest and fastest way is to destroy the thing that is standing so that something new can be built in its place. And I have always been partial to fire."

Mr. Faruk is carefully placing the Conquest pieces back in their starting positions on the board. Dek and I are frozen in our seats as Lady Laroche continues, a look of terrible elation on her face.

"West Spira has kept all the ills of the city away with money and force. They cocoon themselves in luxury and throw their wealth behind the slaughter of witches and the oppression of the lower classes. What happened at the opera today was a message. A new day is dawning in Frayne." She smiles, her face relaxing. "The Rainist overlords can get behind us, or they can be eaten by rats."

EIGHTEEN

It's late but Lirabon Avenue is still busy, people spilling out of bars, and everywhere talk of the rat invasion of West Spira.

"Terrifying, isn't she?" says Dek—referring, I assume, to Lady Laroche. He grins. "I quite like her."

"I can't imagine how she and Mrs. Och would ever have worked together," I say. "No wonder Mrs. Och didn't seem too cut up when we thought she was dead. Well, and vice versa."

"I can't decide if we should be cheering her on or staying well away. I'll see this doctor of hers tomorrow, in any case. Will you get that thing out of your arm now, Julia?"

"Not yet," I say, though I'm tempted. The itching and burning under the skin has moved into my upper arm. I can wait a few more days, I tell myself. If Lady Laroche can't find a way to help Dek, I'll take the *nuyi* out, and I'll . . . what? My heart stalls.

"I'm frightened for you," he says—the fellow with the poison next to his heart. "Suppose you miscalculate and let this thing—the *nuyi*—get too far? And honestly, I'm afraid of the way you're latching on to these ideas about Marike. People, like Mr. Faruk, who think Marike is still alive . . . they're a bit mad, if you ask me, obsessing over a long-dead half-mythical witch. Fanatics."

"Mr. Faruk seems the farthest thing from a fanatic," I say. "And Marike isn't half-mythical. She's a historical figure."

"Well, I mean, the stories about her. Who knows what's true anymore?"

"But it makes a kind of horrible sense, doesn't it? Why did Ma go after Casimir, anyway? *Marike* had a grudge; she had a *reason* to try to destroy him. Casimir had killed Lidari and sent his essence back to Kahge, and he was behind the rise of the Sirillian Empire that set out to kill her as well."

"Any witch had a reason to go after Casimir, especially a Fraynish witch," says Dek. "Julia, don't you *remember* her? How could you honestly think you might be Lidari or she might be Marike? Remember the rag doll you used to carry everywhere? You sucked on its hand when you were going to sleep, and when you lost it in the river you cried for weeks! Remember Ma burning porridge or combing your hair or doing the washing up or scolding us for getting filthy? You talk like none of that means anything, but it's the truth of who you are and who she was."

"That stupid doll is not the truth of who I am," I say, annoyed.

He laughs. "I mean that *I* remember you from infancy to now and you've always been just who you are, so stop winding yourself up about whether Ma put some other essence inside you. You're Julia through and through and you always have been and I would *know* if there were something else in you."

It warms me to hear him say it, but he doesn't know, not

really. He doesn't know how it feels to step out of my body, to disappear right out of the world, to become something else, somewhere else.

"Then why can I vanish? Why can I go to Kahge?"

"Who knows? Ma was a witch—maybe some kind of magic from something she did got rubbed off on you. Don't you think that makes more sense than you being some long-dead monster? And don't you think that Ma being a revolutionary witch makes more sense than her being *Marike*? Why on earth would Marike have decided to live as a washerwoman in the Twist? Anyway, if she were alive, she wouldn't have stayed away from us all this time."

"Maybe she had no choice. Or maybe . . . well, the immortals, like the Xianren, I don't think they love like regular people do."

"*Stop it*," he growls. "She *loved us*, Julia. She was our mother and she loved us, and only death could have kept her from us. I remember her, I remember *everything* better than you do. You're talking nonsense."

"I'm sorry."

To my shame, I find myself blinking back tears.

"I just hate to see you twisting yourself into knots," he says more gently. "And I want that thing out of your arm."

"We have a little time still," I mutter.

We cross the bridge into the Twist, where the night is still young.

"I'll walk you back to your hotel," he says, slinging an arm around my shoulders.

I manage a little grin. "No—I'll walk *you* back."

"You just want to terrorize Torne's fellows again."

"Not so!"

But I won't deny it might cheer me up a little.

NINETEEN

Graybeard is at a table with the ferret keeper and a stocky brick of a man I've not seen before. The stranger looks at us with a hostile expression, his blunt, ugly face ringed with silver curls, while the other two cower. I can't help enjoying the terror I inspire.

"The demon," Graybeard spits.

"Torne said to leave 'er be," the ferret keeper reminds him.

"Did 'e tell that demon to leave *me* be?" shrieks Graybeard, diving under the table.

"I thought you were to be *punished*," I say mockingly, squatting to glare at him under the table.

"Come on," says Dek, pulling me to the door behind the bar. We climb the stairs to the second floor and knock on Wyn's door. A gorgeous redhead in a low-cut dress opens it.

"Hullo, you," she says, like Dek is familiar. Then she takes in my fine gown, and her eyes widen.

"Dek!" says Wyn, appearing behind her and looking relieved. "Come in, both of you. Stars, Julia, you look . . . well, different from usual. Guess who's downstairs!"

"A bunch of rats who call themselves men?" I hazard, entering the room and ignoring the redhead.

Dek chuckles, but Wyn is not to be put off. "Bleeding *Emil Lorka*, that's who!" he practically shouts.

"Really?" I ask, surprised. Lorka is a famous painter and Wyn's hero. "What's he doing mixing with these vermin?"

"He wants to join the revolution!" splutters Wyn. "Look—Julia—you need to tell Torne which of those fellows tried to hurt you, and we'll be rid of them. I'll take care of them myself if Torne won't. Most of them are real revolutionaries. They want the old Frayne back, the old ways, before Rainists got to decide how we all ought to live and worship. They're open to witchcraft being legalized, even."

Wyn himself might not have been open to that a few months ago, but there is nothing like traveling with a pretty, charming witch to change one's point of view. My chest feels hollow whenever I think about Bianka.

"Was Lorka the short, ugly one down there?" I ask.

"Gray hair," Wyn says, startled by my rudeness about his hero, and I feel a bit bad.

"I'll talk to Torne another time," I say. "I just wanted to see Dek home."

What I *don't* want is to spend any more time in this room with this stunning redhead in her revealing dress, hanging on Wyn's arm now and staring at me. Perhaps it's her presence that makes me want to show off a little. In Tianshi, I learned to cross the city by vanishing, and I've been thinking how useful it would be to hone that skill. I embrace

Dek quickly, give Wyn a slug on the arm that isn't wrapped around his redhead's tiny waist, and go to the window.

"We're on the second floor," Wyn reminds me as I pull it open. I don't need it open—I can vanish to anyplace that I can see—but I'm going for dramatic effect here.

"I know." I step onto the ledge—no easy task in my heavy dress and stupid shoes.

Julia, says Dek.

The Edge squats below us—this broken crust of the city between the Twist and Limory Cemetery.

"Is she mad?" squeaks Wyn's redhead. "What is she doing?"

I'm afraid of all the unknowns of what I am and what I can do. I'm afraid of how far I can go. But there is this too: it's *fun.* If I can put aside all the whys and hows, I have always loved being able to vanish. My heart speeds up, but I push away the familiar fear that I won't be able to pull it off *this time.* I step off the windowsill. The redhead's screams drown out whatever Wyn and Dek are yelling.

I can do it in under a second. One step back: the world blurs and I am unseen by ordinary eyes as I plunge through the air. Two steps: sight and sound receding farther. Three steps back: a buzzing in my limbs as I lose contact with myself. Four steps: *Whoosh.* The city spreads out underneath me and I am everywhere, nowhere, bodiless. I find West Spira, careful not to focus too closely on anything so I don't go crashing into a building, just casting my perspective over it all until I find the West Spira Grand Hotel and its tenth-floor balcony. *Focus.* I am on the balcony, back inside my own body, heart thundering. Not bad. A single leap from Wyn's window to my own. What can't I do? I hang laughing with delight and relief over the balcony railing for a moment, then pick the lock on the door with shaking fingers and push my way into the room.

"I wondered when you'd be back," says Pia from the darkness.

TWENTY

She's in an armchair in the corner, a shadow in the dark room. I wouldn't have seen her at all if she hadn't spoken.

"Hounds, you're creepy, lurking in the dark like that," I tell her. I drop onto the bed and kick off my pinching shoes. It feels like far too much work to get out of this bleeding dress with all its ties and bindings, the petticoats and the corset, but I don't want to sleep in a corset either. I give a dramatic moan.

"Are you injured?" asks Pia. She actually sounds worried.

"No. I just hate this dress."

I make myself sit up and start fumbling with the ties.

"Lady Laroche is in the city," she says. "Have you seen her?"

I snort at the absurdity of her asking me that, and a seam rips as I struggle too violently out of the top part of my dress. The purse with the sleeping-serum darts tumbles out of my dress and onto the bed. I tug the corset loose and gasp with relief. My bottom ribs feel bruised.

"Here is my report for Casimir," I say, ignoring her question about Lady Laroche. "Sir Victor introduced me to Duke Everard at the opera. The duke is handsome and charming and writes poetry and fancies himself a bit of a freethinking rebel. He's devoted to his mother. Dafne is utterly beautiful, and I'm sure she doesn't need me looking unbeautiful next to her to win him over. Then rats came marauding all over the place, and we didn't see the opera after all."

I toss my dress, corset, and purse on the floor and crawl under the bedcovers in my petticoat, adding, "I hope there aren't any rats in here."

"There were a number in the lobby," says Pia. "But I don't think rats know how to use an elevator. We ought to be safe up here."

"Safe." I repeat the word and laugh.

"Sir Victor wants to see you in a couple of hours."

"Then I'll sleep for a couple of hours."

"Shall I wake you?"

"Fine. Now go away. I don't like the idea of you watching me sleep."

She doesn't move.

"Please," I groan into the satin pillowcase. The metal of her goggles glints in the moonlight that comes through the curtains.

"How is your brother?" she asks.

"Alive."

"I know you better than Casimir does. You won't let him take you. He hopes you will, but I know you won't. But you won't give up on your brother either. So what will you do?"

I say nothing.

"Julia, I know you have met with Lady Laroche. I am not passing this information along to Casimir because it is irrelevant. He is not concerned about the revolution. He has every confidence that Agoston Horthy will take care of it—and if Casimir is not concerned, then neither am I. But I *am* worried that you will do something rash to try to help your brother. I know Lady Laroche. She is clever, but she is not careful, and she has too much faith in her own abilities. Do not let a witch try to help you get the poison out of him. The mechanic made very sure it could only be done by him."

For a moment, I can't even make words. Then I splutter, "You're *worried*? Go away, by the Nameless. Leave me alone."

She rises but does not leave. I pull the covers over my head so her voice is muffled.

"The *nuyi*, even once it reaches the brain, does not control your thoughts," she says. "It is like an outside force exerting pressure. The farther it expands through the brain, the more complete its control of your actions. It will become impossible to resist the compulsion of the *nuyi*, impossible to act against it. Still—while the *nuyi* will eventually control your ability to act or not act, it will not control what you think or feel."

"Can we talk about this tomorrow?"

"The Xianren destroyed most of the *nuyi* long ago. They tried many methods, but poison was the most effective. The herb hermia is lethal to the *nuyi*. Injecting it into the queen resulted in the death of the entire nest. Individual *nuyi* could also be killed merely by being trapped in a jar with the herb. Hermia is also lethal to humans, but poison dosages can be dealt carefully. Poison can be measured out so that it will merely weaken and not kill."

I pull the covers off me and sit up. She leans forward and makes an odd sound in her throat.

"What the bleeding stars is the matter with you?" I ask, staring at her shadowy face.

"Injecting it right into your arm would be too dangerous," she says in a rush. "Too much in the bloodstream ... and if the *nuyi* dies, Casimir will know. But a very little bit, ingested ... a small dose would not kill you. It would not kill the *nuyi* either. But it would sicken it. Slow its growth. Slow it down."

"What are you saying?"

"There would be side effects."

"Slow it down ... as in ... so, it might take *longer* than ten days or two weeks to reach the brain? Longer before it controlled me?"

She steadies herself and says: "Yes, precisely. Casimir will not want to lose you by letting your brother die. If the poison sac is close to disintegrating, he will order the mechanic to operate. He might not know ... I don't know if he can feel it when the *nuyi* has attached to the brain. It might work.

You might keep the *nuyi* from your brain long enough to save your brother, if you are consistent in serving Casimir, if you are useful. Once your brother was safe, you could remove it, if it had not reached the brain."

"What's going on here?"

She is shaking, and I can't figure out why she's telling me this. If it is some trick of Casimir's.

"I am not ordered to keep quiet on this matter in particular," she says. "But his will is woven all through me and it is hard . . . sometimes, it is hard even to speak. To think about a thing too closely . . . if it is not aligned with his will."

I ask in disbelief: "Are you trying to *help* me?"

"I *cannot* help you, Julia." Half-collapsed against the door-frame, she manages a ghost of a grin. "But let's say that, in spite of the odds, I am betting on you."

Telegram to Lord Casimir, Nago
Island: DUKE EVERARD MALLEABLE
STOP DEVOTED TO MOTHER STOP DAFNE
PROMISING STOP LAROCHE ORCHESTRATES
RAT INVASION OF WEST SPIRA STOP JULIA
COOPERATIVE STOP

DAY 6

OLD ENEMIES, OLD FRIENDS

*"Witches flock to trouble," he says.
"And that's what's coming.
It's a good time to get out of Spira City."*

TWENTY-ONE

I think I won't be able to sleep at all, but I suppose I do, because Pia is waking me up again. It is still black night outside.

"A hackney is waiting," she says.

I stagger into the main room and pull the plainest dress I can find out of the wardrobe—Csilla hung a selection from the trunks of clothing Casimir had sent over. I don't look at the *nuyi*. I don't need to. I can feel it halfway along my upper arm. Squinting at the mirror, I shove the hair extensions back into place with a ribbon.

"No corset?" says Pia.

"Not for visiting Sir Victor before dawn," I mutter.

Pia lights a lamp and says, "You ought to cover that scar, at least."

I blink in the lamplight. The purple scar stands out starkly on my cheek, running from my temple to my top lip. I cover my face with powder, but lacking Csilla's skills, I end up looking as if I've been baking and got a faceful of flour. I wipe some of it off with a handkerchief and stare at my reflection despairingly. I will just have to hope I'm not required to be visible for anybody other than Sir Victor today.

Pia hands me a purse that clinks. It is stuffed with paper money as well as silver coins.

"Use this for bribes or for anything else you need," she says. "Tell me when you need more."

I take it, remembering with a queasy chill the last time Pia handed me a purse full of money. I push the memory aside and tie the purse around my waist. Just in case, I put the sleeping serum darts Dek gave me into this purse as well.

An electric hackney is waiting for me in front of the hotel. As we drive through West Spira, I see a good many soldiers out, carrying lanterns and pistols. Rat-catching. Every now and then a sharp shot rings out.

A woman in a maid's uniform is waiting for me outside the parliament gates. She is cream-puff pale, and her almost lashless eyes make her look like a frightened rabbit.

"Are you Ella?" she asks.

"I suppose I am."

She blinks and hesitates, and then says, "Well, *are* you?"

I sigh and say, "Yes."

She looks me over uncertainly, but she takes me inside.

Sir Victor's offices are quite as beautiful as the hotel, with high ceilings, thick carpets, and windows overlooking the river Syne. Sir Victor himself looks gaunt and exhausted as he wishes me good morning.

"This is Karla," he says, introducing the maid. "She is one

of ours. She will be serving Agoston Horthy breakfast in his office within the hour, and you will go with her, invisible. You will learn the way, where he sleeps and eats. Karla, tell Ella whatever you can."

I look at Karla, who blinks rapidly at me. I wonder what she makes of *invisible*.

"Well, miss, he rises very early. He has no preferences as far as food and drink. In fact, I'd venture to say he cannot taste anything. He's at his desk and in meetings for most of the day. He works very hard. Sometimes his boots are covered in mud in the morning, but I don't know where he goes at night."

"What do you mean, he can't taste anything?" I ask.

"Well, I don't know, miss, only it seems to me that he must not taste very well. The girls made a pudding once and by mistake they put salt in it instead of sugar! I didn't know, I took it to him, but when I got back to the kitchen they was all in hysterics because they'd tasted it and it was so awful, truly inedible. I ran back there to take it from him, but he'd eaten every bite! When I asked him if it was all right, he told me it was fine, and so I took the plate away. But I tried a crumb myself, miss, and I could barely choke it down, it were so terrible!"

I look at Sir Victor.

"I am not interested in his taste buds. I want to know why he has mud on his boots in the mornings. Where does he go, whom does he meet?" He hands me a sheaf of papers. "Memorize these when you have the chance. They are maps of the palace and the parliament buildings. You have a room attached to mine in the guest suites at the palace—I've marked it on the map. There are some clothes and things to make it look as if a girl lives there."

I fold the maps and tuck them into the purse with the sleeping serum and the money from Pia.

"Have you been to bed yet?" I ask him.

He shakes his head. "The city is in an uproar."

"The rats?" I ask, and he nods. Karla looks back and forth between us, wide-eyed.

"It is being considered a direct attack on the Crown by witches," he says. "There will be Cleansings aplenty in the weeks to come. For now, go with Karla, get the lay of the land."

Karla stands up very quickly. I follow her down the hall and the stairs.

"We're almost at the kitchen," she whispers. "You can't just walk in there. Are you going to be . . . ah, invisible?"

"All right," I say, and pull myself out of the world, two steps back so that everything is blurred. Her pale face goes even paler. She hurries down to the large, bustling kitchen.

"There's his lordship's breakfast, there!" a woman barks at Karla, pointing. Karla hurriedly arranges the eggs, sausages, and limp slices of tomato to look a little more attractive on the tray.

I've always been good at staying behind the membrane of the visible and then coming just close enough to the edge of things to snatch something out of the world. I got plenty of practice thieving after Ma died. But to properly take hold of an object, I need to come dangerously close to stepping right back into the visible world. I know I've unsettled market sellers and the like, who believed they saw a flash of *something*, for a moment—but fortunately, people tend to put their faith in their second look. I wait for a moment when nobody's looking my way, and then I grab a bottle and give it a sniff. Vinegar. Perfect.

Once we're back in the hall, I reappear and put a finger to my lips. Karla jumps, the contents of the tray rattling, but she doesn't drop anything. I lift the lid of the teapot and pour in a generous amount of vinegar.

"What are you doing?" she hisses at me.

"I want to see it for myself."

"But suppose he *does* taste it? Can't call that a mistake! It'll be *my* head!"

"It'll be all right," I say, hoping that's true. And then, because she's still waffling, I add: "You can't change sides *now*."

She glares at me and carries on up the stairs. I follow, vanishing again. She goes back in the direction of Sir Victor's offices but takes a different turn, goes up one more flight of stairs, and knocks on a heavy door. A voice thrums within, and she opens the door, balancing the tray on one hand.

There, with his back to us, sitting at a desk and writing with a quill pen, is the prime minister—Agoston Horthy. He does not turn around or pause in his writing, only says, "Leave the tray by me, Karla."

His voice is deep and resonant, but his frame is small,

almost frail. It is hard to believe such a big voice comes from such a small man. Karla, trembling visibly, places the tray next to him and pours out a cup of tea. The pot clatters as she puts it back down on the tray, but the prime minister does not seem to notice her upset.

"You may go," he says. She retreats, then stops with a little gasp. I follow her eyes. There is a rat slinking along the far wall—a fat, sleek thing, its nasty nose twitching. Agoston Horthy reaches for the teacup. Karla is frozen, staring at the rat, then staring at him. I have a horrible feeling she's going to faint or confess everything. He takes a long drink of the tea and puts the cup back on the saucer. I have to hold in the childish urge to laugh at him drinking heavily vinegared tea. She is right: he does not seem to taste it at all. Karla sways a little, and the rat dives at Agoston Horthy's ankle.

Karla screams.

Agoston Horthy turns to glare at her. "What on earth is the matter?"

She is standing with both hands clamped over her mouth, speechless. He looks down at his ankle, where the rat has driven its teeth into his trousers and surely—surely?—his flesh as well. He gives his leg a shake, but the rat is hanging on ferociously.

"Sir!" wails Karla.

He reaches for a letter opener on his desk and in one swift motion drives it into the back of the rat's neck. The rat goes limp, falling away from his foot; blood pours over his sock and shoe. The rat has bitten him deeply.

"Dispose of this thing," he says to Karla, pulling the letter opener out of its neck and kicking the dead animal toward her.

She dissolves into tears. He stares at her rather the way he looked at the rat a moment before, and says, "Never mind. Be on your way."

"Sir, you're bleeding," she blubbers. "Shall I fetch the doctor?"

"No, no, it's nothing." He waves an impatient hand at her. She looks around—for *me!* Stop it, you stupid girl!—then goes stumbling out.

The prime minister examines the wound on his ankle with a look of profound irritation. He takes off his cravat and wraps the ankle firmly. Then he turns back to his work and continues to write, pausing for the odd bite of breakfast or sip of vinegar tea. *If he doesn't get that bite looked at, he's going to die of an infection*, I think, *and that will speed up the revolution somewhat.*

Still, it is difficult to watch a man fail to tend to a wound properly. I remind myself that this is the man who ordered my mother's death and the deaths of hundreds of witches across Frayne, the man who has seen to it that so many of my neighbors were jailed or hanged under his draconian laws. Let him die of a rat bite, then.

I pass a very dull morning watching him write, the cravat on his ankle darkening with blood, until Karla comes back for the breakfast tray, her face white and wobbly as rice pudding. She looks at the dead rat and the bloody cravat and says, "Sir, I will call the doctor."

"Never mind," he mutters at her, not bothering to look up, and she goes out, but soon after there comes a tap at the door, and a weary-looking fellow with a black leather bag comes in.

"Flaming hounds, it's nothing!" Agoston Horthy exclaims.

"So you always say," sighs the doctor.

The prime minister puts down his quill and submits, letting the doctor examine the wound and clean it. He doesn't wince as the alcohol touches the wound, and that is no surprise, I suppose, since he did not even notice the rat clamped on to his ankle in the first place. The doctor sews up the wound with neat little stitches, not bothering to offer any form of anesthetic. I've been stitched up a few times myself, so I know what it's like, and I stare at Agoston Horthy, who is apparently lost in thought, as if he can't feel the needle at all.

"You should rest the foot today," says the doctor. "I hope you do not have many appointments."

"Today, only paperwork," says Horthy, thumping the stack on his desk. "Tomorrow morning I will go and see the king."

"I hope His Majesty is well."

"His Majesty is near death."

"One must never give up hope."

Agoston Horthy does not look impressed by this sentiment. The doctor bandages his ankle, bundles the dead rat up in the ruined cravat, bows to the prime minister, and goes out. Horthy sits back in his chair and stares at nothing for a moment. Then he unlocks a little drawer in the top of his desk, takes out a flat, round object that opens up—I think it is a picture frame—and gazes at it for a long time. I creep closer to look over his shoulder. From my blurred vantage point I can only make out a sepia-toned photograph of a woman and something else before he snaps it shut, slips it into his pocket, and goes back to his work.

The *nuyi* is burning its way up my arm, and it seems to me there's not much point hanging about here, staring at his back while he writes, but with the curtains and door closed there is no way out of the room. I can't vanish myself somewhere else if I can't see it. I'm trapped until a jittery Karla comes back with lunch for him. I reckon I've got something fairly juicy to report already, so I slip out the door after her without reappearing. I wander the parliament halls until I find my way out onto a narrow balcony.

This is a much farther drop than from Wyn's window at the Marrow, but I step up onto the parapet, returning fully to my body because I want to feel and see it clearly. I look down—the straight drop to the street below, where a hackney is trundling by, small boats plying the river Syne. I balance there a moment, arms stretched wide, my heart quickening.

Then I step out into the air and vanish.

TWENTY-TWO

Gennady is on the veranda overlooking Mrs. Och's garden, staring at the lump of bare earth where her cherry tree used to be. Grass does not grow in that spot. I reappear next to him.

"Vanishing Julia," he says in that bone-shuddering baritone—apparently unsurprised by my appearing out of thin air.

"What are you doing?" I ask.

"I am thinking about my life," he says. "I am thinking of all the things I used to care about and wondering why I cared, and I am tallying my failures and regrets and resolving not to care about them either. I do not want to stay in this house, but I do not know where I should go, and I like the food. Mrs. Freeley is a fine cook, a fine person. In fact, I think she is the only person whose company I can stand in the entire world."

Is this what happens when immortals go mad?

"She's a peach," I say.

He scowls at me. "What do you want? Have you come to see Lady Laroche?"

"No. I came to see you."

"If you are not going to tell me where my son is, I do not want to speak to you."

"I don't care what you want," I snap, and then I rein in

my temper. I remind myself that he has been tortured and unmade by Casimir and Shey. That he has suffered. That he did not mean for any of this to turn out the way it has. "I came to ask you about hermia."

"Ah," he says. "Your contract. It won't work, though. The quantity required to kill the *nuyi* would kill you as well."

"I don't want to kill it," I say. "It's true, then? That's what you used to destroy the nests?"

"We used many methods," he says. "But yes—hermia was the most effective."

So Pia was telling the truth. What to make of *that*?

"Julia!" Princess Zara steps out onto the veranda in a dressing gown, her frizzy hair uncombed. "I'm glad to see you!"

"Are you?" I ask. "I suppose nobody can say that sort of thing to *you* unless they really mean it. Where's everybody else?"

"Professor Baranyi has taken your brother to the university to photograph the inside of his chest, and Esme is with them. Gregor and Csilla have gone to the coast to meet with a rebellious count who might give us money. I do not know where Lady Laroche and Idir have gone. They are terribly secretive, those two. Witches are gathering somewhere in the city, but I don't know where. I should *like* to know very much, though."

I stare at her. "Well, *I've* no idea," I say.

"Walk in the garden with me, won't you?" She slips her arm through mine, entirely unselfconscious about the fact that she looks as if she just rolled out of bed. In spite of how young and plain she is, there is no denying that she has about her an extraordinary self-possession that can only be called queenly. We walk down to the pond, where dragonflies flit across the surface of the water and a turtle pokes its head out to glare at us.

"Do you trust me, Julia?" she asks.

"I don't know," I say. There's no point lying to her, after all.

"I hope I will have a chance to prove myself to you," she says. "I want to ask you a favor, and I'm hoping you will keep it quiet. I mean that I do not want Lady Laroche to know."

Ah.

"You don't trust her?" I ask. "Is that because you know what *she's* thinking?"

"I can't read minds. I can only sense emotion and intent. She wants me on the throne, I know that much. But no, I do not trust her. She loves conflict too much. There is something in her that leans toward chaos. She wants to lead the revolution, and this rat business . . . I don't like her methods."

I nod. I'm not wild about her methods either, even if the West Spira nambies deserve a bit of rat trouble.

"I don't mean to sound ungrateful," she says. She is speaking slowly, carefully, with frequent pauses; I realize uncomfortably that she's gauging my reaction as she goes. "But I want to maintain a little distance from her. I would like you to carry a message for me—invisibly, so that nobody can follow you. Esme knows my plans, but I would rather no-body else did as yet."

"A message for whom?"

She lowers her voice. "There is an inn called the Pear Tree, between the Twist and the Plateau. Do you know it?"

"Yes. Bit of a dump."

"Take this letter there and ask for Dorje Tsewang. Deliver it only into her hands and ask her to destroy it when she has read it."

I take the letter she hands me, and then she smiles, like something has amused her.

"It's written in Xanuhan," she says. "I tell you only so you don't waste time opening it."

"And you say you can't read minds," I mutter.

"I wouldn't need my gift to guess at that thought," she replies.

TWENTY-THREE

There are soldiers all over Spira City today, and the Twist is unusually quiet. I have to do a good bit of yelling in the dingy front room of the Pear Tree before an unshaven fellow comes shambling out, doing up his trousers.

"What?" he shouts at me.

"I need to see Dorje Tsewang," I say.

"The furrin lady?" He squints. "What you need to see her for?"

I put one of Pia's coins on the desk. He grabs it and spits on the floor. "She's having tea up on the roof."

The rooftop terrace offers a bleak view of Hostorak on one side and the spiky rooftops of the Twist on the other. The only person up there is a dark-complexioned woman of maybe forty, sitting very straight and reading a book. Her black hair is braided in elaborate loops all over her head. She is wearing a belted crimson tunic over silk trousers and high boots, silk gloves on her hands. She's certainly not trying to blend in.

"Are you Dorje Tsewang?" I ask. As if she might be somebody else.

She puts down her book and looks at me with no expression on her face.

I hand her the envelope Zara gave me. She removes her gloves to take it, and I get a start—her hands are covered in tattoos, old ones, faded. It's writing, but not in any language I recognize. She tears the envelope open with one long fingernail, scans the letter quickly, then reaches into a fold of her tunic and comes out with a match, which she scrapes against the stone balustrade. The match flares, and she sets the letter alight, holding it by the corner as the flames sweep along the edges and the paper curls inward. She closes her other hand over the shrinking fire, extinguishing it, and then opens her fist, blowing away the ashes. I watch, enthralled.

"D'you want to send a message back?"

She shakes her head.

"There are soldiers everywhere right now," I say. "You'd better be careful. They drown witches here."

When she speaks, it is in flawless, upper-class Fraynish: "Don't worry about me, my dear. My papers are in order, and I am not a witch."

"But the fire . . ."

"I do not fear fire, though I can burn. In Xanuha we conquered our witch overlords, you know. Witches seeking power are like a fire seeking fuel. It is a difficult thing to conquer a raging fire that has spread over vast distances, but a small flame can be squashed quickly and painlessly. It is a useful skill—the finding and squashing of small fires."

Startled by her fluency, I ask: "Do you live in Frayne, then?"

"I am visiting," she says, picking up her book again. "Thank you for the message."

I take it I am dismissed. I'll have to ask Esme what dealings the princess has with a Fraynish-speaking Xanuhan expatriate and why Zara doesn't want Lady Laroche to know about it. There is something about this woman—I can't say what it is, only I wish I could sit down and talk to her, find out all about her. But I've no reason to stay—indeed, I've got other, urgent things to do—and she clearly doesn't want me here, anyway.

"Be careful," I say again.

She cocks her head at me curiously but doesn't reply.

TWENTY-FOUR

On a steep hill descending from the Twist into the Edge, there is a shop with a picture of a boot hanging above the door. I knock and enter. The shop itself, with its attractively displayed shoes and boots, its smell of leather and grease, is empty. But a deep voice calls out, "Come in," from the back, so I go through the door into Liddy's room.

A liver-spotted hand flies to her chest when she sees me. For a moment she just stares, and then her face relaxes, her mouth creasing into a smile.

"Hullo, Liddy," I say, helping myself to coffee from the pot on the cast iron stove. "I'm back."

My old friend looks me over, head to toe, and I wonder what she makes of what she sees. "So you are," she says.

There are fresh rolls cooling on the rack by the stove, and I grab one. I've had no lunch, and I'm ravenous. There is no bread in the world as soft and light and always fresh as the bread Liddy makes.

"You won't believe all that's happened," I say, sitting across from her. I can't help grinning at her like an idiot around my mouthful of bread. It is good to see Liddy again. She caught me thieving in the market when I was seven years old, after our mother was drowned, and she took Dek and me to Esme. In a sense, I owe her everything.

She studies my face, her smile closing up slowly like a purse. "You are changed, Julia."

"Knife fight with monsters," I say, drawing the scar on my cheek with my finger and trying to sound cavalier.

"I don't mean the scar. I mean you are *changed*."

And I suppose that's true. We're getting right down to it, then—no small talk. That's always been the way with Liddy.

"You told me once that the world was full of *something elses* if I learned to look for them," I say. "Well, I've been halfway across the world and back since last I saw you, and I've seen more than my share of *something elses*. Actually, it turns out that I *am* one."

Her eyes narrow to pebble-black slits.

"What do you know about Agoston Horthy?" I ask, grabbing a second roll.

"Little that is not common knowledge."

"I think he might be *something else* too. He can't taste anything, and he doesn't seem to . . . feel anything. Like pain."

"There are entirely human disorders that leave their victims with loss of sensation," she says. "You may be leaping to conclusions."

Seems to be the general opinion of every theory I come up with. I pull up my sleeve and show her the silver disk in my wrist, the red line crawling up my arm. The *nuyi* is nearly at my shoulder now. If this thing with the hermia doesn't work, I'm going to have to get it out very soon.

"Do you know what it is?" I ask her, and she nods. Of course she does. Liddy always seems to know everything. "It's not all the way to my brain yet."

"How far?"

I touch the spot on my upper arm.

"Take it out now," she says hoarsely. "I'll do it for you."

"I can't," I say. "He's put a sac of poison inside Dek. It's disintegrating slowly. He'll take it out in a week or so, but only if I leave the *nuyi* be."

She absorbs this information, looking at me closely, and then says: "Word is spreading that Mrs. Och is dead."

"She's dead." I leave it at that. Now is not the moment for my full confession.

"And this . . ." She gestures at my dress, finer than anything she's ever seen me wear. "Oh, Julia, what have you gotten yourself into?"

"I'll explain everything . . . later. Right now I need two things and I don't have much time. Pia told me that the herb hermia would slow the *nuyi* down."

"Hermia is not an *herb*," she says sharply. "It is highly toxic, a poison."

"All right—but it's true, isn't it, that it would slow down the *nuyi*?"

"It would sicken *you*. Pia has never acted in your interests, Julia. She will never act in anyone's interests but Casimir's."

"I know. It's hard to explain . . . but I think she wants to help me."

"Julia, listen to me." She leans forward, fixing me with her sharp eyes, and she says, very slowly: "You are *mistaken* about that."

"Well, it's the only idea I've got right now. I've got to try it, unless *you* know someone who could safely get this poison out of Dek."

"I will ask my friends for advice."

Liddy and her mysterious friends.

"Fine. In the meantime, where can I find hermia?"

"In the forests of Middle Arrekem," she says, her eyes nearly disappearing into the pouches and folds around them.

"So you aren't going to help me?"

"I am telling you not to poison yourself with hermia."

"I hoped you'd help me with the dosage."

"I want no part of it."

"Then I'll find someone else. I wanted help from someone I trust. Someone who cares about me."

"And that's me?"

"Am I wrong?"

Her hands are shaking slightly. She says, "If you are determined to poison yourself, come to me, and I will make sure you do not take too much."

"Can I get it in Spira City?"

"Goro, the alchemist, will have some."

"Thank you."

"I don't like it."

"I don't *like* it either," I say. "One more thing. Have you heard of a witch called Silver Moya?"

"Julia!" She gapes at me like I've sprouted a second head. "You must not go there."

"Frederick told me there was a Silver Moya in Spira City. I need to know where."

She says nothing.

"Fine. I'll ask Lady Laroche," I say.

I swear she tenses at that.

"Marek and Son," she snaps. "The clock maker. They are all in clock shops. You'll need to tell them that your clock at home chimes every thirteen minutes. Julia—great stars!—I don't know what is happening, but you should not tempt powers that can swallow you up."

"Too late," I say. "I've *been* swallowed. Now I'm just trying not to be fully digested. So you know about Lady Laroche, then?"

She nods and sags in her chair. She looks so old and feeble that my heart flutters a little.

"You all right, Liddy?"

"As well as can be expected, at my age."

"How old *is* that?"

"Cheeky." She manages a little grin. "This body is a weary sort of scaffolding, that's all. Things are turning dark in Spira City. I am glad to see you again. I would not have wanted you to come looking and find me gone. But I'm thinking of moving on."

"Moving on?" It is impossible to imagine Spira City without Liddy. To me, she is as much a part of it as Mount Heriot or the river Syne. "Where would you *go*?"

"The world is full of other places."

"Are things here really worse than they used to be?" I ask.

"Witches have been fleeing Frayne for twenty years. Anyone who could get out got out. Now witches are flocking *to* Frayne, witches who were safe elsewhere, witches with no previous allegiance to Frayne, coming to a country that crushed the last attempt at revolution and drowned witches by the hundreds. They are coming in boats from Ingle, through the forests of Prasha, across the sea from Sirillia and North Arrekem. Why do you think that is?"

"I don't know."

"Perhaps you ought to find out."

TWENTY-FIVE

The door to the Adder's Switch is unlocked. Goro, the alchemist, is packing things into boxes while a sullen boy covered in blisters carries the full boxes out to a hackney in the street. I appear in the middle of the room, and the boy skitters out of my way, backing up against the wall, gawping at my fine dress. Goro looks up, his eyes milky with cataracts. I can't resist a dramatic entrance sometimes.

"I need hermia," I tell him. "Liddy sent me."

That isn't exactly true, but I know her name will save us the dance of whether I can be trusted.

He releases a squeaky sigh. "Hermia? There are faster poisons."

"That's the one I need."

"It is costly."

"How much?"

"For an ounce . . . ten silver freyns. An ounce is enough to kill a man. If you want to poison a witch, you might need five or six ounces. Something else . . . well, it depends."

"An ounce will do," I say.

He puts on a pair of gloves and goes rummaging through his boxes. He takes a delicate bronze scale from one box, a bag of some curling brown root from another. He shaves a bit off the root, weighs it, and wraps it up for me with brisk professionalism.

"A lot of witches coming through lately," he says softly as I count out the money for him.

"I'm not a witch," I say, taking the package. "Why all the boxes? You going somewhere?"

"South, to wait out the storm."

"The storm?"

"Good luck. You should know it is an ugly death by hermia."

"Nobody is going to die, I hope. Why *are* witches coming to Frayne?"

"Witches flock to trouble," he says. "And that's what's coming. It's a good time to get out of Spira City. There's some advice for free."

I stop at the market for lettuce and apples, and then go straight to the clock shop—Marek and Son. There's a freckled boy at the desk, about my age.

"You must be son and not Marek," I say.

"Dad passed away last year," he says, bobbing his head.

"Oh. I'm sorry."

"Can I help you, miss?"

"I'm looking for Silver Moya," I say, remembering as I speak that I could be arrested and executed for this. Spira City is not Tianshi.

"I'm sorry, I don't understand," he says mildly.

"Liddy sent me," I say. "Oh, right—I mean my clock at home chimes every thirteen minutes."

"Perhaps you should talk to my mother in the back," he says. "Go on through."

He opens a door behind the counter for me, and I pass into a tidy workshop with birdcages hanging from the ceiling. A middle-aged lady in a high-buttoned dress is polishing a grandfather clock.

"Silver Moya?" I ask.

She turns and looks me over, folding up her rag.

"Pardon me?"

"I need to see Ragg Rock," I say.

"*Pardon* me?" she repeats.

"Do I have to say it to you as well? My clock at home chimes every thirteen minutes, all right?"

She looks at me for a long moment and then goes and locks the door behind me. She takes some birdseed from her pocket, tosses it across a desk in the corner, and lets one of the birds out of its cage. The creature flutters over to the desk and starts pecking at the seed. Silver Moya—for I assume this is she—gets out a sheet of paper and a little ink dropper.

"Am I supposed to . . . pay you?" I ask. I didn't pay Silver Moya in Tianshi. I didn't think of it. But nothing is ever free in Spira City.

"This is a calling," she says briskly. "Not a trade." She hands me a pin. "Would you mind pricking your finger and squeezing a bit of blood into the dropper?"

I do so, and she pours the ink mixed with a bit of blood into a cartridge, which she affixes to her modern pen. My blood is the request, revealing to Ragg Rock who wishes to enter and why.

Silver Moya starts writing.

As her pen glides across the paper, one layer after another seems to slip away from the surface of things, and the room begins to thrum. The ink is wet and very black, and I can feel my blood coursing through me, fast and warm, the *nuyi* burrowing its way up my arm, my heart beating, *thud thud*, and then everything goes still except the bird on the desk. A door next to the grandfather clock has opened. It is bright outside the door, a too-still counterfeit of Spira City dangling out there. The bird swoops out the door, and I follow as if a line ran between it and me, pulling me along after it. I dash out into the street, leaving Silver Moya still bent over her paper, immobile, the final drop of ink suspended between pen and paper. Stairs wind up over Cyrambel Temple, the river Syne rippling alongside it, strangely depthless. I climb up over the city, into the sky, after the bird, until it gives a sharp little cry and drops at my feet, feathers singed and smoking.

There is a broken arch before me, and through it a mist and the outline of trees, black and bare. I step through the archway, and the sky below me is gone. The trees close around me, the ground turning soft under my feet, not quite like ground. Something with wings passes over my head with a whoosh. Something brushes against my arm. Strange lights hang in the fog among the trees, which are moving ever closer. I stumble through the wood and then out onto bare rock. A shadowy thing like a weasel but longer moves past me up the hill, fading to nothing as it goes.

The black rock with the hut on top is the same. Coming down the winding path, I see Ragg Rock, red against the sky. Frederick limps behind her, pale as dust, and careening past them both, down the hill and into my arms, Theo— bigger, fiercer, *filthy*, and alive.

TWENTY-SIX

Frederick and I sit on a ledge furred with gray moss, looking down at Ragg Rock and Theo. They are crouched at the edge of the stream below us, spearing fish and shouting with triumph whenever they get one. Beyond the stream lies the shadowed, spiky wood I came through, Spira City just a cloudy jumble of almost-buildings somewhere far below. The sky is a whitish gray over the craggy rock rising up behind us.

Ragg Rock looks somehow realer than when I saw her last—her stone eyes set deeper in her face, shining with almost human brightness, her red-mud muscles moving in perfect imitation of the human body. Her expression too is more animated, more *human* and less made-of-mud, in spite of the little thumbprint, one of Theo's, on her cheek. They are talking in some sort of pidgin they've concocted between them, part Fraynish and part who-knows-what.

At first seeing Theo careening down the hill gave me a terrible fright. He was holding a small spear with flint at the end like a tiny warrior, his tight curls full of twigs and dead leaves, and he was covered with the red mud of the place. I half expected his teeth to be pointed when he smiled at me, his eyes to have gone pebble-hard like hers. But he was still Theo: nearly two years old now, sturdy fat legs, wide laughing mouth, his skin a lovely golden brown under the mud, his cheeks round and his belly sticking out. He pranced around the place naked like a fine little lord, hurling his spear at the half-animals that appeared from the wood, and I thought, *I saved him*, but also, *What have I done?* Making a small, motherless child call *this* place home? Giving him this red-mud creature as his nursemaid? After kissing my face and smearing mud all over me, he pulled back and said, "Whey Mama?"

"She's not here."

I could barely choke it out, crouched on the rocky shelf before him, his eyes shining with . . . hope, fear, what? I certainly couldn't make myself say, "She's dead, you'll never see her again, you won't remember her when you grow up, if you grow up, the odds of which are looking ever slimmer."

But as if he could read this, or some of it, in my expression, his face screwed up with sudden fury, he pulled back and punched me in the eye. I nearly fell over backward with the shock of it.

"Mama!" he roared at me, and ran off in a fury—like I'm the one who tossed her over the side of the boat to drown. I didn't manage to save her, that much is true, but I tried, oh, I tried. Now he seems to have forgotten it, busy with the task of spearing half-transparent fish with Ragg Rock. They manage to catch the more substantial fish, but most of them disintegrate into fog as soon as they are speared.

Frederick rubs a pale hand over his face. His beard is long and so fair it looks almost white, his cheeks hollow. I've told him everything that's happened since I saw him last; he listened closely but showed little reaction.

"Theo looks well," I say, not sure how to take his silence. "You, less so."

My voice sounds light. I *feel* light, but not lighthearted. Theo is safe. I did that, at least: I've kept him alive, where Casimir cannot reach him.

"We're managing," says Frederick, in a low voice so Ragg Rock and Theo cannot hear him. "I've been waiting . . . for you, but we can't stay here much longer. We need to find someplace else. Someplace in the world."

"Not yet," I say.

"I do take him to the world, Julia. He wouldn't survive if I didn't."

"What do you mean?" My heart plunges.

"He needs proper food. *Real* food. This stuff we eat here . . . it tastes like it's disappearing as you eat it. It's not just the food either. It's the air, or the light, I don't know. There's no sun. We lasted a week, and I thought we were dying. Theo looked terrible, sort of vacant in the eyes, and his stomach was hurting. It was Ragg Rock's idea. She could see he wouldn't survive. She can let us into the world anywhere, so every other day we go to the Silver Moya in Vassali, in Southern Ishti. Ragg Rock trusts her. We stay in the courtyard of her shop. We don't venture into town. She brings us food to eat and some to take back with us, and he can spend an afternoon playing in the sun. It does us both a world of good. He spends most of the time trying to get out of the courtyard, of course, and he cries and screams like anything when we have to come back. He adores Ragg Rock, but he feels trapped here."

"He *is* trapped," I say, trying to wrap my head around the idea of them popping into Southern Ishti for visits. "Does he talk about Bianka?"

"He asks for her, and cries in bursts, and then he seems to forget. I don't know how much he understands. He sleeps poorly. Ragg Rock likes to comfort him—she doesn't sleep, and I think she gets lonely when we do. It's difficult, anyway—there's no night or day here. I seem to need a great deal more sleep than I used to. Hounds, I feel so helpless, Julia." He drops his face into his hands.

I was seven when I lost my own mother, far older than Theo. Old enough to understand that she was gone for good, and how, and why. But I remember how sometimes, in the weeks and months and even years that followed, I would almost forget—busy with my life and the things I was doing, laughing and having a good time with Dek or my friends—and it would seem that she was still at home, waiting for me. I would remember, or be reminded, and each time I was winded by the truth that came snatching my joy away all over again, the same breathless horror and twisting grief, as fresh and vivid as ever.

I don't know how a child as young as Theo is supposed to grieve if he can't even understand why she's gone, where she's gone. Does he know she did everything she could to save him? That she untied him from her as the water pulled her down, let me take him, thinking in her last moments only of him? She gave him to me, and I've left him here with a man too weakened to protect him. There were no good choices, but was this the best one? Could I have done better? What would she say to me, if she saw how I am trying to save him? Oh, Bianka. She trusted me with her child, but I've never wronged anybody so much as her and Theo.

"Ragg Rock is getting very attached to Theo," says Frederick. "It frightens me a bit, watching her rocking him and singing to him when he can't sleep. I don't think it's . . . he shouldn't bond so closely with whatever she is, nor she with him. But I can't intervene. She sees me mainly as competition for his affection and as the person who might take him away from her. Though even she can see he needs the sunlight and food we get in Vassali, and she cannot take him there herself. I can't tell what she's thinking."

Indeed, where once she helped me, she is wary of me this time and stays close to Theo. She asked me if I'd come to take him back and was visibly relieved when I said no. I wonder what she would have done if I'd said yes. If she might not let me in, another time.

"I don't know what to do," I say. "Maybe the hermia will buy me a little time, but even then . . ."

"If you can get Zara on the throne, you'll have an ally in a position of real power," he says. "With an army of witches too. It might be enough to take on Casimir." He pauses. "What is Lady Laroche like?"

"A bit mad, I think," I tell him. "Quite glamorous."

"Mrs. Och held her in high regard," says Frederick. "She considered her an impressive person, but unpredictable. Be careful with her."

"I'll be careful."

"Good. Perhaps I can even help you from here. Frayne has destroyed most of its old texts that reference magic and folklore, but Vassali has an impressive library. I'll see if I can find out anything about the *nuyi*."

Ragg Rock and Theo head up the hill with their shadowy fish.

"Come," says Ragg Rock, gesturing at us imperiously.

I help Frederick to his feet. He stumbles a few times walking up the hill, holding on to my shoulder and leaning heavily on me. He is thinner than I've ever seen him, his back stooped. By the time we reach the top, he is gasping for breath.

"Is it being in Ragg Rock that's doing this to you?" I ask anxiously.

"I don't think so. Mrs. Och took too much of my life-force that last time. She left me enough to survive, but only just. Not enough to fully recover."

Ragg Rock and Theo light a fire outside the hut now, fastening their fish to a spit. Most of them crumble instantly to ash, but a few of them sizzle, like real fish.

"How is Professor Baranyi?" asks Frederick.

"I haven't spoken to him," I confess. "He was very upset when I told them about Mrs. Och."

"I imagine he was."

His voice is gentle and there is no accusation in his eyes. I tell myself that if Frederick believes I did only what I had to do, surely it must be true.

"I've been thinking," he says, and then laughs a little, a glimmer of defiance coming into his expression. "I have a lot of time to think these days. I can't take part in the revolution, but when this is over, I hope to be part of building the new Frayne. I'd like to collaborate on a book with Professor Baranyi—give a thorough account of the history of magic in Frayne, lay out some of my ideas for a just world. If you do speak to him, tell him I am sustained by the things we talked about, and that I look forward to working with him again."

A just world. Oh, Frederick. I've missed him.

"Of course," I say.

Apparently forgetting that he punched me on arrival,

Theo comes into the hut, grabs the dog-eared book of Yongwen fairy tales we brought here with him, and throws himself into my lap.

"My stoy!" he says, opening it and pointing at the first page.

"I can't read Yongwen," I say, kissing the top of his curly head.

"Make it stoy!" he says, as if I'm very stupid, and then begins to tell the story himself, turning the pages and nestling comfortably against me.

Ragg Rock stands in the entrance, watching us.

"He hasn't tried to draw anything, then?" I ask. Theo is not a witch, but he has a fragment of *The Book of Disruption* inside him. We can't know all of its effects, but one of them seems to be that he can will the things he draws into being.

Frederick and Ragg Rock exchange a look.

"We try to keep a close eye, but there have been . . . some small incidents," says Frederick uneasily. "There's a three-headed rabbit-like creature about Theo's size loping around here somewhere. Sometimes it sings in Bianka's voice, which is distressing for all of us."

"Holy Nameless," I say in a strangled voice.

"Indeed. A few other odd little creatures that fit in fine here. Nothing big, thank the Nameless. It does seem that whatever he draws comes to life, but fortunately it is restricted to drawing. So far, anyway. I hope as he gets older he will be able to control it."

"No modeling clay for him, then," I mutter.

"Dwaw is bad," says Theo placidly, as if by rote. And then he says something in his made-up language to Ragg Rock. She laughs and looks away from us.

"I wanted to ask you something," I say to Ragg Rock.

"Not surprised," she snaps back, in my own accent and tone.

"You let my mother, Ammi, take Lidari into the world using the Ankh-nu," I say. "There are some who think that she . . . my mother, I mean . . . was actually Marike. In a new body."

Ragg Rock recoils at that, making a muddy hissing sound in her throat. Theo looks up from his book, startled.

"No," she says. "I would not let Marike come back here. No."

"I wondered if she might have found a way to . . . trick you. But maybe it's not true."

"Not true!" she shouts.

"I just can't figure how my mother came to have the Ankh-nu in the first place."

She shakes her head, still hissing.

"You're sure?" I ask, and she turns her back on me, goes out to check on the fish. I listen to Theo's half-Fraynish babble, telling me the stories from his book. I'd like to stay, holding on to him, but it's clear I'm not going to get any more answers from Ragg Rock, and I can feel the *nuyi* in my arm. I have so little time.

Ragg Rock brings in a cooked fish. "This is because of him," she says proudly.

"My fish!" cries Theo.

"What do you mean, because of him?" I ask, but she clams up again, looking at me with something disconcertingly close to hatred in those pebble eyes.

I promise to return as soon as I can. When he realizes I'm leaving, Theo howls and clings to my leg. Ragg Rock has to peel him off me. I can hear him screaming *Lala! Lala!* as I go down the hill and into the strange wood. Emerging from the wood onto the stairs that wind down toward Cyrambel Temple and the city, I look back, but Ragg Rock is gone. With each step the stairs suspended in the sky melt to nothing behind me, the city a disjointed puzzle below, like a badly made model of a city. When I step off the last stair into the street, it vanishes behind me and there is a shift: the false city comes to life again, everything so real it hurts, the air bursting with sound, and I am home.

Telegram to Lord Casimir, Nago
Island: HORTHY IN OFFICE ALL DAY STOP
BITTEN BY RAT STOP FEELS NO PAIN
TASTES NOTHING STOP WILL VISIT KING
TOMORROW STOP JULIA COOPERATIVE STOP

DAY 7

HORNETS AND POISONS

*"Innocent people!" snorts Lady Laroche.
"That is a fantasy! You might as well
talk to me of unicorns."*

TWENTY-SEVEN

There is no place bleaker than the Edge at dawn. It is gray and damp, an unpleasant chill in the air, the shabby buildings and narrow lanes holding close the violence, the terrible choices and terrible luck, the dead ends and lost hopes, the hundreds of commonplace tragedies that have made up its night. At this hour, you can feel the despair of it, wrung out and weary.

I'd imagined everyone at the Marrow would be asleep, but when I go down I find the scarred old woman in the bar gathering up filthy plates. One of the tables has been knocked over, and she rights it with a grunt.

"Hello," I say, and she swivels her ruined face to look at me.

I remember how she cheered them on when they had a go at me. In fairness I ought to hate her too, but a single look at her is enough to know what kind of muck her life has dragged her through. I can't help but pity any woman who has wound up in the Edge with men like these. Perhaps I ought to pity the men too, but I've only so much pity to spare and it doesn't go to those who once tried to rip my clothes off.

"Oho, you," she says, a glint in her eye. "All these fine dresses you've got now! Must be nice."

I slept only a few hours at the hotel and put on a new dress in a hurry this morning, making another poor attempt to powder my face in the half-light, but I still look terribly grand for the Edge.

"Is Dek asleep?"

"Oughtn't to tell you, but I s'pose it don't matter if I do or if I don't, given you can slip around invisible," she says, and cackles. "They're all upstairs. Far left door is Torne's."

I go up and knock. Esme opens the door, shirtsleeves rolled up over her powerful forearms, pistol at her hip. She pulls me inside, relief breaking across her face.

Torne, Dek, Princess Zara, and Dorje Tsewang, the woman I delivered the letter to at the Pear Tree Inn, are sitting around a table together. I won't deny I'm surprised at this particular grouping.

"Julia!" cries Dek cheerfully.

"What are you doing here?" I ask Zara. "I mean, aren't you supposed to be . . . in hiding?"

"I took a hackney," she says. "I ought to be getting back, though."

She is wearing a plain dress and a hooded cloak, damp from the light drizzle. She looks like a merchant's daughter.

I suppose it would not occur to anybody, least of all a hackney driver, that this stout girl with an overlong nose intends to overthrow the Crown and rule Frayne.

Torne sees me glancing at the chart full of figures spread across the table, and he hastily rolls it up.

"I'm not here to pry into your revolutionary secrets," I scoff at him, though in fact I'm wildly curious.

"She works for Casimir," says Torne quietly, to the table-top, but I know this is meant for Esme.

"I understand the situation," Esme tells him sharply. "We are finished here, are we not?"

"I will send a message this evening," says Dorje Tsewang, rising smoothly. I see a curved blade at her belt as she pulls on her coat. She gives me the briefest smile and goes out, with Torne close behind her.

"Lady Laroche is eager to see you again," Zara says to me, pulling her hood over her head and making to follow the other two.

"I'll stop by later," I reply.

When it is just Esme and Dek and me, Dek reaches over and tousles my hair.

"Stop it!" I say. "Do you know how long it took Csilla to get these bleeding hair extensions on? I came looking for you, actually. I'm going to visit Liddy. She said she was going to ask around about your poison problem. What happened with the magical photographs yesterday?"

"It's not magic," he says. "But I did get to see some odd gray pictures that they claim are of my heart. There is *something* there—other than my heart, I mean. Presumably the poison. The surgeon said he couldn't see how it was attached or what the nature of the sac was. He was awfully jittery when we asked if it would be possible to remove it without rupture, so it looks like that's out, which we'd rather suspected, anyway."

I'd let myself hope too hard. For a moment, it's a struggle to take a breath. But I do, and then another. Despair is a strong current, but I need to keep swimming against it as long as I've got strength to do so.

"We need to get our hands on this mechanic," says Esme.

"No good. It's Casimir we've got to persuade," I say.

Esme's jaw works briefly and then she says, "Dek, I'd like to speak with Julia privately."

Dek nods and goes out, and Esme closes the door behind him.

"Early meeting," I say, suddenly nervous. "Does Lady Laroche know the princess is meeting you here? I know she doesn't know about Dorje Tsewang. Who *is* she, anyway? Why is the princess dealing with Xanuhans?"

I'm babbling. Esme doesn't answer me, her gaze unwavering.

"Hounds, you don't have to tell me anything. I know you're all worried Casimir will get it out of me."

"Tell me how to help you," says Esme.

That nearly brings me to tears all of a sudden. "Well, Liddy's going to help," I say. "There's this herb that will slow the *nuyi* down a bit. If I can keep it from reaching my brain long enough but fool Casimir into thinking it's attached, we reckon he'll have his mechanic take the poison out of Dek. Then I can take the *nuyi* out too."

When I say it out loud, it sounds ludicrous, hopeless.

"We? Who is *we?*"

"Well, me. And Liddy."

Nameless knows I'm not going to tell her this was Pia's idea.

"And Liddy thinks it will work?"

Blast, if she talks to Liddy, she'll know how opposed Liddy is to the whole thing. I nod. Esme's busy. I hope she won't be visiting Liddy anytime soon.

"Julia," she sighs. "Why didn't you tell me?"

"About . . . what?"

There's so much I didn't tell her.

"Kahge," she says, and I shrivel inside.

"I just . . . couldn't." I stare at my hands. "It's too strange and horrible. I didn't want you to see me differently."

"Sit, please," she says, gesturing at a chair.

I sit, because when Esme tells you to do something, generally you do it. She has that way about her.

"I do not like your plan," she says. "You risk everything in allowing Casimir's *thing* inside you. We'll take it out today and find another way to help Dek."

"No," I say. "No. You heard what he said—they can't operate on him. This is the only way."

"Julia!" She crashes her fist onto the table, and I jump out of the chair. I've never been on the receiving end of one of Esme's short, brutal explosions of violence, but I know enough to fear her anger. "Casimir is trying to take *possession* of you. Under no circumstances must you give him that chance. We will take the *nuyi* out *now*. I have a doctor in the Twist who can do it. I will not accept refusal."

There's no point arguing with her, so I dash for the door. She takes one long step toward me, grabs my arm. I shake her loose and vanish.

TWENTY-EIGHT

"Esme's *very* upset."

Thank the Nameless: Dek is waiting for me outside Liddy's, and Esme isn't.

"Does she know you're here?" I ask.

"No—she had to leave. There's a lot going on. Anyway, she knows she can't actually make you do anything."

"Good."

"She's not wrong, though, Julia. You *do* need to get that thing out of your arm. We're all agreed on that."

"I will," I say. "*Please* trust me. Come on. You haven't seen Liddy in an age."

Liddy is very interested to see Dek's new arm and leg. She examines the hinges at his knuckles and a big one at his elbow I hadn't seen yet, then holds his face in her liver-spotted hands and peers at his glass eye. His Scourge scars and the stitched-shut empty socket never bothered me, but that staring glass eyeball makes me shiver.

"What do you think of all this?" she asks him.

He hesitates for a long moment, and I wonder why I hadn't thought to ask him that myself. Why I assumed he'd be glad to have a more functional arm and leg than before. But in fact, I can see for myself that trying to use his new limbs slows him down.

"It's easier to go out," he says at last. "I don't look like a Scourge survivor anymore."

"Ah," she says, and waits for the rest. It comes in a rush.

"The mechanic said it would get easier to use the limbs as I got used to them. I reckon he's right. But my problem was never that I couldn't use my arm and leg. Everything is designed for two hands, two legs, two eyes—that's how it is, but I learned to get around well enough. The problem was that people could *see* the Scourge on me, and the world didn't want me. Now I go where I like, but if I could have chosen, I'd have wanted the world to change rather than me. I feel as if I'm in disguise. Every time a shopkeeper takes my money or a barkeep brings me a drink, I think that if they knew the truth, if they saw my face as it was before, they'd turn me out. I'm getting *angry* about how I was treated. I couldn't afford to be angry before. It might have eaten me up. But now that I can go where I like, do as I like, be treated like anyone else, I *am* angry that they ever dared to stop me, *spit* at me." He stops abruptly, flushed and a little breathless. "It tires me out, honestly, feeling so angry. And then there's knowing that something next to my heart is going to kill me in a week or two."

"Thirteen days," I say.

"I have asked my friends about your problem," says Liddy. "But Casimir's mechanic is renowned for being ... thorough. Have you had breakfast?"

We haven't. She fetches us fresh rolls and sliced ham and jarred pears from the larder.

"Tell me about the princess," she says, setting the table.

"She's remarkable," says Dek. I'm a little taken aback by his enthusiasm. "She has a real vision for Frayne, but she's very detail-oriented too. It's rare to find people who can think big and also understand all the small moving parts. It's the kind of talent inventors need, of course, but listening to her, I think more leaders ought to have it too. You know the result you want, but you also have to understand the minute steps to make it happen, all the things that need to be working together properly to achieve that result. Honestly, I think she's one of the most brilliant people I've ever met."

"I am glad to hear it," says Liddy. "It gives me something to hope for. There are no doubts as to her identity?"

"Esme thinks she has proof enough to put any doubts to rest," says Dek. "She came to see me after my meeting with the doctor who photographed my heart."

"That was nice of her," I say.

"She is nice," he laughs. "But it was to ask me for help. Esme told her a bit about the sort of thing I'm good at. She wanted to hear about the cannons and sleeping-gas canisters I made for our getaway from Casimir that first time on Nago Island. She wants something on a larger scale." His real eye is shining. "If I'm going to die in a week, at least I'll be useful in the meantime."

"Thirteen days," I repeat crossly. "And you're not going to."

When we've finished eating, I take out the packet I got from Goro. Liddy's wrinkled face takes on a masklike expression. She puts a kettle on to boil and ties a handkerchief around her face. Then she leans over the packet, snipping at the curled brown shavings. She puts a minuscule amount in a mug with some tea leaves, wrapping up the rest and giving it back to me, and pours the steaming water into the mug.

"We'll start off with a small dose," she says. "You can eat the leaves directly, but it will be easier on the stomach to soak them in water first."

I take the cup from her and knock half of it back as fast as I can, scalding my tongue.

"So what are the side effects, exactly?" I ask, wincing.

"Most people would ask before drinking."

"Not if the alternative was to be enslaved forever to a mad, murderous immortal."

"Fair enough. Headaches, fever, some nausea or stomach cramping. Muscle and joint pain. Blurred vision. It can have a hallucinatory effect, though probably not at this dosage. Still, as we increase the dose you may hear things or even see things. And of course, it can affect every person differently. You are an unusual girl, and the effects may be unusual."

I finish the poisoned tea as quickly as I can.

"We don't have time to go easy on the dosage," I say. "It's nearly up to my shoulder."

A wave of dizziness hits me, and I put my head between my knees.

"You all right?" asks Dek, alarmed.

169

I breathe deeply until it passes. "I'm fine," I say, and hope it's true. I glance uneasily at the clock—it is nearly eight o'clock, and I want to be there when Agoston Horthy goes to see the king. "I'd better go. This plan still depends on me actually being a useful spy for Casimir."

"How you came to be mixed up with such people," Liddy mutters.

But it wasn't an accident. Casimir sought me out for a job, knowing who I was and a little—oh, but just a little—of what I could do. Which one of us will pay more dearly for the association remains to be seen.

We say goodbye to Liddy. I feel a little unsteady getting up but not too bad. At the door to the shop we meet a young woman with a great bruise on her temple. Her cheeks are hollow with hunger, but there is something else in her expression—a kind of fear that goes beyond deprivation. She is holding herself oddly—broken rib, maybe. Two frightened-looking children are hiding behind her skirts. One of the children has a bandaged arm. A sorry lot, in other words.

"You looking for Liddy?" Dek asks her kindly.

She stares at him and then at me, eyes darting back and forth, throat working with panic, as if trying to assess the danger. The kids move closer to her. Six and four, maybe— or seven and five—and underfed.

"She's through there," says Dek, pointing. "We're just leaving."

We step out into the street, and she pulls the kids in front of her. They go into the shop clinging to one another, the woman shuffling sideways so she doesn't entirely turn her back on us. She slams the door behind her.

"Friendly girl," I say, then ask Dek: "Where are you going now?"

"Weapons dealer." He grins. "If these are to be my last days, at least they won't be dull."

"We're going to survive this," I tell him, and try to believe it.

"My sister, the endless optimist. Go find something useful for Casimir."

And so that is what I do.

TWENTY-NINE

I enter the palace by a balcony with its doors open wide, returning to my body enough that I can feel my feet on the ground, but not so much as to be seen.

"I told them no pork," a man in courtly dress is saying to a woman seated before a mirror. The room is lavishly furnished, everything jeweled, gilt, covered in velvet and tassels.

"You can't expect them to accommodate every little thing," the woman says, patting her hair and staring at her reflection rather challengingly, like she might set up arguing the opposite point at any moment.

"I do not," says the man as I slip through the room to a

connecting chamber. "But I hold that the pig is too intelligent an animal to be served as *dinner*. I have known pigs more curious, charming, loving, and clever than many people, as a matter of fact, and we do not set about cooking our ignorant cousins, do we?"

"Perhaps we should. Evangeline is a bore, but I bet she'd be delicious."

In the next room, a servant is cleaning up and the door is firmly closed. I position myself by the door and wait until she has her back to me. Then I turn the knob and slip out, pulling the door almost closed but not fully, so the click does not startle her. She will just think she forgot to pull it shut, I hope.

In the hall, I take the palace maps Sir Victor gave me from my purse and examine them. I reckon these are the guest suites. I want to get across the palace to King Zey's residence, a few stories down. I descend the curving, carpeted staircase. The walls are hung with long, frowning paintings of dead kings and queens, not a jolly, smiling face among them. No fun being royal, if these portraits are anything to go by.

At the bottom of the stairs, I come to a hall at the center of which stands a statue of Zey's great-grandfather, King Zedar. The queen's chambers, closed up for years now since her death, are to the left, and the king's suite is to the right. A guard stands by the door, fiddling with his cuff links. I go lean on the wall near him, and we wait together—though he doesn't know it—until Agoston Horthy arrives. The guard bows and opens the door for the prime minister. I slip in as fast as I can behind him, trying not to brush against him before the guard shuts the door.

We pass through the anteroom into an empty and rather untended parlor. Agoston Horthy knocks briefly on the door at the far end and goes in, pulling it shut so quickly that this time I have to leap straight out of my body and focus on the corner of the next room I'm able to glimpse through the closing door. I almost crash into the wall by King Zey's bed, drawing back quickly, trying not to cry out. Horthy sits at the king's bedside and shows no sign of hearing or seeing any of my blundering about at the edge of the visible world.

King Zey is propped up in the bed against a pile of cushions. I remember seeing him once when I was a little girl. He rode through the city in a carriage pulled by towering dappled horses and waved a gloved hand out the window. I saw a white beard and a gold crown as the carriage clattered by. He looked ancient even then. Now his beard lies in a yellowing tangle on his chest, his skin the texture of a withered old leaf. I feel a little thrill. The truth is that if I were working for anyone but Casimir, this job would be a kind of dream come true—spying on the grand powers that dictate all of our lives, here in the room with the king of Frayne and his mighty, terrible prime minister. In spite of the stakes and all my fears, there is a part of me that loves this.

"Your Majesty, you look as if you are in pain," says Agoston Horthy.

"Lord Horthy," wheezes the king. "I welcome whatever pain the Nameless One bestows on me. This slow death is mine to bear. This too is His gift."

Agoston Horthy bows his head.

"Today I was able to sit a while and read Scripture," says the king. "I have been well enough to pray. I thank the Nameless One for this."

"The Nameless One loves you," says Agoston Horthy flatly.

"I am fortunate indeed," says the king. "I would like to meet my heir. Not today. Today I am tired already."

"It is early morning still, Your Majesty."

"Tomorrow. Let me meet him tomorrow."

"Very well, Your Majesty."

"What do you think of him, my friend?"

"I think he is young. I think he knows very little."

The king chuckles. "He will have you to guide him. You will serve him well, and you will serve Frayne, as you have done for many years now as my prime minister."

"If he chooses to keep me, so I shall, Your Majesty. It is the king's prerogative to appoint a new prime minister if he wishes."

"He is not too arrogant?"

"I think he will welcome counsel."

"Good."

"Sir Victor has suggested a girl of great piety who might make him a good wife and help guide him in spiritual matters," adds Agoston Horthy.

"Good, good, a wife is the best spiritual helpmeet. You will guide him in matters of state, and she will guide him in matters of the soul. That is good. Anything else?"

"There are rumors that a girl posing as your niece has come to Frayne. Nothing more than rumor yet. But the rat invasion of West Spira suggests a gathering of witches, a new confidence. Perhaps they have found someone to rally behind. The rumor strikes me as plausible enough to warrant our attention. We know Och Farya was in Yongguo recently, and that a girl claiming to be Zara was living there for a time."

King Zey looks very agitated at this. He begins clawing at his tattered beard.

"Is it possible? You *told me* Roparzh's child was dead."

"We believed she was. It is possible the death was faked to throw off her pursuers. I am investigating."

"Suppose the girl *is* alive and has come to Frayne? Who will help her, now that Och Farya is dead?"

"Lady Laroche escaped, as you know."

"Yes, that fiend!" wheezes the king, sitting up some more. "You must hunt her down!"

"We will, Your Majesty, do not worry yourself. Witches have been gathering in the villages north of the city. I sent troops in the night, and they rounded up twenty-three witches. They are in Hostorak now. One of them will give up their leader, I am sure. Put your heart at ease. Concentrate on your maker, who is coming for you."

Something in my chest squeezes painfully. I missed what would have been crucial information for Lady Laroche while I was fetching hermia and visiting Ragg Rock yesterday. Now those witches will likely drown.

"If you find the girl, I want to see her," says the king.

A long pause, and then Horthy says: "Why?"

Zey rocks back and forth on the pillows a bit. "I would know. If she is my niece, I would recognize her."

"You never laid eyes on her, even as a babe, Your Majesty."

"I would recognize my flesh and blood!" he cries. "My brother's daughter! Oh, my friend, there are things that weigh on my soul. Do you not think of it? My brother. His *children*! Do you remember little Davin, such a clever boy? *He* should be my heir."

The king begins to weep, a wild hiccupping sound, waving his hands near his face like his grief is attacking him from the outside and he can shoo it away.

"Your Majesty, we did what had to be done. You should not torment yourself."

"My brother and I used to go hunting in the forest to the south!" He practically screams this. "If my mother had lived . . . oh, my soul, does she know what I have done? Will I have to explain myself to her in the afterlife?"

Agoston Horthy folds his hands on his lap and waits for the wailing and sobbing to subside.

"Bring me the girl when you find her," rasps the king, exhausted by his outburst.

Agoston Horthy says nothing.

"Please!" Zey's eyes widen; he starts trying to sit up again.

"You should rest, Your Majesty," says the prime minister, standing. "Do not think of the past."

"Yes," mutters the king, sinking back into the pillows. "I will rest."

"I will bring Duke Everard tomorrow. Try not to upset him with your morbid musings."

"Oh," murmurs the king, shutting his eyes, like he has been vanquished.

Horthy pulls the blankets right up to Zey's chin, tucking them around the king's frail frame, and goes out. I follow him through the grand hall and out onto the palace grounds, my mind humming with all I've seen and heard. He walks among the fruit trees to a small temple by a pond. He goes inside, and my pulse quickens. He seems so purposeful that I expect him to be meeting somebody here, but the place is empty. He lights a candle and sets it on a table at the side of the temple, and then he kneels on the bare floor. I watch him for a while, but he doesn't move. He's just come here to pray, and who knows how long he will be. There is a faint buzzing from outside—distant enough that I don't pay it any mind at first, but then it gets louder and closer, and I go out to see what it is.

THIRTY

The first thing I see outside the temple is a great clamoring cloud at the far end of the royal gardens. The second thing I see is the heir to the throne, Duke Everard, standing in an azalea bush with a panicked look on his face. I reappear next to the bush, the grass softening under my satin shoes, the world coming into focus. The noisy cloud breaks into pieces.

"Why are you standing in the azaleas, my lord?" I ask him, mainly for the pleasure of making him jump halfway out of his skin, which he does.

"Great stars, you're sneaky!" he cries. "I didn't see you coming!"

Well, no, you wouldn't, princeling. He is dressed less formally than the other day at the opera; his boots are worn, his jacket clearly lived in. As I inhabit my body fully again, the effects of the hermia hit me—my head throbs and my stomach roils.

"What *is* that?" I point at the dark cloud. The buzzing has become a roar. A group of uniformed soldiers are running across the grounds toward the temple. I tense, wanting to vanish, but of course I can't, not right in front of the duke.

"We'd better get out of here," says Duke Everard. "Come this way."

He grabs my hand and pulls me around the row of bushes. I follow, too startled to protest. We run across the lawn to one of the servants' entries to the palace.

"My lord!" says the man on the stairs, flattening against the wall as we race by. "Someone told me there's a swarm of bees outside!"

"A great many swarms," replies the duke. "And I think they are hornets. Stay inside and shut all the doors and windows! Spread the word!"

He is still holding my hand, pulling me up the stairs, out

into a hallway, up another set of stairs and down another hall. We burst into a grand bedroom, and Duke Everard pulls back the curtains to look out the window at the palace grounds. The black swarm of hornets, or whatever they are, is making its way right toward us. There are bells ringing in the palace and voices shouting somewhere down the hall now.

"Sir!" I cry, and he turns toward me, a peculiar smile on his face.

"Call me Luca," he says.

The swarm comes at the window and crashes into it, battering their shiny, striped bodies against the glass, the awful buzz quite deafening even with the window closed.

"Draw the curtains," I say, flinching away from the onslaught.

He pulls the curtains shut.

"Are you all right?" He looks me up and down, eyes snagging on my scar. Only then do I remember that I am not wearing a corset, my hair is crooked, and I powdered my own face very poorly this morning. "You look . . . well, to be honest, you look as if somebody has been pulling your hair."

I catch a glimpse of myself in the long mirror and wince. How stupid of me to appear before him! I'd better make a quick exit. I ignore his question and say, "What's going on? How could there be so many . . ."

"Witchcraft," he says. "Will your uncle send you home, now it's clear that we're under siege?"

"Under siege?"

"Witches attacking us," he says. "Or, I suppose, they are attacking *me*, as it coincides with my arrival in the city. People said there were hardly any witches left in Frayne thanks to Agoston Horthy, and yet look at what's happening! One wonders why they haven't wrought such horrors before now. Are you sure you're all right, Ella? I can call you Ella, can't I?"

I touch a hand to my lopsided hair extensions and change the subject: "What *were* you doing in the azalea bush?"

"Oh . . ." He looks sheepish, which is rather becoming on him. "I saw the prime minister, and I . . . well, I was having a pleasant walk and I thought I'd just . . . duck into the bushes. He's invited me to pray with him a few times."

"He's very devout," I say, smothering an urge to laugh.

"He is, yes. I've never been much good at praying, myself."

This admission surprises me, coming from the heir to the throne, but I just raise an eyebrow at him.

"I'd *like* to be better at it," he says, watching my reaction from under his long eyelashes. "I can't shake the feeling that nobody is listening. I tie myself in knots over it. My mother is very spiritual, she talks about a feeling of deep communion with some greater power, but I've never felt it. Have you?"

I don't think I've ever met somebody so frank about such matters, other than perhaps Frederick.

"No," I say. "Well—perhaps sometimes. Or perhaps it's just that there've been a few times I've hoped so hard someone was listening, it almost felt as if it might be true."

"I knew I could speak plainly to you," he says, smiling. "You strike me as . . . honest."

Well, that's a laugh.

"I'm honored when Agoston Horthy invites me to pray with him, of course," he continues. "It's only that at home I have a great deal of time to roam and enjoy my solitude, and there has not been much of that lately. *Everybody* wants to accost me and give me advice."

"Hence the hiding in the azaleas," I say, laughing in spite of myself. "And then I came along to interrupt your solitude."

"That's all right. You don't look as if you're about to give me any advice."

"I feel some coming on, as a matter of fact. Here: as heir to the throne of Frayne, don't get caught hiding in the bushes. It isn't very *royal* somehow."

He laughs at that, a golden, full-throated laugh that catches at me somewhere just below my rib cage.

"The best advice I've had so far," he says, and his smile pushes everything else to the back of my mind—my throbbing headache, the swarm outside, the *nuyi* crawling through me, Horthy and the king.

"What other sort of advice are you getting?"

"What to say, how to dress, how to behave, who to talk to, who to avoid—and everybody is quite sure I can trust them and only them. Your uncle has been very kind and helpful— I don't mean him," he hastens to add.

"Well, you are to be king," I say. "It's only natural for everybody to want to help you, or establish their influence, depending on how you see it."

"Your uncle and a good many others are very keen on my getting to know your friend Dafne," he adds, studying my face for a reaction.

"She's a wonderful girl."

"Indeed, nobody has a bad word to say about her. I'm being regaled with stories of her kindness and piety."

I get the feeling that kindness and piety are not the keys to this young man's heart.

"She is kind and pious," I say. I'm supposed to keep Casimir happy by doing my job, after all. "But she's very clever too. She has a mind of her own."

"You're going to sing her praises as well?" he asks dryly.

"To know her is to love her. But I can see how it might be boring to be told it over and over."

"Not boring, only strange, to have a girl apparently picked out for me."

"That's quite normal for royals, isn't it? Don't you like her? You could do much worse, and it would be hard to do better."

He laughs again. "I do like her. Well, I don't really know her, but she's extraordinarily pretty."

"As lovely on the inside as the outside would suggest," I tell him, and he all but rolls his eyes. I suspect if there is anything that could make him *not* gravitate to Dafne, it's knowing that everybody means him to.

"It's hard to imagine Dafne running about the palace grounds in such a state of ... ah, disarray," he says, eyes twinkling, gesturing at my general state of untidiness. "Are you going to tell me what *you* were doing when you startled me in the bushes?"

I draw myself up and try to look haughty. "I heard the buzzing and ran out to see what it was. I was not expecting to meet you."

He raises his eyebrows. "And this is what you look like in your rooms, is it?"

"None of your business what I look like in my rooms," I snap, and am gratified that he actually blushes. The drone of the hornets has moved away, and I begin to relax.

"The worst thing about this witch business is that they aren't letting us out into the city," he says. "But I think I've persuaded my *minders* to let me go riding outside the city. Do you ride?"

"Not really. I *have* ridden a horse before," I say, which is true.

"Perhaps if I invited Miss Besnik as well they'd consider it a worthwhile use of my time and agree to a riding party." He looks mischievous, and I laugh.

"That's a very good idea."

"Will you come too? I'll arrange it for tomorrow. We'll make a day of it!"

He's standing quite close to me now, by the thick curtain, and even though we're not touching, I can feel the warmth of him. I look up into his eyes and think, *If he is not already practiced at charming young women out of their petticoats on his little island kingdom, he's going to learn his power very soon in Spira City.*

"I'm not very good at riding," I say. "You and Dafne would have a better time without me."

"I doubt that," he says. "I've been thinking about you, actually. At the opera, when everybody panicked about the rats, you barely seemed frightened at all."

"I grew up in the countryside," I say. "Rats don't bother me."

He bends closer. "Come riding tomorrow. We could talk about all the things we aren't afraid of."

Hounds, he's a rogue after all. To my annoyance, I find my heart beating faster. I'm sure he's about to kiss me, and my head tilts up almost of its own accord. It's a terrible idea, but suddenly I'm desperate to know what it would be like to kiss this bold, golden princeling—even while I'm telling myself by all the stars *not* to go moony for the heir to the Fraynish throne. But given how dire everything is, don't I deserve a bit of kissing?

There are voices at the door and his amber eyes go wide.

Only then does it strike me how inappropriate it is that we are in his room together. Julia left all sense of propriety behind her a long time ago and had few rules to abide by in the first place, but Ella Penn Witzel ought to be thinking of her reputation. What must *he* think, that I made no protest, stayed chatting intimately with him in his bedroom? No wonder he was leaning in for a kiss.

"*Hide*," he whispers, pushing me hurriedly behind the curtains.

I vanish and peer through the crack in the curtains. To my horror, the duchess comes in with, of all people, Lord Skaal behind her.

I have seen him twice before. Once, he was at Agoston Horthy's side while the prime minister tried to bargain with Mrs. Och. The second time, he was in Tianshi, trying to persuade the grand librarian to hand over Princess Zara. Worse, he was able to *smell* me even when I was vanished. His gray hair is swept back, a patch over one eye, the other eye a piercing yellow in his brown face.

"There you are, my dear! Everybody is looking for you in an absolute panic!" says the duchess. "I want you to meet Lord Skaal. He's come back to deal with this witch business. Do you remember, the prime minister spoke of him?"

"Pleased to meet you, sir," says Luca, holding out his hand. Lord Skaal shakes it, smiling affably. Then something shifts in his expression. He lifts his head with a sniff and turns his yellow eye toward the curtains. Toward me.

"Somebody is here," he says.

Horror breaks across Luca's face as Lord Skaal stalks over and pulls the curtains wide. But I am gone before his hand reaches the curtains, vanished over the palace grounds, out beyond West Spira and over the Scola, aiming myself at the crow-spiked house that belonged to Mrs. Och.

I return to myself on the back lawn, by the upturned earth where the great cherry tree used to be. I kneel on the grass to catch my breath while the crows shriek at me and Lady Laroche steps out onto the back veranda.

THIRTY-ONE

"Julia! Come inside!"

I stagger to my feet. My knees are wobbly, but I pretend it's nothing special to appear from halfway across the city in a matter of seconds. I follow Lady Laroche indoors to the front parlor, where Princess Zara and Esme are sitting on the sofa. Zara is wearing an elegant dress that fits her poorly. Esme has blood all over her jacket.

"Are you all right?" I ask Esme, startled.

"It's not my blood," she says hoarsely.

"Oh." I don't ask: *Whose is it, then?* I say to Lady Laroche, "I've just come from the palace. Agoston Horthy told the king they captured twenty-three witches last night from villages in the north and threw them in Hostorak. He's going to try to get your location out of them."

The color drains from her face. She has a pen and a roll of paper in her hand so quickly I'm not sure where they came from. She must keep them in her sleeves. Like Esme, she is a lightning-fast draw with her weapon of choice. The room hums as soon as the pen touches the paper, everything coming too sharply into focus. My nostrils and throat begin to burn and my eyes water. Her magic does not smell like anything I recognize, but it is strong and hot. The crows on the lawn take off in unison, crying out in their ugly voices.

"Are we still safe here?" asks Zara.

"*We* are perfectly safe. None of them know where I am."

Lady Laroche lights a cigar with trembling fingers. "Twenty-three. *Blast.* Thank you, Julia. Mrs. Freeley is sleeping, but I can make some coffee if you'd like."

"No, thanks."

Esme is watching me. I hope she's not going to dive at me again.

"You've just come from the palace?" Zara asks. "Then you must have seen . . ."

Lady Laroche heaves a sigh and flops into a chair.

"We've been discussing my methods," she says. "*Endlessly.*"

"The hornets?" I ask.

"It is reckless," says Princess Zara. "And it is cruel."

"The princess believes revolutions ought to be dainty and well mannered," drawls Lady Laroche. "I am trying to explain that there is usually bloodshed involved. Wars are not won by being considerate toward one's enemies."

"I've seen bloodshed, and I've known war," says the princess coolly. "A mass of hornets is likeliest to kill groundsmen, cabriolet drivers, and ordinary folk going about their day, while our true enemies will keep themselves inside. I object on moral grounds to the killing of innocents, *and* I object on strategic grounds. Sowing panic and a deeper hatred of witches will win us no friends. Without the people behind me, even if we *can* overthrow the Crown and Agoston Horthy, I will not be able to rule Frayne. I must be seen as benevolent, a friend to the people, not a murderer employing witches. You have done great harm to my cause without consulting me."

Lady Laroche puffs out a row of bluish smoke rings and

then directs herself to me again: "You know she can read your mind, essentially? There is no point in being anything other than blunt with her, which is mostly refreshing, if occasionally a little annoying."

"I cannot read minds, only sense intent," says Zara. "I am afraid that you would just as soon see Frayne burn as see peace."

"That depends on the peace and what it means for witches," says Lady Laroche. "I would rather see Frayne burn than tolerate the *peace* we've known under Agoston Horthy for the last two decades. But you and I need each other, princess. You cannot take the throne without the support of the Sidhar witches, and there is no real, legitimate future for *us* in Frayne without you."

"Do you care at all that unleashing rats and hornets on West Spira will result in the suffering and deaths of innocent people?"

"Innocent people!" snorts Lady Laroche. "That is a fantasy! You might as well talk to me of unicorns."

I look at Esme, who is sitting there like a statue while they argue back and forth. Her eyes flick to mine but give nothing away.

"There are children in West Spira too," says Zara.

"You think children are innocent?" cries Lady Laroche. "You must not remember being a child."

"They haven't had a chance yet to choose their place in the world," says Zara. "In that sense, at least, they are guiltless."

"They will choose to inherit all the wealth, privilege,

power, and hardheadedness of their parents, as children born to the upper classes always do."

"You didn't," says Zara.

"Because I was born a witch. My very survival depended on rebellion." Lady Laroche sighs. "Princess, I agree that war is horrible, but we cannot stage a revolution if we are wringing our hands at every turn and saying *What about the children?* It simply won't do! The wonderful thing about magic is that we can manage this with minimum blood on the streets, but there is going to be *some* blood, and the sooner you get used to the idea, the easier this will be."

"But what is the purpose?" cries Zara. "Rats and hornets! You are simply confirming all the worst fears people have about witchcraft!"

"I am sending a message. The *people* will soon see that witches are on their side and can fight for them. Tell me that in the Twist and the Edge people aren't applauding these assaults on West Spira! Esme, what do you think?"

"The fear of witches runs too deep in Frayne," says Esme woodenly. "The poor might applaud an assault on the rich, but they are not going to embrace witches anytime soon. That will be a long, slow process *after* the princess has the throne. To take it, she should not appear to be too strongly allied with magic."

"*Exactly*," says Zara.

"Witches have been hunted and murdered for hundreds of years in this country!" cries Lady Laroche. "Do not speak to me of a long, slow process. We need justice and freedom, and we cannot *wait* for them. I intend to *terrify* Agoston Horthy and the new heir, along with all their West Spira supporters, and then I will destroy them. You will see—the people will turn on them soon enough."

The princess narrows her eyes. "What aren't you telling me?"

Lady Laroche laughs. "Keep to your own plans. I promise I will do everything in my power to clear the way to the throne for you. We may disagree on the details, princess, but never doubt that I am *on your side*."

Princess Zara is quiet, but she does not look happy.

The doorbell chimes. Esme draws her pistol and retreats to a corner of the room.

"That will be Gregor and Csilla and our friend," says Zara, getting up. "I'll let them in."

"What friend?" I ask, but nobody answers me.

"Julia, why don't we go upstairs to my room?" says Lady Laroche. "I need to speak to you, and we had better be out of the way for this. Esme, do you mind?"

"Not at all," says Esme. She's taken the safety off her pistol.

I'm not sure how I feel about that—her asking Esme as if I belong to her, and Esme answering in the same vein—but I follow her up the stairs as Princess Zara answers the door. I peer down from the landing as Gregor leads a finely dressed man with a blindfold over his eyes into the house.

"We'll take that off in a moment, my good fellow," bellows Gregor in the man's ear. He spies me on the landing and gives me a wink.

"Come into the parlor, please," says Zara politely.

"He can't hear you yet—we've stopped his ears with wax!" Gregor tells her. Csilla comes in behind them, and they all four disappear into the parlor. Bewildered, I follow Lady Laroche up to the second floor.

THIRTY-TWO

I wondered what Lady Laroche meant by *her* room. It turns out she means Mrs. Och's reading room. She sits down at the desk, gesturing at the chair across from her.

"Who was that down there?" I ask.

"A very rich and influential fellow. He doesn't hold a government post officially, but he has a great many government officials in his pocket, which is even better. He says he'll back Zara if she takes the throne. Zara is going to see if he's sincere."

"And if he's not?"

She ignores my question. "Csilla and Gregor have managed to bring in a few members of the aristocracy. Professor Baranyi has been even more successful in recruiting allies among the literati. A number of newspaper editors swear up and down they will come out in favor of Zara—but all *after* the revolution. Everybody wants to throw their lot in with us *after* the revolution. People are cowards, Julia. It is tiresome."

"What about the witches in Hostorak?"

"I won't desert them. It is time Hostorak came down."

I remember looking up at the impenetrable prison as a little girl after my mother was taken, the stone walls mocking me, for what could I do against them? The thought of those walls coming down fills me with violent joy, and for a moment I think that if Lady Laroche can do that, I will follow her anywhere.

"What else did you hear at the palace today?" she asks me, all business.

I try to match her crisp tone. "They suspect the princess is here and that witches are rallying behind her. Horthy seems very confident. If he smashed the last revolution to bits before it was even under way, what makes you so sure this time will be different?"

"Because of Zara. Horthy's great strength is his spy network. He infiltrated the Lorian Uprising. We could not look into a person's mind and see their true intent. But Zara *can*. Everyone who claims to be loyal to her, to the revolution, will meet with her privately. If she sees treachery, they will be dealt with. If they are loyal, we can be sure of them."

I don't ask again what *dealt with* means. Zara can argue ethics with Lady Laroche. I need to save my brother.

"She will make a good queen," continues Lady Laroche. "And while mercy is a fine quality, *somebody* has to be ruthless to get the whole thing going. I'll play the part of the wicked witch if it will get her on the throne and make a better Frayne for the witches who come after me."

She is jotting things down on a piece of paper as she talks, and I remember what Bianka told me about how she felt when she held a pen—the sense that the pen might overpower her. But Lady Laroche seems quite in control, wielding the pen like a favorite weapon. It is an elegant instrument, with purple-black feathers along its hilt and a bright, coppery tip. She puts it down, blots the ink, and then takes a glass vial the size of my little finger out of her desk. It is full of a sand-colored powder.

"Where do you stand, my dear, on the idea that the end justifies the means?"

"I'm not sure," I say. "What is that?"

"Poison. I want you to put it in Agoston Horthy's drink. It will save us a good deal of trouble to get him out of the way early. The Crown and parliament will be in utter chaos without him, struggling to fill the power vacuum and making it that much easier for us to take the throne."

My mouth goes dry. I used to fantasize about killing him when I was a child. Dek and I went so far as to buy poison from an unsavory character in the Edge—we were going to make poison-tipped arrows. Ridiculous. I was eight years old. Esme spanked me soundly for it and confiscated the poison. Dek was eleven, and she gave him ten strokes with a switch because he was older and should have known better. Now the poison is being handed to me and I can walk right into Horthy's room, unseen. But I know a bit about death and killing that I didn't know when I was eight years old. The idea of being his executioner turns my stomach. Still, I reach my hand out and take the vial.

"I need to think about it," I say.

She laughs in disbelief. "How did I end up with such an absurdly principled bunch of allies? I suppose I should be grateful not to be working with rogues and wretches, but all this hesitation is impeding our progress. How is your brother, Julia?"

"He's holding up."

"You've met the heir, Duke Everard?"

Suddenly I'm afraid I'm going to blush. "Yes," I say, adding quickly, "He's very young."

"Everyone is young compared to Zey," she says. She opens her desk and takes out a mirrored glass sphere that fits in the palm of her hand. "Do you know what this is, Julia?"

I shake my head.

"It is a besilik mirror—for searching the mind. Particularly useful for unearthing old memories. Shall we see how far back you can go in yours? See if you can find Lidari?"

My heart clenches with fear. "How does it work?"

"I will write the magic to start it off, and the mirror will take you back through your memories. It is disorienting, I've heard, but you will control the journey—how far back you go, where you pause to look deeper. You should try to go back beyond your birth to see if there is anything there."

"Will you be able to see the memories too?" I ask, thinking about Theo hidden in Ragg Rock. I don't want her to see that.

"Only the person under the spell can see what the mirror reveals," she says. "But I hope you will share what you see with me, Julia. I only want to help you."

I don't much like the idea, but if there is something inside me, I have to know.

"I'm ready," I say.

THIRTY-THREE

Lady Laroche unscrews the cap of her inkpot and lays sheets of thick paper across the desk. She places the mirrored sphere at the center of the desk.

"Relax, Julia. Look into the mirror and lay your hands palms upward on the desk."

I do so, and she puts pen to paper. The hot scent of her magic fills the room.

The mirror shows the room and ourselves wrapped around it, misshapen—and then the room changes. The walls are undulating, birds are calling overhead, the carpet shifting and darkening. Clouds race along the ceiling, and it isn't the ceiling anymore but open sky. We are on a desolate moor. The desk is floating across the moor like a ship, Lady Laroche still frowning at the paper before her. The wind blows around us, but I hold still, my hands on the desk. Lady Laroche places a hand on my wrist and writes something on my palm. The ink runs in little spiderwebby lines up my arm, shooting under my dress, and then I can *feel* it, like thin threads going through me. I try to pull away, but she is holding me fast, apparently unaware of how we are flying through the air. The threads of ink reach my neck, climb up my face, they are diving into my nose mouth ears eyes, and then my mind is a cloud of winding ink-threads, wrapping themselves in knots—maybe there are words, maybe somebody is shouting something, maybe the sky is going ink-black now and the moor falling into shadow and I am falling and the wind is roaring in my ears and I am falling into nothingness I am falling I am falling.

Images from my own life flash by and are gone. I race back in time, beyond anything I remember, and while in some way I am choosing this, it feels wild and uncontrolled, the visions moving faster and faster. I see Ragg Rock—a broken, burning city—ships at sea and the clash of swords—a bed with a woman sleeping in it—the sun rising out the window over a bloody field where corpses rot—a feast and music—a child laughing—running down a crowded alley—an old man begging—a bear in a cage roaring—a woman by the sea, *stop*.

The unbelievable blue of the West Arrekem sea lies before us. The sand is fine and white. Behind us the jungle rises up out of the coastline. Her secret house is hidden among the trees, guards blending into the jungle. She stands at the edge of the water, the foam lapping over her feet. She is beautiful. She is always beautiful. She dresses simply here, lets her hair loose in a black cloud around her head instead of oiled and twisted into elaborate braids.

"I'm going to stop being Phar," she says.

I say nothing. She has said this kind of thing before. I let her continue.

"I know what you're thinking. But this current heir will do very well. I've had enough of ruling the world."

She looks over her shoulder and smiles a little at that, because we both know she's joking. She will never be tired of ruling the world.

"You'll do as you like," I say. "You always do."

"You'll watch over our son, won't you?" she says. "He still listens to you."

"He does not listen to me," I say. "He is like you. He'll do as he pleases too."

She keeps her face turned away, as she always does when we speak of the boy. Not really a boy anymore.

"He thinks me a monster. He will not see me."

I say nothing to that. There is no mending what has broken between them. They are both too much what they are.

"I only want you to know . . . I mean to try out some different sorts of lives, but in giving up the influence that comes with being Phar, it may not always be so easy for me to protect you."

"I've never asked you to protect me."

"You could come with me, if you like."

"Where will you go?"

I would go anywhere with her, for her, if she wanted me to. But I can't follow her for all eternity. "If you like" is not enough. There is enough world for the both of us, except sometimes she shines so brightly the rest of the world pales in comparison. It's not true. I've gotten spoiled, and this body is the best yet, tireless, strong and full of desire, which only makes me love her more. Perhaps I should take an old man's body next time, give myself some peace.

"Where won't I go?" she says. "I want to go everywhere. I want to be everything."

"And you're sure your empire will hold without you?"

"It will hold."

"Nothing lasts forever."

She looks at me—I cannot tell if it is anger in her face, or something else. I should know by now, but this is a new face for a new life.

"We'll see," she says.

I lurch forward, not sure what I'm searching for. Deserts, oceans, spired cities and muddy villages, fields of wheat, shadowed temples, bitter fruit, an empty fireplace in a cold room, my hands making bread. When I see him, I stop, panic rising in my throat.

Casimir, power coiled in his every movement, so vital it nearly hurts to look at him. His blood-sworn twelve are with him, ash-white warriors in golden armor, with wild, flowing white hair. The story goes that they were soldiers near death who swallowed enchanted stones he stole from a dragon. When one of them falls, he cuts the stone out of him to put in another man. We are on the edge of a cliff, gulls swooping, the waves crashing against rocks far below. He has cornered me, and there is nowhere left for me to run.

"She'll find out," I say. I am surprised at my own fear. Just a body, after all. No Ankh-nu to save me this time, though.

"That's why we're here," he says.

He draws his sword. I am unarmed, but I have the potion she gave me. The potion that would release me. I take a step back, toward the cliff.

"I can give you a sword," he says. "If you would prefer to die fighting."

As if some hero's code means anything to me. Being immortal, *he could never understand. All this is only because I loved her and I wanted to live. I only ever wanted to live. I fear death as much as any man. Maybe more so. I've known the centuries of half-life and I do not want to go back there, except that from there I might find some chink to slip through, some way back into the world, a body to hold my life again. There is no way back from death. I feel the edge of the cliff at my heels. I take out the vial and tip it into my mouth.*

He shrieks, pouncing toward me, but I feel it already, the pulling apart. I let the body I've worn and loved for twenty-eight years fall—down, down, to break on the rocks, to be washed away by the sea, to fall to bone and ash, or for him to find and behead, sending the head to Marike. My sorrow is wide as the sky as I break away from it, the world whirling away from me like water pulled fast down a drain, gone, gone—until I am only part of what I was, crouched again on those black rocks, shadow cities burning below me.

My first thought is that I have lost her forever.

A jolt, and I'm fighting for air at Mrs. Och's desk. Lady Laroche is pressing my hand to a large green blotter, and ink is pouring out from under my fingernails, seeping out of my hand onto the blotter.

"There, take a breath, you're all right," she says, panting. I manage a huge gasp. The blotter has turned black with ink. The last of it slips out from under my nails, leaving me limp, wrung out.

"Perhaps a bit of brandy," she says, beads of sweat standing out on her forehead. "Or tea?"

"Water," I croak. She goes out and returns with a glass

of water for me. My mouth feels scorched, and I pour the water down my throat as Lady Laroche tidies up the desk. Papers are all across the room, as if a great wind scattered them. The mirror is still on the desk, rocking a little as if we've just settled.

"What did you see?" she asks eagerly.

"I think it was Lidari talking to Marike before she gave up being Phar. And then Casimir . . . killing Lidari."

"How did you choose where to stop?"

"I'm not sure. It was hard to control it. They were just moments that seemed important. I recognized Casimir."

She lights a cigarette, staring at me hard. "What else?"

"That's it. That's what I saw. Does it mean Lidari *is* inside me?"

I want to peel him out, be only myself.

"It seems that his memories are, at the very least," she says. "It does not necessarily follow that his *essence* is. I'm sorry I could not hold the spell longer—I haven't done it before and it is surprisingly strenuous. But perhaps we can try again sometime."

Not a chance, I think but don't say.

Then she chuckles a little and says, "Oh, Ammi! Such mischief! Why didn't she *tell* me?"

A crow appears at the window and taps on the glass with its beak. I'm surprised to realize it's dark out—I've been here much longer than I thought, and I'm desperately hungry. I lost all sense of time inside the spell, but it must have taken hours.

Lady Laroche runs to the window and throws it open. The crow has a piece of paper in its beak, drops it into her hand. When she looks at the paper, her face breaks into an expression of pure exultation.

"What is it?" I ask.

She laughs—a rather mad laugh. "The best of all possible news!" she cries, snatching her hat from the stand in the corner and pulling on a pair of gloves. "Do stay for dinner, Julia. Mrs. Freeley will make you something nice."

It is unusual for middle-aged ladies to run—I can't think when I last saw it—but in spite of her limp Lady Laroche *runs* out the door, leaving me at her desk. A moment later, Mr. Faruk comes in, dressed like an ordinary Fraynish merchant.

"I don't suppose she told you where she's off to," he says, without saying hello.

"No." I'm quite shaky when I get up, though I can't be sure if that's from the spell, from hunger, or from the hermia I took this morning. I need to take some more.

He goes around to the front of Lady Laroche's desk, opening it and taking out her papers, looking through them as if I weren't there. That rather shocks me, and I'm not sure if I ought to say anything, but I decide it's not my business. Surely she would have locked the drawer if she wanted to keep her papers secret.

"Well, I'm off," I say awkwardly.

He offers a distant smile and goes back to his snooping.

THIRTY-FOUR

I can hear the others in the dining room—the rumble of Gennady's voice, the music of Zara's. I try to slip out quietly but am startled at the door by a voice from the front parlor: "Julia."

I freeze. Professor Baranyi comes out into the hall. He has lost weight, his full cheeks gone pouchy, his eyes sad behind his spectacles.

"Princess Zara said you were here," he says flatly.

"I had no choice," I tell him. "About Mrs. Och."

I hadn't meant to blurt it out like that, and I don't know if it's true, though it seemed so at the time. I killed her—or nearly—in such a storm of rage and grief and fear that I can barely think about it or wonder how else it might have gone. He didn't see what I saw. The way she tossed Bianka into the water like a rag doll. The way she swung her blade at Theo. My only thought was to *stop* her—completely.

"She was a great lady, and she made her choices with a wisdom and a perspective earned over millennia. You took from us the greatest ally this revolution could have."

"She hurt Frederick too. I've seen him. He asked me to tell you . . . he wants to work on a book with you after . . . when all this is over. He said that the things you talked about are, um, sustaining him."

I'm babbling. Professor Baranyi frowns, as if he isn't sure whether to believe me or not.

"Is he all right?"

"Barely. But he's safe for now, and so is Theo."

"They are here in Spira City?"

"No."

"How can I believe you?"

"Whatever you think of me, you know I'd never harm him or Theo."

"You did harm Theo, once. I don't know anything about you for certain."

I want to get away from him and the unhappy look he's giving me.

"About Mrs. Och . . . I wish I could change things, but it happened so fast and she was going for Theo with a *knife*." I stumble over my words.

He shakes his head sadly. "She was never your enemy, Julia. You were mistaken."

There's nothing much I can say to that, so I just say good night.

Telegram to Lord Casimir, Nago
Island: KING ZEY NEAR DEATH STOP
HORTHY CAPTURED WITCHES NORTH OF
CITY STOP DOES NOT KNOW WHEREABOUTS
OF LAROCHE STOP SKAAL RETURNED TO
SPIRA CITY STOP LAROCHE BEHIND HORNET
ATTACK STOP JULIA COOPERATIVE STOP

DAY 8

ARISTOCRATS AND MONSTERS

*We go down another set of stairs,
and the screaming gets much louder.
Suddenly I don't want to know
where he goes at night.*

THIRTY-FIVE

The riding gown Csilla picks out for me is the nicest of the dresses I've worn so far. It is a rich burgundy that suits me well, and I look—perhaps for the first time in my life—genuinely *pretty*. Except that it's not really me, with the fake hair coiled on top of my head and a hat pinned on top of that, a tight waist courtesy of the corset squeezing the breath out of me, my face pale with powder, my lips and eyes and cheekbones changed by Csilla's artful lining and shading. I look rather blank and not myself, but still pretty. More or less.

Csilla is tugging at my gown, adjusting it in places. I asked her to come, knowing I wouldn't be able to dress myself properly for the riding party. My guts are churning from the single leaf of hermia I ate this morning. I'll go back later today and ask Liddy to up the dosage, but I can barely ride at the best of times and didn't want to overdo it. It does seem to be working—the *nuyi* has not climbed right up into my neck. But it is an inch farther up my shoulder than it was last night. It's still moving. I don't have time to slow it down just a little. I need to *stop* it.

I've been filling Csilla in on some of my discoveries as we stand before the mirror.

"If Agoston Horthy can't taste anything and he doesn't feel pain," says Csilla, "do you think he's really human?"

"As far as I know, he is a man," says Pia. She is sprawled across the sofa, her boots up on the cushions, eating oranges from a crate of them and leaving the peels all over the carpet. "But he must be more than that, or have powerful friends, because he commanded the Gethin somehow, and they can be commanded only by magic. It would be very funny if Agoston Horthy turned out to be a man-witch, but I think Casimir would have known."

"He told Mrs. Och he inherited the Gethin," I say, thinking with a shudder of the sad-eyed creature I shot and beheaded in Mrs. Och's hallway. Liddy told me it was the last of its tribe—one of the half-beings from Kahge that Marike somehow brought into the world and gave physical form, creating for herself a monstrous and nearly invincible army.

Csilla yanks at the back of my dress again, and I wince.

"Inherited from whom, I wonder," says Pia, peeling the fifth orange in a row with her knife—a swift swirl and the peel is on the floor. "It is surprising how little there is to be found out about him. He comes from a wealthy landowning family. His younger brother drowned, his mother went mad and was shut away or perhaps died, and he was raised after that by his father—by all accounts a stern and pious man.

Horthy is said to have admired his father very much, but the man died some years ago of natural causes."

"His brother drowned?" I say. "Was *he* a witch?"

"There is no evidence to suggest it," says Pia. "The official account is that they were playing by the river, and he slipped, struck his head on a rock, and was carried off by the current. Who knows the truth of it? Horthy's hatred of witches is genuine; he is driven by fanaticism, not greed. He does not revel in the trappings of power, nor does he particularly seem to relish power itself. He does not hoard riches or seek out the company of women or men; he has neither married nor taken a lover. But he is *human*, to the best of our knowledge."

"The maid who serves him breakfast says he goes out of the city at night and comes back with mud all over his boots."

"I doubt Agoston Horthy is going on pleasant countryside rambles. Find out where he goes."

"Stars, imagine drinking tea full of vinegar. Even if he can't taste it, do you suppose he had an upset stomach later?" asks Csilla, fitting a neat little riding jacket over my gown.

"I've no idea," I reply. "I didn't follow him to the privy."

"You were supposed to follow him all day," says Pia.

"Well, I *did* follow him, but then I had some errands to run." I look at her in the mirror, her goggles fixed on me. "What am I going to do, just sit in his room all day?"

"For your brother's sake, I need something interesting to tell Casimir."

I tuck my sleeping-serum darts into one pocket of my

riding jacket, and the hermia packet and the poison Lady Laroche gave me into the other. I'm a regular walking poison factory here. I stare at my reflection in the long mirror, Pia's glare over my shoulder.

"Perfect," says Csilla, satisfied.

THIRTY-SIX

We go by carriage out of the city, westward, where the fine country houses are, and beyond them toward the king's summer palace, though I reckon he won't live to see it this summer.

My lovely dress proves too warm for the weather, and by the time we reach the royal stables, I am bathed in sweat and sick to death of the stilted conversation between Sir Victor, Lord Besnik, Dafne, and myself. Sir Victor and Lord Besnik go to talk to the stable manager, and Dafne pulls me aside, her tone suddenly quite different.

"What do you think of him?"

"My uncle?" I ask, because she is staring at Sir Victor's back.

"The *duke*," she says, with barely concealed impatience.

"Oh! Well, he seems . . . I'm sure he'll be a fine king."

"He's very young," she says. Funny, given she is surely a couple of years younger. "Do you think he's intelligent?"

"We know he can read. And write. But he can't think up his own rhymes."

"He will do whatever Horthy tells him to do," she says, with a hint of scorn, and I am taken aback by the casual way she says *Horthy*. "He doesn't seem like the arrogant type. I'd guess he's quite aware of how unsuited he is to take the seat of power so young, and with so little experience of the country he is to rule. But really, I meant what sort of *husband* do you think he will make?"

"Oh!" I look at her in surprise. "I can't imagine."

"I can. Come, Ella, let's not pretend. I am supposed to marry him, and my understanding is that you are meant to help me win him. Sir Victor told my parents that you are very clever and read people well. What do you think? How am I to win him?"

I laugh in surprise and relief. "I think I am meant to help you only by being less beautiful and less interesting and making you seem all the more appealing in comparison," I say bluntly. "I don't think you need help."

"I'm not sure," she says, unembarrassed by my assessment. "I don't think he is pious, so my piety will mean little to him, and I know that men like beauty but they look for more than that in their wives, particularly if their wife is to be queen of Frayne."

"Does it matter to you that he isn't pious?"

"No," she says. "I can pray enough for both of us. I'm relieved to find him pleasant and handsome. I see no signs of temper. I expect he will be a good husband, and Horthy will see to it that he is a good king. Only I'm not sure I interest him much."

I feel more relaxed now that we are being open about the purpose of our friendship.

"He's interested in poetry, but he didn't like the poet you mentioned at the opera. Too conventional, I'd wager," I say. "He'll like a girl who challenges him. Don't be too docile or predictable. He adores his mother, and you told me she was a madcap in her youth."

Dafne rolls her eyes. "She's a terrifying old crow, isn't she? Here they are bringing the horses out. I'm glad to have someone to discuss this with, Ella."

She smiles at me, a real smile, and I smile back. She's not so bad. Like me, she's got a job to do, and she means to do it well.

THIRTY-SEVEN

Riding sidesaddle is the stupidest thing I have ever attempted. I don't know why Fraynish women try to ride at all. It was one thing in Yongguo, when I could straddle the horse like a man, but I don't like my odds of staying on this poor creature.

Dafne is dressed in cornflower blue, and she looks like a fairy on a powerful-flanked dappled mare. My own horse is a gentle roan, as I told Sir Victor I can barely ride.

The duke arrives soon after with an entourage of men I don't recognize. His eyebrows go up when he sees me. I've not thought of an explanation for how I vanished from his

room when Lord Skaal came in—indeed, there is none—
and I hope it will be enough that the truth is, as far as he
knows, impossible. He does not seem to have said anything
to anybody, or Sir Victor would have heard of it.

Soon the duke and Dafne are riding ahead, Lord Besnik
and some of the duke's entourage cantering along after them.
Sir Victor ambles next to me on a black-nostrilled stallion
that towers over my own horse.

"This is going well," he says, jerking his chin toward Dafne
and the duke riding side by side.

"Easy job," I say.

"Have you spoken to Lady Laroche?"

I give him a sharp look.

He flashes the disk at his wrist. "The purpose of *this* is
only to keep me reporting on Agoston Horthy. And I do. I
have no qualms about pitting Horthy and Casimir against
each other, but I am frightened for my daughter. Mrs. Och
is gone. If there is to be a revolution, and if it is true that
Roparzh's daughter would not execute witches, I would be
glad to help. But in the meantime I need to keep Elisha
safe."

When I was a spy in Mrs. Och's house, before I knew
Sir Victor's real identity, I found letters in his room from
Agoston Horthy: *Elisha seems content at court and, as always,
we will keep her close to us while you are gone.* Most of the letters
made reference to Elisha, the threat only hinted at. Professor Baranyi told me later that Sir Victor's daughter, Elisha,
was a witch, and that Sir Victor served Horthy because it

was the only way to protect her. I gather she is still a kind of hostage.

"Where *is* she, exactly?" I ask.

"She is still living at court under Horthy's eye, with a governess and servants chosen by him—essentially her keepers. I wonder if Lady Laroche could help her."

"I'll ask," I say. No point pretending I'm not in contact with Lady Laroche. "But what about the witches in Hostorak? Are they to be drowned?"

"Not immediately. I spent yesterday interrogating a group of them, and will continue this evening."

I don't want to think what his interrogations entail.

"They don't know where Lady Laroche is," I say. "Just to save you the trouble."

He nods briefly, but I don't know if he believes me. "You're to follow Horthy tonight," he says. "And the report will go straight to Pia. I will be busy."

"Busy interrogating witches who have nothing to tell you?"

"I'm to investigate this princess of yours as well," he says. "Horthy hopes she is a fraud."

"What do you mean?"

"He hopes she is not really Roparzh's daughter, but merely a pretender, a puppet of the Sidhar Coven."

"She's nobody's puppet," I say. "Sounds like you've got two missions that aren't going anywhere."

"It doesn't matter to me what I find," he says impatiently. "I do my job, and you should be doing yours. Casimir is not patient or easily fooled, any more than Agoston Horthy. Both of them require results."

We are quiet for a moment, and then, because it's been needling at me, I ask him: "Why didn't you come with me—after you helped me on Nago Island? The mechanic had only just put the *nuyi* in you, so you weren't really bound. You said it was too late, but it wasn't. You could have escaped with us."

"And then what?" he asks. "Horthy had Elisha, and Casimir still has his claws in Horthy, if not as surely as he'd like. Even without the contract, there was no way for me to defy him. Mrs. Och couldn't have protected me or my daughter."

"So you just let him take over your *mind*?"

"I have been trapped into obedience for a long time. The lack of choice is something I am used to."

"And is it worth it? All the things you do for him? *Interrogating* witches and so on?"

His face closes up. "My daughter is still alive, and you are asking too many questions. You should focus on your own job."

Sir Victor pulls away from me on his horse and vaults a fence up ahead. I am certainly not going to try to do any such thing. I tug the reins, telling my horse, "Go *around* the bleeding fence, will you?" but she is confused and runs at it and then pulls back, sending me tumbling to the ground.

Pain shoots through my shoulder and arm. I lie there in the grass, stunned, trying to figure out if I've broken anything. I decide I haven't and get slowly to my feet.

Sir Victor doesn't notice I've fallen, but Duke Everard has swung around and is galloping toward me. He swings down to my side, looking absurdly dashing in his riding clothes, while my lovely dress is all stuck with mud and grass and wildflowers now.

"Are you hurt?"

"I don't think so," I say. He offers me his arm, but I stagger to the fence and lean on that instead. My horse is nibbling at the wildflowers. The poor creature is surely glad to be rid of me for the moment.

The others have stopped, but the duke waves them on, shouting: "She's all right! We'll catch up!" Then he leans toward me and whispers: "Time for your confession! How in the name of the holies did you get out of my room yesterday?"

"I'm very stealthy," I tell him.

He smells of grass and horse and fresh air. He is frowning at me, eyebrows lowered. Not frightened, but not credulous either.

"I've thought it through, and it's impossible," he says. "There was nowhere to go."

"Depends on how quick you are," I say. "I'll bet you were surprised."

"That's putting it mildly. Gobsmacked, more like it."

This is getting risky, and I'm distracted by how close he is standing, the cleft in his handsome chin, the curve of his lips, those bright eyes fixed on mine.

I pivot to an accusatory tone. "All would have been forgiven for *you*, heir to the throne, behaving as young men do, but did it occur to you that by dragging me into your room you might have destroyed my reputation completely?"

He looks a bit chastened. "I hadn't. I wasn't thinking. And I'm sorry."

"If you're going to go around womanizing, you shouldn't be so careless with your would-be conquests. What can a girl do, once she's ruined?"

"I'm not going around womanizing!" he cries. "I'm grateful you came today. I can tell you aren't fond of riding."

"I'm not, but my uncle insisted I come."

"That's because *I* insisted you come." He grins.

"I don't like being told what to do. I like to be asked," I snap, although honestly about half of my annoyance comes from the effect his nearness has on me, my heart leaping every time he leans close. "Here they come. Dafne looks very fine on a horse, doesn't she?"

He laughs and says, "Yes, she does. Listen, I'm sorry for . . . everything. There's going to be a soirée at the palace tomorrow, in defiance of rats and hornets. Will you come? I'm asking you, not insisting." His eyes twinkle. "I'll bet you're a better dancer than you are a rider."

"Not much," I say, exasperated. "I don't know many dances. I mean, not the sort that are danced at royal soirées."

"I'll teach you. And you could tell me all about how stealthy you are."

"I don't think that would go over well."

"I don't care."

The sky is bright and my heart is thumping, but not from the fall off the horse. He has such a wide and appealing mouth and such an impossible, slightly wicked and yet sweet way of looking at me from under his lashes that if there weren't several riders approaching us I might find the idea of tumbling about in the grass with him almost irresistible, heir to the throne or no. I've always been a sucker for a pretty face and a fine figure.

"Ask Dafne," I hiss at him. "You're going to be king. You'd better learn to follow a script!"

I stumble over to my horse and take the reins. She gives me a baleful, resigned look. Luca helps me back into the saddle and says, all soulful eyes and kissable lips, "I've never been any good at following a script. I just want to dance with you."

And then Dafne is at my side on her own horse.

"Are you all right, my dear?" she asks.

"Fine, only a bit bruised and feeling clumsy," I say. "You two ought to go on ahead. You're much better riders than I am. I don't want to hold you back."

The duke gives me such a look as he leaps back onto his own horse that I find myself blushing, and then he and Dafne gallop off together. She is acting quite the daredevil on the horse now, which is surely the right thing to do. Lord Besnik asks me if I am all right with an expression of barely veiled contempt.

"Fine," I say, and lead my horse around the fence, hot and irritated and embarrassed because I'm still thinking about Luca's mouth, his large, warm hands. *Oh hounds, stop it, Julia.*

My horse and I try to put on a good-natured front for the rest of the outing, but we are very glad to say goodbye to each other by midafternoon. I return to Spira City to the news that five cases of Scourge have been reported in West Spira.

THIRTY-EIGHT

I am trembling with anger across from Lady Laroche, who insists on my waiting while she finishes a letter. I do not like sitting here while she is wielding her pen, and I watch her closely. She signs the letter with a flourish, blots it, tucks it into an envelope, then smiles at me.

"Yes?"

"The rats," I say. "They were spreading Scourge."

"Yes."

"*Scourge!*" I shout at her. Her jaw muscles tense, but otherwise she doesn't move. "Nearly a quarter of this *city* was killed by Scourge when I was a child. My brother was maimed and crippled by it; he nearly *died*!"

"Did you know that very few members of the upper classes died of Scourge the last time it savaged this country?" she asks mildly.

"It spread fastest where people were crammed together, sharing latrines and eating quarters," I say. "The rich just shut themselves away for the duration."

"No," she says, her lips tightening. "No. They have an antidote."

All the air goes out of me.

"It wasn't enough for everyone. But those who could pay for it got it, and they did not die. They fared better than your brother."

All I can do is repeat what she's just told me, like an idiot: "An antidote. They had an antidote."

"Word has already spread of the outbreak. Watch how it clears up. There will be talk of the antidote by tomorrow. We have doctors on our side who will share what they know to be true. Professor Baranyi is drafting a pamphlet, and we will post it around the city. There will not be any Scourge deaths."

I stand there speechless, blood humming in my ears. Though really, why am I so shocked? Should it be such a shock that the elite of Frayne never cared if people like me lived or died?

"Are you busy tonight?" she asks, looking a little smug.

"I'm to follow Agoston Horthy," I manage to say.

"Ah. I need to get a letter into Hostorak. Never mind. I have a few ideas."

"Sir Victor is interrogating the witches they captured."

"He won't get much out of them," she says, but she doesn't look as cavalier as she sounds.

"Did you know that his daughter is a witch?"

"Elisha," she spits. "He let Horthy put him on a leash to save her."

"Sir Victor might help us . . . if you could help Elisha."

"Few have done as much damage to us as Sir Victor Penn

Ostoway," she says. "I do not care what his reasons are. He had other choices, could have taken other chances, and he did not. He yoked himself to Horthy. I would not trust him even if he placed his daughter in my hands. I will make no deals with that man. I pity his daughter, but I have other things to do than save the child of my enemy."

"But don't you think he could be useful? He's so close to Agoston Horthy . . ." and also bound to Casimir. I'm not sure I'm convinced, myself, that Sir Victor would be a good ally. He's certainly high-risk.

"He has chosen his side."

"If you need my help with Hostorak, I'm in," I say.

A moment ago, I thought I was done with her, but the revelation about an antidote to Scourge has shaken me badly, changes everything, and I am longing to see the prison that swallowed my mother come down.

"I have another ally who will take care of it," she says, her eyes crinkling upward as she smiles. "I hope your mission tonight is fruitful. Have you thought any more about the poison? I should like Horthy gone. I thought you might be glad to be the one to take care of it. For Ammi."

My heart gives a heavy thud. She looks sincere, but I can't help feeling she's wielding my mother as a weapon.

"I need to get information for Casimir first. He has to think I'm bound to him or he won't take the poison out of Dek."

"Of course. But if vengeance isn't motivation enough, you might think of the lives you would be saving by removing that butcher of witches from power. Including Sir Victor's daughter, Elisha." She opens her desk and takes out the besilik mirror, balancing it in her palm and looking at me almost coquettishly. "Since you're here, shall we have another peek at Lidari?"

I take a step back toward the door. "I've got to go."

"May I ask you for a favor, Julia? A simple one?"

"Depends what it is."

"I want you to follow Idir. He went to his room to change a while ago, which usually means he is going out. He's meeting someone in the city—someone he takes care to wash and dress for—but I don't know who, and I should like to know. He'll be on his way out soon."

"All right," I say, more out of curiosity than because I care to help her. I remember him going through her desk yesterday and wonder if I should tell her. I'd prefer to know what he's up to before I make that decision, though. "Why? Do you think *he's* spying for Agoston Horthy?"

"I doubt that very much," she says. "But stranger things have happened."

She picks up the pen again as I close the door on her.

THIRTY-NINE

Downstairs, I hear Zara and an unfamiliar male voice. They appear to be heading straight for me. I step into the scullery to avoid meeting them in the hall and find Gennady standing next to Mrs. Freeley, his massive hands a powdery white.

"There you are," says Mrs. Freeley, looking over her shoulder before I can vanish. "I'm teaching your friend here to make a cobbler."

"We're not friends," Gennady rumbles, and I realize with some relief that it's flour all over his hands.

"Never mind that," she says. "You know what he told me? That he's useless! That's the trouble with these immortals. Can't see the trees for the forest. He needs to learn to make a cobbler."

"She's mad," sighs Gennady. "I have lived thousands of years without learning to cook."

"That's exactly your problem," she says. "Care to lend a hand, Julia? Is *that* your real name?"

"It is," I say. "Who's visiting Zara this time?"

"A man," she says. "None of your beeswax. They blindfold 'em, drive 'em around in endless circles, switch 'em from one hackney to another and so on, till the fellas can't guess where they are. Still, he'll know he's been in a fine house in the city, which narrows it down a little."

"Doesn't narrow it down much," I say. "But perhaps they ought to meet elsewhere."

"Safest here," she says. "If it goes wrong."

"*Has* it gone wrong?"

"Oh, indeed. Dragged a fellow out this morning after stripping him of his memories."

"Stripping him of his memories?"

"Something of that kind. They know what they're doing. No no *no*, not like that or you'll just have a mush!"

Gennady looks crestfallen. "Is it ruined?"

"Nothing we can't fix. Come now, pay attention."

Zara is wishing the stranger goodbye. I hear Csilla say sweetly, "I will see you home, Sir Winderlay."

"May I take the blindfold off?" says a plummy male voice. "*Rather* uncomfortable."

"If you don't mind, not yet," says Zara. "It is safer for all of us if you don't know where we are. But we will be in touch."

Csilla and the man go out, and I hear Zara on the stairs. Once the foyer is empty, I wait there, vanished, until Mr. Faruk comes down in one of his elegant suits and ruffled cravats, takes his coat and hat, and goes out the front door.

FORTY

M̲r̲. Faruk walks north through the Scola and crosses the river into the Twist. Then he veers straight downhill toward the Edge. I figure he must be going to the Marrow, but instead he stops at Liddy's door and knocks. Reeling with surprise, I go in after him.

"Are you there?" he calls.

Liddy's voice comes from the back room. "Come in!"

He goes in, and so do I, two steps back from the world so that she will not see me. Liddy is in her chair in the back room—a whitish blur from my perspective.

He settles into the chair I usually sit in. "You've heard the latest?"

"Scourge," says Liddy. "Stars, but she's reckless." Then she sighs in my direction and says, "I thought we were friends, Julia. This is not friendly."

Mr. Faruk looks around the room, perplexed. Blast Liddy. Even Mrs. Och couldn't see me when I pulled back this far, but Liddy—somehow Liddy can. I reappear, and Mr. Faruk gives a startled laugh.

"Lady Laroche told you to follow me?" he asks, apparently rather pleased by the idea.

"I just wondered where you were off to so suddenly," I say. I don't know enough to sell out Lady Laroche just yet. I look accusingly at Liddy. "Why could you see me?"

"Nobody can come into my shop without my knowing it, visible or not," says Liddy. "I knew *somebody* was here, and since I couldn't see anybody, I assumed it was you. I don't know anybody else who can be invisible, after all. My, you look very glamorous. A little grass-stained."

Mr. Faruk is chuckling and shaking his head like this is all tremendously funny. It's the most cheerful I've ever seen him.

I fold my arms across my chest. "How do the two of you know each other?"

"I have many friends," says Liddy. "We're meeting with another friend today, and the matter has no bearing on Lady Laroche, the revolution, or you. It is, simply put, none of your business. But, Julia—I would rather *not* have Lady

Laroche breathing down my neck. I support her cause in the loosest sense, and apart from that, I want nothing to do with her. If we are friends, please do not mention me to her."

I nod. I don't yet know what Lady Laroche is to me, but I've years of reasons to trust and be loyal to Liddy, no matter how many secrets she keeps from me.

"I was going to come by, anyway," I say. "I need . . . you know."

"Oh yes, you're taking hermia," says Mr. Faruk. "I must say, I agree with Liddy. It is too dangerous."

"Look, this thing is nearly at my neck," I say crossly, taking the packet out of my riding jacket pocket and tossing it on the table. "That means it's a day or so from my *brain*, which means I'm a day or so from belonging to Casimir unless I eat this poison. So I'm eating poison."

Liddy puts on a kettle and bows over my little packet, chopping up a couple of leaves and soaking them in hot water. I swallow them quickly. They burn going down. A sharp sliver of pain runs up the side of my head.

"Come back tomorrow and we'll increase the dosage," says Liddy. "You should rest. But not here, if you don't mind. Our friend is coming soon, and I should like *some* privacy."

Embarrassed now, I apologize and make my way for the door. The sun is going down. In the doorway, I meet the young woman Dek and I saw yesterday, her two children still in tow.

"You again?" I say.

She goes past me into the shop, eyes averted. The children

cling to her skirts and gape at me. I wink at the little boy, who looks away quickly. I'm curious, but I suppose Liddy is right to say that some things are none of my business. Dark is falling and I've got a possibly inhuman prime minister to follow.

FORTY-ONE

Two hours after sundown, Agoston Horthy is still in his room, praying. I am in a chair in the corner, vanished. I found dust coating the pillow and the coverlet of his bed in the next room. *He does not sleep.* I file that away to tell Pia and finger the vial of poison in my pocket. There are a carafe of water and a glass at his desk. It would be as simple as pouring the contents of the vial into his drink. I keep telling myself to do it, reminding myself of what *he* has done—and then I remember Ko Dan's horrible death, choking on poison, and I can't.

I huddle in the chair, a viselike pressure wrapped around my skull, my gut cramping. The hermia is crueler this time, but I feel it less when I'm vanished. At last the prime minister stands up, unlocks his desk, and takes out the closed frame he was looking at the other day. He opens it and gazes at the photograph, his lips moving like he's still praying. I move closer, hoping to get a peek, but he snaps it shut and puts it back in the desk, locking the drawer.

I'm curious about the picture, but right now I don't want

to lose him, so I stay close when he opens the door, casting myself farther out of my body and into the hallway as he leaves. I follow him down the stairs to the servants' quarters, through another door, and down another set of stairs.

Every door down here is locked, and Agoston Horthy has a key to each on a chain in his coat pocket. We are under the parliament now. The walls are stone, dark and cold. He takes a lantern from the wall, lighting it and striding down this hall that feels more like a tunnel. I hear something . . . it sounds like an animal screaming. We go down yet another set of stairs, and the screaming gets louder. Suddenly I *don't* want to know where he goes at night, but I suppose this is it, I'm finally going to find out the secret of the great and terrible Agoston Horthy, prime minister of Frayne, bane of witches.

We round a corner. The screaming is very close now. Two armed guards at the end of the hall bow when Agoston Horthy approaches. One of them takes the lantern from him, and the other unlocks the door with the screaming behind it.

The screaming becomes a howl. A small figure comes hurtling out of the door as soon as it opens and crashes straight into Horthy, who grapples with it. The guards help him to pin the thing against the wall. At first I think the prime minister is trying to strangle it, but then I realize he is embracing it; the howling becomes a pathetic sort of whine.

The whining creature is shaped and dressed like a child, but when I catch a glimpse of its head, I recoil. The head is bloated and pale, nearly hairless, with swollen features and eyes like gray stones. Hands and fingers emerge from the sleeves of its jacket like whitish balloons, and the clothes, for all that they are very fine, appear to have been tugged on over a body that is not the right shape for them. Not a child, then. Agoston Horthy holds the creature by the arm, helping it to lurch past me down the hall. The two guards follow, eyes on the ground.

They take a turn I had not seen, and we follow a long tunnel that, as far as I can tell, is taking us in the direction of the river, away from the parliament building. We climb a long, narrow set of stairs. Agoston Horthy knocks once on a door at the top, and it opens. We step out into a dark room, and he opens the door at the side onto the moonlit river. We emerge from a jetty cabin that has been familiar to me all my life. I'd always presumed it to hold boating equipment of some kind. A cabriolet is waiting on the upper path. The driver jumps down and swings the door open.

Horthy, the ill-figured creature, and the two guards enter the cabriolet. I step onto the back panel and hang on as the cab crosses the bridge, passing through the Scola and Forrestal and out of the city, into the thick woods to the south. It bumps along a path through the woods, eventually coming to stop at a clearing with a creek running to one side. The creature lurches out of the cabriolet first, turning its horrible face up to the moonlight, and it goes loping about, moaning softly. Horthy gets out after it. The two guards set lanterns around the clearing.

Horthy and the creature build a tower of pinecones, then throw rocks at it to knock it over. They eat a picnic by the water and cast lines in to fish with. The thing tries to climb a tree, and Horthy, sweating and grunting, tries to help it. The guards crouch by the cabriolet, sharing a pipe with the driver.

I watch the scene with bafflement, fingering the poison in my pocket. I can't help but wonder if they are performing experiments on this poor creature. Yet Horthy treats it with a disconcerting tenderness, and this outing appears to be designed for its pleasure. The moon is high, and I am getting restless. It must be approaching midnight. When I hear a crack farther in among the trees, I go to investigate, vanishing from one spot to the next.

A shadow is moving fast through the woods, away from the clearing. A woman, I reckon as I get closer. I'm judging by size, for she wears a cloak with a hood and she is moving very quickly. She comes to a shelter made of branches. Another woman is lighting a small fire just outside it. The first woman approaches, dumping a handful of dirt over the fire to extinguish it and putting a finger to her lips. They go into the shelter, and I go right up to the entrance, peering in, though I can barely see in the dark. She is writing in the earth with a stick. The smell of rotten fruit rolls out of the entrance. The other woman opens a little cage, and a bird shoots out of it, swooping off low through the trees. Then the two of them nestle together in the shelter. I wait there for a while, but nothing happens, so I return to the clearing, where Agoston Horthy and his monster are now sharing tea and cake.

FORTY-TWO

"Did you eat that entire crate of oranges?" I ask, staring at the empty crate and the peelings all over the carpet.

Pia's goggles whir at me. She is still sprawled across the sofa. I wonder if she was actually asleep. It is almost dawn, and I am bone-tired. I'm hungry too, but the hermia I just swallowed is roiling my stomach, and I'm not sure eating is a good idea.

"Julia," she says, her voice a creak. I think she *was* asleep. "I am late with my report to Casimir. He will be worried."

"Well, Horthy was out all night. I don't think he sleeps. There's dust on his bed."

"Where did he go?"

"The woods south of Forrestal. He's got some kind of monster locked underneath the parliament. It's the size of a big dog but it walks on two legs, or kind of lurches along, and it makes disgusting noises. He treats it like a pet. He took it to the woods and they ... I don't know, they played games and had cake. He just took it back and locked it in its room. It was making the most dreadful fuss, like a child refusing to go to bed."

I shudder. I'm making light of it, but in fact the sounds the creature made were utterly pitiful, and I swear there were tears on the prime minister's cheeks as he walked away from that locked door and the wrenching wails behind it. I don't tell Pia about the witches in the woods.

"The prime minister has shown himself quite willing to make use of magical creatures—the Gethin, and Lord Skaal. Find out what this thing is and how it serves him." She sits up, spilling orange peels off her lap. "Sir Victor sent a message and a map. There will be a meeting at six o'clock tomorrow evening, and he wants you there—it is a war council. He will need to focus on playing his part. You might notice things he does not."

"All right."

"You need to fit in more spying for Casimir, Julia, between fomenting revolution and whatever else you're up to."

I don't answer that. I can't tell what she thinks, where she stands. What does it mean, that she's *betting* on me? Does she really mean it? To change the subject, I touch the base of my neck and say: "It's still moving."

"Take more hermia," she says sharply.

"I just did. I hope the little beast is feeling it worse than I am."

My hand is resting on the back of the sofa, and she puts her own hand next to it. Hers is much paler, with slender fingers—surprisingly smooth and unmarked given all the weapons handling she does, but I suppose she's usually wearing gloves. No broken knuckles. Casimir left her hands intact. The silver disk in her wrist is just like mine, but there is no mark left where the *nuyi* passed. With her other hand, she touches the back of her head, above her neck.

"Mine is deep inside here somewhere," she says. "What was that girl's name . . . in Tianshi?"

"Ling."

"She really pulled it out?"

She has already made me describe this to her several times. Ling worked for Casimir because he threatened her sister and promised great rewards. Why not? In her place, knowing as little as she knew about the players, I would have done the same. I *did* do the same, once. But I think she really loved Dek, and before the *nuyi* reached her brain, she pulled it out. I shudder, remembering the silvery thread, slick with blood, the scuttling creature at the end of it, her ashen face.

"Do you think she survived?" asks Pia.

"I've no idea," I say. "If she went straight to a doctor, maybe."

"Mine is too deep. I cannot pull it out. But I wonder if others have died to escape it. There are things I cannot do, ways in which I cannot go against Casimir's will. But does that include taking my own life? Could I, for example, cut my own throat against Casimir's wishes?"

I stare at her. "What are you talking about?"

"It has occurred to me that if Casimir should wish me to do something I do not want to do, there may be another choice. Perhaps."

"You're getting very rebellious," I say queasily.

"It is good to consider all one's options."

I don't know why I care about Pia, of all people, but I say, "Don't."

The goggles swivel.

I clear my throat. "Just . . . do your job, and I'll do mine. We'll make it through this."

"We?" she says.

"Go back to sleep. I'm going out for a bit."

She doesn't ask me where I'm going.

FORTY-THREE

I sit with Frederick outside the little hut on the hill, slicing up an apple I brought with me for Ragg Rock's rabbit, George. The rabbit is practically quivering with joy. Theo and Ragg Rock are throwing stones over the edge of the hill into the shifting abyss that is Kahge.

"We went to Vassali earlier today . . . if it was today," Frederick is saying quietly. "The Silver Moya there found me a book at the library that references the *nuyi*. It seems that they are able to absorb the intelligence of the creature they attach themselves to, as well as exerting control. They favor large predators and humans in particular. There was a famous case, just before the rise of the Sirillian Empire, of a Rosshan king renowned for his brutality. It turned out that the king and all his top generals and lords had the *nuyi* in their brains. It is the only recorded instance of a whole country being ostensibly controlled by the *nuyi*. A Xianren-led rebellion overthrew the king, and the queen of the nest was hunted down and captured. Rosshan scientists kept and studied some of the *nuyi*, according to the book. If Ragg

Rock will allow it, I'd like to visit the library in Serpetszo, the capital of Rossha. There will surely be records of the event and whatever discoveries the Rosshan scientists made. I might turn up some way of combating the *nuyi*, besides poison."

"If there's another way, I'll try it," I say. "But I've only got a day or two."

"I want to be useful," he says very softly.

"You're keeping Theo safe," I say. "And keeping him away from Casimir is keeping the whole world safe. You *are* useful."

Theo and Ragg Rock come back up the hill toward us, Theo marching in front.

"Dis!" he declares, holding a plant before him, its roots dangling. It is a large, reptilian-looking flower, scaly-petaled and pale, with a stamen like a vicious tongue and a thorny stalk. Ragg Rock grins behind him.

"There are strange things growing here lately," she says.

"Why?" I ask.

"He makes me feel so alive," she replies, and though I do not wish her ill, that chills something inside me.

"Mama, dis flaffer," says Theo, turning and waving it at Ragg Rock.

It takes a moment for this to sink in.

"Flaffer," she repeats, like he is the one teaching her to speak.

"*Mama?*" I manage to say.

"He calls me Mama now," says Ragg Rock. Her pebble

eyes fix on me like a challenge. "I feel it is true. I *am* his mother. He is my child."

She puts a proprietary mud hand on his shoulder. Theo sniffs at the monstrous flower.

"Stink," he says, and gives me one of his beautiful, wide-open smiles.

Telegram to Lord Casimir, Nago Island: HORTHY HAS MONSTER LOCKED UNDER PARLIAMENT STOP AT NIGHT TAKES IT INTO WOODS STOP PLAYS WITH IT LIKE A PET STOP CASES OF SCOURGE IN WEST SPIRA STOP LAROCHE AWARE OF ANTIDOTE STOP WILL USE IT TO FOMENT DISSENT STOP DUKE RIDING WITH DAFNE BESNIK STOP JULIA COOPERATIVE STOP

DAY 9

CYCLONE

*I'd tell her I understand, that I forgive her,
that I just want to know her as she really is,
and I want her to know me as I really am.*

FORTY-FOUR

I wake up because I can *feel* it moving. I sit bolt upright, sweating. The *nuyi* is sluggish but intractably pushing onward, forcing its way up my neck, under my skin. I leap out of bed and run into the next room, where Pia is sitting in front of an entire roasted chicken, tearing it to pieces and stuffing it in her mouth. She looks up at me, her mouth glistening with grease.

"Can you feel it when it attaches?" I ask her. My voice comes out horribly like a sob.

She gets up quickly, dropping the chicken and wiping her fingers on her jacket. She grabs me by the hair and twists my head to the side, prodding the *nuyi* with her fingers.

"You will know," she says. "You have two days if you do nothing. Take more hermia."

"But will Casimir really take the poison out of Dek? He needs to do it soon!"

"I don't know," she says. "You are not taking enough hermia, Julia. It is still moving."

"I'll up the dose."

"Remember Horthy's war council this evening. Six o'clock. I need more for Casimir or he will get impatient."

"You really *don't* want me to belong to him, do you?" I look at her in bewilderment. "Why not? Why do you even care?"

Her goggles whir, and she says, in that strange, clipped voice: "Is that what this is? Caring?" Then she shrugs. "What I want has never mattered."

I put on the plainest dress I can find in the wardrobe, tie my hair back with a ribbon, and look at myself in the long mirror. I don't look anything like the girl who went riding with the duke yesterday. Nor do I look anything like the girl I was last summer. My chest aches.

"Remember when you said we were alike?" I say to Pia.

She goes back to her chicken. "I was wrong about that. If you were like me, I wouldn't care what became of you at all."

⌒

"How are you?" Liddy asks me.

"I've felt better," I say, and then add, "I've felt worse too."

She gestures at the stovetop, and I take one of her fresh rolls. She puts on a kettle, ties the handkerchief around her face, unwraps my packet of hermia.

"I need more than before," I say. "It's at my neck."

"How are the effects?" she asks.

"Bad dreams. Headache. Stomachache. But I'm all right. I can take more."

She nods and bends over the hermia, plucking several

leaves from the small pile with tweezers. She dips them in hot water, rolls them into a little ball with the tweezers, and drops the ball into my open palm. I pop it in my mouth and swallow it, feeling the pulse of the *nuyi*. Let me not be ruled. My dearest and most desperate hope: let me not be ruled. This thing of Casimir's, crawling through me—at least I know it's there, I have some idea of what it is and how I can fight it. I am fighting so hard to be me, but how can I fight the other thing that might be inside me, the creature whose memories are buried in my mind? How can I be sure Lidari never rules me?

"Did you know my father?" I ask Liddy.

"I never met him, no."

"I wonder . . . if he was really my father."

She looks genuinely surprised at that. It isn't easy to surprise Liddy.

"Do you have reason to believe your mother was with somebody else?"

"No, it's not that. Before I was born, Ma made a deal with . . . something . . . in Kahge. A creature called Lidari. Did you know about that?"

There's no reason she should know, except that Liddy always seems to know everything. She shakes her head.

"She brought him—it—into the world. Right before she tried to kill Casimir. Have you heard of something called the Ankh-nu?"

She raises her eyebrows. "Yes—Marike's mythical pot. I have my doubts as to its existence."

"It exists. Ma had it. She *used* it. And when I vanish, I can go to Kahge. I look like something else there. The shadows in Kahge thought *I* was Lidari. His memories are inside me." I'm talking faster and faster. I can't stop. "Mrs. Och thought that Ma put his essence in me somehow. I wonder . . . if my mother and Lidari *made* me somehow, or if he's *in* me. And if he is, then can I get him out, or what if I'm really . . . that, and not me?"

"There is only one way to make a human, Julia."

"But what kind of human am I, if I can go to Kahge?"

"There are many ways a person can be changed that do not make them any less of a person. Believe me, I know."

"How well did you know my mother?"

"She asked me to look out for you, and I have."

"Do you ever get frightened, Liddy?"

"Yes," she says. "But it is a different kind of fear from the fear I remember when I was young. I have lived a long time, and my fear is not for myself anymore but for the world, which I love. I fear that we will come to the darkest times the world has known if Casimir is successful. I have never stopped hoping for humanity." She peers at me from under her hooded lids, and her eyes are kind. Or maybe they are just familiar from a time when I still accepted kindness easily. "The effects of the hermia will be hard this time, my dear. Here—this is a chorintha flower capsule. Go somewhere safe and take it. It will help you to sleep through the worst of it."

She hands me a little capsule, and I pocket it gratefully.

FORTY-FIVE

By the time I arrive at the Marrow, a hot throb has started up in my knees, hips, elbows, and shoulders, even my fingers and toes. The tables in the bar have been pushed to the sides of the room, and three enormous banners are spread across the floor. Two of them are blank, but Wyn and Lorka are busy painting the third. There are cans of paint and brushes all over the place. In spite of the burning in my joints, I can't help smiling at Wyn's radiant face as he waves me over. How overjoyed he must be, to be painting alongside his hero.

"Julia! I was just talking about you!"

"What in flaming Kahge is all this?" I ask.

The banner they are working on depicts Agoston Horthy with a crew of cruel-faced soldiers and fat aristocrats, pockets overflowing with jewels and coins, trampling commoners underfoot. At the back of this procession, a golden-hued Princess Zara is helping the trampled commoners to their feet again, while a ghostly image of her hanged family dangles behind her. Lorka adds some delicate touches to the glowing light behind the princess.

"We're going to hang these around the city tonight," says Wyn. "It was my idea. You know, the power of art."

His smile is so huge it looks as if it might split his face in two.

"We need a scout," says Lorka, looking me over mistrustfully. "We will start in the Plateau."

"Can't beat an invisible scout, I was saying," says Wyn. "Want to come along?"

"I've got a lot on my plate just now," I reply, and his face falls. He glances at Lorka. I feel bad. Wyn is trying so hard to impress the artist, who grunts and goes back to the banner.

"When are you doing it?" I ask.

"Tonight," says Wyn hopefully. "Around midnight, when things are quiet. We'll start on the southeast end of the parliament walls."

"I'll do my best to be there," I say. "But I can't promise anything. Is Dek here?"

"In the cellar," says Wyn. "He's got it set up as a secret laboratory. Go on down and you'll see."

Lorka puts down his brush, giving Wyn a hard look.

"She's his *sister*," says Wyn.

And inches from being Casimir's puppet. I don't blame Lorka for being wary of me.

Wyn takes me behind the bar, shoving a box of dirty cloths aside and rolling back a mat to reveal a trapdoor in the floor. He heaves it open.

"Julia's here to see you!" he hollers down. To me, he says, "Try to come tonight, won't you? We could use you."

"I'll do my best," I reply. My joints are on fire, and a dull pounding has set up inside my temples. Liddy said to go somewhere safe, and the only safe place I can think of is with Dek. I climb down to the lamplit cellar.

"Dek?"

Something clangs, like metal on stone, as I reach the bottom of the ladder. The cellar is full of stacked crates. A sickly-sweet smell hangs in the air. Lanterns blaze at either end of a long steel table, and Dek is silhouetted behind the table, holding an enormous pair of pliers.

"Hounds, I wasn't expecting you here!" he says, smiling as I approach. He's scrubbed up, in polished boots and a decent suit, his hair combed out of his face. The right side of his face is still strange, too pale, the skin pulled tight, with silvery streaks like hints of scars, but you don't really notice unless you look closely.

"What's all this?" I ask, surveying the odd assortment of objects on the table: two halves of a metal sphere that would fit in the palm of my hand, parts of what looks like a telescope the size of my arm, several pressurized metal canisters in a row, an empty wine bottle, and two glasses. *Two* glasses?

Every part of me hurts. I make to sit down on a crate by the table, but Dek yells, "Don't sit on that!" and I leap away from it.

"Sorry," he says. "It's amazing how sloppily some people will pack toxic material and the like. Stars, you really don't look well at all."

"It's the hermia." I gesture at the two wineglasses. "Was somebody here?"

"People are in and out all the time. I keep telling them I'm working with dangerous stuff down here, but they all want a look."

He picks up the two halves of the metal sphere and twists them together. He pulls a small sliding lever at the join and tosses the sphere lightly into the air. It flies across the room, executing several startling loops, and then it pops open and clatters to the ground. He looks pleased.

"I just took quite a lot . . . ," I start to say—or I think I say it. Halfway through the sentence, the pain in my joints flares white-hot. A flash of blinding light obliterates everything, and my knees buckle.

"Have some water."

I'm kneeling on the floor, and Dek is crouched next to me, holding a cup to my lips. I drink, but I can barely feel the water going down. My mouth and throat have gone numb. The bright light fades from my vision, leaving the room colorless and dim.

"Sorry," I mutter. "Liddy said to sleep off the worst."

He helps me up and leads me to a cot at the back of the room. There's a large grate in the wall above that looks like it doesn't fit right.

"Where does that go?" I point at it, and think of the clanging sound I heard as I was coming down the ladder. "Did somebody just leave?"

"Always the spy." He tousles my hair.

Color seeps back into the world, starting at the edges, but a tearing sensation has set up in my bones now, like I'm coming apart. My throat feels scraped raw, and a second sip of water tastes like blood and iron—or maybe my throat is bleeding and that's what I taste. Blast, I've really taken too much hermia this time. I fumble the capsule of chorintha flower Liddy gave me out of my purse. Dek watches me swallow it.

In a horribly calm voice, he says, "Julia—you've got to face the truth. I'm going to be dead soon, and you need to let me go. Take out the *nuyi*."

"No," I whisper. "We'll be all right. I need you to be all right."

I don't remember lying down, but I'm sprawled across the cot now, couldn't move if I tried, and he's put a blanket over me.

"It was such a narrow, hurting little life I had for so long," he says. "I watched you going about, so free, and I felt as if I was *starving* for joy. I found it for a while, in Tianshi, and I'm grateful for that. It changed me. Or maybe it reminded me of who I used to be. If I only have a few days left, I mean to be useful, and I mean to be joyful. But I need you to let me go."

No, Dek. You have always been stronger and surer, you are indestructible, you have to be. I will never, ever let you go. But I can't speak. The chorintha has taken hold, sweeping over me, erasing the pain. The next moment, sleep slams into me, like hitting a wall.

When I wake up, Dek is gone. I climb out of the cot tentatively. I'm still aching all over, but I can move well enough, and I can form a coherent thought, so that's good. I've no idea what time it is, though. On a hunch, I stand on top of the cot and reach for the lopsided grate. It comes easily out of the wall. I leave the grate on the cot, haul myself up into the narrow passage, and crawl through filth toward the light at the end. Not so surprisingly, it leads to a grate in the lane outside the Marrow. So who is sneaking into Dek's laboratory under the Marrow and drinking wine with him? I'll have to ask him directly later; right now I have a war council to spy on.

I vanish and drag myself out into the evening streets of the Edge.

FORTY-SIX

The war council is made up of eight men remarkably similar in appearance, and Luca, who stands out for being young and beautiful and having a kind of softness to him. The others are all over fifty, with the beefiness of men well fed since childhood and overfed in adulthood. They have large shoulders, large guts, pouches under their eyes, fine doublets, gold monocles, clean fingernails, brutal faces. They all rise when Agoston Horthy enters the room. The prime minister is diminutive and rather scruffy compared to the rest of them, but something shifts in the air with his presence. Even tossing acorns in the woods with his monster, there was no sense of frivolity about him. He cannot shed his terrible purposefulness.

I still feel weak, but the farther I vanish, the freer I am from my poisoned body—from the ache in my joints, the pounding in my skull. I become like a phantom of myself, this sickness a distant thing I can only half feel.

"Let us begin," says Horthy with no preamble. "Gorensi."

A man with eyes like black pools and a green snake around his neck . . . no, I am hallucinating, it is only a cravat . . . begins to speak. I blink away the image, come a little closer to the edge of the world, and struggle to focus on what this Gorensi is saying.

"Three spies have gotten close enough to the revolutionaries that they've received invitations to meet with the girl alleging to be Roparzh's daughter. Same story each time. They go to the appointed place, are blindfolded and taken in a hackney. Each time we have lost them in the city—there are a number of changes, and they move very quickly, clearly aware of being followed. Each of our spies has turned up later with no memory of what happened. One of them has simply forgotten what happened after he got in the hackney. He found himself in a pub in Forrestal hours later and could not say how he came to be there. The other two remember almost nothing of their lives. One of them has forgotten even his name, his family, he cannot read or write anymore, can barely speak."

"How horrible!" cries Luca.

"Witchcraft is a clumsy tool," says a fellow whose monocle gruesomely magnifies one of his blue eyes. "They try to rip out the relevant memory and end up ripping out half a man's self."

"You don't think it was deliberate, Sir Oswell?" says Gorensi.

"Oh, it may have been, but memory is a fragile, intricate thing," replies the old monocle-wearer, Sir Oswell. "Removing *one* memory with witchcraft would be like trying to perform delicate surgery with a shovel. It is remarkable they managed it with even one of the spies. He is lucky."

"Then our spies have nothing for us," says Agoston Horthy, uninterested in the rest.

"We know that witches are coming to Frayne in large numbers," says the baldest of the assembled men. "And we've had letters from New Porian officials about Xanuhan missionaries passing through their countries, as well as Xanuhan ships in the New Porian sea. *That* is something to be concerned about, I think. The Xanuhans are not known for sending out missions, and they are headed for Frayne."

"The Xanuhans are not friends to witches, surely," says Agoston Horthy. "Their great fame lies in having overthrown their witch overlords."

"They might be refugee witches from Xanuha posing as missionaries," says Sir Oswell. "They should not be allowed to enter Frayne."

"How will we stop them?" asks Agoston Horthy. "With over two thousand miles of coastline and a mostly unprotected border between ourselves and Prasha?"

"This morning we found another witch camp in the forest south of the city," says Sir Oswell. "A small one, but no doubt there are more. We have troops combing the forest. I am willing to bet they are in the mountains to the east too, and somewhere in the west. These large spells would tax any group of witches, even working together. They are likely surrounding the city, writing magic from different compass points around their target."

I gather Sir Oswell is the magic expert.

"We'll send more men into the mountains and the woods, then," says Agoston Horthy. "But what about West Spira?"

"The spells have been concentrated there. The most powerful group of witches must be close by—either on the edge of the city or somewhere in West Spira itself."

"The witches in Hostorak gave you nothing?" Horthy directs this at Sir Victor.

"Nothing useful," replies Sir Victor. "They received instruction from Lady Laroche via messenger birds, but they did not know her location or the location of any other groups of witches, though they were aware of the existence of other groups. However, I do have a lead in Ibhara regarding the princess. I should like to go there as soon as possible."

"Go now," says Agoston Horthy. "I want you back with answers tomorrow."

Sir Victor nods. There is a pause.

"*Immediately!*" says Agoston Horthy. Sir Victor rises, bows, and goes out.

"I will send a telegram to the queen of Xanuha to ask about these missions," says Agoston Horthy. "They have had success against witches. Perhaps we should have forged stronger ties with them. They remain free of witch rule even under the shadow of the Yongguo Empire."

"Yongguo is not witch-ruled," says Sir Oswell. "Only witch-tolerant."

"Let us not pretend witches don't pull the strings there," says Agoston Horthy.

"I don't believe they do," says Sir Oswell mildly. "That empire keeps witches very effectively under its thumb. But it is no matter. We should keep the Xanuhans out. They think very differently about magic there. They did not want to be ruled by witches, but they do not view witchcraft as inherently evil, and they do not worship the Nameless One. They still keep shrines to the elemental spirits."

"Right now I only want assurances that their missionaries are not in league with forces that mean us ill," says Agoston Horthy.

Something is tightening around my spine. At first it is gradual, but then there is a sudden, sharp squeeze, pain shooting up my spine, and I cry out.

"What is that?" Gorensi screams, leaping to his feet and pointing straight at me. I pull back again, vanishing away from the pain in my spine and the terrified officials.

"I saw it too!" I hear Sir Oswell. "It's gone. What was it?"

Blast—I must have reappeared for a moment without realizing it. They are all scrambling to their feet, drawing weapons, shouting. I vanish back back back, out the window, over the city, farther and farther.

I rest on the steaming streets of Kahge. The shadow-creatures there watch me with ghostly eyes.

"*Lidari*," one of them hisses at me. But they can't touch me anymore. I am strong here, not ill and poisoned. I crouch on powerful limbs, averting my eyes from my scaled arms, my clawed hands. Everything here is changed, a monstrous reflection of the world, but I can't reconcile myself to this other body. I feel my neck, and there it is, the lump of the *nuyi*, even here. I rest awhile as the shadow of my city burns around me, free of pain, but not Julia, not really.

FORTY-SEVEN

Lady Laroche and Zara are both out. I leave a message about the war council with Mrs. Freeley. She and Gennady are busy making sponge cake, so I help myself to some bread and cheese from the larder and sit on the veranda as the sun goes down and night falls. No Lady Laroche. No Zara. The lights in the house go out, and I stay in the dark of the garden. I should take my report to Pia, but instead I fall asleep in a chair as the evening cools and the pain of the hermia fades. I am startled awake when little Strig leaps onto my lap with a *hooo-hoo*, walks in a circle, and curls up, purring. I stroke his soft mix of feathers and fur, and I think with a deep pang of Bianka, and of everything I've done that I can never undo.

The sky is black, the moon a yellow crescent. I need to take more hermia, but the *nuyi* hasn't started moving in my neck again yet, still stunned by the last onslaught. To put off the necessary next dose a little longer, I lift Strig gently off my lap and go out looking for Wyn and Lorka. I walk along the river, vanished, toward the Plateau. I've never passed the river without thinking about my mother, and now I wonder if her bones are down there at all, or if she's still out in the world somewhere. I wish I could call her to me. I'd tell her I understand, that I forgive her, that I just want to know her as she really is, and I want her to know me as I really am.

I see two shadows—one tall, one stout—at the southwest corner of the parliament building wall. A third figure is under the streetlamp, wearing a red dress and smoking ostentatiously. I go closer. Oh, for heaven's sake, it's bleeding Arly Winters, the girl Wyn was shagging on the side while he was still with me. The two figures by the wall are Wyn and Lorka, hanging one of their banners.

"Flaming Kahge, Julia! What are you doing here?" cries Wyn when I reappear next to him.

"You *asked* me to come," I remind him, annoyed.

"Oh, right. I didn't think you'd make it," he says, a little sheepishly. He gestures at the banner. "What do you think?"

It's the one they were working on this morning, depicting Agoston Horthy and the aristocracy trampling people and Zara coming to the rescue. This is a busy street by day, and I can see why they've chosen it: riverside cafés, newsstands, groceries, tobacconists—shops where people will come early in the morning and see the banner right on the parliament wall. It won't stay up long, but plenty of people will see it before it is taken down.

"It's . . . very large," I say uncertainly.

And here is Arly, coming to join us.

"*Julia?*" she says, squinting at me.

"Hello, Arly."

"You look . . . different." She stares at my dress and my scar.

"You look just the same," I say.

She tosses her hair and gives Wyn a questioning look.

"Are you supposed to be scouting?" I ask her. "Or just diverting attention?"

"Bit of both," says Wyn cheerfully.

"We've got two more to go," says Lorka, hoisting a ladder onto his shoulder. Wyn bends to pick up the rolled banners and a heavy-looking rucksack. "The palace, then Hostorak. You'll scout for us, Julia?"

"All right."

I'd like to pretend I don't feel remotely star-struck around Lorka, but it would be a lie. I've heard his name spoken reverently too many times not to feel a little thrill at his knowing *my* name. We head west, along the river.

"Lorka told me I've got a real eye for the human element," Wyn whispers to me.

"I miss the sort of thing you used to draw," I say.

"I was just drawing the world around me," says Wyn. "I wasn't drawing with any vision. I had nothing to *say*."

"I thought your drawings were nice, though." I see immediately from his expression that *nice* is the wrong word to use. "I mean, your pictures showed what our lives were really like. There was so much love in them. That was worth something, wasn't it?"

Arly is practically skipping to keep up with us.

"I'm not disowning them, but I'm growing as an artist," says Wyn. "Did you ever think art could be like a weapon? As powerful as or even *more* powerful than a gun or a sword? A means of changing the world?"

"Not so long ago you asked Gregor if it really made any difference—this king, that queen," I say. "Seems like you've changed your mind."

"I have," he says very seriously. "Agoston Horthy's been a blight on this country. You and I never knew anything else—we grew up in a defeated country, among a cowed people. I just wanted to make the best of my own life. But Lorka says it's our duty to fight for a better world even when there's no hope. He says an artist's job is to tell the truth at any cost. I don't know if he really believes a better world is possible—he's not exactly an optimist about human nature—but he believes in challenging all that is worst in the world. He believes in telling the truth about it, right into the face of power."

"I never thought I'd hear *you* talking this way."

He smiles ruefully. "I know. I've always been a selfish sod, and truth is that I reckon I still am. But when somebody makes right and wrong so stark before your eyes—well, even doing nothing is taking a position. There's no opting out."

"I think you're *wonderfully* brave," says Arly, fed up with being left out of the conversation.

I do not roll my eyes. No, that's a lie: I do roll my eyes.

"I need to talk to Wyn privately," I tell her.

She raises her perfectly plucked black eyebrows.

"Please," says Wyn, mollifying her with one of his irresistible smiles. She shrugs and skips ahead to join Lorka.

"You and Arly Winters again?" I say dryly. "What happened to the blonde? Or the redhead?"

"Well," he says, with an awkward shrug. "Nothing."

"You're going to have some girl coming to you with a baby, or worse."

"You know I'm careful," he mutters.

I let it go. "How does Dek seem to you?" I ask.

His expression turns somber. "He's very focused. Calm. I think he's . . . I don't know, resigned."

That was what I was afraid he would say. A chill coils around my heart. "You'll keep a close eye on him, won't you?"

He gives me a sad smile. "He's worried about you. We all are."

"I'm fine," I say, which is stupid, because obviously none of us are *fine*.

Lorka has picked a spot in front of the palace wall. He gestures at me to position myself down the street. I wait, vanished, watching over the river, which reflects the city lights. They are almost done hanging the second banner when I hear a soft thunk behind me. I spin around and see a rope ladder sliding down the palace wall.

I toss a handful of pebbles down the street so they go clattering past Wyn and Lorka. They pack their things up again quickly, crossing to the river and ducking down the stairs to the low path, where they are hidden from view. The banner hangs lopsidedly from the wall to the west. Arly goes trotting off too, but I stay where I am. The rope ladder is dangling right in front of me.

A familiar figure comes climbing down it.

FORTY-EIGHT

Luca descends the ladder and leaves it hanging there. He stuffs his hands in his pockets and goes sauntering down the street in the direction of the Plateau, in the opposite direction from the newly hung banner. Without a second thought, I leave Wyn, Lorka, and Arly behind and follow him. What by the holies is he *doing?*

He is dressed differently than usual—in a pair of trousers and rough boots that seem to actually fit him, and a leather vest over a loose shirt. He looks like a well-to-do farmer. Still, his large frame and tousled mop of coppery hair are instantly recognizable to anybody who has laid eyes on him before.

The train station is a clamor of noise, but otherwise the Plateau is quiet at this time of night. He heads in among the narrow streets of the Twist, and I think, *What a fool, he's going to get robbed in three seconds flat!*

And indeed, that is exactly what happens. Two fellows smoking in the street exchange a glance at his approach.

"Hullo, sir!" one of them calls.

Luca gives a small nod as he passes them, not slowing his pace.

"You wouldn't happen to have the time?" asks the fellow.

Luca reaches into his breast pocket—oh, he really *is* a fool!—and pulls out a gold timepiece, flicking it open.

"Half past midnight," he says.

"That's a fine watch you have," says the first man, stepping right in front of him. The other man circles behind him. Luca's shoulders stiffen—he has understood too late what is happening—and he slips the watch back into his pocket, his hands forming very large fists. He starts to shoulder his way past the first fellow.

"Give us a look," says the first man, putting a hand out to stop him. "Never seen such a fine watch as that."

"Got anything else as pretty?" asks the other.

Luca takes the measure of them and seems to relax. It's true he is bigger than they are, but that is what makes me nervous. They would not be targeting him if they were unarmed. I wish he'd just give them the bleeding watch. He's about to be king; I'm sure he can get his hands on another.

"You'd best let me by," says Luca, pitching his voice a bit lower than usual. The first man grabs his vest. Luca smashes a fist right into his face—an impressive punch for such close range. The fellow goes down hard, but the other one is coming at Luca from behind with a knife. I reappear, grabbing the man's knife hand and twisting it. He yelps in surprise, and I kick his feet out from under him. Once he's down, I stomp on his hand and snatch up his knife.

He scrambles back to his feet, hollering and cradling his

hand, but seeing me with a knife beside Luca and his companion still on the ground, he makes a dash for it.

"Let him go," I say to Luca. "He'll go straight to his friends, and then we'll be outnumbered. We'd better get out of here."

Luca's eyes are wide with disbelief.

"*Ella?*" he says, and an amazed laugh bursts out of him. Hounds, but I do love the sound of his laugh. It sends tremors right through me. This is not the time or place for tremors, though. I should have vanished as soon as I got the fellow's knife and let Luca think he was imagining things.

I toss the knife into the gutter. "Come *on*."

I drag him to one of the more crowded eveningtime streets, where the Twist's popular bars, music halls, and brothels are jumbled together, and choose a saloon where I'm unlikely to know anybody. It's an older crowd here. Esme would know them, but it's not a place I've ever frequented. I find us a table near the back, and the barmaid brings us a carafe of wine.

"I *knew* it!" Luca is practically crowing. "I *knew* you had a secret! Now you're going to have to tell me."

I am horribly conscious, now, of my bare, scarred face and my dress filthy from crawling through that passageway out of the Marrow.

"I don't have to tell you a bleeding thing," I retort. "I just saved your sorry life. What are you thinking, wandering the streets by yourself, looking like that?"

"Looking like *what?*"

"Like you're not from Spira City and might have a fancy watch tucked away in your pocket."

"Oh." He ducks his head sheepishly. "I wanted to see the city. It was becoming obvious that I was never going to get an actual look at any of my subjects except the tremendously rich ones. I had this idea, you know, that I'd be like the legend of King Olevar, roaming the country in disguise, talking with the poor, finding out about their lives and being a better king for it."

I roll my eyes, and he laughs.

"It's a poor first attempt, I'll grant you. But you can't expect me to be a master of disguise right off the bat!"

"Why didn't you just hand over the watch? You might have been killed if I hadn't been there."

"It was my father's," he says, some of the light going out of his eyes. Ah. He brightens again almost immediately, though. "But that spot of bad luck has turned into very *good* luck, because here you are, and I am going to *insist* that you tell me what you're doing here. If you don't tell me, I shall tell your uncle."

"Would you really?" I ask.

His eyes gleam. "No. But I'm dying of curiosity. You didn't come to the soirée tonight. I kept watching the door, hoping to see you. Clearly you had something else to do."

I take a sip of the horrible wine to stall for a moment.

"It's just that I happen to know some people here," I say, putting down my glass. "Where I come from, we're all very close with our household staff and their children. They're like family. Our cook's daughter came to Spira City and found work in the Twist, but I heard she'd fallen ill. I promised I'd look in on her."

"In the middle of the night."

"I came after dinner, but she was very unwell and I stayed to help. *Please* don't tell my uncle. He'll be so cross with me for staying out so late."

His eyes stray to my scar, but he's too polite to mention it. He waves the barmaid over and orders two bowls of stew.

"You do have a way of appearing suddenly. Or disappearing, for that matter. Let's say I believe your story about your cook's daughter. I still think you've got secrets."

This is turning out to be a very bad idea, and I'm not sure why I brought him here to eat and drink in the first place, but I don't want to leave either. The truth is that I *like* the way he's looking at me—his hungry, wondering gaze. I like the quiver behind my ribs when he laughs. There is this thrill going through me and through me at having him to myself in this dark corner, imagining we can step out of our respective stories and do as we please for the night. But I know it's a fantasy.

"We've all got secrets," I say.

"I'm dying to know yours." He reaches across the table and takes my hand, turns it slowly in his and studies my palm. For a wild moment, I think he's doing palmistry, which is illegal and has been since I was born. His fingers are hot on my wrist. Just an inch farther up, under my sleeve, *one* of my secrets—that silvery disk where the *nuyi* entered— is very visible indeed. I start to pull my hand away, but he holds on to it and looks up at me, suddenly intense.

"I've spent this whole evening bored out of my mind, having that beautiful, dull girl thrown at me, and talking to people I have *nothing* in common with."

"*We* have nothing in common," I say.

"Maybe we do. I don't know anything about you. But you're from the countryside, like me."

"I think that is the extent of what we share," I say. Not even that, in fact.

"I've met lots of country girls. And now I've met lots of city girls. But I've never met anyone like you."

I pull my hand free, and the stew comes to save me. I'm thinking I ought to get out of here, but it's hard to walk away from the bright, warming beam of his gaze, into the shadows, back to that hotel to eat more poison. Besides, I'm hungry.

"I suppose you've met plenty of men like me, though," he says.

"Are you fishing for compliments?" I ask, laughing. "You know that's unlikely."

"Is it?"

"You are the first duke I've known."

"That means nothing. It's a title."

"You don't think titles mean anything? Odd position for the future king to take."

"I'm not talking about family or position. If I were, I'd say I had a great deal in common with the people I met tonight. We are all nobility, but I'm talking about who we are in a more profound way. Am I being foolish or romantic if I say that you are wonderfully mysterious?"

I make a face and keep shoveling back the stew, though I rather like that image of myself.

"I haven't been able to stop thinking about you since you appeared in the azalea bush the other day, and then *disappeared* from behind my curtain. You are a puzzle I'm stuck on."

"You *are* a rogue," I say.

"You made me feel ashamed of treating your reputation so lightly, but I don't think you care one whit about your reputation or you wouldn't be running around the Twist at midnight!"

"I told you why," I protest.

"I don't believe you. If you won't tell me what you're up to, I can find out everything I want, anyway. I'm going to be king soon."

Hounds, I don't need Luca digging into my nonexistent personal history.

"I don't like to be threatened," I shoot back. "I've told you my business in the Twist, and I would not have chosen to show myself to you at all except that I feared for your life."

"I'm not threatening you!" He looks confused.

"You are lording your position over me, telling me you will dig into my private affairs with the power of the throne!

How do you think that makes me feel? I will tell you: powerless and afraid. It is not a nice way to feel, and it does not endear you to me one bit. I *helped* you tonight, and you are repaying my kindness with bullying. You think that because you are going to be king you can have me if you like, but you can't. I am not yours to have or to know."

"Ella, I'm sorry!" he cries, appalled. "I didn't mean to offend you. I was joking."

"You weren't," I say, although I'm less angry with him than I'm pretending, and more angry with myself for being such a sap for his charms.

"Can you blame a fellow for being curious? I feel so out of place with the people here, but it's different with you. I keep thinking—or hoping—that you and I might be alike in some way."

"You ride and dance and write poetry," I say. "I dislike all of those things. You are jolly, and I am not. You are about to be king, and I am nobody. I can't think of anything we share."

"Why don't you tell me what you like?"

"I like this stew," I say, finishing it.

He grins. "You have a healthy appetite—that's something we share! Don't you worry about your dress size?"

I give him an evil look. "You're not going to cut such a fine figure in a few years either, Your Almost-Majesty."

He throws back his head and laughs at that. "We should dance, then, while we're still young and can make some small claim to beauty."

"You can claim it more than I can," I say. "And I told you—I can't dance."

"I believe you just paid me a compliment!" His jaw drops in mock astonishment. "Surely you know how to dance a reel! Come—we are from the countryside, are we not? How can we claim our true, wild homes if we cannot dance a reel?"

And of course, I *do* know how to dance a reel, at least. The music has been getting louder, and a great many drunken louts are making their clumsy hash of the reel. My foot is tapping to the music, and the wine and the stew are warm in my belly. The hermia has worn off, and while that means I ought to take more, I am giddy with relief at being free of the ache and burn of it. He reaches for my hand, a pleading, helpless look on his face that I expect got him terribly spoiled as a boy. I put my hand in his, and he gives a yelp of happiness that makes me laugh in spite of myself. He pulls me to my feet and into the crowd.

His arm goes around me, his hot hand tight on my waist, and I'm facing straight into that great barrel chest of his. If I tilt my head up to look at him, our lips are inches apart. I reckon he thinks he's going to bed me. The worst of it is how much I want the same thing. I am behaving like an utter fool for the heir to the Fraynish throne, but it's hard to remind myself of what he is when those long-lashed amber eyes are blinking down at me and I'm pressed right up against the gorgeous length of him.

So we dance. I can't help laughing at the expression of

mock despair on his face as he passes me off to the next red-faced reveler. I go spinning down the line. I'm still laughing when I find myself staring right into my brother's face, his mechanical right arm around my waist, the glass eye blank and his other eye wide with shock.

FORTY-NINE

"Dek?" I whisper, and then I'm whirling back along the line toward Luca. Luca catches me and spins me around, holding me closer than would be considered appropriate at a royal soirée, but anything goes in the Twist. I crane my neck, trying to see Dek again. He twirls by us, staring, and I gasp audibly because *Zara* is in his arms, white-faced and gaping at us as well.

"Do you know that fellow?" asks Luca.

I shake my head, forcing a smile. He dances me back into the line and sends me spinning down it a second time. I bump against Zara as we pass each other. She's wearing a ruffled peasant-girl dress and her lips are painted red.

Dek catches me and turns me around, hissing in my ear, "Is that the bleeding heir to the throne you've come here with?"

Zara is in Luca's arms, smiling up at him prettily, and he is looking at me over her head. I don't have time to answer Dek, and no idea what I'd say, anyway. Back down the line I go to Luca, around and around and around.

"He's still staring at you," says Luca.

What the bleeding stars are they *doing* here? In spite of my shock, Luca's arm tight around my waist and his face bent right over mine make me feel wild and wide-awake again. I see Dek and Zara slipping out the door, hand in hand. Dek looks back at me once and then they are gone. The dance is breaking up, more and more people rushing the door, and then I hear the roaring behind the music. The players stop, the fiddle trailing off last. A howl outside, not human or animal.

Everything hot and reckless and alive in me goes cold as ice. I break out of Luca's arms, pushing through the press of bodies and out into the street. The wind is blowing hats from heads, papers and baskets and bonnets whirling through the night. I can't see Dek or Zara anywhere.

For a moment, looking at the westward sky, I think it is Kahge come to earth. My heart contracts—*Theo, he's found Theo*—but somebody near me says in an awed voice, "It's a twister!"

It is hard to make it out in the dark, but the speaker is right. Somewhere over West Spira, a whirling column of wind is descending, a screaming cyclone. It touches down, and there is a distant tearing sound as it moves through the city. People are running as if they've got somewhere safer to go.

Magic fills my nostrils, a disturbing mix of smells—spice and salt, singed feathers and honey and wet stone. The cyclone cuts through West Spira and then rises again, breaking apart into black streaks. The wind that blasts over us makes me reel backward. Somebody crashes into me. I let myself get swept up in the running crowd. I run and then I vanish. The wind is gone almost as quickly as it came, and there are cries of "witchery!" everywhere. Hanging over the scene, I still can't find Dek, but I see Luca racing along the street looking for me, calling frantically: "Ella! *Ella!*"

⁂

The cyclone cut a path half a mile long through West Spira in a matter of seconds. The streets are full of rubble and broken tiles, half-destroyed houses and ruined gardens, trees torn up by the roots. The storm did not quite reach the palace, stopping short of the streets surrounding it. Ambulances and police cabriolets are all over the place surrounding the wreckage, and I can hear screaming and weeping from every direction.

I don't want to talk to Pia. My mind is too full of other things. I remember that Sir Victor told me I have a room of my own at the palace, so I check the maps he gave me and find my way there. It's something, isn't it, for a girl from the Twist, daughter of a witch, Esme's little thief, to be able to choose between a fine West Spira hotel room and guest quarters at the royal palace? Well, such is Casimir's reach. For a half second, as I return to myself on the balcony and step quietly onto the soft carpet, I imagine this being my life. Even if the *nuyi* took me, I reason, would it be so bad? Dek rich and protected. Me spying on royal families around the world, living in luxury, as fearless and terrifying as Pia. My name sending shudders through my enemies. Always gold, always a fine meal and a comfortable bed, baths up to my neck, and nobody to tell me what to do or how to be. Nobody but the evil thing that owns me. I shake off the fantasy. It's only that I'm so tired of being afraid.

There is somebody in the bed, asleep. I stand frozen with shock—have I got the wrong room? But no, she's not asleep. She turns over and sits up, golden tresses falling loose about her shoulders, and even in the dark I can see the look of triumph on her face.

"Aha," says Dafne Besnik. "*There* you are."

FIFTY

"What are you doing here?" I ask.

"Waiting for you," she says. "Did you just come in from the *balcony?*"

I ignore that impossible question and find myself babbling: "The daughter of our old cook has taken ill—she lives in the city—I've been sitting up with her. I'm exhausted. But Sir Victor will be *so* cross if he knows I've been out at night."

"Of course he will. Did you *see* the storm? It was coming right at us and then vanished. It's witches attacking the city because they're afraid of Duke Everard—a young, strong ruler about to take control of the country. That's what everyone is saying."

"Are they?"

She looks at me contemplatively, head tilted to one side, and says: "I knew you couldn't be as dull as you've been pretending to be."

"Excuse me?"

"Don't worry, I'm not going to tell anybody." She gets up and steps closer to me. "Once, I snuck out to a masked ball with my friends—*not* a respectable ball! My parents never knew I'd left the house. We drank liquor and danced and smoked something . . . I don't know what, it gave me a terrible headache." She licks her lips nervously. "Wherever you've been, I won't be shocked."

I doubt that, but an astonished laugh escapes me all the same.

"How did you get up on the *balcony?*" she asks again.

I throw something out to distract her from the balcony: "I was at a music hall in the Scola. With a man."

That does the trick.

"*Who?*" she gasps.

"I can't tell you."

"Why not?"

"My uncle would say he is below my station."

Her eyes widen. "Are you in love with him?"

"Desperately," I deadpan. I go to the vanity and rummage through the jars of powder and ointments, just to give myself something to do. Sir Victor meant it when he said the room would look as if a girl lived here.

Dafne stands right next to me, staring at my reflection

and her own in the mirror. "Do you let him kiss you?" she whispers.

"Yes," I whisper back.

"What is it like?"

I think of Luca, his mouth against my ear. How the first time I met him, I felt the heat of his mouth even through my glove.

"Heavenly," I say. "A bit dizzy-making."

"Is he handsome?"

"Too handsome for his own good."

She half-swoons back onto the bed with a whoop of happiness.

"Now we shall *really* be friends!" she cries. "Oh, I'm glad you're not just some dull girl stuck with me for the season! Things will be so much better now that I know I can be myself with you. You *must* tell me more about this man!"

I try to put her off, but she is so insistent that I start making things up about my imaginary beau, turning him into a rebellious young painter who doesn't want to take over his father's rubber import business. I get rather dramatic, thinking of the sorts of books I used to read aloud to Wyn. I'd read the overwrought lovemaking scenes again and again and we'd hoot with laughter and then make our own kind of love. I miss it, in spite of everything that's happened since.

I invent a first meeting, stolen kisses, my parents forbidding the relationship and sending me away to the palace to visit my uncle. But my lover followed me to the city, I tell her, and we've been continuing our secret trysts by night.

Dafne is practically falling off the bed in excitement.

"I've got to meet him!" she cries wildly.

Bleeding hounds! I hadn't expected *that*.

"We've got to be very careful. I don't know when I'm going to be able to see him again."

"I'll help you in any way I can," she whispers. "And you can help me too!"

"What do you need help with?"

"Oh, nothing *yet*. I've never had an affair of the heart. Not a real one. The boys I see are all very boring."

"What about Duke Everard?" I say, my voice too light.

"Oh, he's very handsome, and more interesting than the other boys my parents have considered for me. I'm relieved he's not horrible or ugly. It'll be such a lark to be queen!"

"Will it?"

"Of course it will! I wonder what it will be like to kiss him. And do other things. He must know how, mustn't he?" For a moment, a look of panic comes into her eyes, and then it's gone. "I'll throw the most fantastic parties! Nobody will be able to tell me what to do or how to behave. Not even my parents. Not when I'm queen of Frayne!"

"It might be somewhat burdensome too," I say. "Ruling over such a troubled country."

"Oh, I'll fix ever so many problems," she says, waving a hand dismissively. "I'm sure I'll be very well loved. In the daytimes I'll visit hospitals and give money to the poor and so on, and then throw fabulous parties at night."

"It sounds like you've got it all worked out," I say, feeling suddenly, absurdly, rather sorry for her.

"I don't think he's actually so very religious, the duke—do you?"

"Are *you*, really?"

"Oh yes! Only I don't believe the Nameless One really cares about the sort of morality people like my parents go on about. I've felt it, you know, at temple—the true power of the Nameless One. This vast, encompassing goodness and goodwill. It's so beautiful, so pure, not like . . . well, not like anything in *this* world. I do *not* believe such an awesome power would be as petty and shallow and nitpicky as my parents are! Scripture was all written by men, after all. *I* believe the Nameless One wants goodness and love in the world, and truth, and beauty. Oh, I pass the time imagining what my life is going to be like when I'm queen. I'm going to make up for the miserable life I've had so far!"

"Has it been miserable?"

I doubt this girl has seen much of misery, but then what do I know?

"Yes," she says savagely. "Nobody tells the truth about anything."

"Well, what would the world be like if everyone told the truth?"

"The world will never be that way. But I intend to be free of all the pretense that makes up my life now."

"You are not what anyone imagines, that's certain," I say, trying not to laugh at the fact that *this* is the girl Casimir and Agoston Horthy are trying to push at the heir in the hopes that she will control him. But of course, it's not Rainism they care about specifically, but someone who will support the persecution of witches. I can't imagine either Luca or Dafne knowing or caring enough to stand in Agoston Horthy's way.

"Had you fooled, didn't I?" Her eyes gleam.

"You did. But now I *must* sleep!"

"I suppose real kissing is very tiring?"

"Very," I assure her.

"I'm so glad we'll be friends for real now," she says. "We'll tell each other everything!"

Speak for yourself, my girl. I squeeze her hand and finally she leaves me alone. I desperately want to sleep, but I can feel the push and crawl in my neck again, so I take a few leaves of hermia from the paper in my pocket and roll them into a ball. Deep breath and I eat it.

Shadows with long arms and legs come from the corners of the room and crowd around my bed. They are made of darkness—only their teeth are glittering and bright. They bend over me and begin to eat my skin with those shining teeth, and I can't move or make a sound. I see my mother and father by the door, whispering together. "I thought as much," says Dek, hovering over my bed, smoke pouring out of his empty eye socket. The shadows peel back my skin, pull open my rib cage. There is something curled up inside the hollow space of my chest—something white and damp and hairless. It unfurls, climbs out of my body, its horrible face grinning. My face on the pillow is cracked like a mask, my body split open like a shell. I wake and lunge out of the bed, screaming, my joints on fire, thunder beating against the inside of my skull, and I throw up violently all over the carpet.

Telegram to Pia Kos, West Spira Grand Hotel, 10th floor: SEND REPORT STOP

Telegram to Lord Casimir, Nago Island: JULIA HAS NOT RETURNED STOP WILL REPORT ONCE SHE IS BACK STOP

Telegram to Pia Kos, West Spira Grand Hotel, 10th floor: FIND HER STOP CHECK HER BODY STOP HOW CLOSE IS SHE STOP

Telegram to Pia Kos, West Spira Grand Hotel, 10th floor: ANSWER ME STOP

DAY 10

WITCH BONES

*I can't say if comfort is the right word
for her voice or her hands holding mine.
But she is there, she stays with me all night.*

FIFTY-ONE

Agoston Horthy's speech will surely be printed in newspapers across Frayne tomorrow, but the crowd that gathers along the river to hear it this morning is formidable. I push my way through the mob and bribe my way onto a riverboat. The wardrobe in my room at the palace was full of dresses that did not fit, so I'm wearing the same grubby dress I wore yesterday. Light and shadow flicker together at the periphery of my vision, and the pain behind my eyes is terrible. Last night's dose of hermia has me wrung out like a rag, aching and dazed, but even so the *nuyi* has climbed another inch up my neck. Wretched, determined little thing.

It's bold of Horthy to appear in person when he knows the city is full of witches and a revolution is brewing. It makes me wonder if assassination might be harder than one would think. I think of him drinking the vinegar tea, the rat savaging his leg while he wrote on, oblivious, and the strange, bloated creature in the woods with him. There is much more to Agoston Horthy than a landowner's son risen to terrible power, that's certain.

"My brothers and sisters," he begins. He doesn't need a bullhorn for his powerful voice to carry over the hushed crowds. "You have seen the death and destruction that witches have wrought in our city. You are afraid, and you are right to be afraid, but I am here to ask you to be brave. I have kept you safe for twenty years, and I will stop at nothing to make this country safe again. The witches that threaten us will be routed from this city, they will be plucked from their hiding places, and you will see them drowned in this very river while I watch."

Applause and shouting. Horthy raises his voice, and the crowd quiets.

"You have heard that Scourge has touched our city again, spread by bewitched rats. Since the last outbreak a decade ago, our scientists have been working night and day to find a cure, and they have developed a new medicine that shows great promise. Rest assured that anyone in the city who develops Scourge, rich or poor, young or old, *will* have access to this new medicine. For now, we are holding the spread of the sickness at bay, though our enemies hoped it would ravage the city as it did before."

A rumbling of rage and he holds up his hand. This is not what Lady Laroche hoped for, but I think she should have predicted how easy it would be for him to manipulate the public.

"Let these dark days serve as a reminder of the threat that

magic poses. I do not mean only this particular group of witches, who seek to put a puppet on the throne and raise up a magical elite. I am talking about magic itself. There are some in this city arguing that magic might be used for good, that it might be used to cure sickness or end drought. Do not be deceived. Witches will never seek to help us—it is not in their nature—but beyond even that, consider the consequences of disruption. We all live with losses we think unbearable. The consequences of altering nature carry far into the future, setting off chains of events and unimaginable further disruptions. We *must* submit to the perfect pattern the Nameless One has created for us. With grace and humility we must accept both the bounty and the losses that life brings us, embrace the mystery and the order that we cannot conceive. If we allow witches to meddle with the perfection of nature, to disrupt the threads of a larger pattern, we risk everything. We cannot allow beings with no souls, no moral compass, to lead our world over a precipice into a madness where anything is possible, where nothing is certain or inevitable, where the destiny the Nameless One has chosen for us is fractured and a thousand dangerous paths all open before us without guidance. We must hold firm in our faith, hold steady our hearts. We will make a new world, a world without magic, where we live and die by the light of the Nameless, accepting our fates and enlarging our souls. Who stands with me?"

The applause is deafening. I should have had the courage to kill him after all. Sweat is pouring down my sides and,

for a moment, I wonder if the hermia has made me feverish, but amid the applause, troubled cries are rising up. The
fellow whose boat I'm on is rowing furiously for the edge of
the river.

"The water!" someone cries out.

Steam thickens the air. A splash scalds my thigh. Arms
pull me out of the boat onto the low path, everybody backing away from the river, surging up the narrow steps. The
river is *boiling*, and the terrible smells on the breeze are the
smells of magic, not my own sickness.

"Do not fear them!" shouts Agoston Horthy. The river
surges and froths, and something lands next to me with a
thunk. It is a bone, vividly white. Another one strikes my
ankle, hot as coal, and I jump away with a cry. People on the
low path are cramming onto the narrow steps, desperate to
get away.

"I am not afraid!" roars Agoston Horthy, while his guards
cower around him. "Hear me, you witches, you demons and
fiends! The Nameless One will shine His light on your per-
version, the disruptions of your bodies and souls, and we
will tear you from the earth, that she might be pure again!"

There is some cheering, mingling with the shouts of terror, as the river spits out the bones of witches. They land
clattering and steaming in piles along the sides of the water,
landing on the barge around Agoston Horthy like so much
debris, and he stands there with his arms outstretched, his
face alight with something almost like ecstasy, shouting over
and over: "I am not afraid!"

FIFTY-TWO

"Try this," says Gennady when I appear on the terrace in Mrs. Och's back garden. He hands me a slice of pie on a porcelain plate.

"Why are you giving me pie?" I ask suspiciously. "Is it poisoned?"

"No," he says, almost regretfully. "I made it under Mrs. Freeley's tutelage. I had not realized the art that goes into making the crust."

"So this is your new calling? You're going to be an immortal chef?" I take a bite. My hermia-wracked stomach rebels immediately, and I hand the plate back to him.

"I am passing the time," he says. "Nobody has asked for my help, except Mrs. Freeley."

"If you want to fight Casimir, *do that*," I say impatiently. "Go find one of the other fragments of *The Book of Disruption* and destroy it! Or look for his queen of the *nuyi* and destroy *that*."

"If I go back, they will tear me apart."

"Then don't go," I say. "Make pie. I don't care. Where is Lady Laroche?"

"I don't know."

My elbow flares and throbs. Then my knee. I leave him with his pie and go inside. Gregor and Csilla are in the parlor, holding hands and glancing nervously at the ceiling.

"Hullo, Julia!" says Csilla. "Stars, your dress is filthy!"

Before I can reply, I hear shouting from above. Lady Laroche's voice.

"What's going on?" I point at the ceiling.

"Lady Laroche and Princess Zara," says Gregor. "They're having an awful row."

"About the twister that tore up West Spira last night?"

"Among other things."

I flop down in a chair opposite them. Gregor grins at me and, as rotten as I feel, I can't help smiling back. Revolution suits him.

"You look awfully well, Gregor."

"I *feel* well," he says. "You're not looking your best, though, if you don't mind my saying so. You all right?"

"For now," I say.

More shouting from upstairs. A door slams, and Gregor jumps a little. Csilla pats his arm. "I'll put on coffee," she says.

She glides out, and he watches her go. When he turns back to me, the anguish on his face gives me a start.

"How is Dek?" he asks.

"I don't know." I think again of the two wineglasses in the cellar of the Marrow, the way he looked like he was dressed for a night out, and then he and Zara dancing in the Twist, slipping out hand in hand. I really *don't* know how my brother is. *I mean to be useful, and I mean to be joyful,* he said. What I want him to say is that he means to *live,* that he will fight to live.

"Csilla never wanted children," says Gregor quietly. "Or rather ... she couldn't. Her own childhood was a kind of hell you can't imagine. And what sort of father would I have been? No better than yours, but still, I think of you and Dek and Wyn as ... well, not my *children* exactly, but ..."

I've never thought of Gregor as any kind of a father figure, but he's been family of some kind for more than half my life now, so I say, "I know what you mean."

He looks relieved. "Well. If there's anything I can do ... for you, or for Dek ... I've been wracking my brain, but I'm such a bleeding useless sod. I couldn't bear it if—"

I cut him off: "I know."

I don't want to hear him say out loud what he can't bear, what I can hardly allow myself to think.

Csilla comes back with a coffeepot and three cups on a tray. I sip at the coffee, but I can barely taste anything, my stomach gurgling its protest. Strig comes leaping into the room with a *yowwwww* like he's shouting *"Surprise!"* and Zara follows. She looks almost as bad as I feel—hair limp around her pale face, dark circles under her eyes.

"Julia. Hello."

"Can we talk outside?" I ask her.

Gregor and Csilla exchange a look, but Zara just nods wearily, and we go out onto the veranda.

"What's between you and Dek?" I ask bluntly.

"Your brother is a brilliant man," she says. "I value his counsel."

"Are you shagging him?"

291

Her face turns prim, and a little pink. "I don't see that that's any of your business."

Oh hounds, she *is* shagging him.

"Fine, it's none of my business. Why are Xanuhans coming to Frayne?"

She glances anxiously back at the parlor. "Keep your voice down."

"Lady Laroche doesn't know about it?"

She looks impatient. "I need allies I can trust," she says. I don't know if this is a dig at Lady Laroche, or at me. "Why don't you go up to her room—knock on her door—and ask her about it?"

"About the Xanuhans?" I ask, confused.

"About whatever you like," she says. "Go on. Knock on her door."

I'm not sure what point Zara is trying to make, but I came here to tell Lady Laroche about Horthy's speech and to make sure she got my message about the war council. Since Zara doesn't look set to tell me anything else, I go upstairs and knock on the door of Mrs. Och's old reading room. There is no reply. I try the knob, but it's locked. I bang on the door and call "Lady Laroche?"

Mr. Faruk comes out of the library, holding a book. "Why are you pounding on the door?"

"Is she even *in* there?"

"It would appear not."

He watches me, smiling, as I take a pin out of my fake hair and jig the lock open. The room is empty, the window wide open.

I go back downstairs, where Zara is sitting in the parlor with Gregor and Csilla now.

"She's not there."

I am trying to think how to say that she might have gone out the window, but Zara just nods and says, "She goes out often, in secret, pretending to be working in her room. She does not want me—or any of us—to *know* she is going out. It makes me uneasy. I know you agree with me, Julia—the rats, Scourge, the hornets, the twister. She is reckless, and there is no talking to her." She pauses, looking at me carefully, and then says, "She can't have gone far yet. She was upstairs a few minutes ago, shouting at me."

I almost laugh. "You want me to follow her?"

Ridiculous—the people in this house supposedly working together but asking me to tail each other. Still, I'd quite like to know where Lady Laroche sneaks off to as well.

"If *you* want to follow her, you should hurry," says Zara.

And she claims she can't bleeding read minds.

FIFTY-THREE

Vanishing is a relief now—anything to give myself a little distance from my poisoned body. Lady Laroche, in a sleek dress and a jaunty hat, is boarding a hackney at the corner of Lirabon Avenue. When the driver shuts her door and turns to climb into his own seat, I recognize Torne. I suppose I shouldn't be surprised. He has worked for the Sidhar Coven for a long time. I'd forgotten that, or failed to consider its significance. I climb onto the luggage rack and hang on as the hackney takes off through the Scola.

Torne drives out to West Spira and stops in front of a grand house near the river. Lady Laroche climbs out, murmuring something to him that I don't catch, and then she strides up the path, letting herself in through a side door.

A housemaid is stoking the oven in the scullery. She looks up when Lady Laroche comes in. For half a second, she looks startled; then her eyes glaze over and she goes back to her work. Lady Laroche passes swiftly through the kitchen and goes down into the cellar. Before a heavy door, she takes a notepad and cartridge pen from her purse and writes something down. Even vanished, I feel a wave of heat from her magic washing over me. The door swings open.

Six women are gathered inside a comfortably furnished room. I take them in quickly. A tall, fair girl is bent over a book next to a white-haired old woman, possibly from Yong-guo. There is an enormous Ishtan woman wrapped in silks and writing in a notebook, her eyes rolled back in her head so only the whites are visible. Another young woman, dark as Mr. Faruk, hair wrapped in a kind of turban, is feeding papers into the fire. Two middle-aged New Porian women are weaving something together in a corner of the room, and one of them calls out "Ariane!" when Lady Laroche comes in, causing the others to pause and look up. The Ishtan in her odd trance comes back to herself, her eyes focusing. The young turbaned woman stops burning paper, straightening up and smiling.

"Hello, my dears!" cries Lady Laroche.

"Some tea, love," says the weaver who first called out, getting up and going to a little stove at one end of the room. She has a foreign accent, but I can't place it. This is a truly international assemblage.

"Thank you," says Lady Laroche, taking off her hat and gloves. "Well done, all of you. That was absolutely *beautiful*."

The blond girl looses an odd, horsey laugh. "I wish I could've seen it." She has a lower-class accent. The sort of girl I might run into in the Twist, though I've never seen her before. "Bet we gave Horthy a scare."

"You gave the whole city a scare," says Lady Laroche. She is different here. Warm, relaxed, not posturing. The mask is gone. I recognize this kind of ease. These are her people, her real crew. "You must be tired."

"We're getting better at working together," says the Ishtan in fluent Fraynish.

"I think so too," says Lady Laroche. "We shall be ready when Zey is dead."

"And the princess?"

Lady Laroche sighs. "She does not trust me. I'm not sure how far she will support us."

"Then why should we support her?" demands the girl in the turban.

The weaver brings Lady Laroche her tea. Lady Laroche squeezes her hand and takes the cup, thanking her before continuing to speak.

"She is still our best chance. She can only be better than

Horthy. I'd hoped she would be a true advocate, but she seems to think she can do this without us. She is cutting me out, keeping secrets."

"Let them fight each other," says the Ishtan. "Let them weaken each other. And then we can topple both."

"No, that would be chaos," says the old woman. "Frayne hates witches too much for our kind to rule outright. This princess is our only chance at change. You really think she would betray us?"

"All I know is that she favors a cautious, conciliatory approach, she does not like the spells we work, and she goes out at night to meet with the other revolutionaries. I intercepted a message she sent to someone in the Twist—written in Xanuhan! It was in code, I could not make sense of it, but why is she sending coded messages in Xanuhan? The Xanuhans have ways of combating spells, it is said."

"What about the vanishing girl, Ammi's daughter?"

"I'm not sure where her loyalties lie," says Lady Laroche.

"She is *Ammi's* daughter," the Ishtan says in an urgent voice. "She would help us! Bring her here and we will talk to her! *She* could find out what the princess intends."

"No," says Lady Laroche. "I'm not bringing her *here*. Nobody must know about this place. Besides, Ammi—well, she was far more secretive than I realized. There is so much she never told me." For a moment, she looks genuinely sad. Then she brightens again. "The princess may yet be . . . if not the friend we'd hoped, something of an ally. If the throne is ours to give or take away and we give it to Zara—first, she will see we mean to work with her, but also she will not be able to deny that she is a friend to witches. She will not be able to put off change by arguing that it must happen piecemeal. We must force her hand, *force* her to acknowledge her alliance with us."

"Difficult to do if she is *not* allied with us," says one of the weavers.

"We'll see," says Lady Laroche. "Let's get to work. Our time is almost come, and we have sisters still suffering in Hostorak."

"I want to begin on the branches," says the fair-haired girl, going over to a pile of fir branches stacked against one wall.

"I'm making progress with our fiery friend," says Lady Laroche, putting down her tea and approaching a steel door at the opposite end of the room. "I'll pay another visit now."

To my amazement, she unties her dress. The Ishtan comes over to undo the stays and helps her out of all her things—dress, corset, petticoats, stockings, and so on—folding it all neatly and placing it on a chair. None of the other witches seems in the least perturbed by their leader undressing before them. Completely naked, Lady Laroche twists the handle of the steel door and swings it open. I mean to follow her, but the incredible blast of heat that comes out sends me reeling back to the far corners of the room. Then she is inside, slamming the door behind her, and I am left trapped in the room with the other six witches. They go back to their tasks—weaving and writing, the smells of their magic a thick, dizzying mix filling the enclosed air of the cellar.

I wait and wait for Lady Laroche, growing hungrier and more desperate. The hours pass, but she does not come back out the steel door, which is buckling slightly from the heat behind it. When at last the Ishtan gets up and bids the others goodbye, I make my escape with her, unsure of when I might have another chance. She goes into the back garden and, to my horror and amazement, writes something on her hand and then collapses, shrinking, the folds of her garments falling to the ground. Out slinks a red fox, and my heart gives a lurch. I watch her slip through the gate and head west, to the outskirts of the city. I make my way around the house, wondering what this place is, but it seems an ordinary house, just an elderly couple and their servants, apparently unaware of the witches gathered in their cellar.

Evening is falling, and I am too worn down and hungry to wait for Lady Laroche or to try to follow the fox. I need a meal, I need a privy, and I need to take more hermia. I go back to the hotel.

FIFTY-FOUR

"Where have you been?"

Pia looks strange. Stranger than usual, I mean. Her white skin is shiny with sweat, and her fingers are trembling.

"Busy," I say. "Are you all right?"

"What am I to tell Casimir?" Her voice rises to a shattering pitch. "You think he will treat you like a cherished pet if you belong to him? You think he will overlook it if you disobey him? He will *destroy* you, but he will do it cleverly and slowly, and it will all be worse, so much worse than you can imagine. You *stupid* fool!" She collapses on the sofa, shaking.

"Do you need a doctor?" I ask anxiously.

"I must send him a telegram," she rasps. "You do not know what it *costs* me . . ." Then she catapults off the sofa and grabs my hair, slamming me against the wall and pulling my head to the side so she can see the *nuyi* halfway up my neck.

"Still . . . moving . . . ," she mutters.

"Barely," I gasp. "I mean, slowly. I'll take more."

"First find Agoston Horthy and tell me what he is doing. You had better hope that it is something interesting," Pia hisses. "Tomorrow evening there will be a dance at the palace. All the talk will be about King Zey's health. Go and report back on how close to death he is."

"Does it matter, at this point? Even with the hermia, I'm either his or it's over in a couple of days! Is he going to take the poison out of Dek?"

She makes a choking sound like a laugh. "Go. Find something for me to tell him."

"Tell him Dafne and Luca are madly in love. Tell him Luca worships Agoston Horthy. Tell him Horthy is closing in on the witches and has the revolution in hand. Tell him Zey is a week from death. Tell him all that."

"Is it true?" shrieks Pia. "I cannot lie to him, Julia!"

"You can tell him that is what I *report*," I shout back.

A knock at the door, and my heart plunges into my dirty satin shoes. We stare at each other, then she draws her knife with a hiss and strides over to the door, swinging it open. I wouldn't want to be on the other side of that door. Indeed, Gregor's face turns almost gray as he backs away from it. His eyes snag on mine.

She jams her knife back into her belt and goes out on the balcony.

"What are you doing here?" I ask.

He looks not right. At first I think it's just the scare Pia gave him. But he is not quite meeting my eyes.

"It's Wyn."

"No," I whisper, everything inside me going icy with dread.

"He's . . . it's not that. He's alive," says Gregor. "But he's been arrested. Esme wants you. Will you come?"

"Of course," I say, and I follow him out, without saying goodbye to Pia.

FIFTY-FIVE

They are gathered in Mrs. Och's parlor: Zara, Esme, Csilla, Mr. Faruk, and, to my bewilderment, Arly Winters. I gather Lady Laroche is not back. A map of a building complex is spread out across the floor.

"How did it happen?" I ask.

"It was last night, after you left," says Arly, her pretty face all puffed up from crying. "Wyn and Lorka were hanging another banner. Then Garny came—he said Torne sent him to help—and Wyn tried to send him off. They got in a fight. Soldiers arrived, and I ran."

"Who's Garny?"

"The fellow with the gray beard," says Esme.

Oh, blast it all. Torne knew full well that Wyn wouldn't work with Graybeard. Why would he send him?

"They are all three in Arrimer," says Esme grimly. The prison for political dissidents. "They're to be hanged at noon tomorrow for treason. I have offered my fortune in bribes, to no avail."

"*Hanged?*" I can barely get the word out, my throat constricting.

The map on the table is a map of the prison, I realize. If there is one thing Agoston Horthy's Frayne has excelled at, it is the building of nearly impregnable prisons. You need someone on the inside to have even a chance of getting a body out of the place. Unless you're me, that is.

"I'll get them out," I say.

Esme looks at me, her eyes terrible. "Can you do it?"

"Yes," I say. I'm reasonably sure of it, anyway. "I can go in vanished."

Here at least is something I can do. A fight I can win.

"How can we help?" asks Esme.

"You can't," I say. "I'll go now. Where's Dek?"

"He is meeting with someone for supplies this morning," says Esme. "He doesn't know yet. We haven't been able to reach him."

Zara rises. "A moment, Julia?"

I follow her onto the veranda, drop into one of the chairs, and let my face fall into my hands. Everything hurts, and I am so tired.

Zara sits next to me, lowering her voice. "Where did Lady Laroche go today? Did you see?"

"It's a house in West Spira, cellar full of witches," I mutter. "Far as I can tell they've cast some kind of spell over the people who live there. But they aren't plotting against *you*. They're worried you won't support them once you've got the throne."

"They want too much too quickly, and they don't care how they get it."

"They're being hunted and drowned. That would make me a little impatient too."

"The Cleansings will stop when I am queen," she says firmly. "But we have to move slowly, and witches who use magic outside the law will be punished. Even in Yongguo, that is true. I too dream of the day when we pull down Hostorak, but we need to plot our course with care."

"Torne is loyal to Lady Laroche," I add. "He took her to the West Spira house."

"Ah," says Zara thoughtfully. "So he knows where the place is."

And Torne sent Garny to stir up trouble with Wyn and Lorka. Why? Did he mean for them to be arrested?

"I'll find Dek and let him know what has happened," she says.

All my despair comes back like a wave that threatens to

pull me right under. Again and again I try to push it down and keep going as the tide rises around me.

"I've got to get the *nuyi* out of my neck soon. I don't know what to do. I don't know how I'm going to help him."

"Zey is going to die any day, and when he does I will claim the crown," says Zara fiercely. "Whatever power I have and however I can use it, I am not going to let your brother die. Frayne needs him."

"I need him!"

Without looking at me, she says, "So do I."

We just sit with that for a moment, and then she says, "The house Lady Laroche went to—what is the address?"

I don't know what the right thing to do here is. I don't know what side I'm on. But I figure I'd best be on the side of the girl who wants to help my brother. So I give it to her.

FIFTY-SIX

The prison is impossible. I can get over the outer wall, but there are no windows, so I can't get inside without raising all hell. I spend half the night waiting for someone to come in or out before giving up and leaving a message for Esme at the Marrow. The hanging will be public, outdoors. I'll make sure that Wyn, at least, doesn't make it to the noose.

When I get to Liddy's in the middle of the night, the bruised young woman with the bandaged arm is there. She looks at me fearfully. Liddy puts a finger to her lips, nodding at the two children curled together by the stove, sleeping. They are terribly thin, such little rags of things, like so many kids around here. Dek and I never looked like that. Too good at thieving to go hungry.

"Julia, this is Flora. A friend."

"Hullo," I say.

Flora looks away and murmurs, "I'd better go."

"You are welcome to stay as long as you wish," says Liddy—but in a perfunctory way, as though she's offered before and been refused.

Flora kneels down gingerly and rouses the two children. They get up like little puppets, used to uncomplaining obedience.

"Julia could see you home," says Liddy. "She'd keep you safe, at least on the way."

"Nobody can keep me safe," says Flora.

"I can," I say. I'm not looking for distractions, but nor do I like to see this woman like a broken bird heading out into the night with her kids. This is a dangerous part of the city for a woman alone.

"Wait in the shop. We won't be long," Liddy tells her. "And remember, you will need to make a decision soon about the matter we discussed."

Flora nods and goes out.

"Let me see it," says Liddy. I show her the *nuyi* in my neck. She hisses between her teeth. "It is getting too close. Can you take a higher dose of hermia?"

"I won't be much good if I do," I say, sick at the thought.

"But I'm not really needed until tomorrow at noon. That would be long enough to get through the worst of it, I reckon."

"I will give you some chorintha to take with it," she says, snipping a few leaves from the packet of hermia and soaking them in boiling water. She rolls the poison into a damp ball and wraps it in paper for me, along with the little capsule of chorintha. "See Flora home. Then get yourself somewhere safe before you take this. The worst will wear off by noon tomorrow. Then take a little more. That should stall it a day. You will only have a day after that, I think."

"Thank you, Liddy."

"Don't let him have you, Julia."

I shake my head. *I won't, I won't.*

I walk Flora and her two small children into the Edge. At one point I say, "How d'you know Liddy?" but she just pulls her children closer and says nothing, so I stop trying to talk to her. There is nobody about. When we come to a row of wooden shacks not far from the cemetery, she whispers to me, "Thank you, now please go away."

I linger outside as she ushers the children into a shack with boarded-up windows. Silence. I watch the place for a few minutes and then turn and head back down the road. There is a figure coming toward me, staggering a little. A big man, heavyset and losing his hair, his face pouchy and miserable with drink. He reeks of cheap liquor. He barely looks at me, meaty hands dangling at his sides. On a hunch I follow him back the way I've come, and indeed, he goes into the same shack. My hands curl into fists. I don't need to rely on hunches to guess he's responsible for the bruises and broken bones of Flora and her children. I hope Liddy's business with Flora involves getting her free of this brute and him getting his just deserts. But whatever that business is, it's not *my* business. I wait outside awhile, but there is no sound, so I turn and go back to the hotel.

FIFTY-SEVEN

At first I think it will be all right—or no worse than what I've already endured. But then the hernia twists itself into a snake in my chest, crawls up my throat, and batters itself against my teeth. I'm strangling on it, hands clamped over my mouth, sweating on the bed.

"It's not real."

Her high, strange voice. I'm burning up, and she washes my forehead to cool me down. Snake after snake uncoils in my chest, each one crawling up my throat so I can't breathe. They force my teeth apart and slither out of my mouth, and I gasp for air while the next one forms. The snakes writhe on the ground, twisting about her legs. I try to point at them, but she repeats, "It's not real," and I have to breathe before vomiting up the next one.

I fall at last into a fretful sleep. I wake because somebody is putting metal rings all over me, around my ankles, my fingers, my neck. He is a large grayish thing, no features on his face besides a sharp-toothed grin. He twists a knob on the wall, and all the rings tighten, cutting into me. My screams burst out of me like live things.

Her metal goggles whirr over me. She tries to give me water from a cup, but it turns to gray sludge, like him, and his horrible mouth is laughing at me over her shoulder.

"There's nothing there," she says. He swings a hatchet at her head, and I lunge off the bed. I'm falling so far, dizzy and spinning through nothing.

He grabs me with a hook, swings me back into the bed, but it is not my bed; it is a pit seething with bugs that bite and suck. There will be nothing left of me by morning.

"There's nothing there. Drink this."

I can't say if *comfort* is the right word for her voice or her hands holding mine. But she is there, she stays with me all night until sleep comes up from under the bed, grabbing me with heavy hands and yanking me down into blessed unconsciousness, punctuated with boiling, painful dreams, my skin cracking, my teeth coming out, my bones splintering. When I wake up, my eyes are crusted, my lips bloody, my throat raw.

"Here."

She offers water. She washes the crust of blood and snot and tears from my face. She feeds me broth from a spoon while the morning light and a summer breeze come through the curtains.

Telegram to Lord Casimir, Nago
Island: HORTHY SECURING BORDERS STOP
DUKE AND DAFNE PROSPECT V PROMISING
STOP NUYI VERY CLOSE STOP JULIA
COOPERATIVE STOP

Telegram to Pia Kos, West Spira Grand
Hotel, 10th floor: I AM COMING TO
SPIRA CITY STOP

DAY 11

THIS DANCE

I see the knife in his hand.
"Can you die like an ordinary girl?" he asks.
"Do you know? Have you ever wondered?"

FIFTY-EIGHT

Arrimer Prison is in the northernmost part of the Plateau. The district gets shabbier the farther north one goes from the train station. Beyond the edges of the city there are pretty villages in the hills, but first you have to pass through a shambling sort of ghost town, empty homes and failing factories. That is where the prison stands, its outer wall looped with barbed wire, guards posted in towers. Just outside the prison is the hanging yard, Deadman's Square, where people gather to watch criminals die. It is not as popular as watching a Cleansing, but it will still draw a crowd.

In spite of the short distance from the prison to the hanging yard, they come in an armored hackney. A small crowd has already gathered. I'm wearing another of the dresses Csilla chose, with a shawl around my shoulders and a bonnet on my head. I've not taken any hermia this morning—I can't do something like this through a fog, or in pain—and the *nuyi* is coming awake, sensing its reprieve, burrowing its way up my neck.

They come stumbling out of the hackney, hands and feet chained. Lorka and Garny look defiant, but Wyn's expression of sick terror tugs at my heart. He's the only one I can be sure of saving—I may not get more than one shot at this—so I vanish right there. A shout behind me—below me—it doesn't matter. I'm up over the square, scattering out above the crowd, and then right down behind Wyn. I whisper in his ear, "Don't be frightened."

He jumps half a foot as I reappear just long enough to grab him. The guards don't have time to react—I see their startled faces and then we are gone, a cry from the crowd following us and fading as we soar, vanished, over the rooftops of Spira City, up and out. I aim us for the Scola.

I've gotten good at this, and it is exhilarating. There is Mrs. Och's house. They've left the back door open, as I asked. I focus on that door. Everything comes into sharp relief. I even manage not to stagger, reappearing in the back parlor, but Wyn stumbles onto his hands and knees.

Esme is crouching at his side, and I am gone already, back over the city, back over the Plateau and Deadman's Square, which has erupted into chaos. The soldiers have their guns out, and the crowd is mobbing closer. I don't see Garny right away, but Lorka is on the ground, a soldier pinning him. If I appear in the middle of this, I'm afraid I might get shot.

I go in anyway, fast. I grab Lorka and vanish. I can hear shots and shouts, but it's as if it's happening in another world. This time I bring us down on Anopine Bridge, because I've somehow got ahold of the soldier who was pinning him as well. I reappear and hit the stunned soldier in the face with my elbow. He reels, dropping his gun, and I am gone again with Lorka.

Wyn is still on his knees in Mrs. Och's back parlor. I drop Lorka in front of him.

"Garny . . . ," says Torne. I hadn't even noticed he was there.

Esme is saying something, but Garny will be dead if I linger. I don't much want to rescue the man who assaulted me—but nor do I want more blood on my hands, and surely that's what it is, if I choose not to save him.

So I go back.

Two soldiers are dragging him to the hackney. He is limp in their arms. I slip two sleeping-serum darts out of the purse tucked in my bodice. A dart in either hand, I jab the two soldiers holding him, each in the back. They fall—more shouts—Garny falling between them, but I drop the darts and catch him, barely reappearing at all, and we vanish. Something sears my side as I disappear. I hear the sound oddly after I feel it. The crack of a gun.

When I return to Mrs. Och's parlor, the pain comes sharp and hot. I've been shot. I am too stunned for a moment to think. I stand there, and the only thought in my head is that if I am standing, it can't be that bad. I don't want to look.

Esme sees the blood soaking my dress and tears the seam open to look at the wound.

"Just a graze," she says, and I'm too relieved even to mind

having my dress ripped open in front of everybody. "Disinfect it and put some dressing on it."

I think she's talking to me at first, and I'm rather annoyed at being ordered to disinfect and dress my own wound, but then Mr. Faruk says, "Of course. Come with me, Julia."

I let Mr. Faruk take my arm. I'm weak-kneed, dizzy, and I don't know if that's the bullet grazing me, the hermia-wracked night, or just the whooshing back and forth, in and out of my body, over the city. But I did it. All three of them are here in the parlor, though Garny might be dead already, sprawled openmouthed on the settee while Torne checks for a pulse. His temple is bleeding badly.

"You really are extraordinary," says Mr. Faruk as we go up the stairs. I can't help grinning at that. Then I notice he's wearing a dress. It's a colorful silk gown of the sort rich ladies wear in the northern Arrekem kingdoms. I'm startled enough that I blurt out: "What are you wearing?"

He raises an eyebrow at me and says coolly, "I wear whatever I like."

I'm hardly going to argue with that. We go all the way up to the little attic room where I used to sleep when I was posing as a housemaid here. Strig is sleeping on the bed in a beam of sunlight. He opens one eye as we come in and hoots like an owl. Then he jumps off the bed and looks around, startled by his own owl noise.

"Who sleeps here now?" I ask.

"I do," says Mr. Faruk. "I like to be high up. Sit on the bed, please."

I obey, still feeling light-headed. He undoes the top of my dress and pulls it right off very matter-of-factly. I think I ought to protest, but honestly I'm just too tired, and he is entirely clinical about it, cleaning the wound as expertly as Esme would have done. I squeeze my eyes shut while he washes it and bandages it neatly.

"Your clothes are covered in blood," he says. "Here, wear this."

He takes another Arrekem dress from a trunk by the wall and turns his back to let me change. The dress is big on me, but not ridiculously so. There is only a small mirror on the wall, showing my face and shoulders, so I can't see how it looks.

"Do you think Garny is dead?" I ask.

"I don't know," he says, sounding supremely indifferent.

I'd like to bask in my success, that thrilling rescue, but I can feel the creep and push and crawl in my neck. I touch the bulge of the *nuyi*.

"It's getting close," he says with a nod.

"I need to take more hermia."

"You can rest here, if you like," he says.

I daren't take as much as last night, but I roll a couple of leaves together and pop them into my mouth. This time the poison hits me like lightning along my spine, and I remember nothing more.

FIFTY-NINE

It is evening, judging by the sky. Mr. Faruk is reading a book by what remains of the light from the window. I am lying on the bed. My tongue feels fat in my mouth when I ask him what happened.

"You had a seizure," he says mildly. "You are taking too much hermia."

I sit up, my side twingeing where the bullet grazed me.

"What time is it?"

"Suppertime."

"Everyone's all right?"

"I do not know whom you mean by *everyone*," he says. "Garny will probably survive. He took a bad blow to the head. Your Esme has a remarkable level of skill for somebody not formally trained in medicine."

"She's had a lot of opportunities to practice."

I stand up, my knees wobbling. The Arrekem dress falls loosely around me.

"It is too big," says Mr. Faruk, smiling at me. "But still, you look very nice. A little like her. Just a little."

"Ammi," I say. Not a question.

He nods.

"Seems everybody knew her. How well did *you* know her?"

"Well enough to like her and to mourn her passing," says Mr. Faruk. "She was brave. Everybody will tell you that—

318

how brave she was. But it wasn't for her courage that I liked her. She had a great heart. You know that, of course. She did not parcel out her love. She gave it whole and unharnessed. She loved her friends. She loved her husband. She loved her children. She loved the *world*. She fought and gave her life because she loved the world. It was love more than courage that drove her. I think perhaps you are the same way."

A knock on the door, and Wyn comes bursting in.

"Brown Eyes," he says, catching me up in his arms. I wince a little because my side hurts, but all in all, his arms are still a good place to be. "I thought I was going to die. Flaming Kahge, I'm *not* ready to die. I never knew I was such a coward!"

"You're not a coward," I say, half-reluctantly pulling out of his embrace. "I don't want to die either."

Something changes in his face as he looks me over. "What are you *wearing*?"

"It's . . . Mr. Faruk's," I say. "My things were ruined."

Wyn stares at Mr. Faruk's dress now.

"I'll give the two of you a minute, shall I?" says Mr. Faruk, and he goes down the narrow stairs.

"Incredible, Brown Eyes. That's the second time you've saved my life, isn't it?"

"Arly said you got caught because you picked a fight with Garny," I say.

Wyn's mouth turns down. "Don't know why Torne sent him! I've told Esme what he did. She fixed him up anyway, since you'd gone to the trouble of saving him, but when he recovers, he's out on his ear, or maybe she'll decide to bust him into pieces after patching him up."

"I don't want anybody knocked around. I've had enough of it to last a lifetime."

"Well, he's got no place in the revolution," says Wyn. "If he's clever, he'll run for it as soon as he can. And before he's well enough for any of us to feel he can take the beating he deserves. Why don't you come down? We're having dinner. Everybody has a million questions for you. Lorka wants to thank you in person."

"Is Dek here?"

He shakes his head. "Haven't seen him."

I'm not in the mood for a crowd right now, and I have to give Pia a report, real or not. I pull open the attic window.

"I wish you'd stop jumping out of windows," says Wyn. "It gives me the creeps."

I grin at him over my shoulder. Then I haul myself out of the window, drop, and vanish.

SIXTY

I find Pia kneeling in front of the window and making a high keening noise.

"Are you praying?" I ask in amazement. She buckles forward on the carpet, and I run to her side. "What's wrong?"

Her mouth is twisted in a horrible grimace. She lies there clinging to herself, knuckles white, fingers clenched on the leather of her jacket, neck straining. Then her goggles swivel, focusing on me.

"Julia," she says, as if she's only just seen me. "Casimir is coming."

"What, here?"

"To Spira City," she says.

Terror chokes me first, but with it comes a tiny spark of desperate hope.

"With his mechanic? Can we get him to operate on Dek?"

"I don't know," she rasps. "Go to this party at the palace. Come back with something I can tell him. Something true. It will be better if he does not arrive angry or disappointed by you."

I'd forgotten the party. And blast it all, if Casimir is coming and *if* there's even the slightest chance he might take the poison out of Dek, I had better be a good little spy just a bit longer. Maybe I *can* convince him the *nuyi* has me—if I let it get a little deeper, just a little deeper. Maybe we can convince him that Dek could be of use. Maybe there's still hope. Hard to find it and hold on to it through my horror at the idea of seeing him again.

"I'll call the maid to help you get ready," mutters Pia. She winces as she drags herself to her feet.

"Is the *nuyi* hurting you? Because I asked you to make a false report?"

"Because my will is pulling hard at his," she says. "It is painful, and also pointless, because it cannot pull loose. And yet I cannot stop it."

She rings the bell for the maid, and I take a moss-green dress with flowers embroidered along the bodice out of the wardrobe.

The maid looks terrified as she ties my stays, not commenting on my gasp of pain, the dressed bullet wound, the red-mud scars. She paints and powders a smooth, blank face over my angry, scarred one until I just look like a girl from a good family going to a party.

Pia gives me a ghastly grin.

"Go," she says. "Dance. Report back soon."

SIXTY-ONE

Sir Victor finds me immediately in the palace ballroom.

"Where have you been?"

"Busy."

"Helping your princess?" he says coldly, and then he sighs. "If something happens to me, will you help Elisha? Get her out?"

"Why should anything happen to you? Seems like you're making everybody happy."

"It won't last," he says, and slips a piece of paper into my glove. "Here is a map to her chambers. Just in case. Please." He looks tired and old.

"All right," I say. "How was your visit to Ibhara?"

"Illuminating. Your princess is a fraud, I'm afraid."

"What do you mean?"

"I mean that she is not Roparzh's daughter. We suspected as much. The real Zara died of a fever in Ishti more than ten years ago. Lord Skaal had already obtained sworn depositions from the Ishtan lord she was living with, his family, and the doctor who tended her when she was ill. Witches tried to heal her and failed, then took her body and burned it after she died. That story has been about for a long time, of course. But now I have confirmed that, after Roparzh's daughter died, the Sidhar Coven found a replacement in Ibhara."

"Replacement?" I echo, my bewilderment turning into a slow-dawning horror.

"Yes. She *is* Fraynish, at least. She is a year older than Zara was. A peasant girl. They chose her for her abilities. She is apparently brilliant—an intellectual prodigy—but beyond that, I'm told this girl can sense a person's true feelings, their *intent*. Such a gift! The witches interviewed her, and shortly afterward her whole family was struck down with Scourge. Witchcraft, the villagers now believe. The witches took her in. They educated her and trained her and brought her up to be queen, but she has no blood claim to the throne at all. She is an impostor. There is no true heir but Luca."

I am cold with shock, unable to even find the right question. Sir Victor's manner changes abruptly, and he bows at Luca, who is approaching with his mother.

"Miss Ella!" cries Luca, too loud and jolly. "Dance with me!"

He pulls me into the crowd.

"Agoston Horthy is insisting we go about our lives as normal, in spite of everything that's happening," he says, holding me closer than he should. "But it's a bit difficult, isn't it?"

"I suppose."

He laughs harshly. "*You're* not frightened. You've got something else on your mind. Your cook's daughter, no doubt. Sick with worry?"

"Yes, I'm worried."

"I can't believe I fell for that," he says, his voice almost a growl. "You look nothing like you did the other night, nor even like you did the first time I met you, or when we went riding. You're always in disguise, but I'm not sure *which* Ella is the disguise. Perhaps all of them!"

"You ought to have other things on your mind besides what I look like."

"I really ought to! I visited old Zey again today. He's making no sense. He looks terrible. What an end for a king. But that fading away is the best-case scenario for all of us. What a thing, to be human! I don't know how to rule a country. I just want to write poems and go riding and find a nice girl."

"A *nice* girl?" I say. "Why are you chasing me, then?"

"Very well. A fascinating girl," he says. "Maybe I *want* a girl with secrets—but I want a girl who tells them to me. I want a girl who can fall off a horse and act like it's nothing, who can hide behind a curtain and disappear, who wanders the city in the middle of the night and tells tremendous lies and eats like a man and dances like a clumsy child. I really don't know—can *you* imagine what I see in you?"

"Not a bit," I say, dizzy. "Are you spinning me this much on purpose?"

"There's a trick to not getting dizzy," he says. "I'd like to kiss you."

"That's not the trick, is it?"

"No. Just me wishing out loud. Can we talk somewhere private? I promise I'm not trying to ruin your reputation."

"I can't sneak off in private with you."

"But you can go to the Twist at midnight! You didn't think anything of coming to my room last week."

"Stop turning me about so much. You're holding on too tight. People are staring at us."

"People are staring at me all the time," he says savagely. "They are staring at you because I'm dancing with you."

"Not only that. Because you're hanging on to me like we're lovers, you have this terrible expression on your face, you're dancing like a maniac, and I can't dance at all. We're making a scene."

"I don't care."

"I'm the one with the fragile reputation, if you remember."

"I don't think *you* care."

"My uncle might."

"Please let me kiss you."

"Not *here*."

"But somewhere?"

"Stop it."

I pull free of him and stumble over to Sir Victor. Luca follows but is waylaid by someone, and I don't know if I'm relieved or not. I feel flushed and giddy, and then his mother is leaning over me.

"Leave him alone," she says quietly.

I give her a startled look. She smiles over my head at Sir Victor, moving the topic on smoothly to the music: "We do not have such talented musicians playing for us on Corf, to be sure."

Having broken free of whoever accosted him, Luca joins us.

"Another dance, Ella?" His expression is caught between defiance and pleading. "I think we're getting better."

I bite back a tart reply, and then my heart plunges. Behind the duchess, Lord Skaal is heading straight toward us. I can't vanish in front of everybody—not without blowing my cover entirely and putting Sir Victor in danger—although I suppose that is what is going to happen, anyway, once Lord Skaal gets a sniff of me.

"Sir Victor," says Lord Skaal, smiling toothily. "Is this your niece? Somebody told me she was dancing with our Duke Everard."

Blast him, *blast* him for drawing attention to me. I hadn't known Lord Skaal was here or I'd never have let Luca make such a spectacle of me. I wouldn't have come at all.

"Yes, this is my niece," says Sir Victor. "Ella, may I introduce Lord Skaal."

I offer my gloved hand, my knees shaking, and Lord Skaal

bends over it. His nostrils flare. His yellow eye flicks up to meet mine.

"Ah," he says softly. "May I have this dance?"

Without waiting for my reply, he yanks me with him into the sea of dancing bodies.

SIXTY-TWO

"What an unexpected pleasure," says Lord Skaal, and all I can see is wolf in his long jaw, his gray sweep of hair, the yellow eye, the yellow teeth.

He is better at leading me in a dance than Luca. I don't know the steps, but I skip my feet along as fast as I can, and he practically lifts me off the floor with every turn.

"Earlier today, three traitors sentenced to hang were rescued by magic from Deadman's Square," he says conversationally. "There were glimpses of a person—in a dress and bonnet, no less!—who disappeared and reappeared. A soldier holding on to one of these vermin described a sense of losing his body, being pulled right out of it, seeing the city far below, and then being left suddenly in a different part of the city seconds later. Witchcraft is everywhere right now and people are frightened. Some who witnessed the rescue described glimpses of a creature, half girl, half demon. A long tail, coils of dark hair escaping from the bonnet, a scarred face."

"A long tail?" I manage to say.

"Fear has a powerful effect on the memory. You should hear some of the descriptions of *me* floating around."

He spins me out and pulls me back in, dragging his thumb under my glove so it presses on the hot silvery disk left behind by the *nuyi*.

"I thought so," he hisses between his teeth.

I can disappear anytime. I keep telling myself that. Surely he isn't going to kill me in front of everybody. Still, my cover is blown, so that's that. I feel a pang of sadness at the thought of never seeing Luca again.

"Why are you taking poison?" asks Lord Skaal.

"What?"

"I smell hermia on your breath. Hermia was used against the *nuyi*."

He slides one hand up my neck and presses on the *nuyi*. He is bending over me so close it must look as if he's going to kiss me, spinning me so fast I think I'm going to be sick. I really *am* a spectacle tonight, hazily aware of the scandalized looks we're attracting.

"You are employed by Casimir," he says. "But his hold on you is not finalized yet, and you do not want it to be. Fascinating. You are spying on Horthy, I assume. What does Casimir think he'll uncover? And if you do not *want* to belong to Casimir, might you entertain an offer from the other side? Agoston Horthy does not require one's entire will. He pays well, and you can walk away whenever you want. You would be free."

"I'll think about it when I hear an offer from Horthy himself," I say.

"Shall I arrange a meeting?"

"If he wants one."

I'm just stalling, and a little bit curious. What kind of offer would Agoston Horthy make to a girl like me? What might I say to him, face to face? *You signed my mother's death sentence.* And then? I still have the poison Lady Laroche gave me, meant for him.

"Of course, if you're rescuing revolutionaries of the kind that disappeared today, I suppose you already have a second employer. Unless *Casimir* is supporting the revolution? One can never be sure, with him." His breath in my ear is hot and damp. "Have you heard that Dafne Besnik has been stricken with Scourge?"

"Dafne?" I cry, in spite of myself.

"Such an indiscriminate, vicious attack. It's a horrible disease. Have you known anybody touched by Scourge?"

"I grew up in the Twist," I say. "A good quarter of the people I knew as a child were killed by it. It affected poor neighborhoods most of all, remember."

"And I suppose this is different and therefore just," he sneers. "But Dafne is innocent."

I think of Lady Laroche saying, *You might as well talk to me of unicorns.*

"What a puzzle, what a puzzle," he murmurs. "You smell like a girl, just a girl. But a girl who can vanish, working for Casimir, taking poison to protect her will from him, and working for revolutionaries as well, but not a witch—I can smell a witch easily. Perhaps you are like me. Some strange mix."

"I don't know what I am," I tell him honestly.

"Ah," he says. "That is hard."

There is something almost like empathy in his one yellow eye, which throws me off balance. Not that I need my balance. He is holding me fast, and my toes are barely skimming the floor.

"We received some interesting intelligence today," he continues. "We have been searching in vain for a group of witches hiding out near West Spira. Suddenly the address comes to us by messenger! A house by the university. An old couple lives there with their servants, but they were all under a spell, and do you know what we found in the cellar?"

My heart drops. *Oh, Zara—did you really betray them to Agoston Horthy?*

"I don't know," I say, my mouth dry.

"I think you do," he murmurs. "We flooded the cellar. I imagine that will put an end to the trouble in West Spira. We've found witches in the forests to the south, the mountains to the east, and the villages to the north. I'm sure there are more, but not enough of them anymore, not organized enough, and the witches in West Spira were at the heart of this magic-making."

"What a triumph for you," I choke out.

"Agoston Horthy was pleased. I wish I could thank our mysterious source." He feels my rabbiting pulse with a brush of his fingertips and continues: "Your uncle is an interesting man. He's very effective, though it turns out he has fingers in some other pies as well. Something will have to be done about those fingers, and those pies."

I try to look around for Sir Victor, but I can't see him.

"Are you fond of him?" asks Lord Skaal.

"He's a good man," I say, though I can't really be sure that's true. Perhaps Lady Laroche is right about the choices he's made. I've been spared the gruesome details of what he's done to save his daughter.

Lord Skaal sighs. "I hadn't expected you to *actually* be a naïve young girl. A man cannot serve Agoston Horthy for years without committing terrible acts. But, in the end, it's an eat-or-be-eaten world, isn't it? Sometimes I think I should rather go and join the wolves, but they have their own conflicts, and there are pleasures in being human that I cannot quite bring myself to give up. All of it is just so *interesting*. You, working for Casimir and perhaps also for Lady Laroche—do you think you can serve either one for long without committing atrocities yourself? Perhaps you've already had a hand in deeds you shudder to think back on."

Theo, Theo, Theo.

"I see I've hit the mark there. I don't think you're a good bet for Agoston Horthy after all. You wouldn't be reliable, and there's no way to keep an eye on you."

He lets go of me suddenly, and I see the knife in his hand.

"Can you die like an ordinary girl?" he asks. "Do you know? Have you ever wondered?"

"Lord Skaal!" shouts a man in uniform, racing through the crowd. "Lord Skaal! You are needed!"

The knife flashes toward me, and I vanish, back and back, out over the dancing crowd. Shouts of alarm go up from those who were watching us—a good many. Lord Skaal is

331

left alone on the dance floor, the knife disappearing back into his sleeve. He turns toward the uniformed man, who has stopped in his tracks. From my vanished vantage point I search for Sir Victor, but I can't find him. There is Luca at his mother's side, though—one hand gone to his heart and all the color drained from his face, staring at Lord Skaal and the place where I was. Lord Skaal leaves the ballroom at a brisk pace, as if nothing has happened, the man in uniform whispering in his ear as they go.

Sir Victor's chambers are empty. So is his office.

I leave a note in Luca's room, using some paper and a quill I find at his desk among his rough drafts of poems, mostly crossed-out lines and lists of rhymes.

I'm sorry, I write, and then I don't know what else to say, so I just leave it on his pillow, unsigned.

SIXTY-THREE

"Julia! You frightened me!"

Zara lowers the pistol. Hounds, she must sleep with one hand on it, she had it pointed at me so fast when I climbed through her window.

"I need to talk to you," I say.

She pulls her hair out of her face, fixing me with her clear gaze. "In the middle of the night?"

"Right now."

She gets out of bed and takes a robe from a hook on the wall, wrapping it around her. She slips her feet into a pair of fur slippers. She has pretty, tiny feet—the only princess-like thing about her.

"Let's go down and fix some coffee," she says.

She boils water in the scullery, sets about grinding the coffee beans, and I think of how I once marveled at a princess doing such things, dishes and laundry, simple labor. But of course, she's not a princess. She's just a peasant girl from the coast. She was probably raised carrying water and firewood and taking care of the hens.

"How did your parents die?" I ask, as the smell of freshly ground coffee fills the scullery.

She turns and studies me.

"Oh," she says. "You're *very* angry."

"If you can really see my intentions, you know I'm not going to hurt you. But I want the truth."

"Scourge," she says.

"Haven't you wondered if it was really an accident?"

Her expression shifts subtly. For the briefest of moments, a startling rage surfaces and is submerged again. She, who can read people so easily, knows all too well how to mask her own feelings. I can't tell if I was meant to see that flash of anger or not. I have the feeling she knows how to play people better than I will ever be able to keep up with.

"I had doubts, sometimes," she says. "Some witches were afraid of me, of what I might see or know; I saw and knew only that. But everyone who knows what I can do is a little afraid of what I might sense. Including you."

"Tonight somebody told me that your family was offed by witches. And now you see they *can* manufacture Scourge."

"Not manufacture," she says faintly, steadying herself on the counter. I narrow my eyes at her. How much is a performance? "But they *can* direct it, it would appear. Like weather, like water, they do not create it, but . . ." She trails off, busies herself with preparing two cups of coffee.

"What are you *doing*?" I half shout. "Why did you betray the witches to Agoston Horthy?"

"Hush," she snaps, suddenly fierce. "You will get me killed."

"But it *was* you. *Why?*"

"They were dangerous and uncontrollable. Witches who *murder* must still pay by drowning! They were harming and *killing* the very citizens I am meant to rule over!"

"*Meant* to rule over? You're just some girl from Ibhara!"

I swear her eyes flicker to the big knives hanging on the wall—but then she composes herself.

"Are you going to tell the others?"

"Of course I am!"

"Dek?"

"Yes."

"Julia, hear me out. Look at this country. Look at what Agoston Horthy and King Zey have *done* to this country!"

"Duke Everard might be different," I say.

"He won't be different. He is just a stupid boy, and ruthless, clever men will make use of him as king. You know what I can do. I have spent my life preparing for this. Do you really believe, deep in your heart, in the blood right of rulers? I can make a new Frayne. I have known witches more than half my life now. I know that they do not deserve to die, every one of them, simply for being what they are. I know they do not choose it. I know that unnatural powers *can* be used for good. I know that Frayne can be great and just. *Why* do I have the power I do, if not to make the world better? This is my chance and I shall *take it* and you will not stop me. If you try, you will be my enemy, and you would be surprised at the allies I have. If you tell Lady Laroche about the witches in West Spira, she will kill me, you know that. And then what will happen to Frayne?"

I am breathless at this verbal assault, the threats and pleas strung together at such speed and with such intensity.

"You can't just . . . *pretend* to be queen! What will happen to Duke Everard?"

"Exile, if he accepts it. Execution, if not. I am not playing games, Julia. I am talking about the greater good, for Frayne and for the *world*. I want you on my side."

"Does anybody else know you're not the real Zara?"

"Only a few witches."

"Lady Laroche?"

She nods.

"Esme thinks she's fighting for Roparzh's daughter."

Anxiety flickers across her face. She's got no revolution without Esme, and she knows it.

"We can make a better world. Don't take that away from the people of Frayne because of some misguided notion about bloodlines."

"It's not the bloodlines," I say. "It's not that."

I don't know what it is. The lying and the manipulation. The murder. I need to think. I need to talk to Dek.

"Let *me* tell Dek," she says. "Please."

"You'd better tell him quick, then."

"I will go to him before daybreak. Make me one promise? Talk to *him* before you do anything else and before you go to Esme. Listen to *him*, if you won't listen to me."

I feel a deep, cold flash of anger. "Are you so sure he'll see things your way?"

"Dek is very intelligent."

"He's my brother." I don't know what I'm trying to say. He's *mine*. He's on *my* side. "You'd better tell him *everything*," I add.

She puts a finger to her lips.

The side door opens and in comes Lady Laroche. Her face is terribly white, her eyes blazing with a strange light.

"Well," she says, a bit breathlessly, looking from me to Zara and back again. "What are you two scheming about in the middle of the night?"

"Dafne Besnik has Scourge," I snarl at her.

"The bloody Besniks," she says. "I've always hated them. But don't worry, if you *are* worried—she'll get the antidote. Nobody that rich is going to die of Scourge."

"She knows," says Zara. "About me."

"Ah," says Lady Laroche. "How?"

336

"Sir Victor," I say.

Lady Laroche picks up one of the cups of coffee we've left sitting out, ignored, drinks half of it, and puts it back down on the counter with a clatter, so that the remaining coffee sloshes over the side.

"Torne betrayed me," she says in a distant voice, staring at the knives on the wall.

I remember Zara noting that Torne knew the address of the witches in West Spira, and I have a horrible feeling she intended Lady Laroche to blame him.

"My friends ... some of the most powerful witches in New Poria and beyond ... they came to Frayne because I *asked* them to come." Lady Laroche's eyes are flitting about in an alarming way, not resting on either of us, on anything. "Now they are dead. Drowned in a cellar. *Nobody* knew their hiding place besides me and Torne."

"Torne?" says Zara. "That is a surprise. He has always been loyal."

I want to get out of here, away from these awful people, but I can't move.

Lady Laroche stares at the counter, and then looks at Zara. "Perhaps he formed other alliances."

But she cannot read Zara's mind the way Zara can read hers.

"I am sorry," Zara says. "Whatever our differences, I would not have wished them dead."

She sounds so sincere, I almost believe her myself. It's terrifying what a good liar she is. I could tell Lady Laroche right now that it was Zara who betrayed her, but I don't.

Not because I want to protect Zara, but I don't want to be responsible for her death either. And I resent that Zara must know this, surely knows all my feelings as I stand here next to her.

"Well, never mind. Guess where I've been?" says Lady Laroche, suddenly smiling. *Hounds, she's mad.* "I've just burned Hostorak to the ground."

"Burned?" says Zara faintly. "Hostorak cannot be burned. It is stone."

Lady Laroche laughs, as if Zara is being witty. My knees go weak.

"Things are coming to a head," she says. "Julia, I'm so glad you're here. I need to speak to you about your brother and the *nuyi*. We are almost out of time. Will you come upstairs?"

We leave Zara chewing her lip in the scullery. Lady Laroche lights the lamp in Mrs. Och's reading room, humming to herself.

"Did you really burn Hostorak?" I ask, remembering how Lord Skaal was called with such urgency from the party at the palace.

"Yes. You must approve of *that*, at least."

I sit opposite her, Mrs. Och's desk between us, staring at her too-pale face, her eyes sparking with some awful energy. She takes a pen out of the desk—the pen with feathers at the end—and begins writing something rapidly on a piece of paper, talking at the same time. I tense, ready to vanish, but I don't smell any magic.

"You know, Zara—the *real* Zara—was not a very bright girl," she says. "It was disappointing. By the time she was seven, it was obvious to all of us that she was stupid and temperamental and would make a terrible queen. I can't pretend I was so very sorry when she took ill and died. Hereditary rule just makes for inbreeding and all kinds of unqualified people wielding unmitigated power. Not that I am for the idea of a republic either of the sort they used to have in Gyesa. People are too stupid, by and large, to choose good rulers. Look at the world's most successful empires. The Eshriki Phars, or the Yongguo Empire. Empires either ruled by witches or in cooperation with them. Does our power not set us apart?"

"I'm not a witch, remember," I say coldly.

"You are special, Julia. That is what I am talking about. And Zara is special too. We *chose* her from thousands of girls of the right age because of her talent, her intelligence, her particular gift. The kind of country she will rule— Ammi would have thrived in such a country; she gave her life trying to bring it to fruition. This girl is our best chance at changing everything. She is young. If she lives a long life and rules well, she will leave behind her a country that is completely different, *better* than this one."

She is still jotting notes and talking at the same time. Something shifts, and I blink. "What?"

"Everything might be different," she says. My arm stings, and I have this odd feeling of time having skipped ahead.

"Don't act rashly," she continues. "You may not like my

tactics, but we share the same ultimate goal and should be working together, *helping* each other."

"But it's a lie," I say faintly. Something is not right here. Something has happened, but I can't put my finger on it. "And her name isn't Zara. What is it?"

"That is her name now," says Lady Laroche firmly. "Now, we need to remove the *nuyi*. It is getting too close. Surely you recognize how dangerous you will be to all of us if Casimir controls you."

"No," I say. "Casimir is coming to Spira City. If I can convince him . . . there might be a chance he'll have his mechanic take the poison out of Dek."

"Casimir is coming?" She blanches and sits up straighter. "Are you sure?"

"That's what Pia told me."

She looks suddenly exhausted. "My best hopes are coming to nothing," she says, and tosses her pen childishly across the room. "Zara might be better than Zey, but by how much? Witches are *dying*, and we cannot wait for change. You understand, don't you, Julia? Ammi could not stifle who she was or cease to fulfill her potential. That is itself a sort of death, a slow kind of drowning. I am tired. I have been fighting for so long, and now my friends are dead, murdered by that fanatic . . ."

She falls silent. I can't sit here with the knowledge of what Zara has done weighing on me. And I need to take more hermia if I'm going to hold out until Casimir arrives. I stand up. She looks at me bleakly.

"Where are you going?"

I am done with these horrible people. I am done a thousand times over. I am never coming back to this house. I just leave, without saying goodbye.

SIXTY-FOUR

The elevator goes clank-clanking up. In the main room of our hotel suite, Pia stands with her head bowed over a metal box on the table.

"What's that?" I ask, closing the door behind me.

The goggles swivel as she looks up.

"Sir Victor's head," she says.

My knees go loose, and I lean back against the door.

"Is that a joke?"

"No. Look."

"No," I say. But I have to look. I have to know.

I peer into the box and spin away again immediately, but the image is already seared in my mind: blood pooled and congealed along the bottom of the box like a cushion for his head, his whitish-gray face, eyes wide and mouth open. I lurch to the bathroom and throw up in the tub. Sinking to the floor, all I can think through the buzz in my skull is that it's my fault.

Pia puts the lid back on the box.

"Agoston Horthy just had it delivered as a gift for Casimir," she says. "I am amazed at the gall of him, especially when he is facing a threat to his power."

"I don't know how seriously he takes the threat," I say

hollowly. *Oh, Sir Victor. I am so sorry.* And then I remember his daughter, Elisha. I promised him I'd help her if anything happened to him. I have a map to her room tucked into my glove.

"Is it true about Hostorak?" I ask from the floor.

"Come and see."

She helps me to my feet, and we go out onto the balcony. Beyond the palace, there is a flaming hole in Spira City, so bright it leaves spots on the inside of my eyelids. That is no natural fire. The entire prison is gone.

"The witches inside simply walked out of the fire," she says. "The guards were burned alive, along with anyone who got close."

"How?"

"Nothing burns stone except dragon flame, according to the old stories, but there have not been dragons in the world for a thousand years or more."

I remember the steel door buckling with heat in the cellar in West Spira. Lady Laroche mentioning her fiery friend.

"She's got a dragon," I whisper. I'm not sure if it's a statement or a question. Pia's goggles swivel at me.

"I have to go," I say, and she follows me back inside.

"Be careful, Julia." She raps on the box with Sir Victor's head inside. "Casimir is on his way, and Agoston Horthy is not playing games."

"Elisha," I whisper.

The girl sits up in her bed. She stares at me, her big eyes filling with alarm.

"I'm a friend of your father's," I say.

"Why are you in my room?"

"Your father asked me to help you." Hounds. How am I going to tell her that he's dead? "You're not safe."

I don't know what I was expecting, but I am entirely taken aback when she picks up a bell at her bedside and rings it wildly.

"Stop it!" I hiss at her, trying to grab the bell, but she leaps off the bed and runs for the door, still clanging the blasted thing. I catch her, and she screams.

"What are you doing?" I cry, clapping a hand over her mouth.

"I know what you are!" she shouts into my hand. "I know all about you and my *father!*"

"I mean to get you *out* of here. Somewhere safe."

The door opens, and Lord Skaal saunters in. Elisha tears herself out of my grasp, running to his side.

"You were right," she says in a trembling voice. "She came."

"These people are not your friends!" I cry.

"They *saved* me—from the demons within." Her face goes soft and damp like a balled-up rag, her eyes filling with tears.

"We are very much her friends," says Lord Skaal. "Agoston Horthy has been like a father to dear Lisha for years now. A *real* father, not the kind who's always running off on peculiar missions and stabbing his friends in the back. And indeed, she's been taught how to use her curse for good, her soul having been cleansed of its wickedness."

"Elisha, your father has been murdered, probably by this man here!"

"She's quite right," he says mildly. "But I told you, didn't I?"

Elisha's expression does not change. Lord Skaal's one eye narrows at me. "I was hoping to finish our conversation earlier, but I was interrupted by an incident at Hostorak. Where were we? Oh yes, I was about to kill you."

And then he is a wolf. There is barely a second for the transformation. He is enormous, silver fur bristling, with one yellow eye and one eye scarred over. He leaps, and I vanish—right out of the window, over the city. Shaking outside Marek and Son in the Twist, I can still feel his hot breath on my face. I bang on the door of the clock shop.

SIXTY-FIVE

Theo and Ragg Rock are there to greet me when I emerge from the half-real wood. Theo is brandishing a windup soldier in a fur hat and coat, a sword carved against the side of its leg. When he twists the knob on its back, its wooden arms and legs swing jerkily. Jigging with delight, he sets it walking along the path in front of us until it topples onto its face. Its little arms and legs keep moving after it falls, making it pivot awkwardly on the path. He runs to set it right again, twisting the knob expertly with his fat little fingers.

"Where did that come from?" I ask Ragg Rock.

"Serpetszo."

"The capital of Rossha? They really went there?"

She shrugs and says something to Theo in their private pidgin language.

"Stay wif Lala," he says firmly, grabbing my hand and hugging the soldier with his other arm. The look Ragg Rock gives me with those almost-real pebble eyes chills me.

"I can't stay long," I say. "I just need to talk to Frederick."

We walk up the hill to the hut. Frederick is hunched over his papers, George the rabbit nestled against the warmth of his leg. Theo gives the rabbit a stroke and then sets his soldier walking along the Kahge side of the hut, Ragg Rock shadowing him.

"What's the news?" Frederick asks eagerly. It's still a shock to see him each time—like a ghost of himself, the color and vigor leached out of him.

"Casimir is coming to Spira City," I say, squatting next to him.

He sucks in a sharp breath. "That cannot be good."

The thought of it fills me with dread, but I am still clinging to my pathetic plan. "It might work in our favor—if I can get him to take the poison out of Dek. If the *nuyi* is close enough, if we can persuade him my will is bound and that Dek could be useful too . . . I think his mechanic *liked* Dek."

He nods, but I can tell he's unconvinced. And he's right—the odds are against us, and Casimir would not be coming on a mercy mission.

"How goes the revolution?" he asks.

I don't know where to begin, but once I do, I don't know where to stop. It all comes pouring out of me—Sir Victor's murder, Elisha's defection, the Scourge antidote, Zara betraying Lady Laroche, Zara not really being Zara at all, Hostorak reduced to a flaming hole in the ground. Something like panic is tightening in my chest as I tell him everything.

"Does Professor Baranyi know about Zara?" he asks gently.

"I don't think so. We've mostly been avoiding each other. I'm not having cozy chats with him about the situation, anyway."

Frederick is quiet for a while, thinking, and somehow that calms me down. I know I can trust Frederick's judgment of what is right, what matters.

"My feeling at the moment is that if there is an opportunity to oust Agoston Horthy, we must take it," he says at last. "I don't know what to say about Zara, but if people believe she is the lawful heir . . . it's possible she could unite Frayne and bring about real change."

"But she's just some girl from Ibhara, Frederick! She doesn't *belong* on the throne!"

"Nobody belongs on a throne. When Agoston Horthy came to power and changed the face of Frayne, those who opposed him failed to act soon enough. We make the world with our inaction as much as with our actions. I do not like our choices either, but still I think we cannot let this chance to rid Frayne of Horthy pass us by."

"I won't help Zara. I need to save my brother and get this thing out of my neck."

"And if you succeed? Then what?"

"Then—I figure out how to stop Casimir. Either destroy the other book fragments or kill him. Then you and Theo can come home." I lower my voice here, so that Ragg Rock and Theo don't hear me. "I'm not helping the revolution. It's a fraud, the whole thing. I just want the people I love to make it through this alive."

"It's all very well to try to save the ones you love, but they still have to live in the world, along with all the people you *don't* know or love," he says. "You are going to have to decide where you stand, even if it means choosing the lesser of two evils."

"Hounds, Frederick, I can barely think straight. If you think Zara's the best bet for Frayne, I won't stand in her way, but I'm not helping her either. Look at this thing!" I show him the *nuyi* in my neck—an inch below my ear.

"I've found some interesting things about the *nuyi* and Casimir," he says, hunting through his stack of books and papers and pulling out a few pages of cramped writing in an unfamiliar script. "Ragg Rock let me and Theo go to the great Rosshan library in Serpetszo. It is incredible, this place as a potential doorway to anywhere in the world! I was able to copy parts of the diary of a witch who worked with the Xianren—and Casimir in particular—to defeat the *nuyi* a thousand years ago. Look—here is an illustration of the *nuyi* queen they captured! It is life-sized, so you can see why only the soldiers can enter the brain."

He hands me an illustration of a spider-shaped thing about the size of my palm, with hundreds of tentacle-limbs spread out around it, and what appear to be tiny crab-claw pincers at the ends of the tentacles.

"It is described as translucent and flexible, a sort of jelly-fish consistency, but able to move very quickly on land. The Rosshans and Casimir did all kinds of experiments. The *nuyi* queen seemed able to understand and even manipulate the experiments it was subjected to. It gives off a kind of pulse, and the witches theorized that this was how the queen communicated with her foot soldiers. They are bound to her, however far they or the vessels carrying them travel."

"What does the diary say?"

"I'm struggling with the translation. The dictionary I bought in Serpetszo is not very good and is missing pages! I ought to go demand my money back." He laughs feebly, and I just stare at him. "Sorry. It used to be that the foot soldiers sought out apex predators, but eventually the *nuyi* began to focus on humans in particular, the more powerful the better. The will to power, more than survival and reproduction, is what compels them. When I say they are bound to the queen, I mean their very lives. When the queen dies, so does the entire nest."

"What about the queens? How long do *they* live?"

"Nobody knows. Casimir was particularly interested in the pulse the queen gives off and how she controls her soldiers. This witch complains at length in her diary that the Xianren were supposed to be destroying the *nuyi*, wiping them from the earth, but that Casimir was mostly intent on understanding them. She claims—though the claim is unsubstantiated anywhere else—that he forced her to put the queen inside his own head."

"*What?*" I shout.

"We can't be sure it's true, but we know he controls the *nuyi* somehow, and he took with him an entire nest when he left Rossha. He has found a way to replace the queen himself, whether by putting her physically inside him or by some other means. History shows that he broke with his siblings after that, and his pursuit of power became more marked—beginning with his involvement in the Sirillian Empire and the hunting down of Marike. If it *is* in his head, it may have effected some change in him. Or perhaps the change in him came first, and that is why he decided to put it in his head. There's no way of knowing."

"Hang on—Casimir is being *controlled* by some power-hungry blob that looks like a cross between a jellyfish and a giant spider?"

"I think it's unlikely he would have simply surrendered his will to the *nuyi*, but it is irrelevant whether he controls the queen or the queen controls him or if there is some sort of mutual cooperation. If it *is* in his brain, and if you could kill it, that would be the end of his power over you and anyone he has bound with the *nuyi*."

The mechanic. *Pia.* My freedom and theirs.

Except I can't touch him.

"He's coming to Spira City," I say again, slowly.

Frederick waves the papers unhappily. "None of this tells us how to defeat either Casimir *or* the *nuyi*."

"It's something," I say.

If Casimir isn't coming to take the poison out of Dek, I need to find a way into his skull.

DAY 12

BLOOD THIEF

"This would all be different if Mrs. Och had lived,"
he says, and I think, Well, that's my fault—
he'll be singing that same tune forever,
and it's my fault.

SIXTY-SIX

In Agoston Horthy's room, my hand trembles as I open the packet of poison Lady Laroche gave me five days ago. I think of Sir Victor's head in the box, my mother on the barge years ago, the Gethin murdering innocents, the way this country has cowered and suffered since before I was born. I think of Elisha. I pour the sand-colored powder into his water jug. It fizzes and dissolves.

Then I wait. I keep seeing him come in, but these are only visions from the hermia I took this morning—I can tell because he walks straight through the door without opening it, and also by the strange grin on his face. I've never seen Agoston Horthy smile. These grinning, half-translucent Horthys come in, drink, and then dissolve into a gray sludge at my feet, reminding me of the gray-sludge monster that tortured me during the worst of my hermia-plagued nights. I squeeze my eyes shut and succumb to feverish half-dreams of witches falling off a barge into the sky, falling and falling, my mother's white nightgown billowing, the Ankh-nu in her hands, white smoke pouring out of its two spouts.

I wake to the sound of a key in the door, and for a disorienting moment I'm not sure if I'm vanished or not. I am *not*. I pull back only just in time as Agoston Horthy—the real Horthy, not a hallucination—comes into the room. He goes to the corner and kneels, facing the wall and clasping his hands together in prayer.

I'm going to watch him die. Not because I want to watch, but I refuse to do this thing and be too squeamish to see it happen. This is my third murder. The Gethin. Mrs. Och. Agoston Horthy. If all goes well, it will not be my last— Casimir is coming—but it will not be said that I ever looked away.

Horthy rises after a long while. He goes to his desk and pours himself a glass of water. My heart stutters, but instead of drinking it he puts it down on the desk. Some part of me is relieved, but mostly I can't stand the wait, knowing what will happen. He unlocks a drawer and takes out the picture frame I saw him looking at before. As he opens it, a sharp knock at the door makes us both jump. Every human thing he does—like startling at a sound—makes me horribly aware of what I am doing, makes me second-guess it all over again. I'm still not sure I can let him drink the poisoned water. I'm not sure. *The Gethin. The Cleansings. The Hangings. My Mother. My Mother. My Mother.*

He shuts the frame and slips it into his pocket before calling out: "Come in!"

Lord Skaal enters. I pull back farther, out of my body. I

can see them from every angle, I can hear Lord Skaal's panting breath, I can smell the sweat on him, the damp fur odor he carries.

"What is it, Lord Skaal?"

"The king . . . ," says Lord Skaal, and then he stops and sniffs. He grabs the water glass off the desk and smells it. Relief and despair twine together inside me.

"This is poisoned," he says. He turns slowly, nostrils flaring, showing the edges of his teeth. He calls to me, a snarl in his throat: "Come out, come out, Casimir's little pet!"

"She's here?" asks Agoston Horthy, his voice blurring into a thousand voices, all of them so far away. "Are you sure?"

"If she is not here now, she was here very recently."

He strides over to the chair I was sitting in. I come right up to the edge of the visible world, next to Horthy. *Focus, focus.* Lord Skaal whirls toward me, drawing his pistol. He is so fast, but I am fast too, and this is something I've always been good at. I slip my hand into Horthy's pocket as I reappear. As soon as I feel the frame in my hand—Horthy startling, Lord Skaal aiming his gun—I'm gone, hurtling right out of myself, and the window shatters with Lord Skaal's gunshot.

⌒

Temple bells are tolling all over the city. It takes me a moment to understand: the king is dead. I reappear in Fitch Square. No reason to choose this place in particular, except that it is familiar, and Esme's building is the last place that felt like home. I dressed myself in Pia's clothes today, for comfort and for courage—I'm done being Ella Penn Witzel, after all—so I can't stay visible for long. Even in the Twist, a girl in trousers will attract attention, and the city is crawling with soldiers.

My fingers feel clumsy, but I open the frame and look at the faded sepia photograph of a young woman in old-fashioned country clothes, posed with two little boys wearing their temple best. I look harder at their faces.

How could I fail to see him, in that serious little boy's face? Agoston Horthy, perhaps eight years old, but the ferocity and determination are there already in his expression. This is the face of a child who will grow up to terrorize his country, casting the shadow of his fanaticism across all of New Poria. The brother, smaller than him, though not by much, is a doughy-faced sepia blur, smiling. He looks happy, but who can tell?

I freeze on the woman. She is younger, much younger, her expression solemn but not yet sad. Still, I recognize her. I recognize her plain, round face, her steady gaze, her shoulders hunched under the shawl that seeks to disguise the curve of her spine. Casimir's witch: Shey.

SIXTY-SEVEN

Luca comes back to his room late in the afternoon. He shuts the door behind him, and then he sees me and freezes. I am by the window, just in case. We look at each other across the room for a moment that seems to stretch on forever, and then he says, "What's your real name?"

"Julia," I say, feeling an immense relief as I say it.

"Your uncle," he begins, and the first flash of anger crosses his expression. "I suppose he's not really your uncle."

I shake my head.

"He's dead."

"I know."

"He was a spy, they said. And so are you. Is this getup what you wear when you're not pretending to be a noble girl?"

"Sometimes."

"They told me you tried to poison Agoston Horthy this morning. They told me you would likely try to kill me too. Is that why you're here? To kill me?"

"I'd never hurt you," I say, my voice wobbling a bit. "The rest is true."

"Why?" he whispers.

"It's complicated."

"You're one of them . . . the revolutionaries."

"I'm not, really," I say. "But the revolution is coming, and you aren't safe here. That's why I came. You have to get out of Frayne. They'll execute you."

He goes pale. "I can't run away like a coward."

"Not like a coward," I say. "Like a man who wants to *live*. Do you even *want* to be king?"

"Not much," he admits. "But I can't go home. That's all over. It's exile or fight for the crown, isn't it?"

"I suppose so."

He lifts his chin. "I didn't ask for this, but I'm not going to run away while a bunch of witches take over my country and put their puppet on the throne—some commoner pretending to be Zey's niece. You can tell your friends that."

I wince.

"You left me that note saying you were sorry. It was you, wasn't it? I've been wondering what you meant. Sorry for what? All the lies?"

"Yes," I say. "Sorry for all the lies."

He laughs unhappily. "I knew you had secrets, but I really hadn't considered that you might be a *spy*. I mean, you're barely older than my sister. I think you like me, though, don't you? Or was that all part of the ruse?"

"I do like you."

"Why are you here, really?"

"I can get you out of Frayne. You and your family."

"Can we pretend for a few minutes that none of this is happening? Can we sit down and tell each other the truth?" He locks the door and gestures to a chair by the gleaming mahogany tea table. I sit, and he sits in the next chair. I wish he were sitting closer. I wish I could touch him.

"They sent Sir Victor's head to my ... colleague ... in a box," I say, in lieu of reaching for his hand.

He goes a pale greenish color, and I wish I hadn't said anything. In some strange way, I feel he's pure and ought not to have to face the horror and madness that the rest of us are mired in. He is just a beautiful, happy boy who loves riding and poetry, who has been lucky all his life, and now his luck has run out. I wish I could protect him from the awful truth—heads in boxes and all the rest.

"When will they crown you?" I ask.

"The day after tomorrow," he says in a strangled voice. "Tomorrow is Zey's funeral. Are *you* a witch?"

"No," I say, and he looks relieved. "But my mother was. You don't know anything about witches. They aren't evil. Well, some of them are, I suppose. Just like ordinary people. They have power, but they don't choose it, and many of them don't use it. It's just . . . something they can do. Like me disappearing."

"Why don't you start there? I *saw* you disappear. How?"

"I just can. The way you can run or jump, I can vanish."

I'm not really telling the truth, but we don't have time for the whole truth. I don't even *know* the whole truth, not for sure. Who my mother is. If she's still alive. What happened to Lidari. If he's inside me.

"How is Dafne?" I ask. "Have you seen her?"

"I visited her this morning. She's getting better, but she'll have scars and blots on her face and some nerve damage to her hands, so she won't be able to play the harp anymore. That lovely face was what she had going for her, and it's ruined."

"She has more going for her than a lovely face," I say. "Now perhaps she'll have a chance to figure that out."

"That's cold. You know as well as I do that a girl like that won't get far without her beauty."

"I like her, actually, and I *do* feel sorry for her. I'm sorry she won't be able to play the harp, and I know about scars. But there are so many people who live in fear, so many people who *won't* be all right. . . . Dafne has money, and she has spirit, and she's not stupid. I know it's awful, but she *will* be all right."

I find myself thinking about Flora, the bruised young woman with the starving kids, hanging about Liddy's shop. I hope *she* will be all right. She might be, if Liddy has taken an interest in her plight—the way she took an interest in my plight ten years ago, plucked me off the streets, a thieving little orphan, and gave me a shot at something slightly better.

"You really think witches ought to rule Frayne?" Luca is wearing the unhappy expression of a little boy being unjustly punished.

"Zara's not a witch."

"I ought to hate you. But from the day we met I've just wanted to understand you. Now I think I'm farther from knowing you than ever."

"Here is the truth," I say, and against my better judgment I reach for his hand. He lets me take it, moves quickly to kneel before my chair, looking up into my face. He is so lovely, I think I'll choke on my own words. "I grew up in the Twist. My mother was a witch and my father was an opium addict. I have a brother, and I love him more than anybody in the world. My mother was kind. She always tried to help people. But Agoston Horthy signed her death sentence, and she was drowned when I was seven. Our father left us, and we were taken in by the queen of crooks. I earned my keep as a thief and a spy. I've done some terrible things, and I can't claim to be a good person, but I try to take care of the people who need me. I don't believe witches are evil—no more than anybody else—and I *do* think it is evil to drown them. I think the world would be better without Agoston Horthy, but I don't know if that gives me or anyone else the right to end his life. Right now I don't know what the right thing is. I wish you would leave and go somewhere safe. I don't want you to be hurt. *There* is the truth."

He is kneeling in front of me, but he's so tall that his face is nearly level with mine, and he is holding both my hands tightly in his. I feel unsteady, like we are at sea and clinging to each other in a storm.

"When I went out that night, I wanted to know the city," he tells me. "I want to understand the country I'm to rule. I wouldn't be a bad king, Julia. Oh, I like that name. It suits you. Julia. You've seen things I can't imagine, you know things I don't. You could advise me! If I had Agoston Horthy *and* you on my side, surely I could understand the whole of Frayne. I'm willing to meet and talk with the revolutionaries . . . not the witches, but the Lorians and the others . . ."

"Why not the witches?" I shoot back. "I've been trying to tell you, they needn't be your enemies."

He looks so lost. He pulls my hands to his lips and kisses my knuckles, then rests his rough golden cheek against one of my hands. I feel close to tears.

"You don't understand anything," I whisper. "You *have* to talk to the witches."

"Then set up a meeting for me."

"Really?" I ask him. "Do you mean it?"

He lets go of my hands and, floating free suddenly, they twine around the back of his neck as if of their own accord. I feel his silky curls between my fingers. He slides his hands up my trousered thighs to my waist, pulls me toward him.

"Yes," he says. "Stay with me. Advise me. Be my ... be with me."

I'm not sure if he pulls me or if I push him, but I'm sliding off the chair into his arms and we are in a heap on the floor, legs tangled together, my hands in his hair, my mouth against his. It is impossible to get as near to him as I want to be. He is slow and tender, and his slowness is unbearable, my blood battering against my skin, this desire conquering everything else, every thought and fear. I can't get out of Pia's clothes fast enough, and if I could speak clearly I would tell him, *here* is the truth, *here* is who I am, but I show him what I can't put into words, I show him.

He runs his hands over the red-mud scars on my arm and side, the mark of the *nuyi* running up my left arm. He traces the scar on my cheek.

"What ...?" he says, and kisses me again, and I'm lost, utterly lost.

"I just wanted to save him," I babble.

"Save who?" he murmurs into my hair, and I don't know if I mean Dek or Theo or even him.

He touches the burning disk in my wrist and gasps, pulling his hand away. I take his burnt finger and put it in my mouth. He gasps again, but differently this time.

362

"Stories for every scar," I say.

"I want you to tell me. I want to know everything."

"Later." I pull him out of his clothes—oh hounds, the great glorious length of him.

"Do you promise? Will there be a later? You're not going to disappear and never come back?"

"I promise."

In the moment I believe it, I believe that I can promise such a thing. He lifts me onto the bed, bending over me, and I want him as much as I've ever wanted anything in my life. He fumbles in a drawer by the bed for one of the protective sheaths Wyn first introduced me to. "I don't know how to use this . . . ," he begins. "I do," I say.

I roll over on top of him. He gives a gasping laugh, and I shut out everything else, just for now, just for a while, because there is joy here for the taking and we're going to take it before the city burns.

But for all the half-mad frenzy of my desire, the act itself is clumsy and too quick, too quickly over—him gasping into my neck and me drifting away from him already, still aching for him, but somehow this awful sadness has crept in, and I can't get back the urgency of wanting him. I'm left only with my fading desire and the dismal sense of hunger unsatisfied. He kisses me so sweetly, stroking my arm, and I shut my eyes as if I can hide my feelings that way. His fingers glide over a sore spot on my arm. My eyes fly open, and I sit up, moving his hand to look at the spot. There is a red spot, a bit of bruising around it, on a vein in my inner arm. The right arm, not the arm with the *nuyi*.

"Another story?" he murmurs, bending his big tousled head to kiss the spot.

"I don't know that story," I say quietly. And fear comes creeping back in, cold and weary—a snake returning to its lair.

SIXTY-EIGHT

I leave him, promising I'll set up a meeting between him and the masters of the revolution. We pretend that we are going to orchestrate peace, as if our kisses can seal something, our bodies demonstrate the possibility of crossing the gulf between natural and unnatural Frayne. Deep down I know it's a lost cause. Nobody will listen to me. Nobody will listen to him either, even if he's about to be king. We two cannot reconcile Agoston Horthy's government and the Sidhar Coven. But I don't know how else to say goodbye to him, besides promising that I'll see him again. And maybe I will. I hope I will, looking at his wide-open face, his clear eyes, his lovely mouth. I've never known anybody so open, all his vulnerability and wonder right there on his face for me to read.

"Hang on," he says, sitting up in the bed as I'm pulling Pia's trousers on and looking for my boots. "You know, I've never actually done that before."

"Oh!" I can't help my exclamation of surprise. I hadn't meant to claim the virginity of the heir to the Fraynish throne. Frayne's new king, now that Zey is dead.

"*You* have, though," he says. I do up the buttons on my

jacket as quickly as I can. "Was I ... I'm sorry if I wasn't sure ... I hope ..." He stops and laughs at himself, looking down at his big hands, and I take pity. I am desperate to be gone from this room and all the things I am feeling and all the things I am not feeling, but I remember that fear, after the first time with Wyn—whether it was what he wanted, whether I did it right. I bend and kiss him.

"You are wonderful," I tell him, which is true, if not an answer to the question he is asking. "You are good and sweet and wonderful."

"I mean, as a lover," he says, and then laughs awkwardly again. "I could practice. You could teach me ... what you like."

I kiss him again, a long, slow kiss, taking all the sweetness from it that I can, because I know—I would like to pretend otherwise, I would like to pretend I'll have a chance to teach him what I like—but I know it will be the last time.

"Wait to hear from me," I say.

And that's goodbye. I leave him sprawling, huge and lovely, on the bed. I open the window, climb up onto the parapet, and vanish out over the city.

SIXTY-NINE

"What did you do to me?"

Lady Laroche is at her desk—Mrs. Och's desk—writing and smoking. Her fingers tighten on her pen when I appear before her.

"This mark on my arm." I yank up my sleeve. "Last night, you *did* something to me."

She gives me a puzzled look, but she's a liar and I know it.

"Where is Zara?" I ask.

"In her room."

I go banging up the stairs to the third floor, throw open her door—what used to be Frederick's room, still full of his books.

"I need you."

She tosses whatever message she's reading quickly into the fire. I laugh—oh, the endless plots and secrets in this house!—and I grab her hand, pulling her after me, back down the stairs. Lady Laroche is not in the reading room anymore. Her cigarette smolders in the ashtray. I tear down the next flight of stairs, dragging Zara along with me. Lady Laroche is pulling on her coat, leaving in a hurry.

"Stop!" I shout. I vanish and reappear between her and the front door, slamming it shut with my shoulder. "Tell me what you did to my arm."

She looks at me, and at Zara on the stairs.

"I mean you no harm."

"Is it the truth?" I ask Zara.

"Yes," says Zara, descending the stairs slowly. "She does not want to harm you *or* me. But she is full of harm nonetheless."

Lady Laroche smiles.

"Did you take my blood?" I ask.

She puts on her gloves and says, "No."

"Lie," says Zara.

366

Lady Laroche shrugs. "All right. Yes."

"*Why?*"

She doesn't answer me.

"You can't go stealing my *blood*," I shout. "Give it back!"

"I don't have it anymore."

"Lie," says Zara again.

"Oh, shut up," says Lady Laroche.

"Did you put a spell on me?"

"Only so you wouldn't notice or remember."

"What do you want it for?"

"I am not going to bewitch you with it."

"True," murmurs Zara.

Lady Laroche and I stare at each other. Her arm is behind her back—moving—she's got a pen, of course she has, she wouldn't be unarmed. I grab her arm and try to wrestle the pen from her. She pushes me off, sends me sprawling across the bottom stairs into Zara, flings open the door, and then she's gone, folding up suddenly into a small, black, winged shape and shooting off into the sky. I scramble back to my feet, bruised and shaky, the heat of her magic scorching my throat.

"I told Dek," says Zara, lifting her chin. She looks so young and ordinary. "I told him everything. He agreed we ought not to tell Esme. Are you changing sides, Julia?"

"It was never about sides," I say. "I just want to save my brother."

"So do I. Can we work together in that regard, at least? I could help him if I were queen."

"Will you meet with Duke Everard? He's open to talking to . . . well, you."

"Don't be ridiculous. The throne is almost mine, and I am going to take it. I hope you will be at my side, with your brother, and not standing in my way. Not standing in *his* way. Frayne will be generous to men of talent, men like Dek, when I rule it. But I need power if I'm going to save him."

"How will you save him just by being queen?" I shout at her.

"You can't imagine the resources I'll have," she begins, but I stop listening.

I feel the raised line in my neck with my fingers, searching for the lump of the *nuyi*. I can't feel it. The line stops in the soft place at the base of my skull. It has gone inward. A horrible, sick chill snakes through my veins.

I run back up the stairs to Mrs. Och's reading room and yank open the desk, scattering Lady Laroche's papers, tearing through them, looking for something, *anything* that might tell me what she's doing. But there is nothing useful here. I stand there with a scream stuck in my chest, and I don't know what to do. The weight of it all is hanging over me: the *nuyi* creeping toward my brain, the poison next to Dek's heart, Luca's life in the balance, Lady Laroche doing *what* with my blood? I look up, and Professor Baranyi is watching me from the doorway.

"She did something to me," I say. My voice sounds far-off, garbled. "She took my blood."

"This would all be different if Mrs. Och had lived," he

says, and I think, *Well, that's my fault*—*he'll be singing that same tune forever, and it's my fault.*

"I honestly can't imagine Mrs. Och managing Lady Laroche," I say.

"Some of Mrs. Och's contacts—witches who could have helped us—refused to join the revolution. I tried to speak on her behalf, but they had no reason to trust me, and every reason not to trust Lady Laroche. In the end, the only witches who came were those loyal to the Sidhar Coven. The ones who want witches to rule."

"Well, it's all a great bleeding disaster now, isn't it?" I say. "But I'm a bit preoccupied with staying alive and not being enslaved to Casimir at the moment. Why did she take my blood?"

"I don't know. I'd hoped Lady Laroche might fill Mrs. Och's shoes. But she is not . . . like her."

Poor Professor Baranyi. Seeking to attach himself to another powerful, magical woman in the wake of Mrs. Och's loss.

"I was mistaken in her. I would like to talk to Frederick." He peers at me over his spectacles. "*Are* you Lidari? You don't actually know, do you?"

I shake my head.

He looks down. "I cannot forgive you," he says quietly. "I can never forgive you."

"I didn't ask for your forgiveness," I say.

I'm sweating like mad now, a cold sweat. I push by him and go back downstairs. Zara is in the scullery, whispering with Mrs. Freeley, while Gennady rolls dough for bread. They all freeze as I go by. I don't care what they are whispering about. I go crashing out into the cool evening. I run through the city instead of vanishing, just to feel my body move, my human body, my girl's body. I don't want to let it go.

SEVENTY

Mr. Faruk is at Liddy's again, wearing a splendid New Porian suit. They are drinking wine by candlelight and looking absurdly cheerful.

"She took my blood," I say, without greeting them.

"Lady Laroche?" Mr. Faruk looks genuinely surprised, but I don't trust anybody anymore. "Whatever for?"

"I don't know!"

"You don't want a mad witch hanging on to your blood. You should get it back."

"Casimir will be here tomorrow," I say. "I need more hermia. I need to stop the *nuyi*, just until tomorrow."

"I don't think your plan is going to work," says Mr. Faruk. "If the *nuyi* hasn't taken you, what's to stop him just replacing the sac of poison in your brother's chest with a new one and starting the clock over?"

"We don't know if he can feel it when the *nuyi* attaches," I gabble. "It's gone inside now. He won't know. He might not know. Give me a dose that will stall it till tomorrow."

Liddy and Mr. Faruk exchange a look.

"If Casimir takes me . . . ," I gasp.

"If that happens, we'll finish you off, love," says Liddy coolly. "Quick and painless. You can be sure."

She prepares the hermia. I swallow it and the room goes dim. I am lying with my cheek against the floor, staring at their feet, and I can hear their conversation carrying on above me, like echoes in a cave. I feel as if I'm lying at the bottom of a pit, where nothing and no one can reach me. Their voices might as well be the sound of the sea.

Later—much later, it seems—I am leaning on somebody. It is Mr. Faruk. I struggle to focus my eyes. We are walking past the old, broken fountain in Fitch Square, and he is encouraging me with every step, like I'm a child.

"Can you get up the stairs?" he asks, opening the door at the bottom of Esme's building. Even through this fog of confusion I notice the lockpick in his hand, how swift and skilled he is, the lock giving way in an instant. When I was a girl, that was my great ambition—to be able to open locks. It wasn't the theft that appealed to me so much as the forbidden space. Surely that is what draws all thieves and spies. If it is not desperation, then it is the refusal to be told where you can go, what you can know, how you can live. Nine years old and I ran through Spira City like the whole place was mine. I felt *powerful*. I thought nobody would ever be able to bar my way.

Mr. Faruk is gone. He has left me at the foot of the stairs—a long, dark tunnel with a light at the top. Home. I crawl up the stairs, and it seems to take forever, it seems as if this is the whole of my life, crawling slowly up these dark, familiar steps toward something I hope is safe.

I try to count their faces, concerned and hovering, talking at me out of double mouths, everything doubled. Two Gregors on the sofa with two Csillas in his lap. Two Esmes lifting me. Two women in red silk and elaborate braids. I remember her: Dorje Tsewang, the Xanuhan spy. Two Deks at the table, slouched over a glass of something amber. Two Wyns and two Lorkas. Both Lorkas look like cross little goblins. Two Arly Winterses, for heaven's sake. *Since when is Arly Winters inner circle?* I want to say. *Because of a little scouting while you hung your silly banners?*

Esme's voice rumbles over me. I remember being ill once, and she sang me to sleep—or until I pretended to sleep. She was a terrible singer and her maternal moments always unnerved me, and yet I was glad to have her at my bedside too. Sometimes it is enough to know you are protected, that someone is at your side, standing between you and the darkness out there. I stare at my booted feet propped up on a chaise. I feel as if I'm looking at Pia's legs. A breeze comes in through the window, and I want to lap it up, I'm so hot.

Esme's voice is rising, and everyone is staring at me.

"Sorry," I say, my voice thick and strange in my throat. "What did you say?"

"Torne has been murdered." Esme's voice again. "Lady

Laroche blamed him for betraying the witches in West Spira. She is becoming increasingly unstable. That's why we came back here, rather than stay at the Marrow. But I'm afraid for the princess."

"I will go now and make sure she is safe," says Dorje Tsewang, rising fluidly.

"Shall I go with you?" asks Gregor, not looking like he wants to go anywhere.

"No," she says. "I will be faster alone."

This is an odd moment for a thunderbolt revelation, but it comes all the same. I'm looking at Dorje Tsewang, still doubled, and then the two halves merge into one woman, tall and straight-backed and fearless. She's fastening a wicked-looking blade to her hip and pulling her coat on over it, and I keep hearing again and again the cool insouciance of her voice—*I will be faster alone—I will be faster alone—I will be faster alone.*

I used to look around at the women in my world and wonder what the future held, what kind of woman I wanted to be, but I saw nothing that appealed. Now, fevered and hallucinating, I think: *I want to be like* her. A woman up to her neck in adventure and intrigue—not petty crime but matters of real importance, with real stakes—but beholden to nobody. The kind of woman who makes her own choices, follows her own laws, sure of her power, and walks into danger saying *I will be faster alone.* I don't know if I will get a chance to be that woman. The kind of woman Pia should have been, instead of Casimir's slave.

Dek is bending over me. Such a sad look on his face.

"You all right?" I mumble.

He nods. "I'm sorry about this, Julia."

He slides the needle into my arm.

I wake up because somebody is shaking me. It's still dark out, and it requires a tremendous effort to open my eyes. Pia's mechanical goggles are inches from my face. I force myself to sit up and look around. I'm in my old room, my old bed.

"Your friend came to see me," Pia croaks. "I have been looking for you everywhere."

"My friend?" I ask blearily.

"Lady Laroche." She hands me a crumpled paper. "She wanted to send a telegram to Casimir, so he would get it when he docked in Nim. He will be here in the morning. This just arrived for her. I must deliver the message to her now. I have no choice."

It comes back to me: Dek with the needle. I try to leap out of the bed, but my limbs are rubbery and I go crashing to the floor. I feel the back of my neck, rip off the bandage I find there. Fresh stitches.

"He took it out. Oh, flaming hounds, he's taken the *nuyi* out."

Horror sweeps over me. Too late, then—too late to save him. What can I do? I try to get up. Pia is hunched on the floor, enduring whatever she is enduring. I squint at the paper she gave me, but I can't read it in the dark. I drag my-self over to the stove and light a match. By the flickering light, I read the telegram:

REGINALD'S AT NOON STOP.

DAY 13
BETRAYALS

Casimir steps out of the shop,
blood on his boots.

SEVENTY-ONE

Huge crowds turn out for Zey's funeral. Frightened as they are, still they turn out, most of them looking rather stunned that the man who has sat on the throne for half a century is really gone.

"Look what I got!" says Wyn. He's bought little Fraynish flags for Arly, Dek, and me from a roadside stall. People throughout the crowd are waving them, waiting for the carriage carrying Zey's coffin to pass.

"Brilliant," says Dek. "I love seeing somebody make a killing off a clever idea."

He is so cheerful. I look away.

"Stop sulking," he says to me. "It was a bleeding *inch* from your brain, Julia. I had to do it."

Oh, Dek. This isn't sulking. I am annihilated by despair.

I won't belong to Casimir. There is that. But in a week, that sac of poison inside my brother . . . a howling blank panic fills my head before I can really think it. I'd hoped so hard—but it was for nothing, all that hermia, everything I've done.

Bells are chiming all over the city. Arly and Wyn are sharing a mug of cold tea and whispering to each other. Dek puts his arm around me.

"Forgive me," he says.

There is no way to live with this terror and grief. And yet here I am, alive, with him. For now.

"I've been working like mad," he says. "It's . . . invigorating, this sense of purpose. I won't spend my last days waiting to die. I'm going to see the revolution through." He pauses and then says very quietly, "Can we talk about Zara?"

I make myself nod. He lowers his voice, his mouth next to my ear.

"I know how you feel. It's hardly comfortable to support a lie. But Zara is one of the most brilliant people I've ever met. She can change things. Hounds, Julia, please *speak* to me!"

I force the words out around the lump in my throat. "Will you tell Esme?"

"No. Their generation is . . . well, they think they're fighting the same old fight, for Roparzh. It's bigger than that, but we can't have doubts and dissent now. Please, Julia, promise you won't ruin our chance to change the world? I'm talking about making a country that wouldn't have drowned our mother. Call it my dying wish."

My gorge rises at that, and I struggle not to throw up. Deep breaths. Our mother. Surely if she were alive, even if she *is* Marike, she would be here for this—the fall of Zey's Frayne and the possible rise of a new Frayne. Whoever she was, whoever she might have been before she was Ammi, as Ammi she fought for that for years. But maybe she really is at the bottom of the river.

"Zara betrayed Lady Laroche's friends, the witches, to *Horthy*," I whisper. "They were drowned. She's *not* a friend to witches."

"She told me. Don't think she takes these choices lightly. We're fighting a war, and those witches were murdering innocent people. She *had* to take control back from Lady Laroche, or this revolution wouldn't be her revolution at all. It might have become a witch coup. Witchcraft *is* dangerous, Julia. It still has to be controlled. Lady Laroche would have witches free to use their power as they please. The world can't function that way."

"What about people like me? Am I going to be free to use my power as I please, in Zara's Frayne?"

He kisses the top of my head. "We both know there are no people like you."

I lean into his embrace and listen to his heart beating. I feel as though the sheer force of my desperation ought to be able to draw the poison out of him. How can I be so helpless?

A hush falls over the crowd as boots and hoofbeats approach on the road. Rows of finely dressed soldiers come first, then a horse-drawn carriage with the coffin carrying King Zey's body. Arly is weeping.

"Flaming Kahge, what is she crying for?" Dek asks, irritated.

"She's very softhearted," says Wyn fondly.

I watch the coffin pass and think of the old man raving

on his bed, full of regrets. The carriage goes clattering by, followed by further rows of soldiers, and then I see Luca in a carriage at the rear, flanked by Agoston Horthy and Lord Skaal. He looks young and bewildered seated between those two men, each so terrible in his certainty and purpose.

"I almost feel sorry for him," mutters Wyn. "The duke, I mean."

"Are they planning something today?" I ask sharply. He's very exposed in the carriage, even with Lord Skaal next to him.

Wyn shakes his head. The crowd mobs behind the carriages, following them toward Cyrambel, where the funeral will be held.

"I'd better go," I say.

I have to fix this. I will offer Casimir anything; I will *be* his slave, if that's what it takes. I can't let my brother go, I can't, I can't, I can't.

"It's going to be all right, Julia," says Dek, smiling like he believes it. "Just stay away from the palace tomorrow."

SEVENTY-TWO

In the lane behind Reginald's café in Mount Heriot, an old woman is lighting a small fire. She whispers over it, writing something on a scrap of paper, which she then feeds into the flames. Her magic leaves behind a swampy, unpleasant smell as she shuffles off.

Lady Laroche comes half an hour later in a hackney. She is wearing mourning garb and a huge hat with a dark veil, so I cannot see her expression, just a blur of white and lipstick behind the veil. She has a piece of charcoal in her gloved fingers, and a scorched smell wafting behind her. The waitress shows her to a back room—windowless—and my heart sinks. Once the door is shut, there's no way out for me, even vanished.

The waitress lights the lamp and leaves her there. Lady Laroche pulls back her veil, unpins her hat, rolls the charcoal between her fingers. She sits straight-backed and very still, but up close I can see her pulse in her neck. I want to hold my knife to that leaping vein and demand my blood back, but first I want to know what business she thinks she has with Casimir.

He arrives exactly at noon with Pia at his side. Even vanished I feel my skin crawl. It is strange to see him in Spira City, his finery old-fashioned, his skin bloodless against his dark beard. Pia too looks stiffer and whiter than usual. She has left her gloves behind, and her delicate hands are bare. Those soft girl hands, those killer hands.

"I asked you to come alone," says Lady Laroche, nodding at Pia as Casimir sits opposite her. "Do you not trust me?"

"You have tried to murder me several times. The question is ludicrous. I have come protected, and I do not only mean Pia."

"Of course," she says smoothly. "And you know the greater risk is mine. I have come protected too."

"Why am I here, Lady Laroche?"

"Agoston Horthy has failed you, hasn't he? But suppose the game was upended? Suppose we *both* had what we wanted?"

"How?"

"Zara has failed *me*," she says bitterly. "But still I think a regime change might serve us both. Frayne is my home, my beloved country. I want to be free here. I want *all* witches to be free here. Not hiding, not frightened. I want witches to learn their craft and take pride in it. I want witches to *rule*, as they should! And now something has fallen into my lap that makes me think you and I need not be at cross-purposes at all. I know what *you* seek."

"What do I seek?" he asks dryly.

"The Book of Disruption."

All the air goes out of me. Pia is still as a statue by the door.

"I have befriended Ammi's daughter, Julia," she says. "I have had access to her memories."

"Ah," says Casimir. "You really *do* have something I want."

"Without her knowing—I made sure of that, believe me—I found out what she's done with the little boy, Gennady's son."

Still vanished, I go for her, but there is something between her and me—something in the air. I press against it frantically. It feels like *nothing*, and yet I can't get closer to her. I try to vanish farther and reappear next to her, but that doesn't work either. I hover two steps back from the world, heart thundering. I don't know how to stop what is happening.

"She took him to Ragg Rock," says Lady Laroche.

"How?"

"By requesting it of Silver Moya. So simple! Ragg Rock gave her entry and takes care of the boy where you cannot reach him."

Again I press hard against the invisible barrier in the air around her. I push and push until it starts to give a little. Casimir sits back and strokes his beard.

"Mrs. Och's friend, the professor, told me a little bit, and the rest I took from Julia's memories," Lady Laroche continues eagerly. "You have two parts of the Book, but the other part Gennady put in his boy. If I give you the boy, you could reassemble it, and your power would be tremendous—like the old times when the Xianren ruled the world. Reassembling the Book would also pull Kahge back into the world. All the magic that has been draining out of the world since the Book was broken returned to it. A world disrupted. What would that look like?"

Casimir smiles grimly. "Are you so sure you'd like that world?"

The barrier around her feels like air and yet terribly dense, too thick to move through. I force my way into it and it presses around me, pouring into my lungs, stealing my breath.

"You think we have been at cross-purposes, but we are not!" cries Lady Laroche. "The world is large enough for both of us, and we could wield our powers as we wished. A truce, and the world disrupted completely. No more question of magic being stamped out. Only the magical *could* rule in such a world. We have been playing for Frayne as if it mattered, but it would *not* matter if you held *The Book of Disruption* and Kahge came to earth. You could leave Frayne to witches—to me. Your power would be far greater than ours, after all."

"How will you give me the boy?"

Oh, the awful flatness of his voice, his eyes, and I'm caught in this heavy, airless thing that surrounds her, trying to force my way through it, unable to touch either of them.

"I will show you. But I want your promise that you will give me two things in return."

"Very well."

"I want Frayne and I want Horthy."

"*If* I reassemble *The Book of Disruption* due to your help, you can have Frayne," he says. "But not Agoston Horthy."

"Why?" she cries. "What can he matter to you?"

The pressure of the barrier around me is crushing, but I keep struggling, though it's too late to stop what has already been said.

"He does not matter to me," says Casimir. "But you will let him live or you will suffer the consequences."

"He is a butcher of witches. I *will not* let him live."

"I do not like to repeat myself and will do so only once," says Casimir. "You will let him live or you will suffer the consequences. This point is nonnegotiable."

I still have the picture, *Shey* with Agoston Horthy and the other little boy. The brother who drowned. That wailing, bloated creature under the parliament, playing with Horthy in the woods by night—the drowned child somehow reanimated. Casimir still fears Shey. He won't give up her son to harm. My mind is racing, and all the pieces of this puzzle are before me, but I can't yet assemble them, not quite. I keep inching farther into the barrier.

"Very well," says Lady Laroche, looking like she's just swallowed broken glass. "Frayne, then. I'll leave Horthy be. I have another gift for you. A gift that doubles as a favor to me. Princess Zara and a group of revolutionaries are meeting right now at your sister's old house. Your brother Gennady is with them too. They have betrayed me and shut me out. I've lifted the spells around the house, so there is nothing to keep you out. I want them dead. All of them."

"Pia will see to it," Casimir says, giving Pia a nod.

For a moment, I think I'm through the barrier, and then I hit something scorching hot. I recoil fast, closing my teeth around a cry of pain and fear, struggling to stay vanished. The thick, invisible wall ejects me so quickly that I am staggering back into the room, everything blurred now by my tears as well as by my vanishing, but Lady Laroche shows no sign of having noticed anything and nor does Casimir. Still fixed on each other.

"And?" he says to Lady Laroche. "How will you get me the boy?"

"You can go to Ragg Rock," she says. "With this."

She holds out a vial to him. "Julia's blood. If you force Silver Moya to use it, Ragg Rock will let you pass."

He takes it with his long, pale fingers, and blast it all, I can't touch him to get it back now. "Is it really hers? If you are lying, you will pay for it."

"It is hers."

"Go now," says Casimir to Pia, pocketing the vial of my blood. "Bring the house down quickly, so those inside have no chance to get out."

She opens the door. He is rising from his chair. I'm going to have to move very fast if I'm to beat both of them to their destinations, but they still have to travel across the city, and I can do it in vanishing leaps. The Scola is closer, and Pia will be faster than he is, so I go to Mrs. Och's house first.

SEVENTY-THREE

When I appear suddenly in Mrs. Och's front parlor, crashing into the tea table, six people jump out of their seats: Dek, Zara, Professor Baranyi, Mrs. Freeley, Gennady, and Mr. Faruk.

"Ah, here's Julia," says Mr. Faruk.

"Pia is coming here to kill you all," I say, thinking how just once it would be nice to turn up somewhere and ask what's for lunch. "Casimir just met with Lady Laroche. We need to get out."

"And go where?" asks Zara, blanching.

"The Marrow?" I suggest.

"The university," says Professor Baranyi. "Esme and I

agreed on an emergency meeting place in the planetary studies building. A professor's chambers—he is a friend. There are weapons if we need to defend ourselves."

"All right," I agree. "It'll be faster and safer if I take you vanished." I remember how, when I rescued Lorka from Deadman's Square, I also took the soldier hanging on to him. I've got two hands, and weight means nothing between the world and Kahge. "I can take you two at a time. How do I get there?"

"Go to the Anderov Scole University clock tower, and I will show you the building," says the professor.

"Dek," I say, reaching for him.

"The professor and Zara first," he says.

His face is set, and I don't want to waste time arguing. I take the professor by the hand. His dark eyes meet mine, owlish behind his spectacles. Zara scoops Strig up in one arm and grips my other hand firmly. I yank all three of us back, aiming out the window at the bit of blue summer sky I can see above the garden. Out over the city we go, out of our bodies and then narrowing back into ourselves, over the university, reappearing at the base of the clock tower.

Professor Baranyi staggers away from me, looking sick. Zara has experienced this before, when I was not yet as good at it as I am now, and she is more composed. Strig is wriggling in her arms, hooting and meowing frantically. Luckily, the campus is quiet, nobody in sight. Everybody is either at Zey's funeral or indoors.

"Hurry up," I hiss at the professor. "Which building?"

"That row of windows, you see?" He points across the square. "On the fourth floor."

"I'll get us inside," I say, grabbing them both and vanishing us out of the world again. We reappear in a large study attached to a cozy room with a stove—Professor Baranyi's friend's chambers. Now that I know where it is, I can get my brother safe.

"Take Mr. Faruk and Mrs. Freeley next," he says when I return.

"Dek!" I shout, furious.

"Go on, I know another way if it comes to that," says Mrs. Freeley, and she pushes Dek into my arms. I pull him out of the world before he can struggle and deposit him in the room at the university with the professor and Zara.

"Hurry," he says to me. "Bring the others."

When I get back, Gennady, Mrs. Freeley, and Mr. Faruk are all sitting quite calmly in the parlor.

"Do any of you *want* to be rescued?" I shout at them. I'm half inclined to leave them there and go straight to Silver Moya's.

At that moment, the front door is ripped off its hinges. Pia appears in the doorway of the parlor with a flaming metal canister in her hand. How did she get here so quickly? But then, I can think of two occasions when she's crossed cities at terrible speeds carrying me on her back—I shouldn't be so shocked.

"This will bring the house down around us," says Pia, holding up the canister. "Julia, hurry. I cannot hold out for long."

"Run," I tell everybody.

"Don't run," rasps Pia. She grips the doorframe with one hand. "I'll catch you if you run. Go somewhere I can't find you."

"Come," says Mrs. Freeley briskly. We follow her into the basement. She tears up a panel in the floor of the wine cellar and steps back. "Down you all go."

We scramble down the ladder one at a time and then along a narrow tunnel. There is a tremendous sound, the world rocking, and I am knocked off my feet, pebbles raining down around me. We lie there in the tunnel, no sound but some crashing above and our panting, panicked breathing in the dark.

The dust settles. Mr. Faruk strikes a match.

"The tunnel is clear ahead," he says.

We stumble onward. The tunnel brings us up and out into a small toolshed in a neighboring garden. I can hear shouts from the street and houses nearby.

"We should be all right here for a little bit," says Mr. Faruk. "Long enough for you to get us to the university."

My blood is beating out the seconds. I can't just leave them *here*, but I need to get to Ragg Rock, no time, no time, no time. Casimir won't have made it yet to the clock shop, I tell myself, but I have no real sense of how many minutes have passed.

"Mrs. Freeley and Gennady, please go ahead," says Mr. Faruk politely, like he's holding a carriage door for them. As I pull us up and over the street, I see that Mrs. Och's house is a flaming mass of rubble, soldiers closing in on it. No sign of Pia, and my heart clenches. I'm surprised by how much I hope she is not buried underneath all of that.

I leave Mrs. Freeley and Gennady with the others in the university chambers and go back to the toolshed, but Mr. Faruk is gone.

SEVENTY-FOUR

The clock shop in the Twist has been torn to pieces—the windows broken, the door off its hinges, the street deserted. My heart plunges.

I'm about to go through the doorway when someone steps out of it. *Something.* He is shaped like a man but white as ash. He stands before me naked, all twisted ropey muscles, symbols I don't recognize tattooed across his body. He is holding a bloodstained blade in each hand. His white hair flows down his back, and there is blood in his hair too, blood on his arms, splashes on his chalky face. His eyes are depthless. I remember these creatures—they chased us from Casimir's fortress half a year ago in ships, and I saw them in Lidari's memory, before he plunged off the cliff.

Casimir steps out of the shop, blood on his boots.

"You," he says, pointing a long, ringed finger at me. "You should be *mine* by now. Where is your brother?"

I vanish away from him, landing hard in front of Liddy's shop. I go straight through to the back without announcing myself. Liddy is alone. The room smells of coffee and bread.

A strange oasis in a city about to erupt. Her eyes light up as the door opens, and then something in her expression falls a little when she sees me, like she's disappointed.

"Julia, are you all right?"

"I'm really not. Maybe you guessed this, but I hid Theo in Ragg Rock. Now Casimir has my blood, and I think he tried to use it to get there. Silver Moya is dead. I didn't see Theo, so I'm hoping she refused to help him. I need to get to Ragg Rock and warn them. I need to find another Silver Moya before he does."

"There are a few," she says briskly. "There is one on the coast. It would take Casimir some time to get there. She is cagey, though I'm not sure she'd help you. You can travel quickly and so perhaps somewhere farther is better, out of his reach, where I have friends."

I don't ask how she knows how fast I can travel. She takes out a map and pokes an ancient finger at it.

"Brillimar, in Ingle. Go to this address." She scribbles something down for me on the back of the map. "Ask for Ellis and tell him Liddy in Spira City sent you. He'll remember me, and he'll take you to the Inglese Silver Moya."

I go out into the street with the map, and I vanish. Farther and farther. Spira City tilts below me. I fix my sights on the northern horizon and return to my body, gasping on a hill. A startled goat trots away from me. Up and out again I go, fixing on the next horizon, and the next. A cowshed, scraggled forest, rocks and moor, and then the coastline, the gray, churning channel between Frayne and Ingle.

With trembling hands I take out Liddy's map and examine it, a group of seagulls eyeing me suspiciously. I vanish and pull my perspective high enough that I can see the shape of the Inglese coastline. I come down on the white cliffs, check the map again, shaking and sweating, and then away from my body once more, leaping out and across the world.

SEVENTY-FIVE

It takes me half the day to reach Brillimar. Perhaps I could do it faster if I weren't afraid of unhooking myself completely from the world, being unmoored in the sky, lost to myself. I run through the sleepy town, showing the address Liddy gave me to people I can't talk to, asking for Ellis. Mostly people back away from me, pulling their children clear, frightened of this scarred girl lurching about in trousers like a mad thing. I should have thought to change into a dress. No doubt constables will be coming for me soon, but one woman with a basket of turnips points me to Ellis's house. I bang on the door, and an old man opens it, gawping. He speaks Inglese, sounding worried.

"Liddy sent me from Spira City," I gabble at him. "I need Silver Moya."

"Great stars, a Fraynish girl!" he says, switching languages. His Fraynish is clumsy but easy enough to understand.

"Silver Moya!" I shout. "There's no time!"

"Looks like, looks like," he clucks. He pulls on a coat and

boots and takes me to a little clock shop at the village center. I went right by it and did not notice it. I'd forgotten what Liddy said—*they are all in clock shops.* He knocks on the door and calls through it in Inglese. A woman wrapped in fur with a cloud of white hair around her puffy face opens the door.

"Ragg Rock." I am crying. "I need Ragg Rock."

They hustle me inside. I take my knife from my boot and draw it across my palm, making a thin line of blood that quickly spills over my hand. The woman mops it up, scolding, but she takes a bit for the inkpot too. Birds fly around the shop freely, cheeping and shitting. The man is binding my hand, talking to me in his unfamiliar Inglese. Silver Moya is writing, the world is darkening and slowing down, thank all the holies. The birds slow down too, suddenly moving like snails through the air, all but one, bright-eyed and alert, stopping in midair right in front of me.

I try to say thank you. I try to say I'm sorry. The bird swoops out a bright new door, and I go after it.

SEVENTY-SIX

The archway on the hill to Ragg Rock lies in smoking ruins. The sometime-moat, sometime-forest is all ash now—a scorched ring around the blasted rock. The house at the top is smashed, a shambles. I run screaming up the path, calling them, but there is no answer. This despair is wider than all the world.

I find the pieces of Ragg Rock scattered near the stone dial, which has been riven in two, steam pouring out of the place where it has split. First a leg. Then her shoulder and the top of her arm. A hand. Her head—the face a muddy mess. I pick it up. One pebble eye is missing, but the remaining eye fixes on me. The lips move but nothing comes out; her mouth is full of gravel and dirt. Horrified, I nearly drop the head. With shaking hands, I place it gently on the ground and scramble around, trying to find the rest of her. Once I have most of her laid out in one spot, I think I've figured out what her lips are trying to say: *My. Pot.*

I run to the ruins of the hut, pulling aside the black beams. The smashed rabbit hutch, Frederick's papers scattered and burnt. The pot is overturned but still in one piece, and when I turn it upright it pools with hot red mud again. It is too heavy to lift, so I have to go back to the broken dial and carry Ragg Rock in pieces up the hill. Slowly and painstakingly, I start to put her back together. Once I get her head on her body and one arm roughly reattached, she is able to help. She sculpts herself back into the shape of a woman with swift determination. She grabs a stone from the ground and shoves it into the empty mud eye socket to make a second eye, larger than the first.

"Where are they?" I ask her over and over, until she pulls some of the gravel out of her mouth and works at her tongue with her fingers for a few seconds. Her throat moves, rippling, like she's building herself on the inside.

Then she says, in my voice: "I thought it was you."

"They stole my blood," I sob. "I'm so sorry. Where is Theo?"

"It was the second time. A request that felt like you. The first one was a witch, alone."

So Lady Laroche tried to come and snatch Theo herself, first. I shouldn't be surprised.

"The first one was not so strong," says Ragg Rock, and now she is speaking in Frederick's voice, with his accent and inflections. "When I saw it wasn't you, I shut her out easily and sent her back. Then it happened again . . . a call from your blood. Frederick hid Theo. He promised they'd come back, and I agreed; I didn't want my boy in danger. I thought if it still wasn't you I would send the intruder back again, and we'd know you were dead. But this time it was *her*—the witch who gave the creatures in Kahge their body parts, senses, and feelings. I remembered her, though it was half a century ago. *She* was too strong for me. She pushed right through. She wanted to get to Kahge. She tore this place apart, tore *me* apart, trying to call the shadows from Kahge, but they would not come, of course. And the Xianren was with her—Lan Camshe. Looking for my Theo."

Shey. *Shey* made the deal with the shadows in Kahge, giving them form and feeling. Ragg Rock told me about that witch before, but I didn't know who it was. Why? What does Shey want with Kahge?

"Did you tell them where Theo went?"

"Of course not." Her muddy hand closes around my arm. *"Why haven't they come back?"*

"Tell me where they are. I'll see if they're safe."

Our hurry to rebuild her has left her face lumpy and misshapen, making her expression of despair all the more terrible. "A farm near Spira City. He said a friend of Och Farya's lived there. He *said* they would come back. They don't need Silver Moya, I told him to write to me himself, to write that they are ready to come back, but he hasn't done it. You have to bring my boy back."

"Yes, all right, yes, but you need to take me there."

I'd promise her anything right now.

"It's my fault," she mutters. "I should never have let her come that first time. Her grief was like a whirlwind. I got lost in it."

"You mean Shey? What did she want?"

"The first time, she wanted some of the essence from the shadows—enough to animate a body, give life back to the child she lost, or life of some kind. I didn't see the harm in it at the time, but it didn't turn out like she wanted. It never does. When she tried to come back later, there was so much rage, I was frightened. I wouldn't let her back."

It all comes sharply together at last. Her little boy drowned, and Shey could not accept it. She came to Ragg Rock and met with the shadows from Kahge, those shadows longing for life. She gave them bodies and so much more. In return they gave her enough of their magical essence to resurrect her child. I remember what Ragg Rock told me about the newly embodied shadows and their deal with a witch she did not name—*They can love and feel pain, they can sleep and even eat.* Agoston Horthy cannot feel pain or love, he does not taste or sleep. She took all that away from him and gave it to the shadows, the price for his brother's life. But of course it didn't work, and she made monsters of both her children. Ragg Rock wouldn't let her back to undo it. Is that why she has yoked herself to Casimir? Because *he* can bring Kahge into the world, and then she can undo what she did?

"Will I ever see my boy again?" Ragg Rock wails.

"If it's safe, he can visit, but I have to get him *safe.*"

"*Visit?*" It comes out a terrible hiss. She shoves me onto my back. Muddy tentacles burst out of the ground, wrapping around my arms and legs, pinning me. One of them snakes around my throat and squeezes.

"I'll bring him," I gasp.

"Liar," she snarls.

And yes, I *am* lying, lying desperately. I won't die here, strangled by mud, after everything. "I mean it!" I cry. "You know he isn't safe in the world, they're looking for him, he needs to be here, he needs *you!*"

She bends over me, whispering: "There are *flowers* growing here now. Flowers, like in the world. Real ones. You should see it. There are creatures getting closer and closer to flesh and blood. I feel"—she knocks on her chest with a muddy fist—"a *heartbeat* sometimes, when he is near. This place is coming to life. I understand it now, everybody who has come here suffering, talking about love. I understand it. He has no mother, and this place, me . . . it is turning into a mother. The air is changing. It is transforming itself for him.

Becoming a garden where he can be safe, where he can be happy. I am becoming . . . I am changed . . . I . . ."

"I'll bring him back," I rasp. The mud tentacle tightens its grip on my throat. Her voice veers between mine, Frederick's, other voices I don't recognize.

"I've watched it for thousands of years. Mothers and their children. Now *I* have a child. My own child, my own dear boy. This is his home. You must bring him, but I don't trust you. I know you want to take him away from me. You are using me. You want my help and my protection, but you want to leave me behind as soon as you can. I know." She makes a sound like a sob. "It was wrong, but I helped those poor shadows because they only wanted to live. Lidari, all of them. So desperate to *live*, to feel. Marike, who refused to die, who wanted to rule the world, I *understand*. Nothing is ever enough. The witches come here for more magic, the shadows want more life, people want more love, more power, more of what they have and some of what they don't, but what have *I* ever wanted? I never knew how to want, how to love, until he came and brought this place to life. The heart beating inside the hill. Do you hear? Flowers growing, *here!*"

"They're going to kill him," I beg her. "You can't go to the world to help him. *I* have to do that. If you love him, let me save him."

A growl comes from deep inside her chest. "If you don't bring him back, I will unleash *havoc*. I'll bring down all the boundaries. I'll let the witches and the shadows come together like they did in Marike's time and let them do as they will. Let chaos reign. Do you hear? He is my son!"

400

"I'll bring him."

Because what else can I say? What can I do?

The muddy tentacles fall away from my limbs and my neck. I scramble to my feet, gasping. The rabbit, George, hops out from behind a bush, nose twitching, and I feel absurdly relieved that he survived the ruin of Ragg Rock. She picks him up, tucking him under one arm, and walks me to the ash ring surrounding this outpost between the world and its shadow. Gaslit Spira City tilts below us for a moment and then flits away, the land rushing past, dark rolling fields, what might be wheat but who can say by moonlight, and then: the shadow of a farmhouse.

"There," she says, pointing. Pebble eyes glinting. "Remember what I said."

She holds the rabbit to her chest, and I leave her there, a lonely sentinel in her ruined post, as I make my way down the stairway to the world.

DAY 14

WHAT A MOTHER WILL D

☞

Something *is coming from the w*
Like great dark sails in the sky, or some
Not a bird. No bird is that big

SEVENTY-SEVEN

The stairway from Ragg Rock disappears behind me as soon as I step onto the path leading to the farmhouse door, and something rises up out of the ground in front of me, hissing. A snake. Two more uncoil on either side of me. They raise their hooded heads, tongues flicking in the moonlight, each one as thick as my arm. The first draws back its head as if to strike. I vanish, leaving the snakes twisting on the path, and pull back for a view of the house. The curtains are drawn shut over all the windows so I can't just put myself inside, but then I see a little window at the top without curtains and aim myself for that. In the dark I can see only more darkness through the glass, but I focus on it, anyway, returning to my body in a low-ceilinged room—a storage attic, I reckon. There are boxes all around me, dust and cobwebs, the sound of small, scuttling creatures. I crawl around in the dark until I find a trapdoor, but it opens from the outside. There is no way out of this bleeding cupboard. I bang on the trapdoor recklessly until it falls open and the barrel of a rifle is pointed into my face. A lantern flares and blinds me.

"What by all the bleeding holies are *you*?" asks a gruff female voice with a northern accent.

"Don't shoot," I gasp, sliding through the opening and landing with a thump at her feet. The lantern and the barrel of the gun swing down, still pointing at me.

"How did you get into my attic?"

"Is Theo here?" I ask.

"Ah." She moves the lantern to the side a bit, and I squint up into a black-eyed, big-jowled face topped with hair curlers. "You must be *her*, then. Up on your feet. No sudden moves."

I go in front of her down the hall. She raps on a door and out comes Frederick in ill-fitting nightclothes, leaning on a cane.

"Frederick!"

"Hush, you'll wake the wee one," snaps the woman.

"Thank the Nameless you're all right," he whispers. "Come downstairs."

Dawn is lightening the house already. Frederick looks such a scarecrow, his skin and hair faded, his limbs loose and twig-thin. But his smile is the same. Half a dozen lean cats are perched around the kitchen, some of them winding about the witch's legs and mewing hopefully as she bustles around preparing food. Frederick introduces her as Olivia, but she spares me barely a nod. I am ravenous, devouring everything she puts in front of me, bread and butter and eggs and goose liver and thick milk. Frederick and I are in the middle of telling each other everything when I hear a dear, familiar little voice from the stairs: *"Lala!"*

Theo comes hurtling into my arms.

Theo eats nearly as much as I do, climbing onto my lap and off again, running circles around the table in excitement, followed by a shaggy barking dog. He pauses for huge bites of breakfast, which he shares with the animals, and then demands more. Olivia never stops moving, laying out more food.

"Knew she was trouble. Told the professor I wasn't getting involved." She is talking about Lady Laroche. "Mrs. Och always said she was power-hungry, that one."

I bite back everything I might say about Mrs. Och.

"Why did you come *here*?" I ask Frederick. "Casimir and Shey are in the city now!"

"I can't protect Theo," he says. "Olivia's farm has been a haven for a long time. She took in other witches fleeing the city and never once failed to protect them or send them safely on their way."

"A right mess, a right mess," mutters Olivia, banging into the scullery with the dirty dishes. The dog follows her. Theo is under the table playing with two of the cats now.

"I have to go back to Spira City," I say.

"Don't you think you ought to get some sleep first?" says Frederick gently.

"I'll sleep after." I'm so tired that I'm dizzy, but the food has restored me somewhat. I can do this.

"After what?" he asks me.

I reach into my pocket for the little picture frame.

"Great stars," he whispers when I open it. "Is that Agoston Horthy as a little boy?"

"And Shey. Casimir's witch."

"She's his *mother*?"

"Yes. And I'm going to make a deal with her."

SEVENTY-EIGHT

I find them in our rooms at the West Spira Grand Hotel. Pia is on the floor, her mouth bloody, Casimir's boot on her neck. Shey is watching them from a chair, those doughy hands that can reshape the world folded placidly in her lap.

"After everything I've done for you, you worthless maggot!" Casimir is roaring. "Do you remember the noise? The one that drove you mad, that chattering inside your head?"

"No, please," Pia rasps between bleeding lips.

"I have some more of those little eggs," he says. "I am going to put them inside your ear and let them hatch and watch you go mad for a month or two and then we will see if you come to heel again."

"No. No. *No!*" It rises to a piercing shriek, a horrible, animal wail.

"I remember how you tried to smash your head open the

last time," he says. "We'll bind you fast, put you back in that padded hole, feed you with tubes, sweet thing, and break your will all over again, since it appears it needs to be done."

I return to myself behind him so that Shey will not see me. This is not the moment for a chat with her. I need to get Pia out of here, and if Casimir sees me it will be over before I have a chance to explain anything. I reappear just long enough to dive between his legs and grab Pia by the ankle. As soon as I have a hand on her, I vanish.

But he grabs her when we're half gone. He comes *with* us. Out the window, over the city. I bring us back to our bodies in midair, above the buildings. We go plunging down toward West Spira's streets *fast*.

"Get him off!" I shout at Pia. "I can't touch him!" Past the rooftop of the hotel, down, down, the street hurtling to meet us. "Hurry!"

Pia turns like an eel in midair, me clinging to her ankle, and with the other booted foot she strikes Casimir full in the face. He falls, and we vanish again.

"Did he put them in? Did he do it?" Pia is raking at her ears.

"He didn't get anything into you," I promise her, and hope I'm right. I drag her down the hall of the planetary studies building, bang on the door.

Gennady opens it, pointing a pistol right at Pia.

"She's in this state because she *didn't* blow you to smithereens," I say. "Stop pointing that thing at her!"

He lowers the gun.

"He'll find me!" Pia screams.

"No," I say. "He won't. You're safe here."

"But *you* are not safe from *me*," she hisses, pushing me up against the wall by the door. "I can't fight him, Julia. You should kill me now while I'm willing. I can't do this anymore."

"You *can*," I say. "You wouldn't still be alive if you didn't want to live. You wouldn't have survived everything he's done to you. I know that much. It's the way we're most alike, I think—how badly we want to stay alive."

"Blasted survivor's spirit," she spits, doubling over.

"Let's get you patched up."

Bells are pealing all over the city again. It's coronation day. Revolution day. Dek, Zara, the professor, and Mrs. Freeley are gone. Little Strig is still here, chasing dust motes.

"I've just seen Theo," I tell Gennady. "He's safe for now."

"I'm glad," he says, and adds a moment later: "Thank you."

Angry words rise up in my throat, but I squash them down.

"No need to be completely useless," I tell him unkindly. "Help me."

There is a bathroom with a porcelain tub down the hall of the professor's chambers. We fill it with warm water, Gennady carrying copper pots from the stove. He sits outside the door with his gun, and I help Pia out of her clothes, which are stiff with blood.

Seeing her naked is shocking. She is long and muscled and terribly white, with metal all twisted through her. Bolts and screws in her spine. Wires at her joints. When I wash her hair, I can feel the plates in her head, metal fused with bone. I wipe the dust and blood from her goggles. She heaves herself out of the bath, and I don't know if it is more unsettling to see the hard parts of her, made of metal and wire, or the ordinary softness of her breasts and belly, the ways in which she has a woman's body. I hand her a towel.

"Thank you," she croaks. She dries herself slowly, like it hurts to move.

I rinse her bloodied clothes as best I can in the bathwater and then hang them by the stove in the other room. I find a blanket to wrap around her and bring her to sit by the stove.

"You are not safe from me," she says again. "You are right—I want to live. I can't kill myself. I am begging you to do it."

"Suppose we lock you up and Gennady keeps guard?"

"I've broken out of stronger prisons than this one," she says, gesturing around the room.

"I have sleeping serum. I could knock you out."

"That might work for a short time. But then what?"

"I've got a plan," I say. "Do you know why Shey works for Casimir?"

"No."

"Because she wants to get to Kahge. She wants to undo a spell she did. He hasn't told her that I can cross over, has he?"

"In his fortress, he told me to keep you away from her," she says. "He was angry when I brought you to the room while she was there. That was my first small disobedience, enacted almost without thinking."

"I'm going to make a deal with her. *She* can stop him for us."

"He will not let you near her. And he needs only a second to break you."

"I'll manage something. Trust me."

"I do," she says. "But why are you helping *me*?"

"I asked you the same thing. You told me that you weren't helping me. That you were betting on me."

"Yes."

"Maybe I'm betting on you too."

Something goes slack around her mouth at that. She leans forward, and an odd sound comes out of her throat.

"Are you all right?" I grab her shoulder. The odd sound keeps coming. It takes me a moment to realize she's weeping. She folds herself onto a chair, trying to strangle the sound.

"What you said, about us being alike, do you remember?"

"I was wrong."

"No, you were right," I tell her. "I could have been like you if there'd been nobody on my side."

That's where I've been lucky. I've *always* had people on my side. My mother and Dek. Esme and our gang of thieves. I've always had a family, in one form or another. I've always been loved, and loved properly. I don't think Pia had anyone to show her she was worth something in herself, that nobody had the right to treat her like their dog. I wonder if it's the kind of lesson you need to learn young to believe it in your bones, like I do. If it's too late for her to learn it. I hope not.

"I'm your friend," I tell her, and I mean it. "If anybody

ever tries to hurt you again, I'll kill them. And I'm not letting Casimir near you again either. I'm going to *end* him. You and I are going to survive this and we're going to be free."

The awful sound keeps wheezing out of her. I am kneeling next to the chair, and she rests her forehead against mine. When she is able to speak, she says: "I have to go back to him."

"Lie down," I say, and she does. I take out a dart of sleeping serum.

"You'd better use two," she says.

"We'll start with one. I'll be back. Sleep well."

I stick the dart into her, and her head falls to one side.

"Do I shoot her if she tries to leave?" asks Gennady.

"No," I say, giving him my last two darts. "If she starts to move, stick her again and stay out of her way."

"Where are you going?"

"To find Casimir," I say. "I'm going to bring him down. I just need a minute alone with Shey."

I feel strong again, never mind that I haven't slept.

"Minutes alone with Shey never end well," says Gennady.

There is a sound like thunder.

"A storm?" I say, startled, pulling open the curtains.

"Guns," says Gennady.

The revolution has begun.

Luca.

SEVENTY-NINE

I return to my body on a high balcony at the palace. Soldiers in formation surround the palace and the parliament. Revolutionaries are mobbing through the streets, building ramshackle barricades and being shot down in horrible numbers already. There are fires all over the city. It looks set to be a massacre. Uselessly above it all, I don't know what to do. I meant to get Luca out of here, but perhaps the revolution is going to be cut down before they can get to him.

A shrill keening sound from above. I look up and see witches astride flaming branches. They are flying over the city from every direction, toward the palace. The soldiers start firing pointlessly into the air. The witches fly lower, circling the palace grounds but still out of range of the soldiers' bullets. I huddle behind the balustrade, peering out over it as the witches come in close and hurl what appear to be cylinders of flame through the palace windows. Judging by the smoke rising up all over the city, they've been dropping these fairly indiscriminately. The gates to the palace grounds open, a swarm of soldiers pouring back inside now that the palace is under attack from above. I see close to a hundred people dressed in crimson and black with odd masks over their faces among the armed rabble along the river. The Xanuhans, I'm betting.

A chorus of screams from soldiers and revolutionaries

both—fingers pointing at the sky. *Something* is coming from the west. Like great dark sails in the sky, or some vast bird. Not a bird. No bird is that big. As it gets closer, I feel my heart drop. The keening of the witches gets louder. The formation of panicked soldiers is breaking up, and the Xanuhans are pushing through, into the palace grounds.

The dragon must be twenty feet long at least, its narrow body undulating, rippling and snaking through the air, with two pairs of wings ballooning out like sails on either side of it, keeping it afloat. Something bulges at its neck, swelling and growing whiter, expanding outward, and then a blade of flame comes from the thing's mouth, striking a high tower of the palace. The stone dissolves, runs black and molten.

The palace grounds are in chaos now, more and more revolutionaries making it over the walls. A Xanuhan warrior below holds up what looks from my vantage point like a telescope and fires something into the air. A little metal ball hurtles up into the sky, *way* up, somersaulting. The weapon Dek was building. It pops, and a thick bluish smoke billows out of it, enveloping a few of the witches. They plunge downward, off their flaming branches, falling to the palace grounds far below. I catch a whiff of the gas, and my head spins. I'm about to flee inside when the dragon swoops right past my balcony, and instead I'm frozen with wonder, staring over the edge of the balustrade at the tremendous length of it—its blunt lizard face and that balloon at the neck swelling with white fire again. I see Lady Laroche's face as she flashes by on the dragon's back, hair streaming out behind her, arms raised in triumph, exultant. And then she is past, swooping around the palace. Another blast of dragon flame. Another tower melts blackly over the stone below it.

A witch alights on the balcony next to me, burning cylinder in hand. She stares at me, openmouthed, then makes to throw the cylinder. I vanish across the tower room, swing open the door at the end, and race down the twisting stairs as fast as I can. The room explodes into flames behind me.

The palace is full of shouts and clanging bells and people running. I find Luca in the crown room, wearing heavy new robes, crown askew on his head. He looks stunned. His mother has a pistol in her hand. Both Agoston Horthy and Lord Skaal are with them. Lord Skaal is pulling aside a tapestry on the wall.

"Take them to safety," Horthy is telling Lord Skaal as he opens a door behind the tapestry.

I am poised on the stairs just above them. The door at the other end of the crown room flies open, and the guards posted there fall bonelessly to the floor. In comes Lady Laroche, lit cigarette in hand, her hair pulled into a hasty updo. Three witches in black come in behind her and, slithering on its belly, those great ballooning wings closed up so tightly that they look like a frill along its sides, the dragon, like an enormous snake. The dragon swivels its head up high, some flash about the eyes that makes me avert my gaze, vanished though I am. The duchess shoots the dragon's side, and the creature thrashes its tail angrily. One of the witches is writing on a slate, and the pistol tugs free of the duchess's hand, flying across the room and clattering against the far wall.

Lord Skaal curls a lip and snarls.

"Lord Skaal, you've always been an opportunist," says Lady Laroche pleasantly. "This might be a good moment to switch sides."

Lord Skaal nods in Horthy's direction. "Until I see his dead body laid out, I would not bet on this man being defeated." Then he sniffs the air and turns to where I am vanished at the top of the stairs. "And who are *you* here for?"

Lady Laroche stiffens.

I reappear, and they all go still, looking up at me. Agoston Horthy meets my eyes for the first time while the dragon slides across the floor.

"Julia!" cries Luca. The poor boy looks terrified.

"I'm glad you're here, Julia," says Lady Laroche, though I'm sure she's anything but. "This is our moment. Here before us is the man who murdered Ammi!"

"I thought you just made a deal with Casimir to leave him alone."

She looks alarmed that I know this, but she doesn't miss a beat: "*You* didn't, though."

Then everything seems to happen at once.

Lord Skaal turns into a wolf and lunges at Lady Laroche. The dragon swivels toward him, the balloon at its neck swelling hugely, and this close I can see the heat and flame swirling inside it. Agoston Horthy shoots the translucent, bulging sac at its neck with a pistol I didn't even see him draw. The dragon makes a horrible screeching sound. Shots are being fired in the hall just outside the crown room. Lady Laroche and the two other witches are trying to strangle the wolf, who snaps and snarls and gives them no moment to write magic. The dragon is slithering fast toward Horthy, its jaws wide, but the balloon at its neck is bulging and sagging, *leaking*. Agoston Horthy shoots another hole in it. Something too bright to look at is pouring out of that sac at its neck, eating away at the floor, melting the marble. Horthy has a knife out now, and he is approaching the wounded dragon, the witches grappling the snarling wolf, one of them immobile and probably dead, the duchess pulling Luca through the door that was hidden behind the tapestry. Black-and-red-clad Xanuhans pour into the room, all of them wearing bulky black masks over their mouths and noses. I recognize Dek's work—the masks are to protect them against sleeping gas.

"Julia!" screams Lady Laroche from beneath the wolf. "Choose your side!"

A Xanuhan tosses a metal ball in the air. It somersaults over and over. I make a vanishing leap to the entrance of the tunnel in the wall, reappear to grab Luca's hand in one of mine, his mother's in the other, and as I hear the *pop* of the metal ball, I pull them with me out of the world, away from the burning palace.

EIGHTY

I take them to Liddy's shop. The door is closed and—for the first time ever—locked. We can still hear gunshots from West Spira. The smell of smoke is everywhere. I bang on the door, but there is no answer.

"What is this place?" cries the duchess.

"I'm rescuing you," I tell her.

"We should go back and fight!" she protests.

"You've already lost," I say, thinking of the Xanuhans pouring into the room, the dragon thrashing on the floor. Zara let the Sidhar Coven attack Horthy's armed forces and then brought both down herself. Everyone will hear how her Xanuhan allies gassed the witches out of the sky. "Zara's going to take the throne, and you'd better not be around for it."

Luca puts his arms around his mother, and they embrace in the street.

"We'll flee to Ingle," the duchess murmurs. "Our ships in Corf can take the rest of the family across the channel without having to touch on Fraynish soil. Oh, thank the Nameless they stayed there!"

"They'll have a few days before anybody gets there, I expect," I say. "Send a telegram and tell them to meet you in Ingle."

I bang on the door again. Suppose Liddy has truly left Spira City? I can't believe somehow that she'd leave without saying goodbye to me.

I haven't got a lockpick or even a hairpin, so I smash a window with a brick lying in the street. Immediately two glowing, hissing spiders the size of my fist appear, flying out the window, forelegs raised threateningly. The rhug. I back away, shouting, "*Liddy! Are you in there?*"

More of the spiders come out the broken window, positioning themselves by the door and windows.

"What are those?" cries the duchess, pulling Luca away from them.

Can I really be barred from Liddy's shop? My heart is thundering in my chest. I hear voices nearby, and Luca is still wearing the bleeding *crown*. I grab their hands to vanish again, but then the door opens.

It isn't Liddy. It's the woman with the bruises—Flora. A fresh bruise blooming on her cheek. And behind her, the brutish-looking fellow I saw going into her house.

"*You*," I say.

Her eyes widen. The brute says gruffly, "Let them in. Hurry."

The rhug make way, obeying this man's command. She pulls the door wide and then closes and locks it behind us.

"Why did you smash the window?" asks the brute angrily.

"Where's Liddy?" I cry.

"Shh." Flora puts a finger to her lips. "The children are asleep upstairs."

Mr. Faruk comes out of the back room, dressed simply for once, in boots and a light coat.

"You certainly know how to pick your moments," he says to me. "Why have you brought the king here?"

"*Where's Liddy?*" I push past him, dread closing around my heart like a fist.

"Julia, wait," he says, grabbing my arm. His grip is hard, but I vanish out of it and reappear by the door at the back of the shop, throwing it open.

Liddy is sprawled across the floor, her throat cut wide

open. Her eyes stare up at nothing, already hard and very dead. I stagger backward, clapping a hand to my mouth, and spin to face Mr. Faruk, Flora, and the young brute.

The brute says, "I suppose we're going to have to explain."

"I don't think that's a good idea," says Mr. Faruk wearily.

"I owe her that much," says the brute, and then to me he adds, "It's not what you think, Julia."

"Isn't it?" asks Mr. Faruk.

Everything has gone cold inside me. Luca and his mother are standing together against the closed door, unsure if it's safer in here or out in the streets.

"How do you know my name?" I ask the brute.

"Look again," he says, pointing into the back room. "What do you see?"

The body of my old friend. I taste iron on my tongue.

"Not there," says the brute. "On the table."

"What are you doing?" asks Mr. Faruk sharply.

"She's not going to *take* it," says the brute.

"*You* said she was a thief, among other things," says Mr. Faruk.

Liddy's dead body seems to take up my whole view. I hear their voices as if from another world. But I pull my gaze up to the table. There it is—the thing I've only seen in pictures and visions—a little double-spouted clay pot with hiero-glyphs on its side.

"The Ankh-nu." I turn to look at them. The answer is right here, but my head is spinning.

"I am Liddy," says the brute. That familiar, easy tone—of

course, I ought to have recognized it, even coming from a different voice and body. "I mean to say, I was never really Liddy, but the Liddy *you* knew is now . . . this. Me."

The Ankh-nu. For switching bodies. I look at the brute, but I can't believe it.

"How?" I say. "Liddy?"

Mr. Faruk looks impatiently at his wristwatch. "The hackney will be here any minute."

A choking laugh bursts out of me. "You're not going to get a hackney in the middle of a revolution!"

"Oh, I am," says Mr. Faruk.

The duchess is pulling on Luca's sleeve, whispering something.

"If you go, you'll be captured," I call to them. "I can get you out safely. But I need to know . . . *what* is going on here."

"I'm sorry, Julia," says the brute. "I wanted to explain things earlier, but it was dangerous and I didn't know . . . well, where to begin."

"Where did you get the Ankh-nu?" I ask. And then a horrible thought strikes me. "Are you . . . were you . . . my *mother?*"

Mr. Faruk gives a bark of impatient laughter.

"No," says the brute. Liddy. Maybe. "Your mother is dead, Julia. Ammi drowned. I am Lidari."

Mr. Faruk goes past me and takes the Ankh-nu off the table. He tucks it into a leather bag and slings it over his shoulder.

"We really do need to go," he says. "Before the city burns down."

I look at him, and it comes together, painfully. My mother dead. Lost all over again. That stupid, bright hope of finding her goes out in a sharp, hard puff of understanding.

"Marike," I say coldly.

"I used to go by that name," says Mr. Faruk.

"*You* put the Book in Theo."

"Yes," says Mr. Faruk. "I thought I'd come up with a very clever way of destroying the fragment—getting it apart from Gennady. I didn't expect Gennady to run off, leaving me with a concussion down at the harbor. Thank goodness I didn't need *that* brain much longer."

Poor Ko Dan. Poor everyone who ever stood in Marike's way. I feel sick, everything in me grasping for answers, for any possible hope.

"Then *you* can take the Book out of him," I say.

"That was always a lost cause," says Mr. Faruk. "Two essences in one body! The Book fragment is completely entwined with Theo's essence, a part of him, to live and die with him. There is no taking it out without taking *him* apart."

I look at the body of my friend again and tears spring to my eyes. I feel so lost. My mother is dead.

"Why did you kill Liddy?"

The brute says gently, "The body is just a casing—a house for the essence. You know the power of the Ankh-nu. Your mother brought me from Kahge to the world, but she was reluctant to take someone's body. The body she consented to put me in . . . a woman who had suffered a stroke, her mind gone, empty . . . it was only ever a temporary home. Like every body I've had."

Liddy. Lidari. Oh, but I'm such a fool. I used to be the best liar I knew. How I miss those days.

"What about the body?" asks Flora, pointing at Liddy's corpse.

"Leave it," says the brute—Lidari—dismissively. I am shocked by this callousness.

"Why is she *dead*?" I ask. "I don't understand."

"Flora's husband was a monster," says Lidari harshly. "He hurt her and he hurt her children. I needed a new body—a strong one, a young one. We made a deal with Flora. She brought him here, we tied him up, and I switched bodies with him. But his reaction to being put into a new body was such that . . . well, killing him was the only way to calm him down, frankly."

"*Calm him down?*" I sputter.

"Call it self-defense, if you like. I have no qualms of conscience concerning the death of such a man."

Flora's face is blank. "Can we shut this door? I don't want the children to see when they wake up."

I take the blanket off the back of the chair where Liddy used to sit—Liddy with her fresh rolls and coffee and easy conversation, Liddy, whom I could always trust—or so I thought. I lay the blanket over the body and close the door.

"I'm going to check on the children," says Flora.

"You'd better wake them," says Mr. Faruk. "Our hackney will be here any minute." At my incredulous expression, he adds: "Do you imagine this is the first time I've fled a city as it falls?"

"What about Lady Laroche and Zara?"

"I've wanted to see this come to fruition for a long time—Zara on the throne, a girl raised and trained to be the perfect ruler—but my role is that of a relatively disinterested observer. I was curious to see whether Lady Laroche could really work with anyone else. It turns out she can't, and now it's time for me to move on. I'll be interested to see how it all plays out, but it's bound to be chaotic."

"First explain it," I beg the brute—Lidari. "Why can I vanish? Why did the shadows in Kahge think I was you? Why do I have your *memories*?"

"Do you know how Marike brought the Gethin from Kahge?" asks Lidari.

Mr. Faruk passes a hand over his brow. "I don't like to revisit that. I was so young then—so ruthless."

"The witches were pregnant," says Lidari. "Using the Ankh-nu to transfer an essence is no simple matter, and bringing a half-life from Kahge into the world had always proved impossible. But when a witch is pregnant, her power is magnified. She is nearly indestructible, and also, of course, the pregnant woman is designed to hold another life within herself—the essence as well as the body makes room for this. Magic and nature work together for a short time. Marike gathered her army of witches and required them to find mates and become pregnant. When they were still in the earliest stages of their pregnancies, she brought them to Ragg Rock one by one. Using the Ankh-nu, she put the essence of the shadow-beings into the small, still-forming lives *inside* the witches. The witches returned to the world and gave birth to creatures not of this world—part human, yes, but infused with the essence and magic of the shadows from Kahge. These grew into the Gethin—an army that could hardly be killed, they were so full of magic, and the longer they lived the less human they became. Yet still they were bound to their bodies and the world."

"That's revolting," I say. My chest has gone cold. "What does it have to do with *me?*"

"Ragg Rock was appalled at the result. After that, Marike was never able to return to Ragg Rock," says Lidari with a nod at Mr. Faruk. "But we had the Gethin army, and we had the Ankh-nu, and for a time the world belonged to us . . . or that is how it felt, in any case. We used the Ankh-nu for centuries to occupy new bodies. We lived on and on. Eventually, with the help of the Sirillian Empire, Casimir tracked me down, drove me to the cliffs of Ingle, defeated me. I had no choice but to abandon my body and return to Kahge. Marike could not come for me. Perhaps she did not try so very hard."

"I thought I had to let you go," says Mr. Faruk. "But then I met Ammi, who had gained favor with Ragg Rock. Unusual for a witch like her to be granted entry, but she wooed Ragg Rock carefully and well. She had been seeking different, stronger magic there. She was beginning to separate herself from Lady Laroche and the Sidhar Coven. I told *her* about Lidari, cast back into Kahge, and a plan by which we could all take revenge on Casimir."

"She meant to try to carry me out of Kahge in her empty womb," says Lidari. "Marike let her bring the Ankh-nu to Ragg Rock, and Ragg Rock let her meet with me. With my essence inside Ammi, she would destroy Casimir, and then I would be given a place in the world. We tried and failed a number of times. When it finally worked—well, I knew why, but I didn't tell her. I was afraid she'd refuse to do it if she knew. She *had* become pregnant—with you, Julia. Using the Ankh-nu, she took me into her, into you—the very beginnings of you."

I can feel Luca and the duchess and Flora all staring at me. I am numb with horror, my feelings far-off, frozen things.

"With me in her womb, my essence a part of you and so a part of her, she could use *my* power and essence as well as her own," continues Lidari. "She belonged to both worlds and could cross over to Kahge. The witches pregnant with the Gethin had the same power but were forbidden to use it—Marike wanted the Gethin bound to the world. But Ammi, while she was pregnant, did a great deal of vanishing. She was able to enter Casimir's fortress undetected. She was full of the magic of Kahge, her powers at a tremendous peak. She couldn't kill him, but she bound him in stone and cast him into the sea. Then she returned to Spira City and found the body I've worn for nearly eighteen years." With an utter lack of attachment, he nods toward the room where Liddy's body lies under the blanket. "When she discovered that she was pregnant, Ammi was furious with me, terrified there would be some damage done to you by all of this, but it seemed that you were fine. You were born without difficulty, a strong and healthy baby girl. A few years later, she came to tell me about your vanishing. We did not know how far it went. It seemed perhaps just a small gift left to you from your formation with my essence as part of yours and all the vanishing she had done during her pregnancy. Or so we hoped. Clearly Kahge and my essence imprinted on you more deeply than we'd realized."

"That's why the things in Kahge thought I was you," I say.

"Yes. But you are *not* me, Julia. I promise you that. You are only yourself, a human girl. It's just that as you were forming in the womb, we shared space for a while. Everything that *I* am left its trace on you."

I stare at the fine shoes displayed around the room, dazed. I am a girl. I am Julia. My mother is dead. I'll never see her again. I don't know if it's a comfort that she really was the woman I remember after all. Not if what I remember is all I have and all I'll ever have. It's not enough. But she loved us. Dek was right—she would never have left us. I hold that certainty close.

An explosion sounds very nearby, and we all jump. One of the children upstairs begins to cry.

Mr. Faruk peers out the broken window. "The hackney is here."

"You could come with us, Julia, if you like," says Lidari.

"No," I say. "But I reckon you owe me a favor or two." I point at the duchess and Luca. "I need you to take them to Ingle. See them safely out of Frayne."

"Your princess will not like that," says Mr. Faruk. "And we were not planning on going to Ingle."

"Why not?" says Lidari. "We're hardly short on *time*." To me, he adds: "Have I not spent this lifetime helping those in need? Helping *you*? I am glad to see the fall of Agoston Horthy, and I am happy to help the innocent to freedom and safety. I will always be ready to help you, if you need it."

I shake my head. "You're not who I thought. You're a murderer."

"So are you," says Lidari. "I have struggled with it, but I have only ever taken the bodies of evil men and women who did such damage in the world that they forfeited their right to live in it, or the body of the mindless woman that I've occupied recently. And I have tried to do whatever good I could do, to balance the scales."

"There's no balancing those scales," I tell him in disgust. "You've stood by Marike. You know what she's done, what she's capable of. She was going to kill Theo."

"To save the world, mind you," says Mr. Faruk irritably. "I suppose you consider that a minor detail."

Lidari says: "Love outweighs everything. You know that."

And I do know—because I've been inside his memories— how Marike loomed larger and mattered more than anything else. But I don't know what to think about such a love, when the loved one is a force of plunder and destruction.

"Come with us," says Luca, grabbing my hand.

I shake my head. Fear hollows my chest again. "There's something I need to do here."

"Your revolution is already won," says Mr. Faruk.

"It wasn't my revolution," I say.

⌒

It is a horse-drawn hackney, the old-fashioned kind, with a wizened little fellow as driver. There is something odd about the horse, something a little too intelligent about the eyes.

Mr. Faruk helps Flora and the sleepy children into the hackney and then turns to me and says, in a newly friendly voice, "If you change your mind, come and find us. The world is larger than these little revolutions, this swapping of crowns and thrones. You have, by luck, a tremendous gift. You might find it easier to be with those who understand."

"And the two of you—you'll just go on living forever, stealing bodies and taking them over?"

"A harsh way of putting it."

I'm thinking of the brute they murdered, even if he was a nasty piece of work, and the old woman they convinced themselves had no more use for or claim to her own body. My mother was part of that too.

"If I come looking for you," I say coldly, "it's going to be to *stop* you."

"Thank you for the warning," says Mr. Faruk. "I suspect there will come a time when we have had enough of life, but I don't fancy oblivion yet. The human story is still, no matter what, an entertaining spectacle."

The duchess and Luca are in the doorway, waiting. The Crown, and then nothing. They look fairly calm, all things considered.

"Come to Ingle when you're done with whatever you have to do here," says Luca. "Come find me. I'll be waiting for you."

"Don't wait for me."

He pulls me into his arms.

"I'll still be waiting."

I let myself think it's true for the moment that he's holding me. His arms are sturdy and feel safe, though the truth of the matter is that his arms are one of the least safe places I could be.

"We owe you our lives," says the duchess, pressing my hand between hers as we say goodbye.

"Good luck," I manage to say. Then they get into the hackney, and it pulls away.

EIGHTY-ONE

They are not at the university. I stand there in the empty room—no sign of a struggle—heart pounding. Where could they be? Mrs. Och's house is a ruin. On a hunch, I go to Esme's. The door is unlocked, so I go up to the parlor.

And there:

Gennady, his face bloodied, is lying in front of the hearth like a creature dragged back from the hunt, bound fast with silver ropes that cut into his flesh. Dek is at the table with a look of pale misery on the half of his face that is really his. Casimir is sitting across from Dek, the bejeweled length of him making the parlor seem smaller and drabber than usual. Pia stands behind Casimir—apparently brought to heel, her arms behind her back, her goggles fixed on me as I come through the door.

And:

Shey. She is sitting by the window in the chair Esme favored, knitting. The room smells of damp earth.

"Julia, go!" Dek shouts as soon as I appear.

I could. I could get Dek out of here, vanish us away somewhere safe. But the poison is still attached to his heart. He has less than a week—unless I can crush Casimir, here, now.

"We've been waiting for you," says Casimir.

Dek's head sags on his neck.

"It looks as if your friends will take the day in Frayne," says Casimir. "I could weigh in, but I think we are close to a larger victory. Let's make this quick. Your brother's life, right now. Where is Gennady's son?"

Quick as a snake, Dek has a blade out of his boot, and quicker than he can reach his own neck, Pia grabs his wrist and snaps it. There is the crack of bone breaking and an awful sound escaping Dek's mouth.

"Shey!" I shout. "I can—"

Casimir is out of his chair, speaking before I'm partway through. His words don't come out of his mouth—they come out of *mine*, not as sound but as a swarm of thread exploding out of my face, crawling up my throat and choking me, my lips stitching closed. His eyes are thunderclouds over me. Dek scrambles out of his chair and is thrown back against the wall with a sickening thud.

Shey stops knitting.

I'm on the floor, twisting, grabbing at my mouth, even my nose stopped up by the threads coming from inside, I can't breathe, my vision is closing. As if from very far away I hear Pia's voice, strangled with effort: "She can take you to Kahge."

Casimir wheels toward Pia, his face white with shock. Shey's fingers move quickly—quicker than him. The threads unravel, and the dark thing in my throat recedes. I sit up, gasping, clawing and wiping at my mouth and nose, but there is nothing there anymore.

Casimir is stopped, still poised to strike Pia with whatever might have come out of his mouth next. Dek is crumpled by the wall, Pia bent over his chair as if in pain, her face contorted, Gennady by the hearth. None of them are even breathing. Shey has frozen them, like she did to my friends in Casimir's fortress half a year ago. Her sad eyes meet mine.

"You were saying?"

"I know Agoston Horthy is your son." My voice is raw from whatever Casimir did to me. "And the other one, the one who drowned ... Horthy keeps him locked under the parliament."

She points a knitting needle at Pia. "Is it true, what she said about Kahge?"

"Yes. You made a deal with the shadows there, didn't you? To bring your son back to life when he drowned. But it went wrong. And you took so much ... from Agoston."

I could tell her she's mad if she's prepared to tear down the world to bring—what?—some imagined measure of peace to her children, lost already. What good would it do? But I can give her what she wants, and as dangerous and foolish as it may be, I've run out of other options. I need her help.

"I can cross over to Kahge," I say. "And I can take you with me."

"How?"

And so I tell her about my mother, and Lidari, and my gift. That Casimir knew all along. Her eyes go deeper and deeper as I talk, a small line appearing in her brow. She stands up, putting her knitting down on the chair.

"Take me."

"You have to promise you won't harm anybody else after this."

"I promise nothing. Casimir will help me or you will help me. If he helps me, I will break you for him. If you help me, I will break him for you. That is all."

I know I might be unleashing something terrible here. I want to ask Frederick, I want to ask Dek, I want to ask *somebody* if I am doing the right thing. But there is nobody to ask, and Spira City is on fire, and I am out of time.

"You have to hold on to me," I say.

"You tried to kill me once. You shot me in the neck."

"I was aiming for the head, and anyway, it didn't work. Can you blame me? We're all just trying to save the ones we love."

"When my boys were small, the love I bore them dwarfed every other feeling that I had ever had," she says. "It was a force I could never have imagined—and with it came fears beyond what I could endure. That is what it means to be a mother—that fear, as much as the love. He was playing by the river. A simple fall and he was gone, quick as that, just gone. No mother could accept that. No, no. My beautiful boy. To have it all turn so wrong—but still, what could I have done differently?"

"You could have grieved, and taken care of your surviving son."

"You are too young, and you have no children. All my worst fears have come to pass, and still love yokes me to my purpose. Still love—but changed, emptied of fear, robbed of joy, and become a pitiless master."

Not love, then, I could say, but it doesn't matter.

"Hold on to me."

She gives me her hands, and I see for a moment that even she is afraid of me, a little. I yank back, so we are spinning through nothingness, through and through, until we land on the shore of the boiling river Syne.

EIGHTY-TWO

She rises from a crouch and surveys the smoking world around her: the shadowy ruins of Spira City. Hollow-eyed half-creatures peer at us from flaming windows. I stand beside her with no certainty of what she will do, of what she *can* do, of whether she might bring all the world to ruination. Is that what I'm willing to risk, for Dek and for Theo?

The answer would have been yes not long ago, but standing here, I think how wrong I was, how wrong I am. How that makes me no different from her.

Her fingers work, moving in the steaming air, beckoning. Slowly they come to us, the ones I remember, the ones who called me Lidari and tried to kill me, limping and dragging their patched-together bodies. Here is antlered Solanze, handless and hulking. They come to her unwilling, struggling and groaning, but drawn inexorably by her magic.

Sweat stands out on Shey's brow. Her knees buckle under her. The whirlwind on the horizon roars louder and louder. She falls to the road and rakes her fingers along the ground, digging symbols out of the stone. The patchwork monsters twist and howl with outrage, unable to resist, drawing still closer, forming a ring around us. I cower next to Shey—her fingers gouging stone, blood beading on her lips, blood pouring from her nose, her eyes turning crimson and black, her body bowing, bending, sweating. The ground itself emits a groan as she tears symbols into it, out of it.

One of her hands seizes up. She gives a wretched shriek. The hand looks like a twisted claw, immovable, but she keeps raking at the road with it. I hear her fingers breaking, her raw gasps of pain with each snap of bone. The symbols on the road are multiplying by themselves now, riving the riverbank. Mist swirls around us, making shapes and changing quickly as if the mist itself were trying to illustrate her intent. She is blowing out symbols with her steaming breath, her broken hands still scratching open the rock, and the whole nebulous, smoking city is groaning now, a sorrowful sound coming up from its depths.

A sharp crack explodes into the air; a ripple goes through the half-alive creatures around us. They sag together limply. Something has gone out of them.

Shey rises, slow and terrible.

She reaches for me with her broken hands, and I recoil instinctively. Her body is swollen, misshapen, her fingers gnarled like twigs, her face bloody and mottled.

"Back," she croaks at me.

The beasts start lurching unsteadily closer. I don't want to touch her but I do. They close around us, snarling, and we vanish out of this place, returning within minutes to Esme's parlor.

Shey crumples to the floor.

"What happened?" I'm shaking so hard I have to kneel on the floor next to her. "What was that?"

"I broke my agreement with them," she whispers. "Took back . . . what I gave . . . and returned . . . what I took."

She looks at me with whirling eyes. A smile forms on her bleeding lips.

"Get me a pen," she says.

EIGHTY-THREE

I can't believe she can hold a pen in that broken claw of a hand, but somehow she does. She writes on the clean sheaf of paper I bring her, and the smell of freshly turned earth fills the room again. Pia comes loose from the wall, tumbling to the floor. Gennady stirs and groans. Dek stumbles forward. The silver bindings loosen from Gennady. Like live things, they uncoil and snake across the floor to wind themselves around Casimir, binding his legs and arms, sealing themselves tightly around his mouth. Then Shey flicks a broken finger, and he falls forward too, toppling to the floor, straining against the silver bindings, his eyes blackening with rage.

Shey packs her knitting awkwardly into her big leather bag on the floor.

"Wait!" I shout. "You told me you would help me . . . break him. I need him dead or he'll come for Theo."

"Dead?" She looks at me. "Easier said than done. Leave him in Kahge."

"We can destroy the other fragments," rumbles Gennady. "When you took me to Kahge, those months ago, I saw the end of things . . . where magic drains out of the world."

"The whirlwind," I say. Dek comes to my side, wrapping his mechanical arm around me so I can lean against him. He holds his other, broken hand to his chest.

"I will take the Book and cast it into the whirlwind," says

Gennady. "Along with Casimir and myself. Our time is done. I am broken beyond repair. But my child can live— like a human child, in a human world."

"But how . . . where will we find the Book?" I ask.

"Ah," says Shey, sighing.

"Please," says Gennady to her. "As a kindness. After all you have done to me."

Shey shuffles to where Casimir is twisting on the ground. With one shattered hand, she tears open his shirt. There are two large symbols tattooed on his chest, below the small symbol protecting him from me. She writes on one of these with her finger. It bulges, something moving under the skin, swelling outward. The flesh splits open like overripe fruit. A blackened ball rolls out of his chest and changes shape, flattening into a row of pale strips of bone scratched with writing. She does the same, and the same sickening thing happens, with the other tattoo.

Shey groans as she gets back up. "Your book. *The Book of Disruption*. Two thirds of it, anyway."

Gennady touches the strips of bone almost reverently.

I think of what Ragg Rock told me when I first brought Theo there. A part of the Book taken out of the world meant that Kahge and the world were farther apart. If we take these two parts of the Book from the world, how wide will the rift be?

Will I be able to get back?

But it would be the end of all this. I don't have a choice.

"I'll take you," I say quickly, so I don't have time to dwell on what the cost might be. "What about the *nuyi*? Is the queen really in his brain?"

"He claims to have mastered it," says Shey. "And maybe he did. What do I know of the Xianren? Although I wonder sometimes if it mastered him. He was different once, I'm told."

"He was," says Gennady. "But if he changed, he changed willingly."

"Where is the mechanic?" I ask.

"Nago Island," says Pia. "I will send for him." She pauses and then says, "I cannot."

She is still bound to Casimir. Her face turns a nasty shade of gray.

"Do you have any more hermia?" Dek asks me. "We don't know how far the *nuyi*'s reach is. We need to make sure it's dead."

I give him the packet, and he sets about boiling the remaining leaves down to sludge, fetching a needle, and filling it with the liquefied hermia. Then he kneels next to Casimir with a knife in his unbroken hand. Gennady holds Casimir down so his body doesn't buck, and Dek shoves his face into the carpet, exposing the back of his head. My stomach turns.

"There is one more thing I need from you," Shey says to me quietly, from the door. "You will hear from me soon, and you will know better than to defy me."

She goes down the stairs. From the window I watch her hunched figure limp across the square because I can't look at what Dek is doing. There are fires all over the neighborhood, smoke in the air. A sudden scream from Dek. I spin around. Something that looks like a blood-soaked pancake goes flying across the room, up the wall, along the ceiling.

"Great hounds!" roars Gennady.

Casimir is lying facedown on the floor, still bound in silver, the back of his head bloody, blood all over the carpet. The thing flies from the ceiling straight at me. I put my hands out to try to stop it. It fastens on to my arms, driving stinging tentacles into my skin, scuttling up my arms toward my face. It is pulsing with fury, soft and slithering, like an organ come to life.

"Get it off!"

I slam it against the wall to no avail, spinning madly. Dek charges right into me and sticks the needle into the creature, pushing the plunger full of hermia all the way down. The thing shudders and goes limp, still fastened to my arms.

"Flaming Kahge," says Dek breathlessly.

He pulls the thorny bits of tentacle out of my arms with tweezers while Gennady stuffs the squashy remains of the *nuyi* queen into his coat pocket. Pia has her back against the wall, watching everything. She looks slowly down at the inside of her wrist, and touches a finger to the silvery disk there. Even from across the room, I can see it has gone dull. She flicks at it with a fingernail, and it flakes right off, a bit of dull thread dangling loose from her wrist. She stares at it for a long moment and then looks up at me. I try to smile, but I think it probably looks more like a grimace. Whatever happens next, Pia is free of Casimir. We've managed that, at least.

Gennady heaves Casimir's bound body over his shoulder and picks up the strips of bone. Casimir's eyes are wide open. They fix on me with such deep hatred that I tremble, even though he's bound, undone.

"Let's go," says Gennady.

EIGHTY-FOUR

We land on the black rock above the smoking city, as close to the whirlwind as I dare to take them. I can feel the pull of it, roaring on the horizon.

"Good luck," I say to Gennady. Who knows what he's going into? I can only hope Casimir never finds a way back. The look on Gennady's face is something close to elation. Perhaps the unknown is the only thrill left for someone who has lived out every possible life.

"Take care of my child," he says.

"Of course." I gesture feebly at the great whorl of wind and smoke. "I hope there are lots of pies on the other side of that thing."

He actually laughs. "I hope I never see another pie," he says, but then he adds: "Please thank Mrs. Freeley for me."

His brother in his arms, he starts to bound toward the whirlwind, into its tug. I vanish—or I try to—but the whirlwind is growing now, expanding to fill the sky, like a mouth opening wider and wider. It swallows Gennady and Casimir, sucking hard at me as I pull and pull against it. The black rock and the shadowy Spira City fall away, but I can't find the world, and the whirlwind wants me. It roars and pulls at me while I pull away please let me go please let me go back please let me be Julia again and for good.

Something snaps. I slam into hard rock.

"What is happening?"

Ragg Rock's mud face is bent over me, etched with fear. The rabbit, George, leaps onto my chest, trembling. We are on top of her hill, but the hill is tilting dangerously toward Kahge on one side, and Kahge is all whirlwind now, still growing and devouring, pulling. Spira City on the other side is spinning away, as if breaking free of its moorings.

"We have to go!" I shout. "We have to go *now*!"

I tuck George into my jacket and take Ragg Rock's mud hand in mine. We run. The moat is breaking into a cliff, crumbling to nothing; there is no stairway at all, Spira City a revolving speck below us, receding. I drag her to the cliff's edge and right over it, a desperate dive toward the retreating world.

We fall through the nothingness, and as we fall, her hand turns soft in mine. A flash of her terrified face as her hand melts to wet mud, as we are caught in a great wind, spinning and tossed about, and then she is simply blown apart, lost in the emptiness between the world and its awful reflection.

I hit something that feels solid but it is moving, everything is moving, I am sliding hard and fast, and then it all goes still and the only thing I can feel is a soft trembling against my palm.

I look up, blink. I still have eyes, then, and a body. I am outside the old laundry shop, boarded up for a few years now, below the flat where I used to live with Dek and my mother and father. I smell smoke and magic blowing across the city on a hot wind. Voices shouting. The trembling under my hand, I realize, is the racing heartbeat of the terrified rabbit. The wind passes over me and is gone. It begins to rain.

Three sets of dirty, scuffed boots run past me. A woman just behind them stops—a roly-poly grandmotherly type.

"You all right, dear?" She reaches out a hand to help me up.

The booted men turn and come back, faces soot-smudged and exultant. One of them is bleeding from his leg and another coughing badly, but they are laughing.

"I'm all right," I say. Hearing my own voice, I think it might even be true. Not so for Ragg Rock. Frightened as I was of her, I feel a wash of pity. I stagger to my feet and tuck the rabbit back into my jacket to shelter it from the rain, which is coming down harder and harder. "What's happening?"

"Roparzh's daughter has returned and taken the throne!" cries one of the men. "Duke Everard has fled the city!"

"They've tossed Agoston Horthy in prison!" says the other. "Along with the witches who were trying to take the city. She's saved us all! She has a special gas to fight witches! She *stopped* them!"

"She pulled those monsters right out of the sky," says the other man. "I saw it. I heard she slew that dragon herself with a *sword*! They've got its head on a pike now!"

"Come, lass, there's going to be a celebration. Come and see."

And they are pulling me along through the rain, which becomes a downpour, the fires in the city going out one by one.

AFTER
THE REVOLUTION

EIGHTY-FIVE

It seems a dark portent for the new queen to begin her reign with the public drowning of a witch. I have had enough of Cleansings in my lifetime, and I've no desire to see Lady Laroche's execution in the traditional manner, or Zara's address to the people. She says she wants to show people that this new Frayne will not tolerate harmful magic, that they will still be protected against witches. I've voiced my objections and now I have other things to do.

Waiting outside the room where Casimir's mechanic performed the surgery on Dek, Zara and I did talk about Mr. Faruk, who was her tutor once. She was skeptical when I said he was Marike.

"Perhaps only a very convincing con man," she said. I told her I was convinced—by the Ankh-nu, by Lidari. But she remained unsure.

"He had secrets piled miles deep, but I could never read him well," she said. "As someone who stepped into the shoes of another and made a life of pretending to be someone else,

I'm inclined to skepticism. The best actors convince themselves."

In the end, it doesn't matter. Marike and Lidari have left the city. The Xianren are gone. Ragg Rock is gone. My mother is gone. But I'm still here. As soon as the mechanic comes out to tell us the surgery was a success, I go to do the thing Shey has asked of me.

There are no windows in Arrimer, but I can't wait for a hanging this time. Getting Agoston Horthy out of his cell involves sleeping-serum darts and a good deal more time and drama than I'd like. The prison locks down, bells clanging, soldiers running everywhere. But they can't see us, and so they can't catch us.

I haven't tried vanishing as far as I can. I don't know if Kahge is still there or if its link to the world has been severed completely by the destruction of the two Book fragments— and if so, where would I go if I kept pulling back? I don't really want to know. I stay close to myself, no farther than four steps from my body. I keep the precious world in my sights.

Leaving the prison in chaos behind us, I take Agoston Horthy out over the city, to Limory Cemetery. At the cemetery gates, I tell him, "I have a brother too. I'd do anything for him. I understand that part."

The former prime minister looks different. Something lighter around his eyes. He doesn't answer me.

"I'm not saving you," I say. "The queen says you have to stand trial, and you will."

"I'm not afraid to die," he says.

"My mother was a witch. You had her drowned."

I face him finally: the monster of my childhood, the first person I ever wished dead, and, like me, made what he is by a mother meddling in Kahge. We are the children of witches who wanted too much, our very natures disrupted.

"My mother was a good woman before my brother died," he says. "But life twists us and breaks us and we must submit. A broken, twisted witch might *not* submit to life's random cruelty, its inevitable losses. She might do terrible things with her anger and grief and regret. Those who *can* disrupt nature eventually will. They are too dangerous to live."

There is no shame or pity in his steady gaze. Such calm certainty, even now.

"You've been sleeping," I say. Those deep hollows under his eyes have receded.

He almost smiles. "I can sleep, I can taste my food, quench my thirst. I even feel pain. It is good—to rest a little, to feel a little—at the end. But it's too late to matter."

He doesn't mention love. She robbed him of that too, and then gave it back, and I wonder how it feels to feel again. I wonder if there is anyone for him to love, now that he can.

At the far end of the cemetery, she is waiting. The body in a casket, the earth already dug up. I walk part of the way with him, until she is in view. She looks up, and their eyes meet. I think I feel him tremble at my side, but it's hard to say.

"You have an hour," I tell him. "Then I have to take you back."

He walks slowly up the path toward his mother and the drowned body of his brother.

EIGHTY-SIX

When I get back, Dek is awake, and Zara is at his bedside.

"Don't you have a country to rule?" I say to her. I confess: I'm upset she was the one there when he woke.

She presses her lips together. "Indeed, it is a difficult time. I've just been told that somebody who can *disappear* took Agoston Horthy from Arrimer."

"He's back in his cell now," I say curtly.

Zara's mouth drops open.

"That's not a very queenly look," I say. "I just needed to borrow him."

"You might have asked me."

"You would have said no."

"Did you take him back alive?"

"Yes. And if you hang him, you're going to have the most powerful witch in the world in a snit. I recommend against it."

"We can't live in fear of witches and their whims," says Zara. "Horthy must stand trial, and he will be hanged as a traitor."

"I hope you're ready for what might come of that," I say.

"We will see."

"What about Lord Skaal?"

"No sign of him. Nor of Duke Everard. His whole family fled Corf. Rumor is they've gone to Ingle."

She gives me a hard look, which I ignore.

"I'd like a moment with my brother."

"Of course."

She leans over and plants a kiss on his forehead. He gives her cheek a caress with his hinged knuckles. I look away.

Before she goes out, she says to me, "Are you a friend of my country, Julia?"

"It's my country too," I say. "And frankly, I'm not sure."

"I should like you to use your powers for good—to serve your country."

"You mean to serve *you*."

"I've granted Pia a pardon, as you asked, and given her citizenship papers. She has taken up permanent residence in the West Spira Grand Hotel. I made her an offer of employment, and she said she would accept it if you did. This new Frayne will have its enemies, magical and otherwise. You could help keep it safe as it grows into a country ruled by justice. There *will* be justice for witches, I promise you. They will be judged by their deeds and not their nature, but the laws will be strict."

I think of Dorje Tsewang standing up and saying, *I will be faster alone.*

"I'll consider jobs on a case-by-case basis," I say.

"Then we will be in touch."

She goes out, and I sit awkwardly on the edge of Dek's bed.

"So you're going to be king of Frayne?" I ask him.

He laughs. "No. She'll make a political marriage. But I'm going to have a *very* well-funded laboratory."

"Developing fancy weapons for the new queen?"

"If you're going to consider jobs of the kind I think you mean, I'm going to make sure you're well armed. But no— not just weapons. I'd rather like to try my hand at things that make peace easier, not war."

"You can be useful and joyful for a good while now," I say.

"That's just what I intend." He smiles, and then his voice softens. "My poor sister. What a time of it you've had."

"Oh, I'm all right," I say. His smile wobbles just a little, and that's enough—my tears come flooding forth. I wrap my arms around him and bury my face in his shoulder. My brother, who is going to live.

EIGHTY-SEVEN

Roughs and beggars and outlaws crowd the ruins of the palace and its grounds for the coronation party. The gates are open to the people. There are soldiers too—Zara has upped their wages and that seems to have been enough for most of them. She's gone digging into Frayne's coffers for this party too, but she's right that she is winning goodwill. Fireflares explode overhead, and music fills the air.

"Well, my girl, we did it," says Esme when I join them in the crown room. Csilla is dressed to the nines and looks as happy as I've ever seen her, jewels glinting in her hair. The crown room is still mostly intact, though there are fissures in the marble floor where the dragon's fire sac leaked.

"*You* did it," I say. "What now?"

"Gregor is taking a government position, believe it or not," Esme says. "Zara still needs to appoint a prime minister. She is considering Sir Oswell."

"Sir Oswell?" I cry, remembering the monocled man at the meeting with Agoston Horthy.

"An olive branch to the old guard," she says. "He is not an extremist, and she needs to keep her enemies close."

"What about you?"

"I'm retiring. I've bought a house in Mount Heriot, as a matter of fact. I'm leaving the place in the Twist to you, Dek, and Wyn."

"Mount Heriot?" I say in surprise.

"I had a bit of money tucked away," she says, her mouth quirking.

Of course she did.

I think of my golden boy—in Ingle by now—and I hope he's all right. He was always innocent, and I'll still fight to save his life if Zara ever finds him. She said she wasn't going to go looking, but I know she's afraid he'll find support abroad and challenge the throne. And I suppose he might. There are threats on every side of this new regime, and I don't yet know which side I'll be on. It depends on where the threat comes from, I reckon, and what Zara does now that she's got the throne. I don't know where I stand on this clever, lying, ruthless, slightly magical peasant girl from Ibhara, raised and betrayed by witches, now queen of Frayne and my brother's lover.

"It's going to be a new start for us all," says Esme.

The men are raising their glasses in a cheer. It's impossible not to feel it, the hope they thought they'd lost forever. A glass finds its way to Gregor's hand, the amber liquid fizzing and foaming. He is shouting and cheering with the others, triumphant after so many years of failure and loss. He raises the glass to his lips and pours the drink down his throat. I feel Csilla go rigid at my side.

Someone slaps him on the back. Lorka. Gregor laughs and slings an arm around the artist. Somebody else fills up his glass again. More cheers—"Long live the queen!" He shouts it too, "Long live the queen!" and empties another drink. The bottle is passed around, the laughter wild and raucous.

Csilla turns and walks out to the balcony, her fine gown trailing behind her. I go after her. We stand on the balcony, but I don't know what to say to her. She lights a cigarette, her eyes dry and depthless.

"He'll try again," she says at last, and I nod. We look out over Spira City, fireflares bursting like brilliant flowers in the sky. It looks like the city is burning again.

EIGHTY-EIGHT

Esme was serious about turning her building in the Twist over to Dek, Wyn, and me. It's in our names and everything. Dek has a laboratory at the university, but he's converted our old ground-floor room into a workshop for "personal" projects—by which I gather he means secret. I've got Esme's old room with its big windows, and Theo sleeps in there with me. Frederick has taken Wyn's room in the attic, which he says he likes, though the stairs are hard on him. The thunk of his cane reminds me of Dek's crutch. Wyn moved into a flat near the train station with Arly Winters, with a sunny back room he can use as a studio. He still treats this place like home, though, and is officially third owner of the building. Everyone is in the big parlor now.

Wyn and Arly are playing cards, while Dek tinkers with a mechanical hinge. Frederick is just back from meeting with Professor Baranyi at the university—they are collaborating on a book about the history of magic and folklore in Frayne—and he is giving Theo his supper. Theo is exhausted, his head nodding over his food.

"I'll just take him to bed," I say, laughing as his eyes droop half shut.

"Wabbit," mutters Theo, pointing at Strig and George playing together on the floor. At least, Strig is trying to play. George is just gnawing on the carrot between his paws while Strig pounces back and forth, alternately meowing and hooting.

"We ought to find a nursemaid for Theo," says Frederick. "Somebody who knows more about children than we do."

"Not a bad idea," says Wyn.

"Can I apply for the job?" asks Arly. "He's such a little poppet!"

"No," I say. "We need someone with qualities. I mean qualifications."

Wyn gives me a look, and Arly pouts crossly. I turn away to hide my grin.

"We should hire a witch, actually," says Frederick. "We'll need someone who knows about magic and can keep him from drawing, or deal with it if something happens."

"That's a sign of the new Frayne," I say. "We'll put an ad in the papers: *Nursemaid wanted for magical little boy. Witch with good cooking skills preferred.* Come to think of it, I don't think she's a witch, but Mrs. Freeley would be perfect."

"I expect her position at the palace is better remunerated than whatever we can offer," says Frederick.

"What *is* her position, exactly?" asks Dek.

"Ask your girl, the queen," I say, a little snidely, and he grins at me.

The doorbell chimes. Wyn leans out the window to see who it is.

"It's your friend with the goggles," he says to me, pulling his body back inside.

"Ugh," says Arly with a shudder. "She gives me the creeps."

"Watch it, or she'll give you worse than that," I say cheerfully, going down to open the door.

"A message from the queen," Pia tells me. "She wants to see us. Says it's urgent."

"Hounds, is there trouble already?"

"Are you surprised?"

"All right, I'll come. But I've got to put Theo to bed."

"Have Frederick do it."

"It'll only take a minute—he's nodding off in his chair. Will you come up?"

"I'll wait."

Maybe Arly gives her the creeps too.

"Be right back, then."

I run back up. Frederick is tidying away Theo's dinner.

"I'll take him to bed," I say, lifting the half-asleep Theo out of his chair. He wraps his chubby arms around my neck, lets his head fall against my shoulder.

I take him potty and then carry him to our room. I pin a diaper on him and tuck him into the sturdy cot Dek built. Theo's hands slide away from me, his eyes already closed. I tell him I love him. I kiss his soft cheek. He is beautiful sleeping; it tugs at me and there is a small part of me that wants to stay here gazing at him. But something else is tugging at me too, something that quickens my pulse and makes me want to break into a run. I know this thrill so well. I can't imagine life without it.

I slip out of the room quietly and go back to the parlor. Arly and Wyn are making doe eyes at each other over the cards, and Frederick is lost in his book, but Dek looks up without my having to say anything. He puts down his hinge.

"Be careful," he says.

I give him a wink in reply. I pull on my gabardine coat, slide my knife into my boot. And then I'm taking the steps two at a time, bursting out into the night.

Pia is silhouetted under a gas lamp, all long limbs and deadly poise, waiting for me. The night is waiting too, wide awake and holding close its secrets, its joys and dangers, and I am full of something like joy and something like danger as well, to say nothing of secrets.

Pia's goggles swivel, once in, once out, as I join her under the light.

"Ready?" she says.

And I am. Oh, I am.

ACKNOWLEDGMENTS

Thank you to my agent, Steve Malk, for always pushing me to do more, and for working some kind of miracle that has allowed me to do my favorite thing in the world and call it my *job*.

Thank you to my editor, Nancy Siscoe, for championing these books, for loving Julia, and for being so much better and smarter and kinder and funnier than even my onetime fantasy of what a Real Live Book Editor would be like. You take top spot on the short list of People I Really Want to Impress.

Thank you to all the wonderful, dedicated people at Knopf and at Doubleday Books for making these books so beautiful and for getting them out into the world and into the hands of readers—my gratitude is boundless. Special thanks to eagle-eyed copy editors for saving me from myself, to Kathy Dunn for guiding me through the Being an Author stuff, and to Alison Impey for the stunning covers.

To my beta readers—Samantha Cohoe, Kip Wilson Rechea, and Dana Alison Levy, all three brilliant authors whose books (and selves!) I adore—thank you, thank you, and thank you!

My heart and my gratitude to the usual suspects, my nearest and dearest, my been-through-some-serious-shit-togetherest, my loved-longest: my parents, my brothers, my grandmother—how lucky am I to have you as my family? And my chosen beloveds, Jon, Giles, Mick—for the biggest laughs, the wildest escapes, and everything we've let go of over the years while still holding on to each other.

And *you*, of course—thank you for reading. I needed to give Julia to someone, and there you were. xo

ABOUT THE AUTHOR

CATHERINE EGAN grew up in Vancouver, Canada. Since then, she has lived on a volcanic island in Japan (which erupted while she was there and sent her hurtling straight into the arms of her now husband), in Tokyo, Kyoto, and Beijing, on an oil rig in the middle of Bohai Bay, then in New Jersey, and now in New Haven, Connecticut.

She is currently occupied with writing books and fighting dragon armies with her warrior children. You can read more about her at catherineegan.com and follow her on Twitter at @ByCatherineEgan.